A SHOW

of Hands

To Pat and Bud Crossman,
my mom and dad, for roots and wings

OLAF INGRAHAM leaned into the light. "I'd like to've seen the look on Bergie's face when he started cuttin' that fish hole and seen her lookin' up at him." Olaf did his impersonation of a young woman frozen in ice and laughed his stupid laugh.

"They got Gammidge over from Rockland. He's up at the funeral parlor now, lookin' at her," said Stuffy Hutchin. In long years of practice, *s*s and *c*s had worn a path around Stuffy's four teeth. That's why they called him Sylvester. But his real nickname was Stuffy. He slurped the foam off his beer and wiped his mouth with his sleeve. "Fifteen for two."

"Blast it, Syl'! Where'd you get that five? Every time I got tens, you got fives." Wendell played a jack. "Twenty-five."

"And every time you got eights, he's got sevens," said Harry, and sipped his Coke. For most of his seventy-odd years, Harry had only rarely been without a six-ounce Coke in the thick green bottle, and he sipped after every sentence—softly for a period, loudly for an exclamation. He wasn't the kind of person to ask questions, so he hadn't developed an interrogatory sip.

Olaf and Bill, cut in half by light and shadow, floated headless in the cigarette smoke behind Stuffy, studying his cards, tossing nods and winks through the shadows of the poolroom.

Stuffy's bottom lip curled over his gums and played a perpetual game of push tag with his tongue. "Thirty-one for two," he said, dropping a six of clubs on the cribbage board.

"Fours, fives, and sixes," Wendell exclaimed. He rose partly out of his chair and slammed down the cards in disgust. "I shoulda known."

"Should have," said Stuffy. "I got fifteen two, fifteen four, fifteen six, and three is nine." He jumped his peg gingerly down the board. "Puts me out with a hole to spare."

Harry smiled. "Nossir, you can't beat luck like that."

"Skill," said Stuffy. "Pay up, Wen'."

"If I'd 'a' had first count . . ."

Stuffy sat back and crammed the overflow of his belly into his pants. "If wishes was horses," he said philosophically, "we'd be up to our necks in fertilizer. That's three dollars, I believe."

"Play me again."

"Nope."

"One more. Double or nothin'."

"Nope."

"Why?"

"I don't want to play no more. No competition. Besides"—he burped—"that was double or nothin'."

Wendell stood up the rest of the way. "That wasn't neither."

"Was so."

"Was so," repeated Harry with an authoritative pull at the visor of his plaid wool cap.

Either Olaf or Bill, floating in clouds of smoke like Zeus, said "was so" from the shadows. That made it so, whether it was or not. Wendell reluctantly dug out his old leather change purse and paid up in quarters, dimes, and nickels. The others watched in silence as he counted out. A glimpse at the inside of Wendell Slocum's purse was a rare thing, like a solar eclipse or Halley's comet, demanding some measure of reverence.

"She musta fell in and banged her head," said Stuffy, counting the coins with his eyes. "Drowned."

"You'll have to take the last ten cents in pennies," said Wendell. He dumped a little pile of pennies into his palm and resumed counting, by ones.

"Could have," said Harry. "You shouldn't go walkin' 'round them quarries if you don't know what you're doin'. Lotta loose rock up there."

"Yup," said Olaf. "Loose rock all over the place."

"Some dangerous," said Bill.

Stuffy waited patiently while the last few coins fell into his hand. "Musta froze over that same night."

Waymond Webber was quietly rolling balls on the billiard table. Nobody cared enough about Waymond to give him a real nickname. Some called him Oozie, but it was more adjective than noun. "She didn't have no clothes on," Waymond said. He was the kind of person who would wait all night to say something like that.

"Leeman Russell was up there when they chipped her out," said Harry. "Fresh as a mornin' in Paris, he said she was, froze like that. Doc Pagitt put her in one've them bags like you seen 'em do on TV. A clear one, like Phyllis Clayton puts the dry cleanin' in, only thicker. You could see right through it."

"She didn't have nothin' on, did she?" said Waymond. Nobody paid any attention. Not paying any attention to Waymond was a community pastime.

The cowbell on the back of the door clanged loudly, and everyone looked to see who had come in.

"Professor," said Stuffy. He lifted a chair from the table behind him and spun it around. "Come have a seat over here. Brenda, get the professor a Moxie."

Harry dropped his bottle among the empties in the crate beside the counter. "Nickel, Brenda," he said, holding out his hand. The bottle deposit was one of those unique economies necessitated by life on the island with its scarcity of disposal space. Harry hadn't lost a nickel yet. Brenda was busy wiping off the grill. "Bergie said he puked when he found her."

"I don't hardly wonder," said Olaf.

"Me neither," said Bill.

Winston Crisp was made from leftovers of Jimmy Stewart—lanky, soft-spoken, pale and milky around the eyes. Gold wire-rimmed spectacles conspired with a pleasant, forgettable face and stooped shoulders to give Crisp a bookish appearance. Hence the nickname "Professor," which the locals had given him when he spent his first summer on the island as a boy of seven or so. They had called him that ever since. Now that Crisp had retired to the island, the nickname had thoroughly supplanted his Christian name even on his mail. Sometimes even Matty called him Professor, though she claimed to hate the name.

Over the rims of his glasses, with eyebrows vaulted in a perpetual query, Crisp surveyed the world that always seemed to be running off without him. He sat down as he was told.

Brenda circumnavigated Harry's outstretched palm and handed the professor his Moxie. "Nickel, Brenda," said Harry, shaking his open palm, eliciting a glare that put a severe strain on two or three of the more popular commandments.

"We're talkin' about that body they found up to the quarry, Professor," said Stuffy. "Some summer girl."

"Oh, yes," said Crisp. "Matty said . . . she told me . . . while I was having my oatmeal. Terrible."

At that moment the cowbell clanged again. The door flew open and an agitated individual burst in and stopped dead in his tracks.

"What's wrong with you, Leeman?" said Olaf, by way of greeting.

Most small towns have a town crier. On Penobscot Island it

was Leeman Russell. He was the one who always managed to get to accident scenes before the blood dried. He could be counted upon to convey the unpleasant news to the rest of the citizenry in the most alarming manner possible—like the evening news. His eyes ransacked each face in the room. "They found out who it is!" he said.

Brenda poured Leeman a coffee. This was going to be news worth a free drink.

"It's that girl who was up at the senator's last summer," said Leeman, lip deep in the ephemeral puddle of attention, "the one the FBI was out here lookin' for last fall."

"The one they was tryin' to keep so quiet about, you mean," said Olaf.

"How many others there been, Olaf?" Stuffy chided.

When Harry finally closed his hand, he found a nickel in it. He went to the refrigerator and took out another Coke. "What're you talkin' about?" he said. "You talkin' 'bout Senator McKenniston? What's she got to do with him?"

Stuffy shuffled the cards habitually. He was one of those people—not as rare on the islands of the Maine coast as elsewhere in the world—whom nothing surprised. The wrath of God could reduce everyone in the room to pocket lint or refrigerator magnets, and he wouldn't bat an eye. He'd suck his lower lip a little and shuffle the cards. "McKenniston's boy, Neddy," he said. "He brought this girl up here last summer."

Harry could make a noise at the back of his throat that was the very embodiment of disgust. He made it twice now. "That boy . . . that boy was never nothin' but trouble!" Big sip. "Always up to somethin'."

"That big outdoor weddin' he had up by TipToe Mountain a couple've years ago don't seem to have settled him down much, did it?" said Wendell.

"They didn't even invite anybody from the island," Olaf recalled.

"Walter Cronkite was there," said Bill.

"So was that opera lady," Olaf said. "Isabelle . . . Elizabeth, somethin'. What was her name, Professor?"

"Beverly Sills, I think you mean."

"I thought it was somethin' like that," said Olaf. "All them jet-setters."

"Not a clam digger in the bunch," said Stuffy. The lobstermen laughed.

"Ain't hardly any clam diggers left in the jet set these days," said Olaf dryly.

Wendell was indignant. "Well, what was Neddy doin' bringin' a girl out here if he's married?"

"He never brought his wife here," Olaf observed.

"Nope," said Bill. "Always left her in Massachusetts."

"That boy chases anything with skirts, I'd say. Got a different girl every time you see him." Harry spat, seeming to forget he didn't have any chewing tobacco. He nearly lost his dentures. "Prob'ly all over the girls who go to work up at the house."

"Like white on rice," said Waymond, whose only ad-libs were things everyone had heard a few thousand times before.

"Well, you know what happened to Sarah Quinn," said Olaf.

"She ain't still workin' up there, is she?" Wendell asked.

"Who?" said Bill. "Sarah? Not since she had that baby, I shouldn't think."

"She'd've had one, one way or the other anyway," Harry observed with a draining pull on his Coke bottle.

Olaf narrowed a critical eye. "What's that s'posed to mean?"

"Ragged Islanders," said Harry, "and rabbits. They both start early with whoever's handy. And if there ain't fresh blood, well, there's friends and family, and up there it's one and the same, ain't it?"

"Oh, here we go," said Olaf. "Everything you ever wanted to know about anything from someone who knows nothin' 'bout everything."

Harry continued. "And when your brother's your father and your uncle, like most of 'em, there prob'ly ain't a Noble Prize in your future, if you know what I mean. Sarah Quinn's a good example."

"Well, if the Nobel Prize was given out for foolishness," Bill interjected contemptuously, "there wouldn't be anyone between you and King Gustav when it come time to pick it up."

"Started work up there when she was fourteen or so," said Stuffy, nudging the subject back on track.

"That's her old man's doin'," said Olaf. "I bet he drug 'er up there."

"That's one thing you can say about Ragged Islanders, you know," said Wendell. "They was always like that. Soon's a kid's old 'nough to make his way, out they go and make it."

"Ain't nothin' wrong with that," said Harry. "I was payin' board when I was thirteen."

"That was over sixty years ago, Harry," said Wendell. "Lotsa things changed in sixty years."

Harry scoffed. "Change don't signify improvement."

"I don't imagine life on Ragged Island did much to make her ready for young Ned," said Olaf.

"No denyin' puberty hits some boys like a drug," said Stuffy. He went into a long, animated stretch. "Anyway, that's why you never read nothin' about it in the papers when that girl run away."

"That's why they had the FBI out here," Leeman added.

"Pays to be a senator, I guess," said Stuffy.

"I 'member thinkin' that was some strange, though," said Olaf. "There was all kinds've people saw her leave the island 'bout that time, 'member? Mostly Sanborn seen her get off the boat in Rockland. So did a couple've others. Becky Gable and Evelyn Swears was over doin' shoppin' that day—they seen her get off."

There was a dull murmur of consent.

"And nobody saw her get back on?" Crisp asked.

All heads shook.

"That's why I couldn't figure out why the FBI come over here lookin' for her," said Olaf in summation.

"Well, she musta got back out here someways," Stuffy said. " 'Cause she sure is here now."

"So, that's the same girl," Wendell sighed. "Well, that's some awful."

There was a brief intermission during which everyone entertained his own thoughts. Crisp slowly rotated the Moxie bottle in his hands. "That was about Labor Day, as I recall, wasn't it—when the FBI came out?"

"Thereabouts," said Stuffy.

"It wasn't more than two, three days after the Calderwood boys' boat blew up, right?" Olaf recollected. "Remember them fellas thought she mighta been on board, since it happened just off McKenniston's float. Not what you'd call startlin' intelligence there."

"You don't s'pose it likely she was out lobsterin' with 'em?" said Harry, to a chorus of laughter.

"Yessir, I bet that's just what it was," said Olaf. "I tell you, I can't hardly beat them summer jerks off my boat with a stick." Olaf waded into the spirit of things with his boots pulled up. "Now Senator, you get your hands outta that bait box! Princess Caroline, I told you to bring your own baitbags!" The good time being had by all was brought to an abrupt end by the epilogue. " 'Course, all they ever found was Herbie and Andy—what was left of 'em."

"Just after Labor Day, you say?" said Crisp, listing toward the speaker with his good ear.

"I said it was just two or three days after Herbert and Andy Calderwood's boat blew up, Professor," said Olaf, a little louder. "He's deaf as a post," he mumbled aside. "The boat blew up the day after Labor Day. Remember?"

"Mmm." Crisp nodded. "Oh, yes. Yes, I remember. But they found her frozen, you say—this girl?"

"Like a fish dinner," said Leeman. "I saw her when they pulled her out."

"You did?" said Crisp thoughtfully. He shuddered. "I shouldn't like to have seen such a thing, myself."

"She didn't have no clothes on, did she, Leeman?" said Waymond. "You could see everything, couldn't you?"

"She had a shirt on," Leeman replied. "Just a sweatshirt or whatever you call it." He looked embarrassed. "That's all I could see."

"That ain't what I heard," said Waymond.

Leeman didn't appreciate having his reportorial integrity questioned. "Well, I was there, f'r pete's sake. I guess I oughta know."

"A gruesome thought," said Crisp. He looked at Leeman over his glasses. "Not a pleasant sight after all that time, I shouldn't think."

"Oh, well, it wasn't . . . I mean . . . it was just like she was asleep, except her eyes were open," said Leeman. "She was funny colors in places. Her face looked strange, but—"

"Asleep?" said Crisp. "You mean she wasn't . . . that is to say . . . after all that time . . ."

"She was froze, Professor," said Olaf. "Bodies don't rot if they're froze."

"No," Crisp replied softly. "No, of course they don't. Not as fast anyway, I understand. But . . . when was the earliest hard freeze last year?"

"Last of October?" Wendell said tentatively. "Early November, maybe?"

"Not 'til the last week in November," said Stuffy unequivocally. "My nephew and nieces was out skatin' just after Thanksgivin'."

"After Thanksgiving, yes. That's what I thought," Crisp said. "And there was even a thaw after that, seems I remember."

Stuffy corroborated Crisp's recollection with expert testimony. "Yup."

"Good long spell, as I recall."

"Almost up to Christmas," said Harry. "I hate it when it don't snow for Christmas. Ever since I was a kid, I hated when it didn't snow for Christmas. All we got was rain last year, right up 'til the day or two 'fore—then the weather turned."

"Mmm," said Crisp and massaged his forehead with two fingers. "Then that's a problem, isn't it?"

"Why?" said Olaf.

"Well," said Crisp, leaning over his Moxie and speaking so low that everyone had to gather around to hear, which, with the exception of Stuffy, they did. "If the girl drowned just after Labor Day, as you suppose, and she couldn't have frozen 'til after Thanksgiving, what happened to the body in the meantime? Assuming she was dead in the interim, that is."

"Professor's right," said Stuffy with a wry smile. "A body don't stay very fresh settin' out for two and a half months."

Curiosity rested a foot in the furrows of Olaf's forehead. "And it woulda been worse floatin' in the quarry the whole time," he said.

"That's right," said Bill. "Remember Benny Howell? They found him not more'n a few days after his boat capsized. He was blue as a moose's balls and half the size of a whale."

There was a murmur of agreement. " 'Course, that was salt water, that was," said Wendell.

Crisp cleared his throat and everyone fell silent. "But you say she was not . . . that is, she was . . ."

"Like she was asleep," said Leeman. "She even had makeup on."

"Makeup?" said Crisp, and reflected a moment. "Makeup, you say?"

Leeman nodded. "That's what Chuckie said. Prob'ly why she looked funny."

"Well, my, my," Crisp said to his reflection in the cigar cabinet. "Imagine that." He looked at Leeman. "I don't suppose any mention was made of how she died."

"I still say she drowned," said Olaf. "Must've."

"You think so?" Crisp replied.

"Well, you find someone dead and they got a four-inch hole in their head, and they're holdin' a thirty ought six, it's a fair bet to say they died of a gunshot," said Olaf.

Everyone but Crisp and Stuffy nodded and made agreeing noises. Stuffy generally withheld agreement on principle. Crisp took a long pull of Moxie and winced. Moxie was good for that. "Makes you less likely to look elsewhere for the cause, I'll say that much," Crisp commented. He stood up, paid Brenda for the drink, and riffled briefly through his pockets, until he remembered that he'd lost what he was looking for, so he quit. "Well, good day, gentlemen."

The cowbell rang in reverse when anyone went out, which it did now as Crisp left. Everyone watched him through the grimy, rippled windows as he stepped out into the cold, tucked his scarf into his collar, pulled his hat down around his ears, and charged off across the street. "Wouldn't take long to count the beans in his jar," said Olaf.

"Don't think so, do ya?" said Stuffy, dealing out the cards for four. Four immediately took their places.

"Don't take much sense to figure he ain't got any," said Olaf.

"Cut for the crib," said Stuffy, drawing an ace. "High card." No one else cut higher than a jack, so Stuffy dropped a five into the crib. "Shows what you know."

Olaf scoffed. "I s'pose you know all about it?"

"Ain't sayin'," said Stuffy. "But I know he worked for the NSA for 'bout half a century, is all."

"What's that?" said Wendell. "Gov'ment?"

"I know he was in gov'ment," said Harry. "Everybody knows that. Argues pretty strong in Olaf's favor, you ask me. Anybody who's been in gov'ment for fifty years is all set for the happy jacket."

Stuffy played thirty for a go. He lit a filterless cigarette and worked it into a damp groove in his lower lip. "National Security Agency is what NSA means," he said in a cloud of smoke, dampened appreciably by ss and cs. "That's just above the CIA. Seventeen for two. You heard of the CIA, ain't you, Olaf?"

"Crisp worked for the CIA?" said Wendell, impressed. He'd imagined the professor more in the spokesman-who-asked-to-remain-anonymous type of work.

"The NSA," Stuffy corrected. "That's more secret. Most folks don't know nothin' about it."

"What'd he do?" said Olaf in a face-saving maneuver. "Shred paper?"

"He ain't pretty enough for that," Bill observed.

Stuffy used his eyebrows to drag Olaf into focus. "Chief code breaker," he said.

The brief silence that followed was heavy with awe. All but Stuffy's eyes turned again to the window. The professor was struggling up the Net Factory Hill, holding his hat, his head, or both against the bitter northwest wind.

"Code breaker," Wendell whispered.

"Twenty-eight for six," said Stuffy, playing a seven. "Chief code breaker," he amended.

WHEN WINSTON CRISP first moved to the island, he'd planned to have the old family cottage winterized and live there year-round. But it was too lonely, even in summer when most of the other cottages along the shore were full. That surprised him. He'd never been lonely before. All those years in the belly of the beast, bent over a microscope, squinting at a computer screen, straining to hear telltale clicks through symphonies of hisses, doodling endlessly in pencil on every available surface, traveling to places no one had ever heard of. He'd never been lonely before. He always had his riddles.

Loneliness lost all pretense when the neighbors left after Labor Day, so he decided to close up the house for the winter and find a place in town.

He'd known Matty Gilchrist most of his life, and they'd always got on pretty well, so he moved into her rooming house. Seemed the natural thing to do. It was a cozy place, with ruffles, porcelain figurines on lace doilies, and gilt-framed portraits of people nobody knew. Little shelves for dishes and pictures of family. Nothing in common with his old digs on Connecticut Avenue in Washington—design by neglect, shades of dried-mustard brown and musty gray, where woman never trod except Miss Flyguard from the Bureau. She'd been there a couple of times, but she was one of those women who'd been neutered by feminism. Alarmingly nice ankles, though.

"Ah, there you are, Winston," said Matty as Crisp came in the front door. Matty always left the kitchen door open so she could see who was coming and going. Of course during the winter it was only Crisp or, on Wednesdays, the telephone men over from the mainland. Still, knowing who it was didn't stop her from checking to make sure. "Any mail?"

Crisp took off his hat, untied his scarf, and carefully draped them on the bentwood stand behind the door. He shuffled through the mail as he headed down the hall toward the kitchen. "Water bill," he said, "something about saving . . . blackflies? Well, I didn't know we had a shortage of blackflies, did you, Matt? I'd always assumed there was a surplus. Seems everything needs saving these . . . Here's something from your sister." He handed her the letter. "And *The Island News.* That's about it."

Matty wiped her hands on her apron. "Nothin' about . . . ?" she said hesitantly.

"No," Crisp replied. "No. Not today."

"Well, then," said Matty. "No news is good news. There's always tomorrow."

Crisp turned his kindly eyes on her and smiled a distant smile. "Always tomorrow, my dear," he said, and squeezed her shoulder.

Matty was the only person in the world who knew about Winston's poetry. It had been their secret for years, and she'd suffered with him through rejection after rejection—form letters most of the time. But once in a while someone had taken the time to jot a note in the margin: "too sentimental," "maudlin," "out-of-date," "what century are you from?" That type of thing.

Matty liked the poems. They rhymed. She thought they were

honest and heartfelt. But the world that valued those things was gone, she knew that. She saw the void every night on TV.

"You sit down there and get comfy," she said with a nod toward one of the old cane-bottomed chairs that lined the table. "I'll put some water on for tea. Just let me get them scones out've the oven and put this potpie in—it's for the church supper—and we'll talk about it." She limped slightly as she went about her business. She'd broken her knee in a fall on the ice three winters ago. It often bothered her when the weather changed.

Winston pulled out the chair and sat down. "They've had this poem a long time," he said softly. "Usually they don't keep it this long. I mean, they usually let you know." As his voice fell in on itself, he fixed his eyes on Matty and followed her back and forth from one end of the counter to the other.

He tried to remember when they'd first met. He often made a game of it, not that it brought him any closer to remembering, but sifting through the memories always turned up one in particular. It was of Matty at about fifteen or sixteen, tumbling over the moors out on James' Island, like a paper doll cut out of the blue sky, her thick, long yellow hair troubled into tangles and edged in gold where the sun tried to peek through. Just the faintest outline of her lithe, young body was visible through the thin blue summer dress. There were lots of little white flowers in the pattern, too. They fell into valleys, danced over the folds, and swept gracefully up to gentle peaks in the most beguiling way.

Matty had aged easily. During the war she was a radio operator with the Coastal Watch. Always practicing her Morse code, ever vigilant. Ever ready for an invasion that never came. Pauline Revere.

The first summer Crisp returned to the island after the war, Matty had taken on a fair amount of what she called "cuddle flesh" and thereafter grew cuddlier and cuddlier as time went on. Never married, she became everyone's favorite aunt. Though she had pretty much overwhelmed the youthful promise of womanhood in almost every respect, she was no less pleasant to behold at the present stage of her life. The overflow was soft and homey and always smelled of something fresh from the oven. Everything about her said "welcome."

Matty lay the crust on the pie as gently as a mother putting a child to bed and crimped the crust with practiced fingers. It was a ballet, perfectly choreographed to the music of her constant chatter. Winston didn't suppose he'd ever write a poem like Matty.

His gaze fell to the table, and he sat quietly for a moment while Matty cleaned up. After a while he was so lost in thought he didn't notice her staring at him.

"Somethin' on your mind?" She poured the tea and put a cup on the table in front of him.

The sound of her voice called him from far away, and he stuttered and stammered a little, as might be expected of any visitor from another dimension. "Huh? Oh, I . . . well, Matty . . . I was just thinking about . . ."

"The girl?"

He nodded.

"Poor thing," said Matty. She had pulled out a chair but didn't sit down; she just wedged it under an ample cheek of her bottom and suspended herself against it, tempting gravity. Through the steam of her tea she regarded her star boarder. When he looked up, she looked down into the cup.

"Poor thing," he echoed.

"Terrible way to die, isn't it? Drowned."

"Oh, I don't think she drowned," said Winston. "I don't think that's very likely."

"What do you mean? They found her up at the quarry, didn't they? Luther told Milly Thompson they found her frozen in ice up there, like I told you this mornin'."

"I know," said Winston. "They were talking about it down at the poolroom. Leeman Russell was telling them how they chipped her out of the ice." Matty turned away. "Sorry, Matty," he said. "But

Leeman was there, you see. Now, what makes it odd is that the girl went missing just after Labor Day and now she turns up frozen, 'fresh as a mornin' in Paris' I think is what Leeman said. Like she was asleep."

Matty lowered herself into the chair. "What do you mean 'went missing'? Who went missing?"

"The girl."

"What girl? That one?" She pointed toward the mortuary.

"Yes, from Senator McKenniston's house."

Matty stood up. "You mean that's the girl young McKenniston was paradin' all over town last summer, the redhead?"

"Seems so."

Matty took her incredulous expression out of mothballs and tried it on. "But she ran away."

"In September," said Crisp.

"Then how'd she turn up froze in the quarry?"

Crisp used his eyebrows to flip the question back to her.

"My word," said Matty. She would have said more, but her eyes had drifted toward the window at the very moment something of interest was happening across the common. "My word," she said. This was clearly an independent remark, to which the previous exclamation was only distantly related. "Looks like they're finished already."

Crisp turned toward the window, pushed the glasses up on his nose, and brought the world into focus. Four men were leaving the mortuary. Luther Kingsbury, the policeman, was easy to tell under his patrolman's-issue blue fur hat with the upturned flaps and a big gold-colored badge. So was Dr. Pagitt, who always walked as if he was leaning on the wind in a force nine gale. Immediately behind them was the only stranger in the trio, undoubtedly Gammidge from the mainland. Last, and most recognizable, was Charles Young, the undertaker. Chuck walked like an inverted pendulum because one leg was a lot shorter than the other.

Matty looked at her watch. "Too late to make the boat."

"What?" said Crisp, cupping his ear. "What'd you say, Matty?"

"That fellow from the mainland—he was goin' to try to make the last boat. Too late now," she said. "He'll be stayin' here tonight, I expect." Her supposition was punctuated by the sound of the boat whistle blowing in the distance. The ferry would return after dark, but the island was effectively severed from the mainland for the long winter's night. Natives slept better in the knowledge. "Better get supper started. Beef stew all right with you, Winston?"

"Fine," Winston replied. He got up from the table and gave her a kiss on the cheek.

"I hate simmerin' stew for less than four hours," she fretted.

"I know you do, my dear," Crisp said. "I'm going up to my room to write for a while."

"You do that," said Matty. "I'll bring you up some scones later on." No one was surprised that Crisp had gained nearly twenty pounds since he moved in with Matty. They would have been surprised if he hadn't. But he was still thin as Salome's veils.

Poetry wouldn't come this afternoon. Every time Crisp closed his eyes to concentrate, all he could see was the dead girl in ice. Of course, his imagination was somewhat handicapped, never having seen her himself. No doubt this accounted for the fact that, in his mind's eye, she looked uncommonly like Olaf Ingraham. This made the vision no less disturbing.

The front hall door opened and Luther Kingsbury's voice searched the premises without a warrant. "Matty! You t'home? Matty!"

For a moment the only reply was the loud ticktock of the grandmother clock over the umbrella stand. Momentarily, though, that worthy lady's footsteps could be heard in the hall. Crisp went to the top of the landing. "Evening, Luther," he said.

"Hi, Professor." Luther turned to the stranger who accompanied him. "Nate, this here's—" But it was too late to make an introduction as Matty entered under full sail.

"There you are, Luther." As usual she was wiping something wonderful off her hands. "I've been expectin' you."

"I told you," Luther said to the stranger. "News travels fast out here."

"News got nothin' to do with it," Matty interceded on her own behalf. "I saw you come out of the mortuary same time as the boat whistle blew. And since I'm the only place open year-round, I put a few extra carrots in the stew. Stew okay with you?" she asked, holding out her hand.

The stranger shook her hand. "Nate Gammidge, ma'am."

"Matty Gilchrist," she said. "Everybody calls me Matty."

"Matty," Nate Gammidge said with a tilt of the head. "Stew's fine with me. Sorry to put you out at the last moment like this."

Matty took his coat, hat, scarf, and gloves and hung them on the stand with all the creases pointed in the same direction. "Only time innkeepers get put out is when they ain't put out. Come on in and have some coffee, or would you rather have tea? Winston generally likes tea this time of day."

Crisp had waited halfway up the stairs for Matty's initial wave of hospitality to subside. She was one of those people who'd practically force her services on you—press your shorts and darn your socks somewhere between "hello" and "walk this way." She needed room to maneuver.

Crisp descended the rest of the way. "She's not referring to the family pet, Mr. Gammidge," said Crisp. "At least not in so many words." He held out his hand. "I'm Winston Crisp."

"Call me Nate," said Gammidge, shaking Crisp's hand warmly and looking him in the eye. Crisp noted what a rare thing that was. "Winston Crisp?" he said thoughtfully.

"Sounds a bit like an after-dinner mint, I'm afraid," said Crisp apologetically.

Gammidge's mind was recalled from elsewhere. "What? Oh . . ." He laughed politely. "No . . . well . . . I was just wondering if I've heard that name before."

"Not likely."

"Seems I have, though. Not a name you're likely to forget."

"Nor a person you're likely to remember," Crisp replied with a smile.

"You stayin' for coffee, Luther?" said Matty.

Luther, who lived in mortal dread of his wife, gathered his wits toward supper, excused himself, and—having informed Matty that "the town will take care of it," meaning the bill—left.

Matty deposited her boarders in the parlor and bounced off to the kitchen to tend dinner.

Winston let Gammidge have his choice of chairs. Gammidge sat in Winston's favorite, by the fireplace. Winston sat opposite him and loaded his pipe. "Do you mind?"

Gammidge shook his head. He looked around the room. "Cozy place you got here," he said.

"Oh, it's . . . it's Matty's," Crisp replied. "I'm just . . . I board here, is all."

Gammidge nodded. "Cozy." He took a magazine from the stand, opened it, and stared at the fire over the top of the pages.

"Your first time on the island?" Crisp asked.

"No. Well, in an official capacity, you could say . . . but I come out here once a year or so, with my wife. She has family out here. Usually we stay down at the Tidewater."

"Oh," said Winston. "That's closed for the winter. Repairs of some kind, I gather."

Gammidge nodded and his eyes reverted to the fire. Crisp let the silence turn the screws (it had the effect with most Americans, he'd observed) and finally force him to speak. "Nasty business."

"Really?" said Crisp. "Oh, you mean the . . . my, yes. Awful business. Awful."

"Nasty," Gammidge reiterated, but he failed to attach the anticipated explanation.

Crisp was not prepared to let the topic lapse. "Terrible," he said. "To die like that."

Gammidge looked at him sharply and seemed about to say something. Instead, he just smiled. "Mmm."

"They say she drowned."

"That's what they say," Gammidge replied.

"She didn't, though, did she?"

Gammidge studied his companion a little more closely. "You don't think so?"

"I would say it was murder."

For some reason Gammidge took hasty inventory of the doorways with his eyes. "Murder?"

"Strangled or poisoned, most likely. Am I right?"

"What makes you say that?"

"Just a hunch," Crisp replied softly. "No water in her lungs, was there?"

Gammidge produced a cigarette.

"Don't let Matty see you with that," Crisp warned.

"But you—"

"She likes the smell of pipe tobacco. At least this kind. It's the same as her father smoked. But she hates cigarettes—foul the air, she says. Burns in the furniture, you know." Gammidge started to put the cigarette back. "You want to go out on the porch and have a smoke?" Crisp offered. "I'll go out with you."

Once they were out on the porch swing, heavily garbed against the cold, the conversation picked up where it had left off. "Why do you think I didn't find water in the lungs?"

"From what I've heard, she wasn't bloated," said Crisp. "She was dead before she went in."

"Well, I expect it'll be all over town by morning anyway," Gammidge sighed. "She was strangled. Pretty brutally, too, from what we can make out. Must've been huge hands to reach clear 'round her neck like that."

"Who could have done such a thing?"

"Well," said Gammidge after a long, satisfying pull at his cigarette, "it won't be a mystery for long."

"How's that?"

"Fingerprints."

"Fingerprints!" said Crisp. "That's quite unusual, isn't it? I mean, if the body had been in the water any length of time."

"Tomorrow I'll put it down to expert detective work, Mr. Crisp," Gammidge confided. "But, just between us, it was pure luck. Seems the girl had fresh makeup on"—his hands went to his neck—"all the way down here."

"And that's where the fingerprints were preserved, in the makeup?"

"In the makeup," Gammidge echoed. "Plain as day. You can see 'em with the naked eye." He smiled. "Somebody's in for it."

A corner of Crisp's mouth smiled all by itself. "No doubt," he said. "No doubt at all." The moment's silence that followed was finally broken by Crisp. "I'm curious, though. You see, I'm . . . that is, in my line of work—well, I'm retired now—but . . . I was a bit of a chemist. I like to do little experiments now and again. Would you happen to know what kind of makeup it was?"

"Haven't the foggiest," Gammidge replied. "Ugly as sin. Must have been some kind of chemical reaction with the water. You'd know better than me. Anyway, I took some samples. They're in my case. But that's more than a little out of my line, if you know what I mean. I'm an appointee—just sign the death certificates, basically. Leave all the hands-on business to doctors and the lab folks up in Augusta. That's who I got the sample for."

"I don't suppose it would be possible to have a look," Crisp asked, only poorly concealing his excitement.

"Oh, no," Gammidge replied quickly. "No. I don't think that'd be a good idea. It's evidence, you see. Not a whole lot of it. That is, I didn't take a lot—"

"Oh, but I only need a dusting, really." Instantly Crisp regretted putting Gammidge in an awkward position. "I'm sorry, Nate," Crisp said with a smile. "I tend to get a little carried away from time to time. Of course I understand . . . evidence, and all . . . you need to—"

"I have to turn it in."

"Turn it in, of course you do," Crisp said.

"Send it up to Augusta," Gammidge said. "That's their job."

"Of course it is," Crisp agreed. "You're right. I shouldn't have mentioned it." He tapped out his pipe on the porch railing and, producing a pipe cleaner from his coat pocket, began a meticulous cleaning process. For a while the noises of the night took over the conversation. "Just curious is all," Crisp said at last, as if to himself. "If it's oil based, well, that's curious."

Gammidge took the bait. "What?"

"Pardon?"

"You said, 'If it's oil based.' What do you mean?"

"Oh, well, I was just thinking out loud, you know, about the makeup. To have stayed on any time in the water . . . is she fair skinned or dark skinned, would you say?"

"Fair," said Gammidge. "Very fair."

"Mmm. Fair. Well, then. To have stayed on any time in the water, the makeup would have to be oil based—anhydrous," said Crisp.

"It would?"

"Most makeup is water based nowadays. It would wash off in less time than it takes for water to freeze, you see? And whatever hadn't washed off—well, it's not likely you'd notice it straight out of the ice like that." Crisp waited. Just a nudge or two in the right direction. "But Leeman said Chuck noticed it as they were chipping her out. Curious."

Gammidge scratched his neck and pulled his collar up a little higher. "What's fair skin got to do with it?"

"Fair skin and dark, or ruddy, skin react differently to makeup. The makeup would probably have congealed on someone with darker skin."

"Don't that beat all," said Gammidge.

"Curious," said Crisp. "A little bit of a puzzle."

Gammidge studied Crisp long and hard while Crisp looked

absentmindedly into the distance, pretending not to notice that he was being stared at. He'd learned a lot about human nature in seventy-odd years. He knew that silence was the midwife of thought.

"I don't see what we'd gain," said Gammidge. "I mean, what difference does it make? She was strangled, then thrown in the quarry." The statement had a rhetorical ring about it, so Crisp left it alone. Gammidge made thinking sounds. "Maybe how long between when she was strangled and thrown in . . . You think it might tell us that?"

Crisp doubted it. "You never know what an investigation will turn up."

"It wouldn't hurt." Gammidge looked again at Crisp. "You're really a chemist?"

"Hmm?" said Crisp as if his train of thought had gone off on another track. "Pardon?"

"You've done that sort of thing before? I mean, have you ever worked for the police? Forensics?"

"The police?" said Crisp. "Well, no. No, I can't say I have . . . worked for the police. No."

It would have made it easier if he had. "Oh," said Gammidge.

"Mmm," said Crisp. "Nope." He paused, laying a foundation of silence upon which to build his addendum. "Unless you count the CIA," he said, more steam than sound. "I don't suppose they're police though, are they?"

"Pardon?"

"I beg your pardon?"

"What did you say about the CIA?"

"Oh," Crisp said. "I was just . . . thinking out loud, you know. I said I've done a little work for the CIA in my time. Well, actually it wasn't the CIA when I started. It was—"

"You worked for the CIA?" said Gammidge, suspended tightly between skepticism and the wish to believe.

"The OSS," said Crisp, who thought it impolite not to finish a sentence, providing you could remember what you wanted to say.

"Not directly, though. I mean, they didn't . . . I was working for another branch of the government at the time, but—"

"But you did work for the CIA? Chemistry work?"

"They'd call me in from time to time for some little problem or other. Yes," said Crisp. "From time to time."

Gammidge would need a moment or two to argue with himself. Meanwhile, Crisp worked at looking like the kind of person with whom Gammidge wouldn't mind entrusting important evidence.

"You have what you need here, up in your room, I suppose?"

"You suppose correctly," said Crisp. "Nothing very elaborate . . . "

Gammidge got up. "It's cold out here," he said, faith having triumphed over reason. "Won't hurt to see what you've got up there, would it?"

"I don't see how it could," said Crisp. "Of course, I wouldn't expect you to do anything you might feel uncomfortable about."

Two hours later, amid a jumble of dinner dishes, ashtrays, and test tubes, Gammidge found himself leaning over Crisp's shoulder as the latter arranged a few specks of residue on a glass slide and fixed it under his old brass microscope.

"Of course, this isn't the real problem, is it?" said Gammidge. "Given what we know about the fingerprints and . . . The question is, what happened to her after she left the island? And why did she come back? And who killed her?"

"I understand she was seen in Rockland," said Crisp, trying to bring the smudge into focus. "Did anyone else see her? I mean, anywhere else?"

"Not that I know of," said Gammidge. " 'Course, the FBI was handling the whole thing. Senator got 'em in on it, so we didn't have a whole lot to do with the case. But she wasn't seen anywhere else, far as I know."

"That's strange," said Crisp.

"What? Do you see something?"

"Oil-based."

"Well, that explains why it didn't come off in the water. Not so strange, I wouldn't say," replied Gammidge.

"No," said Crisp thoughtfully. "No. What's strange is, it contains traces of lead."

"Lead?" Gammidge peered into the microscope. "Lead?"

They looked at each other at close range. "Reddish traces, in the pigment."

"That's awful poisonous to put in makeup, isn't it?"

"It is indeed," said Crisp. "That's why they stopped making it in 1932."

GAMMIDGE PONDERED THE STATEMENT for a moment, then stood abruptly as if he'd been struck. He began to pace, rubbing his forehead in an effort to massage some sense to the front of his brain. "This thing's getting more holes than my car insurance contract, Crisp. First there's this gap between when she turned up missing and when she died. And nobody knows how she got back to the island. Now it turns out she's wearing makeup older than she was. I tell you, this business is getting beyond me in a big hurry."

It was Crisp's turn to study Gammidge, and the scrutiny made Gammidge uncomfortable. "What?"

"I'd like to see the body, Nate," Crisp said flatly. Before Gammidge could protest he added, "It's highly irregular, of course, I realize, but it's not illegal, is it?"

"You know it isn't," said Gammidge. "Mighty irregular, though." A blink or two in punctuation. "Mighty irregular."

"I'll call Mr. Young, if you like."

"Mr. Young?"

"Charlie."

"Oh, the undertaker. Mmm, wouldn't have to if he'd had his way," said Gammidge. "You know I almost had to twist his arm to get him to lock the door. 'She ain't goin' nowhere,' he says. I had to remind him this wasn't another old lobsterman dying of a heart attack. 'She still ain't goin' nowhere,' he says."

Crisp smiled. "Keys aren't much in fashion out here."

"No," said Gammidge. "I can see that." He paused long enough to make it seem as though he hadn't made up his mind. "Go ahead and call him, but for pity sakes just don't tell him about the makeup. Not good to have too much evidence floating around, even if none of it makes any sense." He paused. " 'Specially if none of it makes sense."

Outside the mortuary a lone streetlamp orphaned its light on the doorstep of the dark and the cold. Snowflakes, jostling one another for their turn in the spotlight, parted to make way for a distinctly Charlie Young–shaped shadow that approached, leaning on the wind at an almost supernatural angle.

Winston Crisp and Nate Gammidge were on the porch of the mortuary, keeping as much out of the storm as possible. Charlie had to hold the railing and pull himself up the steps. He dug for the keys in his overcoat pocket and yelled to make himself heard.

"I'd like to know what in blazes is so important it couldn't wait 'til mornin'!" His mittens made his fingers too fat to grab the keys. He took them off. He cursed, or prayed, depending on your point of view. There were only three keys on the ring and one was a car key; nevertheless it took three tries to find the right one. "If you'd've let me leave it open in the first place, I wouldn't've had to—" The wind tore off the rest of his words and ran away with them. Seconds later everyone was inside, dripping on the linoleum.

"Sorry about getting you out on a night like this, Chuck," Crisp said as soon as he had command of his tongue.

The storm had highlighted Charlie's face with white and hung icicles on his eyebrows and mustache. "Why didn't you drive?" Gammidge asked.

"Car's broke," Charlie snapped. "And if it wasn't I don't guess I'm so spleeny I'd drive it up here from the bottom of the hill. I get to that point, you can just lay me on the slab in there and start diggin'." He shook off his hat and stamped his boots. "What'd you want over here, Professor?"

"Well, Mr. Gammidge and I were just talking. You know he's staying over at Matty's."

"Well, I guess he would be, come to think of it, since the motel's closed," said Charlie thoughtfully, thawing now that he was out of the cold. "You get her to make you some've her blueberry muffins, Nate. She makes blueberry muffins good enough to bring a sailor home. Still," he said with a jerk of his head toward the cooling room door, "what's that got to do with her?"

"Seems there's some things that just want explaining," said Gammidge. "The more we talked, the murkier the water got, you know?"

"Well, somethin' awful is all I can say," replied Charlie. "Baby is all she is." He paused. "Was. Had her whole life . . ." Snow seemed to melt in the corner of his eye. He wiped it away. "I don't get too many young ones. Mostly pretty old. Half embalmed already. That ain't so bad." He pushed open the door to the kitchen and turned on the light. "They lived a long time and jus' come through here in the natural flow've things. I've known 'em all my life, most've 'em. I talk to 'em, you know? Sounds crazy, don't it?" He filled the teakettle with water, put it on the stove, and turned on the gas. "Well, I do. Just like I was Doubtful Bailey givin' 'em a haircut, or somethin'. You want tea, Nate?"

It was too cold to say no. "Please."

"Crisp?"

Crisp nodded. Charlie got out two cups. "They all know me, too," he said. "You know what I mean? They all know they'll come to me sooner or later. Makes kind've a bond. I mean, I meet 'em on the street, or down to the hardware store, the post office, or anywhere—it's always kind've in the back've your mind, isn't it? They know, when the time comes, I'll do right by 'em. Do 'em up good. Treat 'em with respect." He extracted tea bags and a little Cool Whip container of sugar from the cupboard. "Same time, they know I ain't countin' the days, though. That's important."

Gammidge looked at Crisp with a smile on his face, but Crisp was craning his head toward the speaker, listening with all his heart. Anticipation perhaps? He was getting on, after all. Seventy-five? Eighty? Not long 'til he'd be a captive audience for one of Charlie Young's monologues.

"But this poor child," Charlie continued. "Some days I hate this job." He shut off the gas and poured steaming water into the cups. "You can leave your coats on them pegs in the hall," he said, putting on his mittens and his hat. He slid the key ring off the counter and handed it to Gammidge. "You want the place locked from now on, you lock it. I ain't gettin' outta bed again tonight."

Gammidge took the keys good-naturedly. "I'll bring them over first thing in the morning."

"No need," said Charlie, making his way to the door. "I'll just come in the back door and unlock it from inside."

"You mean you didn't lock the back door?" said Gammidge.

Charlie grinned. "It don't have a lock."

"But what's the point? Why did you bother?"

"Just wanted to see what you was up to," said Charlie. " 'Night." It was hard to tell if he grinned or not. He closed the door and let the storm carry him homeward.

Crisp was trying not to smile. Fortunately he didn't have to make a living at it.

"That beat's everything," said Gammidge, prepared to be thoroughly put out, until he saw Crisp's expression. Then he laughed to wake the dead.

The wind howled maniacally, driving legions of snowflakes to their death against the mortuary windows. No two died alike. Winston pulled up short with both hands on the cooling room door. "I wish this wasn't necessary," he said. Gammidge put a reassuring hand on his shoulder and nudged the door, letting Winston's weight push it open. Light from the hall painted a doorway on the floor. The shadows it framed stood still a moment. The far edge of the light was draped with the folds of a white cloth, which Crisp presumed to be the shroud. He sniffed. "Formaldehyde."

"You'd think I'd've stopped getting the creeps in these places long ago," said Gammidge, feeling for the light switch. "I can just picture her, sitting up on the table in the dark, looking at us."

Crisp hadn't thought of that. He was relieved when the light clicked on. The body was on the table in the middle of the room, where it belonged. Not that it took a lot to imagine that the folds of the shroud that covered it had just fallen into place.

Gammidge took two pairs of disposable gloves from a dispenser on the wall and handed one pair to Crisp. "Put these on," he said. "Enough fingerprints around here already." Gammidge knew the body, so Crisp let him approach first. He drew the shroud back from her face and looked at Crisp. "Well," he said by way of introduction, "here she is."

Crisp took a few crablike steps toward the body, deaf side forward, and squinted as if to keep as much of the image as possible out of his brain. Once beside the table he stood staring into the air above it. Murder once removed was a mystery. Give it a face and a name, it was a tragedy. He knew that when he looked down, the girl on the table would become part of his life forever.

"We don't have to do this, Mr. Crisp," said Gammidge softly. "My people in Augusta will sort it out. It's their job, you know."

Crisp closed his eyes, swallowed hard, lowered his head, opened his eyes, and absorbed the image of the dead girl.

"Good Lord!" he gasped reflexively.

"Makes you feel like you should whisper, doesn't she?" Gammidge murmured. It was true. There was nothing corpselike about the face. She was simply a beautiful young woman, asleep. Crisp was glad Charlie had closed her eyes. "I tell you," Gammidge continued quietly. "I'll never understand kids and makeup. Look at her—I guess she's about as pretty a girl as I've seen, wife excepted, of course—and look at all that makeup and whatnot. So thick it's practically chipped off in places. Look here."

So it was. But Crisp's thoughts were breathless at that instant. Exclamation marks seldom found a way into his vocabulary, so whatever superlatives he knew had atrophied from disuse. Consequently even his mind was speechless. She was a beautiful child. The ghastly pastels of death, visible beneath the paint, brushed her delicate features—the turn of the nose, the sweep of the lips. She was just the kind of girl he'd have designed if given the assignment. It didn't seem possible that those pale, peaceful lids concealed only the bald, sunken stare of death.

The makeup was all wrong.

Gammidge turned down the shroud. Once again Crisp was jarred to the soul. An ugly ring of rust-colored flesh banded the girl's neck, in sharp contrast to the pale greenish alabaster of her skin. The first stages of decomposition were evident, especially in the area of her larynx, which seemed to have been compressed during the attack.

"Crushed her windpipe," said Gammidge. "You can see the fingerprints—you get right up close."

Crisp removed his bifocals from his coat pocket and wedged them on his nose. He bent over the wound. After a moment's inspection he nodded and stood up. He took off his glasses and rubbed his eyes.

"Make anything of it?"

"Pass me a couple of those, will you?" Crisp pointed at a box of swabs on the counter behind Gammidge.

"What're you gonna do?" said Gammidge, holding out the box.

Crisp once again bent over the body and began sniffing in the vicinity of the shoulder. Then, with the stick end of the swab, he began delicately scraping the skin.

"You're not touching the fingerprints, are you?" said Gammidge, nudging himself into Crisp's frame of reference. "Don't do that!"

"I won't," Crisp replied, raising his eyebrows but not his eyes. "I'm nowhere near . . . that's odd."

Gammidge bent close. "What?"

"Moisture seems to . . . would you mind getting me some water, Mr. Gammidge?"

"Just water?"

"If you would." Crisp had produced a magnifying glass from his pocket and was minutely inspecting the girl's flesh.

"I thought Sherlock Holmes was the only one who used those things," Gammidge said to himself. He went to get the water. By the time he returned, Crisp had extended his survey as far as the toes.

"Here you go," said Gammidge, proffering the water, which Crisp drank.

"Thank you."

Gammidge was flabbergasted. "I thought you wanted it for some experiment or something."

"I beg your pardon?" said Crisp, turning an innocent eye on Gammidge. "Oh, no. I was just . . . I get thirsty in the winter. It's so dry indoors. Well," he said, returning to the business at hand, "I think we can make a few assumptions."

"About the lead?"

Crisp stood up and took off his rubber gloves. "Lead? Oh, I think that's pretty high level in the makeup. No doubt."

"What then?"

"Well," Crisp said thoughtfully. "I think it's safe to say she'd been lying out in the sun within an hour or so before she died and that she'd been wearing a . . . one of those little . . ." Crisp used sign language to supplement his vocabulary.

"Bikinis?"

Crisp nodded and reddened slightly. "Without a . . . that is to say . . ." Once again he let his fingers to the talking.

"No top? You mean to say you think she was naked?"

"Nude. Yes," Crisp said quickly. "On the beach."

"What was on the beach?"

"She was."

"You mean, she was on the beach when she died?"

"If not," Crisp said, "she had been within an hour or so before, I should imagine. You see?" he said, holding up a cotton swab with pepperlike specks on it."

"What is it?"

"Beach sand."

"Sand?"

"Beach sand," Crisp corrected. "There's a big difference between beach sand and gravel sand." Gammidge's expression asked, is there? "Yes. You see, gravel sand is sharper to the touch. Beach sand is almost soft. All that friction . . . washing up and down on the beach, you see . . . every wave—"

"Rounding the edges," Gammidge said, catching on.

"Year after year," said Crisp, concluding his thought. "Exactly. I got this from her toenails. They're smooth on the edges, you see? And I'm sure if we did a chemical analysis, we'd find a trace of salt."

"But she was found in the quarry, Crisp," Gammidge complained. "That's fresh water."

Crisp draped the shroud over the girl's feet as if he was tucking in a beloved grandchild. "I said we could make assumptions, Mr. Gammidge. I didn't say they'd necessarily make sense."

"No. They sure don't," Gammidge agreed. "How did you come up with all these notions anyway?"

Crisp took another swab from the table beside the body and held it up to Gammidge's nose. Gammidge sniffed. "I know that smell," he said, and sniffed again. "Don't tell me." Crisp waited patiently. "Coconut?" he guessed. "Coconut? Suntan oil?"

"I'm sure it is," Crisp replied. "I'm sure it is. And it's only in . . . those places . . . you'd expect to find a tan."

"And not where you wouldn't?" said Gammidge.

"Except for the . . ." Crisp indicated the chest area. "I would have expected . . . ahem. Yes. But, you see there's a film of moisture on the body—residue from the ice, probably, as the body doesn't seem to have absorbed much in those areas where you'd expect to find a tan. It's formed into perfect little drops. Oil, you see? Otherwise, there's no film. If you were to paint the body with a dye, a colored water, it would adhere to the bikini area but not to the rest. It would bead."

"It'd look like she still had the bikini bottom on?"

Crisp stepped to the other end of the table. "You might say that. As if . . . yes. That's why the makeup is peeling off, you see? Because it was put on over the suntan oil. The suntan oil is meant to be absorbed—to a degree—so its molecules are smaller than those of the makeup. In effect, they repel each other."

Gammidge furrowed his brow. "Would they do that?"

"What?"

"Do they put on makeup over suntan oil? That doesn't make sense, does it?"

Crisp shrugged. "Chemically it doesn't, no," he said. "But I'm afraid I can't speak with much confidence as far as fashion goes. Not exactly my . . . some of the things women do. Well." He paused briefly. "Of course I don't suppose you remember the bustle?"

Gammidge replied that, of course, he didn't. But he had seen pictures.

"Well, I've never seen them, either," said Crisp softly, "in person. I'm not quite that old. But my mother . . . well. I'll have to show you my family pictures sometime. I remember my father expressing his amazement that sensible women—doesn't matter what they are, doctors, lawyers, or charwomen—will trample one another in their rush to sacrifice good sense to the god of fashion. I think that's how he put it. I've always liked that."

"Isn't it the truth," Gammidge agreed. "I can't see putting makeup on a face like that."

"Much less makeup forty-odd years old," said Crisp.

Gammidge shook his head. "That's a real stinker. 'Course, I'll still have to send those samples off to Augusta."

"Oh, of course," said Crisp. "As you said, it's all academic, isn't it? Given the fingerprints and . . . well, we're just satisfying our curiosity, aren't we?"

"I wouldn't say my curiosity's feeling very satisfied, Mr. Crisp. In fact, the harder you look at this case, the hungrier it gets."

"There's always that danger when one approaches evidence with an open mind."

"What do you mean, 'open mind'?"

"Well, Mr. Gammidge, to paraphrase an analogy I heard recently, let's assume you heard a shot in a closed room. You entered the room and found a man with a smoking gun in his hand standing over a dead body. The man with the gun was known to hate the dead man passionately. Now, it's your job to provide the court with evidence in the case. What do you do?"

"I search the victim, the room, the murderer, and the weapon and assemble the clues to hang him," said Gammidge.

"That's where the error lies, you see," said Crisp. "You assume the man with the gun is the murderer. Because of that, you approach the evidence with prejudice. So if evidence fits your view of the crime, you accept it; if it doesn't, you ignore it—overlook it."

"But, I mean, it stands to reason. You make certain assumptions—"

"In this instance you assumed wrongly," said Crisp. "So did the jury, as it turns out."

"You mean that actually happened?"

"In Baltimore. About the turn of the century. The suicide note was found under a dresser several days after the gentleman with the smoking gun had been hanged for murder. Insisted on wearing his bowler hat and a scarlet cummerbund for the occasion, as I recall."

"But . . . how could they overlook a suicide note?"

Crisp cocked his head slightly and weighted his words with his eyes. "Because they weren't looking for it," he said. "They didn't—"

". . . have an open mind," Gammidge interjected.

". . . have an open mind," Crisp said. "That's correct. It's important we don't make the same mistake in this case."

"But, I mean, when you've got someone's fingerprints on a strangle victim's neck, that's a lot different than a smoking gun, wouldn't you say? After all, she didn't strangle herself."

"I'd say that's a sensible conclusion," said Crisp. "Still, as someone once said, there are points of interest."

"Points of confusion, you mean."

"I'm simply suggesting that we don't ignore evidence merely because it doesn't fit with what we expect to find," said Crisp. "Anytime facts are being overlooked, chances are the truth is as well," he added. "And truth is the thing, you see."

"Well then, what are the facts so far?" Gammidge asked. "Let's say she'd been at the beach. Why don't you think she was murdered there?"

Crisp rested his slim left buttock comfortably against the marble slab. "Because of the makeup," he said. "I don't pretend to know much about women, but what I gather is they tend to need mirrors for this sort of operation. Larger mirrors than those they carry for general maintenance. Also, if this makeup is as old as . . . old enough to contain lead, it would have come in porcelain jars and tin tubes. A little cumbersome to carry around. Especially someone so . . . lacking in pockets."

"She could have had a bag."

"Possibly," said Crisp. "And a strong arm." He brushed the arm of the corpse lightly through the shroud.

After a brief silence Gammidge resumed his compilation of suppositions. "Okay. She was at the beach, or had been recently. Somebody snuck up on her, after she'd put on makeup over her suntan lotion, and strangled her." Gammidge pantomimed the murder in the air. "Then he took her up to the quarry and dumped her. Craps!

She was frozen. It didn't freeze hard 'til almost December. What was she doing sunbathing on the beach in December?"

"During a hard freeze," Crisp added incidentally. He'd been spinning the magnifying glass between his thumb and fingers. He tucked it into his vest pocket. "I seem to remember someone saying she had a shirt or blouse on?"

"That's right. Sweatshirt. Charlie put it in a bag around here someplace. Probably in one of these . . ." The room was lined with a low bank of built-in wooden drawers. Gammidge began pulling them out and sifting through the contents. "Here it is," he said after a brief search. He held up a plastic grocery bag to which an index card was affixed. "Her name's on here somewhere. Here it is. Amanda Murphy."

"Amanda Murphy," said Crisp softly. Sadly. Now the tragedy had a name, like a ghost ship or shipwreck: the *Andrea Doria,* the *Mary Celeste,* the Amanda Murphy. "Pretty name."

"Pretty girl," said Gammidge.

Crisp took the bag and removed a sweatshirt, which was still wet. "It's a man's shirt." He spread it out on the instrument table, revealing a huge number 33 and the Yale logo. He squeezed one of the sleeves until a drop or two of water fell into his open palm. He tasted it. "Fresh," he said.

Gammidge nodded. "Quarry water."

Gently Crisp turned the shirt over and examined it. "Blood on the collar."

"Just where it would be if she was wearing the shirt when she was . . ." Gammidge let silence finish the sentence. "That's what I figured was some queer, though—how she was wearing that shirt, a man's shirt, and nothing else. I mean, nothing."

Crisp nodded absentmindedly. "Most peculiar," he said, almost in a whisper.

"Queer," Gammidge reiterated. "And if she was wearing one of those bikini things, where did it go?"

Crisp draped the sweatshirt carefully across the table. "It would have to be near the murder scene somewhere," he said to himself.

"What?"

Ignoring the question, Crisp inclined his head confidentially to-ward Gammidge, but he didn't take his eyes from the shirt. "Did you happen to . . . this is rather delicate, Mr. Gammidge—Nate . . . but did you happen to notice . . . that is, did Doctor Pagitt examine the girl to see if she had been—"

"Oh. Well, yes," said Gammidge. "In a case like this—I mean, no clothes to speak of, and strangled—well, it's the first thing you do, you know. No." He reddened slightly. Gammidge didn't make the acquaintance of many young ladies in a professional capacity. "I mean, as far as he could tell. Of course, there still have to be tests and . . . the doctor took samples. But not as far as we could tell. Maybe you could—"

"Oh, no!" said Crisp. He could feel his feet flushing in his imi-tation fur-lined L.L. Bean boots. "No, I couldn't. I'm hardly quali-fied. He removed a kerchief from his vest pocket and mopped his brow. "Gracious. No. I'm quite prepared to take Dr. Pagitt's . . . Mmm." He cleared his throat. "No signs of a struggle?"

"Well . . ."

"Well?"

"Well, it's probably not important, but look at her hands."

"Her hands?" Crisp took one of the hands from beneath the shroud and held it in his own. It was so small. So delicate. So cold. He turned the palm upward and immediately saw what Gammidge was referring to. Across the first joint of each finger was a wound, one that must have originally been thin and superficial but had widened and deepened with decay.

Gammidge peeked over Crisp's shoulder. "Make anything of it?"

Crisp motioned toward the other hand. "Is there the same—"

"Yup." Gammidge nodded. "Same thing on both hands."

"I see," said Crisp. He studied the wound with his magnifying glass. "Something's oxidized here."

"Blood, I should imagine," said Gammidge.

"Do you suppose so?"

Already Gammidge had read enough of Winston Crisp to brace for the sucker punch. "Don't you?" he said feebly.

"Well, that would mean this wound was made after she died," said Crisp. "You see, there's no sign of bleeding. No. I don't think the skin was broken, originally. I would say that whatever did this was rusty."

"You mean," said Gammidge, trying to make out the ledges in the fog, "you mean . . . What in hell do you mean?"

"I would say the wound was made by a wire of some kind."

"A wire?"

"A rusty one."

"A rusty one? You mean they dragged a rusty wire across her hands?"

Crisp gently tucked the arm under the shroud. "No," he said. He began twirling the magnifying glass in his fingers again. The storm was complaining bitterly outside. His eyes drifted toward the window and he stared holes in the deep, angry night. "She was strangled with it."

"Strangled?"

A length of gauze hung from the rim of the gray plastic trash can. Crisp picked it up and wound an end around each fist. "Turn around. I'll show you."

It may have been the fact that they were in a funeral parlor. It may have been because the cold, soulless body of a young woman lay not three feet away. It may have been the storm, moaning through the graveyard of his unconscious, rallying the ghosts of childish fears. Whatever it was, Gammidge didn't particularly want to turn his back on someone who was going to demonstrate a strangling. Chills ran all over him with cleats on.

"I think I'll get the idea if you just tell me," he said.

"It's just gauze, Nate," said Crisp. "You can do it to me, if you want."

Gammidge scolded the ghosts back into their graves and turned his back on Crisp. Without warning Crisp dropped the gauze around Gammidge's neck and began to tighten. Immediately Gammidge's hands flew to his defense, grabbing the cord on either side of his neck.

"See?" said Crisp, loosening the tourniquet.

It took Gammidge a second or two to swallow his heart, but—still holding the gauze with both hands—he got the message at once. "Somebody tried to strangle her with a rusty old wire. She put her hands up, just like I just did. The harder they twisted, the harder she pulled."

"It must have been over fairly quickly," said Crisp. He tugged at the gauze and Gammidge let it fall. "Otherwise her fingers would have been cut through." He rolled the gauze into a ball and dropped it into the trash can. "She didn't suffer."

The rush of blood to Gammidge's brain had a lubricating effect on his thought process. "But what about the fingerprints?" he said indignantly. He pulled down the shroud to reveal the girl's neck. "You can see as clear as day, somebody had their hands around her neck. Are you trying to say he strangled her once with a wire, then again with his hands? Why? To incriminate himself? That makes no sense.

"Nope. I'm afraid you let your imagination run away with you this time, Winston." The look in Gammidge's eyes as he stared at the wound on the girl's neck was that of a man trying to make sense of a senseless tragedy. "She could've got those scars on her hands any number of ways—climbing over a wire fence, tying a postal package, even flying a kite, for pity sakes. I've done it myself." He covered the girl's face again.

"Nope. You just don't strangle someone twice. Besides," Gammidge concluded, "if she was strangled with rusty wire, any kind of wire, there'd be wounds on her neck, all around it, wouldn't there?"

Crisp smiled slightly and looked at the floor.

" 'Course there would," Gammidge said, trying to balance the evidence on his hypothesis.

"You're probably right," said Crisp. He realized he'd trespassed on Gammidge's good will long enough. "They could have come from anywhere."

" 'Course they could have," said Gammidge. They went to the door and turned off the light. "Once we find out who those finger-prints belong to—"

"By the way," Crisp said matter-of-factly. "Did you happen to notice what color her hair is?"

"Her hair?" Gammidge echoed incredulously. "Red as Hades, f'r pity sakes. Hard to miss that."

"That's right," said Crisp. "So was the wig."

"Wig?" mouthed Gammidge. "She was wearing a wig?"

"I took it off and put it in the bag with the sweatshirt."

Gammidge stopped in his tracks. "Why didn't Charlie Young notice it?"

"He wasn't looking for it," replied Crisp. As he pulled the door shut, it creaked loudly on its hinges, like a cry from the dead. He turned and looked at Gammidge. "Curious, isn't it?" he said.

They stepped into the storm at angles and, wading to the far shore of the circle of streetlight, were absorbed by the darkness.

CHAPTER 4

APART FROM LEEMAN RUSSELL and the pool hall, there are two places on the island you can plug into the grapevine: Fifield's hardware store and Irma Louise's House of Beauty. This eminent list once included the barbershop, but Georgy Kirby died. Doubtful Bailey, the new barber, was from away, so nobody talked to him.

Of course the beauty shop was the exclusive domain of the fair sex. There they heaped burning coals upon one another in absentia and, incidentally, did inexplicable things to their hair with foul-smelling fluids. In summer, when the door was open, you had to hold your breath for fifteen seconds on either side as you passed, or risk a lethal dose of whatever it is that turns ladies' hair blue.

Crisp spent his time in the hardware store. He even had his own chair, between Stump Adams's and the door. Seniority would eventually move him closer to the stove, but he'd have to wait his turn. He was lucky anyway, being the only off-islander ever to have his own chair.

Of course, the advantage of being closest to the window was that you got to see who was doing what on Main Street and relate the details to the others. The simplest observation, such as Smo Bodwell going into the post office, would elicit a personal and genealogical commentary that would put to shame the best efforts of those name-search companies advertised in *National Geographic* or the *Enquirer*. Not even the most insignificant event passed unnoticed, and of these events the store's huge square windows offered an unimpeded prospect. Not to mention a clear view of the harbor and the motel. The entertainment there, in season, beat movies hollow.

There was a lot of ice on the sidewalk today, so foot traffic was scarce. Conversation, therefore, turned on the only other topic of interest—the murder of Amanda Murphy. Crisp wedged his boots among the others under the stove, adjusted the green corduroy pillow in his chair, sat back, and propped up his feet on the edge of the display case.

Drew Meesham was waiting on a lady who wanted shelving screws; otherwise, the chairs were full. Drew's, of course, was closest to the stove; he owned the place. Petey Lamont was next. He wasn't senior but had a special dispensation because he couldn't hit the spittoon from any farther away. Beside him was Stump Adams, the island storyteller and oldest in the group. Between him and Crisp was Pharty McPhearson, who was also called Silent but Deadly, S. D. for short, not necessarily for the brevity and pith of his comments.

"I never thought I'd live to see a murder out here," said Stump as the conversation nodded. "Might as well be in New York."

"That's right," said Petey. "Next thing you know we'll have to lock our doors at night . . . take keys out've the car."

Crisp took a butterscotch from the cast-iron skillet Drew kept full of candy for the kids who dropped by after school. The conversation needed a nudge in a more profitable direction. "I suppose the senator will get involved."

"McKenniston?" said Petey. "I doubt it. Ancient history by this time."

"This bein' an election year, he won't want to stir up any closets," Stump observed.

"Rattle any skeletons, you mean," said Pharty.

"Same thing."

Crisp tossed the candy wrapper at the spittoon and missed. He always missed. Petey habitually reached down, picked it up, and sniffed it. He loved butterscotch but the doctor had warned him off candy, so he got by on fumes.

"McKennistons have been up there a long time, haven't they?" said Crisp.

"Since Stedman, the senator's grandfather," said Drew as he sat down. As usual he'd been keeping an ear on the conversation all along. If a customer got a few screws too many as a result, well, as long as they didn't get too few. "Marshall used to come down here once in a while in the old days. Him and Briley was good friends."

There was a moment's silence as everyone remembered Briley, who, though he had died more than twenty years before, old as Methuselah, was no less alive in the collective memory. Petey had Briley's chair these days.

"That was a long time ago," Stump eulogized. They all nodded. Everything was a long time ago.

"Before my time, I'm afraid," said Crisp. His words hardly rippled the silence.

Drew's eyes were animated by memories. "Oh, them was some days, Win'."

"Some days," Petey chorused.

"Yessir." Drew opened the squeaky door on the cast-iron stove and tossed in a birch log. The door slammed shut and the latch dropped into place. The birch bark offered a tattoo of snaps and pops, launching its soul in clouds of ember-trimmed ashes. "People from that end of the island come to town a lot more them days. They was a lot more social.

"Them girls," continued Drew, "always dressed in white . . . linen or muslin or whatever they call it. Just pressed. Some kind of big old straw hat with ribbons on it. I tell you, one've 'em tossed you a glance, you felt about ten feet tall." He dropped his head back and closed his eyes.

" 'Course, they had a look that'd make you feel like the underside of somethin' ugly, too," said Pharty.

"So I hear," said Drew with a smile. " 'Course, I never saw it myself."

The musty air, thick with the smell of linseed oil and turpentine, soaked up the ragged laughter that followed.

"Not like today," said Stump. He launched a lipful of tobacco juice at the spittoon in emphasis. "These girls come off the boat, floppin' and hangin' out like dogs in season. Pants so tight, you might as well strap your imagination to an anchor and heave 'er off the lee'rd bow."

Crisp thought of Matty and smiled. "Not a lot of mystery to it anymore, is there?" he said.

"Mystery? The only mystery is how you stuff a hundred and fifty pounds of meat in a ten-pound sack," said Stump. "Sex," he continued with another spit. "I tell you, without a little mystery, a little romance, it don't mean no more than a sneeze or a good fart."

"Cheap," said Pharty.

Stump turned his milky gray eyes toward the harbor but looked at something much farther away. "I'm glad Cassie ain't alive to see what it's come to." There was a requiem of silence for Stump's wife of fifty years who had been dead ten.

"She was a good woman, Stump," said Drew.

"She was," said Stump. "She was." All eyes turned from him in respect. "Raised four kids, buried three. Worked with me toe-to-toe, stroke for stroke all them years. Never complained. And maybe she was pretty, maybe not." He sniffed. "But she was . . . beautiful."

Crisp measured the time until it was right to say something. "The McKennistons came to town more often in those days, you say?"

"Sure did," said Drew. "Every Sat'dy, at least. 'Course, there was always something goin' on. Dances, plays, band concerts. Something."

"Nothin' like that these days," said Pharty.

With a wag of the head, Petey agreed. "Nope. Not 'ny more."

"Saturdays," said Crisp. If he'd learned one simple lesson in life, it was that patience seldom failed to yield the desired results. And in certain circles his patience was legendary. "Plays, you say?"

"Sure," said Stump. "You remember them plays over to the Memorial Hall, don't you, Pr'fess'r? Gorry, it wasn't that long ago they stopped havin' 'em, was it?"

"Back when TV come in," said Petey.

"TV," said Stump, stuffing a diatribe into the inflection. "Sometimes them actors over to The Ledges'd put one on."

Mention of The Ledges pried a memory loose from one of the dustier parapets in Crisp's brain, and it landed squarely on his heart: Debora Stalsberg, his first genuine summer love. Her father was a famous theatrical producer who had renovated the abandoned inn on James' Island and opened it to Broadway actors in the off-season. An ancient shudder of excitement shimmied up Crisp's back in scratchy woolen knee breeches.

"They'd all live out to The Ledges," said Petey. "Men and women both. Together."

"There was sin b'fore TV," said Stump. "It just wasn't so fashionable."

"Wasn't never really a 'how-to' on the subject before TV," Petey appended.

Drew imagined some lint on his khaki pants and picked it off. "They put on plays they was goin' to do down to New York when theater season come."

Pharty leaned forward and resituated his cushion. "'Falls 'bout same as deer season, don't it? That's why I hardly ever make them plays."

An old ship's clock on the wall opposite the men had the Millberry's Magnesia logo etched in ornate frosted letters on its glass case. None of the men remembered Millberry's Magnesia; that's how long the clock had been there. Drew wound it first thing every morning, last thing every night, and it kept perfect time—seven minutes slow. Always had been. On the island, "I'll be there 'bout Millberry time" meant a little late.

The gentle ticktock of the ancient timepiece synchronized the silence that rushed in to fill the empty spaces. During lapses in conversation old eyes often settled on the pendulum in a ritual of self-hypnosis. It was the only thing that moved, gently knocking aside the seconds like dominoes.

Crisp was having a hard time concentrating. Very unusual. He couldn't get Amanda Murphy out of his mind. His thoughts wouldn't be so troubling if he envisioned her as he had seen her—dead, pale, cold. An image like that sleeps fitfully forever in the subconscious of the beholder. That's to be expected. But it was not the way he saw her. Somehow his brain had resurrected her, dressed her in a thin blue summer dress with tiny white flowers in the pattern, and put her in a big empty house where she wandered from room to room. He never saw her face directly, only in reflections—in windows as she stopped for a moment to peer out into the stark sunlight, or in smoky mirrors as she passed by. Room to room. Slowly. Silently. Room to room. Ticktock, ticktock.

Crisp shook his head and rubbed his eyes.

"Did any of the McKennistons ever get mixed up with those people?"

"What people?" said Drew. "Actors?"

Crisp nodded.

"That's the funniest thing," said Petey. "I was just thinking about her."

"Her?"

"Trudy McKenniston," Petey replied. "She wasn't McKenniston then. Stumpy, what was her name? Her folks had a place in Camden."

"Was it Rockford? Wilford?" Stump's milky old eyes searched the floor for recollection. "Somethin' ended in 'ford.' "

"Rutherford!" said Pharty.

Stump slapped Pharty's knee. "That's it!" he exclaimed. "Trudy Rutherford."

"There was a girl, I hope to tell you," Drew commented with a wheeze of exclamation. "Head turner, she was."

Petey agreed. "She coulda turned an owl's head clear off the sprocket."

"I don't remember her," said Crisp.

A customer came in. Drew slowly disengaged himself from his chair. "She was older'n us, Win'. Musta been eighteen or so when you started comin'. You was still in knee pants."

"But we noticed her," said Petey.

"I guess so," Pharty concurred. "Wasn't she somethin'?"

Crisp applied a poker to the embers of his memory but couldn't come up with Trudy Rutherford. "Nope. I don't remember."

Drew smiled to himself as he followed his customer down one of the aisles overgrown with cast-iron skillets and brass soap dishes no one would ever buy. "You always was a little slow," he said. Everyone laughed.

"She was an actress?"

"Onstage and off," said Petey on the inhale as he passed the yellow butterscotch cellophane under his nose. "You remember that play she was in that time Briley fell outta that tree, Stump?"

"Gorry, I forget that," said Drew.

"What tree?" said Crisp. "What happened?"

"Well . . ." Drew looked at Petey with a distinct twinkle in his eyes. "Speakin' of sex . . . the old-fashioned kind . . . I don't guess it would turn heads today, but those folks were rehearsin' outside—"

"Built a stage right out from the porch on the east side there," Stump said. "I remember. Us boys'd sit up in the trees and watch. Whistle at 'em, you know. Wasn't we some obnoxious in them days!"

"I know a few ladies who'd say we've only got worse with time," said Drew with a laugh. "Anyway, the old man—what was his name?—owned the place."

"Mr. Stalsberg," said Crisp. Everyone was surprised he'd remembered that.

"That's right!" said Drew. "Stalsberg. He'd written this play—"

"Awful play," Petey editorialized.

"Awful," Drew agreed. "Never amounted to anything. Anyways, it was about this Irish girl . . . played by Trudy Rutherford."

"She was the one part worth watchin'," said Stump, smiling to himself.

"I'll say," said Petey. "All of us boys had just about enough of that play by the time she come on, but when she did! . . ."

"Ooo!" said Drew. It had been a long time since he'd said that. Probably longer for Stump and Petey. Nevertheless, they echoed the sentiment. "She had this beautiful long red hair. Shined just like copper in the sunlight."

"I'm surprised you noticed," said Petey. "She coulda been bald, for all I remember."

Stump leaned toward Crisp and spoke into his good ear with earnest confidentiality. "She wasn't overdressed, if you get my meanin'. Had this little skirt on, not much else."

"And the sun was behind her," said Petey. Then he giggled, just like he had sixty-five years ago. Crisp thought of Matty.

"Well, the wind was blowin'," Drew resumed, "and every now and then a gust would come along and lift her skirt up to never-never land. Trouble is, the same gust would push this branch right in the way so we couldn't see. Each time Briley'd lean forward a little more, 'til finally—"

"Out he comes!" Petey exclaimed, jumping from his seat with a peal of joy, tossing his hands in the air and doing an arthritic pantomime of someone falling from a tree. He lowered himself to his seat on a cushion of laughter.

Drew wiped tears from the corner of his eye. "They'd set up this table for a picnic right under the tree."

"Nice and shady," said Stump.

"Nice and shady," Drew concurred. "And he landed smack in the punch bowl!"

"Punch everywhere!" said Stump. "I remember! I remember!"

The laughter that followed dissolved slowly into smiles. Crisp wondered how many places existed where a group of men in their seventies and eighties could share the same memory. "I'm sorry I missed it," he said.

"She was some pretty, though," said Drew. "Looked some nice in that red hair."

"She wasn't a redhead?" Crisp asked.

"I don't believe so," said Petey. "I don't remember what—"

"No," said Drew authoritatively. "She wasn't a redhead. Blond, I think. Dirty blond. Had to give up actin' when she married into the family," Stump said.

"She married the senator's father?" said Crisp.

Petey nodded. "They wasn't thrilled about it, even so."

"Well, I don't suppose she did too bad in the bargain," said Crisp. "Not much stability in acting, from what I've heard."

"Oh, her family had money, Win'," said Stump. "Prob'ly coulda bought an' sold the McKennistons—"

"Couple times over," said Drew, returning to his perch.

"Couple times over is right," Stump continued. "New money, though." From his vest pocket he removed a worn old corncob pipe that he wasn't allowed to smoke and teased his lips with it. "Nope. They was just in love."

"What was the senator's father's name?" Crisp asked.

"Marshall," said Petey.

"He was just as wild as she was at first," said Drew. " 'Member? Over to Rockaway all the time with that crowd, he was. Got old Stedman wound up sump'n fierce."

"They've been in that house the whole time, I suppose," said Crisp. "The McKenniston place . . ."

"Oh, yes," said Stump. "Yes, they have. Don't remember who

had it before they come out here, but, yes, they been there ever since. Big old place, it is."

"Twenty-five rooms," said Petey with an air of authority. "Thirty-seven acres across the neck with deep water on both sides."

Pharty leaned toward Crisp and spoke in confidence. "Petey's cousin Alvin was caretaker up there."

Crisp was impressed. "Oh, I see. Thirty-seven acres you say. Well, now. And twenty-five rooms?"

"In two buildings," Petey said.

"Big job," said Crisp. "Is he still at it?"

"Who, Alvin?" said Pharty. "Heck, no. He shot himself in the knee when they was out jackin' deer one night, back some time now. He don't come out anymore. Stays indoors. Embarrassed, I guess."

Which explained why Crisp didn't know him.

"Should be," said Stump.

"Who's caretakin' up there nowadays, Pete?" Pharty said.

"Mostly Sanborn," Petey replied.

Pharty raised his eyebrows to admit the information and nodded it to the back of his brain. "That's right, too."

"Yup."

"Mostly Sanborn," Crisp echoed, and everyone nodded. Patience was a fruitful tree. He stood up, picked a caramel and a few peanuts from the skillet, and bade good day to his comrades. "Guess I'll go check the mail," he said. He did.

"Well, here's a new one, Matty." With one hand Crisp was hanging his coat up for the third time while holding an envelope and letter in the other. As he walked down the hall toward the kitchen, the coat fell on the floor.

"You sold one?" said Matty. She stopped her little flurry of activity and emerged from the cloud of flour that settled about her— the goddess of baking.

Crisp finger-boxed the glasses back up his nose. "Well, no. No, they didn't buy it, but listen to this: 'Dear C,' that's all it says, 'C,' like this, see?" He showed her the salutation. " 'Dear C, My name is Candace Walpole. I'm Ms. Davis's secretary.' Davis is the editor," Crisp informed Matty over the rim of his spectacles. " 'Part of my job is to send out rejection letters, like the one enclosed, and sign Ms. Davis's name. Whenever I have time, I try to read the poems. It doesn't seem right that I should be sending rejection letters when I haven't even read the material, although I'm doing it on her behalf.

" 'I suppose that sounds silly. Be that as it may, I just wanted you to know I think your poem is wonderful. I cried when I read it. I wish my editor was of the same opinion. It reminded me of my Grandfather Chester, whom I dearly loved.

" 'How little that calls itself art these days is beautiful. I just wanted to thank you.' "

The look that Crisp gave Matty would have been no different if he'd been awarded the Nobel Prize for literature and nominated the nation's Poet Laureate in the same breath. He'd touched the heart of a fellow human being with his words. He looked again at the letter. " 'For what it's worth, Candace.' "

Matty clapped the flour from her hands and patted him on the forearm. "Now, there, Winston. You see? That's somethin', isn't it? I mean, think of all the poetry that woman sees, and she thought enough of yours to write that letter. That's special. It just shows you, it's a question of taste, is all. Just because someone's an editor doesn't mean they know a good thing when they see it. You wait, one of these days you'll get one with sense."

Crisp smiled. He dropped the rejection into the trash without reading it and gently folded the secretary's note and tucked it in his pocket. Matty's eyes, softened at the edges, followed his actions. "May I see?" she said. Crisp laid the poem on the table and went to his room. Matty didn't pick it up. She pulled out a chair, sat down beside the sheet of paper, and read.

Closer to the fire, chair by chair
Grow the old and gray men gathered there.
How vivid now the fire has become
Closer to the fire, one by one.

Closer to the fire, chair by chair
They shift and mumble, nod, and doze and stare
And talk of all the things they've never done
Closer to the fire, one by one.

Closer to the fire, chair by chair
The tide of life withdraws and leaves them there
Despite the battles faced, and lost, and won
Closer to the fire one by one.

Closer to the fire, chair by chair
Ancient faces lined by joy and care
Wonder, now that all is said and done
How they're closer to the fire, one by one.

Matty looked out the window and sighed. Somewhere out there, in the cold canyons of New York, was a kindred spirit named Candace Walpole. "Lasagna," she said. It was Crisp's favorite meal, so she made it every time he got a rejection.

They'd had a lot of lasagna.

MOSTLY SANBORN GOT HIS NICKNAME by virtue of the fact that his father was unknown. His mother, however, was a Sanborn.

He was a lot of person in a small space. Everything about him, taken separately, seemed big—his head, his hands, his feet, his chest and shoulders. Somehow, though, the components were heaped together in such a way that they didn't measure more than five foot five. The adhesive that held the pieces in place was a smile, without which he would have been unrecognizable.

Mostly stumped up the drive as Crisp got off his bike, puffing loudly.

"Helluva pedal, ain't it, Pr'fessor!"

Crisp unsnapped the bindings from his pant legs. For some reason he always found it difficult to keep from laughing when he talked to Mostly. "It's nine miles from town?"

" 'Bout," said Mostly. He shoved his hands behind the bib of his overalls and waited for Crisp to assemble himself. "How long d'it take ya?"

Crisp looked at his watch. "Well, I left about one-thirty . . . What's that? An hour and fifteen, twenty minutes?"

"Not bad," said Mostly. Crisp leaned his bike against the hedge, and they walked toward the house. "I never much got the hang of bicycles myself," Mostly confessed. "My aspirations was pretty much satisfied once I got walkin' down pat." He laughed, and Crisp, embraced by the laughter, laughed, too. "Good day for it, though. I guess when it gets warm like this, people do crazy things. Spring's next week."

Crisp stopped halfway down the hill and sopped up the surroundings with the sponge of his spirit. Already the snow had retreated to soggy pockets in the shadows. Fifty feet away the lawn broke against an outcropping of granite in explosions of juniper and splashes of golden grass. In the Thorofare teams of waves dressed in blue, black, and silver played pitch and toss with handfuls of diamonds. Soon small fleets of East Haven dinghies from the yacht club on the opposite shore would be rounding the buoys, their sails flapping like a spinster's dainties hung out to dry.

Crisp and Mostly bypassed the cottage and made straight for the path to the beach. There were similar cottages on cliff tops all along the shore. Huge summer homes, all cut from the same mold. Weathered shingles. White trim. Green shutters. Reshaped by nature in its own likeness, as much a part of the island as the granite and evergreens themselves.

Mostly puffed a lot as they climbed down the wooden steps to a grassy outcropping just above the beach. "Don't come down here much durin' winter," he said. "Be time to put the floats over, though, 'fore you know it. Senator's sailin' up from Mass'chusetts just after Memorial Day."

Mostly stopped short of the edge. "Up there's where they'd go most've the time," he said, pointing up the long sweep of rocky beach. "'They'd go jus' 'round the corner of that point up there if they wanted a little privacy." He stuck his hands into his overalls again and assumed his "this-is-as-far-as-I-go" stance.

"Is it sandy there? Around the point?"

"I don't know," said Mostly. He took off his Make My Day, Shoot a Tourist hat and scratched his head. "I ain't been up there in so long. Seems there might be a little sandy place." He squinted at the tree-covered point of land as if to stare holes in it. "I wouldn't be surprised."

"Did she spend much time there?" said Crisp. He turned up his collar and tucked his hands into his pockets.

"Mandy? I guess so. She liked bein' alone." Some other emotion tugged at the corners of Mostly's smile. "Don't know what she seen in Neddy."

Crisp pulled a piece of sweet grass from its sheath and stuck it under his tongue. "Not his type?"

"Hardly," said Mostly. He was editing his thoughts. "Finer points of courtship ain't exactly his strong suit." Crisp nodded slowly. So did Mostly. " 'Course, he's still a kid, you know. You never know how they'll turn out." He nodded toward the beach. "Shows a little promise, I guess. He'll come out all right once he grows up. Family'll see to that, I s'pose."

A lobster boat sliced up the Thorofare, the husky shudder of its engine doubling off the rocks and trees. Crisp's watery eyes floated after it as his thoughts jostled one another into order. Mostly hummed tunelessly at the back of his throat.

"Mandy," said Crisp.

"Hmm?"

"Mandy," Crisp repeated. "Is that what they called her?"

Mostly nodded. "She called herself that."

"She was different, you say?"

"Night and day from most of 'em," said Mostly. "Quiet. Kept her own company. I can see what he saw in her, but . . . well, it was a strange relationship." For a moment the smile had gone completely.

"How so?"

"Well," said Mostly, trying to marshal his thoughts. "You didn't hardly ever see them two together. And when they was, it was—I don't know how to say it. I seen him with plenty of girls over the years . . . his wife, too. Poor kid. But it wasn't like he was with the rest of 'em."

"You mean he wasn't as affectionate with her?"

"You can say that."

"Maybe he was, since he was married, he was just trying to—"

"I'll tell you right now," said Mostly, "you could say a lot of things about Neddy McKenniston, but you'd never say he was subtle. Everyone knew what was goin' on. And the senator—"

"And the senator didn't mind if he brought her up here?"

"You know," said Mostly, "this will tell you somethin' about Neddy and the senator. Neddy'd come up only one or two weekends during the summer. He brought her up when he first come, just 'fore the Fourth of July, and left her all summer! So when the senator come up—he usually spent every other week here—he finds her here! His son's mistress! And he's got to play host to her."

"Must have been terribly awkward," Crisp speculated.

"I guess," Mostly agreed. "You'd never know it, though. The senator was real—what's the word . . . graceful—gracious! That's it. He was real gracious to her, far's I could tell. I guess he could be like that 'cause of all those years campaignin'. You have to learn to put a good face on things." Mostly brushed his heavy-toed boots lightly through the grass and thought for a moment. "Some ol' sad."

"Any others like her?"

"Not really," Mostly replied. "Well, he took a fancy to Sarah Quinn for a while. I could never make heads nor tails of that. Got her in a family way, they say. Sure surprised a lot of people up this way. Those that know him."

"The child is his then?" Crisp asked.

Mostly looked across the Thorofare. "That's the story," he said. "I don't think he knew what he was gettin' into with her."

"How do you mean?"

"Well, I guess she had her sleeves rolled up for business," said Mostly. "Marriage. I s'pose he probably made promises—you know how boys are—and, well, she didn't know they wasn't worth salt. How's she s'posed to? Anyway, he got her in a family way. She's never outright said it was him, but she ain't the kind to—"

"Play the field?"

"That's right."

"What does the senator think of all that?"

"Oh, he don't take much notice. Figures it's just wild oats, I guess. He harvested a few acres himself, everyone knows. Still has an eye for the ladies, if you follow the tabloids."

"When did all this happen with Sarah?"

"Summer 'fore last." By degrees the smile had battled the frown from Mostly's face and reasserted itself. "Must be somethin' in the air up here in summertime." He pinned his smile to his earlobes and tucked his hands back behind the bib. "Well, I gotta get down to the boathouse and creosote them pilin's. You need'nything else?" Crisp said he didn't think so. "Well, you need me, just give a holler. Not that it'll do much good. I got Marky Williams over from East Haven helpin' me. You know Marky Williams?"

Crisp tugged his stocking hat into a thoughtful position. "Not that I recall," he said.

"Well, his pa's Loriman. Builds boats over there. Anyways, this boy—I guess he's fifteen or so—he listens to that goshdarn radio all day, an' you wouldn't believe the noises that come outta that thing. Sounds like a load of ball bearin's an' beer cans in the clothes dryer. Drives me right crazy. Whatever happened to good old rock 'n' roll? That's what I want to know."

About halfway through this critique, Mostly had started walking away. He continued to talk, and now and then the breeze nudged the sound of his voice in Crisp's direction. He couldn't make out the words, though an occasional pillow of laughter would bat at his ears.

Crisp stood there for a minute watching until Mostly was gone, then he looked out over the water toward East Haven. The chilly wind had picked up a little, tossing the smells of pine, salt, and snow together with the sounds of gulls and whispering trees. He inhaled deeply and climbed down the rocks to the beach.

There was a time when he could have covered the distance to the point in thirty seconds, jumping fearlessly from rock to rock, heedless of snow, ice, and seaweed. Somewhere in the mass of creaks and wrinkles that he'd become, that fleet-footed boy was hiding, teasing him with the memory. Falling had become Crisp's chief fear.

Fifteen minutes later he rounded the point and was confronted by a recumbent elephant of black granite. He rested a few minutes before beginning the ascent. By the time he reached the summit, he was breathless, but the effort was rewarded. Directly below him was a crescent of rough sand beach hemmed in on all but the ocean side by ledges. A very private place.

Within ten minutes he had circumvented the beach and found a narrow cleft in the rock that provided easy access to the beach from ground level. He shook his head.

"This place was made for murder."

Turning from the cleft he surveyed the area. A field of wave-worn boulders climbed from the beach to the woods, an ancient spruce forest that rested atop a three-foot lip of red soil, veined with tree and juniper roots.

Crisp made his way across the boulders, over the driftwood, and up a well-worn ravine. At the edge of the forest, he peered through a tangle of low branches. The trees had been culled recently. There were no deadfalls, and the new growth was no more than a year or two old. The forest floor was bare except for a thick carpet of spruce needles, a scattering of ferns, and here and there a small pile of ice where the snow had found its way through the canopy of boughs overhead. He smiled.

"That'll save bending," he said. "Now to find the granddaddy." He went from tree to tree, talking softly to each in an old-man whisper. "You're too young, aren't you, fellah?" "You don't have any hiding places, do you?" "No secrets here . . . ah!" Not twenty feet off the path, within a stone's throw of the beach, he found what he was looking for—a huge old spruce tree, stripped of its bark in places, rotten in others, pocked with woodpecker holes and laced with worm trails and hardened rivers of sap. "Hello, grandpa," said Crisp, stroking the smooth, dry trunk. "Got something to tell me, old man?"

He walked slowly around the great tree, bending and bobbing to avoid the naked branches. There were two big holes on the mossy side of the trunk. Standing on tiptoe, he could just reach the bottom lip of the uppermost of these. The lower hole was much more accessible. He took off his bulky down jacket, rolled up the sleeve of his checkered flannel shirt, and thrust in his arm up to the shoulder. His eyes roved their sockets blindly as he directed all his senses to his fingertips. Suddenly they stopped. "Had to be," he said. He withdrew his arm from the trunk. Clutched between his second and third fingers were a small piece of black fabric and a length of rusty wire, in the middle of which was a frozen wad of cloth.

The black fabric was frozen, too. He dropped to a knee and unfolded it over his leg. He stretched out the material. It formed a double triangle of material, very high-sided with thin strings at the corners. He folded the objects together and, standing, tucked the treasures into his coat pocket.

He patted the tree trunk. "Sorry to trouble you, old man," he said. "You'll sleep better, now."

THERE IS AN INDESCRIBABLE but palpable electricity that troubles the atmosphere of a village when big news is afoot. Crisp felt it as he peddled through town. Something had happened in his absence. It was past four-thirty and the hardware store was still open. Nothing testified to the intensity of excitement as alarmingly as this simple fact. It was the equivalent of a news bureau staying open into the wee hours during a national crisis. It had last happened in the hardware store nearly twenty years ago, the night a part-time deputy from the mainland had gone crazy and set fire to the Odd Fellows hall, the bandstand, and Ingrid Libby's prize forsythia all in one night, then disappeared into the woods, never to be heard from again.

Crisp wheeled his bicycle across the sidewalk and propped it against the whitewashed sill of the hardware store window.

"Well, you heard what happened?" asked Fossie Bergstrom. He'd been sitting in Winston's seat near the door. He started to get up. Barring an epidemic, Fossie wouldn't be eligible for Crisp's chair for a few years yet. There were others ahead of him. But some day it would come down to him and Mont Billings. He thought it best to keep the inside track.

"Sit, Foss. Sit. I can't stay," said Crisp. "What happened? I've been up at the other end of the island."

"You ain't heard, then?" said Drew, dangling the information for a moment. "Well, that'll teach you to leave town."

"What happened?" Crisp repeated, still breathless from his ride.

"This big old Coast Guard helicopter landed over in the parkin' lot 'bout forty-five minutes ago," said Petey, dispensing the details like fine wine. "And that coroner from over to Rockland got out've it with this other fella, some state troopers—"

"Two of 'em," said Drew.

". . . two of 'em," Petey continued.

"And Luther Kingsbury," Stump added.

". . . and Luther Kingsbury." Petey nodded. "He had his siren on, lights flashin' and everything."

"Looked like the Fourth of July out there," said Stump.

"Some wind that thing kicked up," said Fossie. "I'd forgot that parkin' lot was paved. Sand and dirt blowed everywhere."

"Why?" said Crisp, his breathlessness increasing.

"I guess they must've found out who them fingerprints b'long to," said Petey. "S'what we figured."

"Most likely," Drew agreed stoically. "I don't guess they'd come out here after ferry hours 'less it's somethin' pretty important. They must know who done it."

". . . and come out to pick 'im up," Petey concluded.

"Pick him up," echoed Stump Adams.

"Somebody's in for it," said Petey.

Crisp was already reaching for the door. "Where did they go?"

At that moment an old green Chevy pickup with stripes of fluorescent orange and lime green down the sides flew by. Its plywood side boards, posted to the bed with two-by-fours, flapped in the wind like the wings of a fallen angel fleeing Judgment.

Drew spat out a crisp epithet, which the rest silently "amened" with gasps, wheezes, and wide eyes.

Excitement propelled Petey to the window with a speed his appearance belied. "Kilby Miller," he said. He leaned over the display ledge as far as physics and his aged equilibrium would allow. "Where in heck you s'pose he's goin' in such a hurry?"

"Don't know," said Stump, "But that truck's gonna fall apart b'fore he gets halfway there if he don't ease up!"

"Somebody must haveta have their septic tank pumped out awful bad," said Drew with a wry smile. "Anyways," he continued, "them others went the same way." He pointed over his shoulder in the direction so emphatically indicated by Miller's truck. "Had half the town in tow."

Crisp immediately made that half the town plus one. The once-weary sinews of his legs, revived by an injection of adrenaline, propelled his bicycle through the street and up the hill at a clip that would almost have done a schoolboy proud. The others looked after him.

"Sometimes you forget he's from away," said Drew.

At the top of the hill Crisp stopped to refill his lungs.

Five roads emanated from the large oval occupied by the new bandstand. Crisp stared down each of these as far as his old eyes and the gathering gray of twilight would allow. Whichever way the procession had gone, no sign of its passing was immediately evident. There was, however, some commotion at the far end of School Street, near the old ball ground. With one leg he pushed himself a few yards in that direction and squinted. He could make out a little knot of women that had tethered itself to the wooden rail of Sadie Mitchell's porch. As he coasted down the hill toward them, he could see that their delicate sensibilities had been animated by something.

The Creator had endowed Sadie with a chest that acted as a natural amplifier for her singsong voice. As a result she was incapable of speech at anything approaching a subdued volume. This peculiar attribute, combined with her tendency to make every sentence an exclamation, made her, Crisp thought, distinctive.

So by the time he had pulled within fifty feet of the group, he was almost fully aware of the situation, at least from Sadie's perspective. Nevertheless, as there remained a few gaps in his knowledge, he applied the hand brakes, dragged his feet, and careened to a graceless stop against the walkway.

"Professor!" yelled Sadie, who had just managed to get out of the way in time to be of no use to him as a cushion. "For half a second there, I thought you was some kid!"

In response to the squeal of brakes, Ginger Foster had hoisted her substantial person halfway up the railing. "Gosh sakes, Crisp. You scared me half to death!"

Emily Minot stood as still as Lot's wife, with her hands crossed over her breast. She blinked once. She blinked twice. "I 'bout had heart failure," she sighed finally.

"One thing right after the other this afternoon!" Sadie proclaimed. "You shoulda seen Kilby Miller go flyin' past here a minute ago."

"He came this way?" said Crisp breathlessly. He extricated the bicycle's front wheel from the walkway, where it had punched a notch in the punky wood, and tugged at the handlebars in an effort to straighten them.

"Like the devil was after him," said Ginger. She dropped both feet daintily to the boards. "Up towards the point."

"That's where the rest of 'em went," said Emily.

Crisp liked island women—honest, strong women who said what was on their minds, took life at face value, and responded in kind. He especially liked Emily Minot. Her story was a long litany of tragedy that would have put Job in a blue mood. But she lived on, uncomplaining, not merely surviving but thriving. He smiled at her, but she wasn't looking.

"What d'you suppose is goin' on, Professor?" said Sadie. "We was wonderin'."

Ginger studied the gathering darkness. "Nothing up there but Robert's cemetery," said Ginger.

"The cemetery," Crisp repeated. Two and two were coming together. "Kilby Miller—he's the grave digger up there, isn't he?"

Ginger and Emily nodded. Sadie proclaimed, "But he wasn't flyin' through here at ninety miles an hour to bury somebody, Professor."

"Maybe somebody trying to get out," said Ginger with a smile.

Sadie laughed. "You don't think it's old Bruce Bennett, do ya? Found out them summer people painted his house pink. That'd do it!"

Clouds had begun to gather when Crisp left the north end of the island. Now the sky had draped its thick gray petticoats over the treetops and was fat and heavy with rain.

"Maybe I'll just take a ride up there and see what's going on," he said casually.

Sadie looked at the sky. "You'll get wet."

"Radio said we're s'posed to get a good blow," said Emily. "Winds up to forty-five knots. Rain, hail, the whole works."

"You'd be better off up to Matty's, Professor," said Sadie. "I don't think it'd be too smart to have you out plowin' down god knows what on that bicycle durin' a drivin' nor'easter, not at your age."

Crisp had no objection to being mothered. Something about him had always invited it, and he'd resigned himself to it long ago. He simply tended to bring out the mother hen in women. Even Miss Flyguard.

Matty, most of all.

"Oh, I think I'll be all right, Sadie," he said, adding an "aw shucks" kick at the grass. "I guess I'm just too curious for my own good." He smiled at the ladies. "Couldn't sleep without knowing what's going on, you know. Good day, ladies."

He pulled the corner of his stocking cap, disengaged himself from the little group, hopped to the roadside, and pushed off down the hill. The women watched after him.

"He's a nice old man," Sadie remarked. "You'd think him and Matty'd get married, wouldn't you?"

"She'd jump at it," Ginger speculated.

Sadie laughed. "I would too, if I was about a hundred years old."

Their eyes followed him a moment in silence.

"Funny man," said Emily.

"Worked for the gover'ment," Sadie explained.

The ladies nodded.

By the time Crisp had pedaled two miles, it was fully dark. The sparse hem of houses that rimmed the dirt road had given way to an ancient canyon of evergreens and undergrowth that towered on either side. Now and then the black clouds would pulse with lightning, making everything, for half a second, bright as midday.

The road was mostly uphill. Crisp had gotten off his bike and was pushing. He felt like Ichabod Crane entering Sleepy Hollow.

Some sixty-odd years ago he and some friends had built a tree house in the woods, somewhere off to the left. In a vain attempt to prime the pump of summer, they had decided to stay there overnight. It was April. There was still snow on the ground in places. Much of the night, with only a storm lantern for light and warmth, they'd sat up in their itchy woolen sleeping bags, telling ghost stories, shivering inside and out.

By midnight they'd worked themselves into such a fright that they climbed, screaming, down the ladder and flew along the narrow path through the woods and down the road to town, and safety.

Crisp was nearing eighty now. His had been a life of constant peril, spanning every continent. He'd seen uprisings, riots, revolts, revolutions, pogroms, wars. He'd even started some. But he'd never again felt the thrill of that innocent fear.

He felt it now. He looked back over his shoulder just as a distant lightning bolt flashed and, in that instant, imagined he saw someone behind him on the road—a woman, keeping close to the trees.

When the lightning flashed again, there was no sign of her. Even at his age it was easy to imagine things. He smiled, but the smile brought no comfort. The wind dragged legions of lost souls through the trees, and he couldn't help but wonder whose they were.

Sweat froze on his brow as he made his way up the last low hill to the cemetery. In the distance he perceived an odd blue light rhythmically pulsing off the underbelly of the clouds.

"That'll be Luther," he said aloud. It was like talking into a pillow. The wind, beating him sharply about his good ear, played pitch and toss with his words.

Cresting the hill he could see the busy blue light on top of Luther Kingbury's truck worrying the darkness with mute cries of alarm. There were other lights, too. Headlights, taillights, flashlights. Now and then someone would walk in front of them casting a giant shadow on the trees. The wind had scooped a handful of raindrops from the brooding clouds and was pelting them about indiscriminately.

"Professor!" yelled a voice from the crowd as Crisp emerged at its periphery from the shadows. "You pedal that thing all the way up here?"

Though the speaker was no more than a black smudge against the background of lights, the sibilant *s*s betrayed him. "Stuffy," said Crisp as he drew within hailing distance. "What's up, what's all this?"

"They're diggin' up Andy Calderwood!" Stuffy bellowed above the wind.

The words halted Crisp in his tracks. "Exhuming!"

Crisp couldn't hear the reply at first. The wind was monopolizing his good ear. "What?" he said as he drew abreast of Stuffy.

Stuffy looked at him sidelong. "The fingerprints they found on that girl was his."

THE STRAIN OF THE BIKE RIDE coupled with the surprise proved a drain on Crisp. The blood drained from his head as if someone had pulled a chain. He got dizzy and began to lose his sight. Everything went black with the exception of one small, indefinite spot of light in the center of his sight. He staggered back half a step into the fender of a truck and braced himself with an outstretched arm.

"They're down," said somebody nearby. "They're openin' 'er up." Suddenly the whole chaotic scene collapsed into baited silence. Kilby slipped down into the grave, his feet landing on the mahogany casket lid with a dull thud. Even the wind seemed to pause for a peek over his shoulder.

Crisp was blinking frantically, trying to focus on the faces in the crowd knotted around the grave. He managed to distill Nate Gammidge down to a single image just in time to see him nod to Luther Kingsbury, who nodded to Kilby Miller, who bent down to loosen the screws and open the lid. Crisp became aware of a hand on his shoulder.

"You all right, Professor?" said Stuffy. "You look like the underbelly of a dead fish. You okay?"

"I'm okay," said Crisp. "I guess it's just . . . I've been doing a lot of riding today."

"Too much," said Stuffy. "Comes a time, you know."

Sage advice, well taken, thought Crisp. He'd had heart trouble in the past, and his doctor had recommended biking as the perfect aid to rehabilitation. It's likely, however, he didn't have the marathon in mind.

The silence was reinstated as the casket lid was swung open. At once the shadows were fractured by camera flashes that went off like popcorn. The elements seemed to take this as their cue and flew into a reckless dance of the supernatural. The lightning flashed, the thunder crashed, and the swollen belly of the clouds gave birth to a torrent of cold spring rain.

It was a scene from a cheap Hollywood movie, but no less chilling for its familiarity. For a minute or two, there was a lot of commotion in the immediate vicinity of the grave. Finally, the lid was closed and fastened by Kilby Miller and his helper, who then climbed out of the muddy hole. The official contingent made their way through the crowd, got into their cars, and drove away.

"Well?" said Mildred Conway. She was holding a newspaper over her head, but it was no proof against the rain. "What'd they find, Syl?"

Stuffy shrugged. Crisp looked at him through the waterfall. Odd that he would come so far on such a night and seem so disinterested. Patience, Crisp thought. He had no doubt that there had been at least one pair of eyes that had not missed the glimpse into the grave, one pair of ears that had heard every word. All he had to do was find Leeman Russell. As the crowd began to disperse, he made his way toward the grave. Stuffy followed.

"What'd he look like?" The speaker was Waymond Webber. He was standing in a pile of dirt at the edge of the grave with his hands thrust deep into the pockets of his brown corduroys under

his bulky Mae West. He was talking to Kilby, who had started fill-
ing in the grave.

"Didn't look," said Kilby. Crisp had never seen Kilby Miller
without a Lucky Strike in his mouth. No doubt it is this appendage
that, over time, had forced Kilby's voice to detour through his nose.
It was a mucusy, cancerous voice. "Only one thing worse'n puttin'
'em in is takin' 'em out."

He was speaking rhetorically. Kilby knew that Waymond
wouldn't appreciate the emotional dimension of grave digging.

"Did he stink?" said Waymond. Kilby ignored him. "I don't
smell nothin'."

"That helicopter ain't goin' back in this weather!" Leeman Russell was speaking. Crisp craned his neck and searched the thinning
crowd. Leeman was one of a small contingent that had taken refuge
in the shelter of a high-boughed spruce. The others in the group,
not interested in information that was up for public consumption,
were talking among themselves in hushed tones. Crisp made his
way to the crowd and gently amputated Leeman from it.

Leeman knew more about Winston Crisp than most people on
the island, and therefore suspected twice as much. For this reason
he held him in the kind of speechless awe that a touch of mystery
creates. "Leeman," said Crisp softly. They began to walk slowly
away from the glare of headlights and the hum of voices. "What
do you make of all this?"

"Oh, I'm not too surprised, Professor," said Leeman, unconsciously adopting Crisp's soft, confidential whisper. "I mean, it's a
shock, and all that. But, when you think about it, somebody had
to do it, didn't they? And why not Andy Calderwood? Just because he's dead don't make him a saint, you know. I mean, I don't
want to say anything disrespectful, but Andy just wasn't a saint
is all."

"Not many are at that age," Crisp observed.

Leeman nodded once. Some rain had dribbled down the back
of his neck and traced his spine like the cold blade of a knife. He

shivered. "Any age," he opined. They withdrew to the slim comfort of a spruce tree beside the road.

"Did they find what they were looking for, do you think?"

"I don't know what they was lookin' for," said Leeman. "All they did was open the lid a half a minute, shine some lights in there, and take all these pictures. You musta seen them flashes go off. They had them professional photographers from the police. Some fast, they was. Automatic winders on them cameras, you know. They had Polaroids, too. Anyway, then they just closed 'er up. I guess whatever it was, they didn't have to look at too close."

The rain, falling with some purpose, had opened up a small rivulet at their feet. They poked at it as they spoke, Crisp with the round toes of his Bean boots, Leeman with the loose rubber flap that had separated from the plastic on his soggy sneakers.

"I don't guess anyone got too close a look then," said Crisp. He dammed the rivulet from one side, Leeman from the other.

"Couldn't hardly see nothin'," said Leeman.

"Oh, you were there, then? I mean, close enough?"

Leeman glanced quickly at Crisp. It was as if his professional integrity had been called into question. "Oh, 'course I was close enough. When they opened that lid, I was right there. And when they shined them lights in, I could see clear to Sunday."

"You mean, you saw the body?"

"Well, yes. Not too good, though," said Leeman, almost apologetically. "There was just that half a second before the flashes all started going off. After that you couldn't hardly see nothin' but stars and spots." He rubbed his eyes vigorously with the heel of his hand. "I still can't hardly see now."

A respectable reservoir had formed behind their pokings. Crisp gently tapped a breach in the dam and the water coursed through, carrying the dam with it.

"But you saw him. You saw the body," Crisp repeated.

"Oh, I saw the body, all right." Leeman replied. "I sure did. I mean, you couldn't recognize him or anything. Not just like that."

He snapped his fingers. "But, well, he hadn't gone nowhere." He paused to reflect. "You know what I think?"

Crisp didn't have to feign interest. He turned his good ear a little more toward the speaker. "What do you think, Leeman?"

"Well," Leeman said, "if Andy done it . . . I'm not sayin' he did, I'm not sayin' he didn't. That's what they got courts for. I can't believe anyone would do such a thing, myself. I mean, we're talkin' about a human life here. That's the kind of thing happens on the mainland where they ain't got sense enough to know better. But if he did, you know, kill that girl, and then he dies a couple days later, how'd she get up to the quarry where Bergie found her?"

He seemed unwilling to speculate further.

"Frozen," said Crisp, catalystically.

"Frozen. That's right. If he killed her, it must've been in August or September, or whenever, 'cause he was dead after that. Then she ends up frozen in the quarry. You was down to the poolroom when I told 'em how they found her, wasn't you? Yes, 'course you was, I remember. Well, like I said, she was fresh as anything." He raised his eyes and looked searchingly at Crisp. "How?" he said.

Crisp shrugged.

"It don't make sense," Leeman continued. "Somethin' had to happen to her between when she was strangled and when she was put in the quarry. It don't make sense. Does it to you, Professor? I mean, if Andy done it, it had to be done before he died. Didn't it?"

Crisp shook his head. There was a song in there somewhere, if not a poem. "Did they do anything else?"

"Who?"

Crisp nodded in the direction of the open grave.

"Oh, them fellas? Well, one of them got down in there. He had these little plastic bags, you know like they put samwiches in?" He raised his hand and held an imaginary sandwich bag between his thumb and forefinger. "I guess they was collectin' somethin' outta there. Evidence, or somethin', prob'ly. Hard to tell. There was a couple of 'em keepin' us back, you know."

"What do you think *might* have been in the bags?"

"Oh, I don't really know," said Leeman, lowering his hand. "I didn't get much of a look when they went by. My eyes was still full of spots from them cameras. Somethin' shiny. Buttons from the coat? That's what it looked like." He laughed. "Could've been mothballs, though, for all I know. Do they put mothballs in caskets?"

The rain fell in crystal curtains that exploded on contact with the ground. One by one the small knots of onlookers untied themselves and the curious drifted to their cars—home to warm stoves, a hot meal, and a week's worth of animated conversation. Leeman Russell and Crisp watched the last of them leave. "Some gosh awful," Leeman said in requiem, "the whole darn business."

Kilby Miller's old truck was parked at the edge of the grave, winking at the proceedings with its one dim eye. Against the soft yellow glow, Kilby's silhouette tossed soggy shadows of dirt into the hole. Waymond's silhouette was there, too, indifferent to the weather. Crisp couldn't help wondering if somehow Waymond repelled rain the way he repelled people.

Leeman glanced at his watch. "I guess I'd best be gettin' home," he said. "You got a ride, P'fessor?"

Minutes later they were bumping down the road in Leeman's Oldsmobile station wagon with Crisp's bicycle stuck halfway out the rear door. Exhaust fumes wafted into the front seat.

"I suppose you knew the Calderwood boys pretty well, Leeman," Crisp said. He examined his companion's features carefully in the glow of the dashboard lights. Leeman had a distinctive profile—a prominent Adam's apple; a strong, jutting chin; deep-set eyes; a lower lip that pouted perpetually outward; a slightly receding hairline, graying at the temples; and what an old friend of Crisp's in Washington would call a "passive" nose. Overall, a pleasant-looking fellow. Crisp wondered why he hadn't been requisitioned by one of the island's eligible womenfolk.

Leeman kept his eyes on the road and both hands on the wheel.

"I knew them well as anyone, I guess. Not what you'd call intimate, you know. But they were cousins back through my aunt Agatha somehow. You know Aggie Pease?" Crisp nodded. "Well, she's my aunt. Back through her, somehow. I think she was a Calderwood. Half the island's been Calderwoods one time or other."

"I don't know much about the Calderwood boys," said Crisp without a smile. "I saw them on the street now and again. I gather they were pretty wild, like most boys that age."

"Andy sure was a rough young fella," said Leeman. "Not real bad, I wouldn't say, but rough. Had arms on him like, well, I don't know what. A gorilla or a football player. Real strong from pullin' all them pots, you know. Never got in much trouble. Drunk a few times and fights and things like that. He wasn't really bad, though, not . . . what's the word? Intentional?"

"Malicious?"

"That's right," Leeman nodded. "I can think of plenty who's worse. I guess that's why it's hard to figure him doin' somethin' like that." He jerked his head in the general direction of the cemetery. "I mean, it had to be somebody, like I said, but . . .

"He came from a good family." They pulled into Matty's driveway. "Besides, he was goin' with Tessy Noble. They was engaged and everything and . . ." He paused, and his eyes bounced self-consciously from the console to Crisp and back to the console again.

"And?"

Leeman looked out the driver's window through the rain. "From what I hear she wasn't makin' him wait for the weddin' night to seal the deal, if you get my drift."

Crisp looked out his window. "Oh, I see," he said. "So, he wouldn't be likely to . . . it's not as if—"

"Yes. That's right," Leeman replied, glad the professor knew how to carry on a conversation without using bald words. "I mean, if you got the run of the candy store . . ."

Crisp nodded out his window. Leeman nodded out his. "He was pretty tall, wasn't he?" said Crisp.

"I can tell you exactly how tall he was," said Leeman. "Six foot three and a half."

Crisp was surprised. "You sound awfully sure."

"Oh, I am," said Leeman. This mystery thing could run both ways. "I'm manager of the basketball team." He grinned. "I like to help out up to the school if I can. They got hardly any budget these days. Well, one of the things I do is get all them figures for the yearbook. Statistics, you know. Andy was the tallest one on the team."

"Six three, you say?"

Leeman nodded. "And a half."

"And a half." Crisp mused. "About an inch and a half taller than I am."

For a moment the only noise was the loud rain on the roof.

"What about the other one, Andy's brother?"

Leeman faced the dashboard again and began running his fingers over the station buttons on the radio. "Herbie."

"Herbie," Crisp echoed. "Pretty much the same?"

Leeman didn't think so. "He was a lot smaller," he said. "Not quite as tall, or so rugged, you know? A lot lighter, too. 'Course, that ain't much of a surprise 'cause him an' Andy had different mothers."

"Oh?" said Crisp. "I didn't know that. Different mothers, you say?"

"Andy's ma died of leukemia or some sickness like that. Maybe cancer."

"Leukemia is a form of cancer."

"Well, that must be what it was, then," said Leeman. "Anyway, that was back when I was fifteen or so. Andy was just goin' into school when I graduated, so I guess he would've been, oh, two or three when his ma died. Prob'ly never knew her."

"And his father remarried?"

"Woman from Stonington," said Leeman. "They had Herbie."

"So there was, what, four or five years between them?"

"If that," said Leeman. "She was five or six months gone by the time they got legal."

"Honeymoon rehearsals, eh?" said Crisp.

Leeman sniffed a note of irony. "That's what happens, ain't it?"

They agreed this was so.

"Some piano player, though."

"Herbie?"

"Yup. He lived up there near Gustav Hobartsen, you know?"

"The concert pianist?"

Leeman nodded and smiled. "My mother says she used to beat him up when they was kids."

"Hobartsen?"

"Yup. She figures that's prob'ly why he left the island. Then he goes off and gets world famous." Leeman looked at him confidentially. "He is, you know."

Crisp did know. "And Herbie learned from him?"

"He was gettin' good, too," said Leeman. "Not that I know much about piano playin', but it sounded some good to me. He'd play up at the gym for school concerts and the alumni banquet. That kind of thing. But I bet he could've played Carnegie Hall or one've them places. He did play over to the Community Center in Rockland once. They announced it on the radio and everything."

"That good?"

Leeman raised his eyebrows and nodded.

They sat quietly for another moment. The engine purred unobtrusively, with only a sputter at irregular intervals to verify its existence. Leeman picked at his cuticles while the rain came down steadily, tracing brief white lines through the broad beams of the headlights; slapping itself to splinters on the roof. There were shadows in the dining room window. Matty had guests.

"Well," said Crisp with a slap at his knees. "Thanks for the ride, Leeman. I'd probably have drowned otherwise."

They got out and Leeman helped him extricate his bicycle from the trunk. "Goshdarn seat's caught on the lip there," he said. "I never seen a seat like that, Pr'fessor. Big as a sofa. Most English bikes have them little seats that crawl up where the sun don't shine. It didn't come like that, did it?"

"No," said Crisp as they lowered the bicycle to the ground. "As a matter of fact, I got it last Fourth of July at the white elephant table. Fifty cents."

"Well, I wish I had one of 'em," said Leeman. "I got one've them French racing bikes—ten speed. Goes some wicked fast. But I don't hardly ever ride it 'cause I got hemorrhoids, you know?" He patted the thick foam-padded leather seat appreciatively. "You ever have hemorrhoids, Pr'fessor?" Crisp hoped it was a rhetorical question. It was. "Some ol' painful, I tell you. Puts that bicycle right off limits." Leeman patted the seat again. "Now, if I had a seat like that, I'd be able to take 'er out, see? Get a little exercise and lose some've this weight I gained over the winter."

If not for the fact they were both soaked to the skin already, one or the other of them might have been in a rush to get out of the rain. Neither was.

" 'Course, it looks awful out of place."

"I suppose it does."

"Wouldn't look so funny on one of them high-risers like the kids have, instead of them banana seats," said Leeman.

Crisp didn't know what a high-riser was. "Hmm."

"They're a lot heftier." Leeman slammed the rear door closed a few times until the latch caught. "I guess when you get to a certain age, you don't much worry what you look like anymore," he said philosophically.

Crisp couldn't think of anything to say in response. "Good night, Leeman."

" 'Night," said Leeman. He got in his car and backed out of the driveway. Crisp stood in the rain, resting a hand on the bicycle seat, and watched the Oldsmobile drive away. He wheeled the bike to the granite steps, leaned it against the latticework under the porch, and went inside.

He stood in the small entry hall and took off his boots, coat, and hat. Through clear spaces in the beveled glass of the frosted windows in the parlor door, he saw Matty busily laying out coffee and muffins. Their warm aroma made its way through the prevailing cloud of early spring dampness. Cranberry and rhubarb. He wasn't willing to subject himself to the scolding he'd get if she saw him in his present condition. He didn't turn on the light.

There were three coats on the pegs behind the door. The dry one was Matty's. The others were as sodden as his own. He smiled, hung up his coat carefully, took off his socks, and waited, watching at the door for Matty to take her departure while his feet froze to the linoleum. It would be a short wait. She never stayed long in one place.

The moment she left he opened the door with all the stealth his shivering hands could muster, closed it softly behind him, and tiptoed across the cold wooden floor to the braided rug by the fireplace. From there it was a hop, skip, and wobble to the hallway runner.

"Coffee's ready!" Matty called from the kitchen.

Just as he got to the bottom of the stairs, two men came through the double doors that led to the living room. One of them was Nate Gammidge. He held out his hand. "Hello, Professor!" he said warmly. "I wondered if we were going to . . . what?"

Crisp had held a silencing finger to his lips, mouthed some words neither of them could make out, and hobbled up the stairs like a tardy husband.

Nate Gammidge looked at his companion, shook his head, and laughed. "Dark doings," he said as they walked down the hall toward the parlor. "That's the fellow I was telling you about. Interesting character."

S AFELY IN HIS ROOM, Crisp draped his wet clothes over the radiator, sponged down in his private half bath, toweled himself off, and climbed inside some warm, dry clothes. Minutes later he joined the other guests over coffee and muffins. Nate's companion had been introduced as Alfred Hanson, medical examiner from the attorney general's office.

"Well, Professor," said Nate, "looks like you were right about that makeup."

"Makeup? Oh, yes. Old, was it?"

"Made in the early thirties, according to the lab in Augusta. Like you said."

Crisp sipped his coffee and nodded. He took a bite of muffin and refused to say what Gammidge seemed to expect him to say. Gammidge looked at Hanson. "The professor said it was old makeup." Hanson nodded. "He was kind of a chemist," Gammidge continued. Hanson nodded and turned his attention to the fire. "Kind of a chemist in your day, weren't you, Professor?"

Crisp smiled a smile of agreement. Gammidge sighed deeply and swallowed half a cup of coffee at a draught. Must be a trick to carrying on a three-way conversation by oneself. "Hot in here," he said, tugging at his collar. "You got the suntan oil right, too, didn't he, Alfred?"

Without moving his head, Hanson raised his eyes from the fire and looked wearily at Gammidge. "That's official information, Mr. Gammidge," he said.

"But he was the one who—"

Hanson turned to Crisp. "I don't mean any disrespect, Mr. Crisp. I don't want to come across as Inspector Lestrade to your Sherlock Holmes, but this is a very delicate business, for a lot of reasons. Very delicate." His eyes amplified his meaning. "Already, in accommodating your requests, Mr. Gammidge has considerably overstepped both his professional and political bounds, and not without jeopardy to his career, I might add."

Gammidge didn't raise his eyes during the monologue. Nor did he raise them now. He turned the gold and silver wedding band nervously around his finger. Hanson continued.

"No doubt life in retirement gets dull for someone with your talents and . . . imagination. I suppose life on an island would be especially so. Be that as it may, this unfortunate girl's death—"

"Murder," Crisp corrected.

Hanson nodded once. ". . . is best handled by professionals. Surely you see the logic in this."

"I do indeed," said Crisp, whose expression betrayed nothing. "As you say, it's a delicate case."

"I don't think you know how delicate," said Hanson.

"That may be," Crisp replied. "That may be. But it's mighty interesting, from an amateur's point of view."

"Oh, I don't know that it's so out of the ordinary as to trouble about, Professor," said Hanson, dismissing Crisp's curiosity.

Gammidge finally raised his eyes, more than a little startled by this appraisal. "Not out of the—!"

Hanson raised his hand and Gammidge fell to earth like a stung duck.

"Well," said Crisp quietly, with a smile, "your experience is a good deal broader than mine if you don't think finding a dead man's fingerprints on Amanda Murphy's neck doesn't fall a little out of the ordinary."

It was Hanson's turn to be startled. Immediately he turned on Gammidge. "I thought you were told—"

"I didn't!" Gammidge protested against the unspoken accusation. "I didn't say anything! He just figured it out."

Crisp poured another cup of coffee. Normally, Matty wouldn't let him have two, because caffeine seemed to make him sleep poorly, and when he didn't sleep well he had nightmares. In the absence of her iron will, he found his own no match for the temptation. "Stuffy told me."

"Stuffy? Stuffy who?"

"Just a town character," Gammidge explained. "Harmless."

"You've never played cribbage with him," Crisp said with a smile.

Hanson flushed. He glared at Gammidge. "So, everyone in town knows the whole business?"

"I didn't breathe a word!" Gammidge defended.

"I can't believe that something this . . . this—"

"Sensitive?" said Crisp.

Hanson swept the room with a glare and riveted it on Crisp, against whose inscrutable, slightly bemused expression it melted. "How did this . . . character . . . find out?"

Crisp shrugged. "Probably Leeman Russell told him."

"And who—"

"Don't bother," Gammidge interrupted. "When it comes to intelligence-gathering, the FBI don't hold a candle to the poolroom."

Hanson stared at the fire and punctuated the ensuing silence with sharp sighs and wags of the head.

"In fact," said Crisp, in an effort to break the tension, "I think Einstein might have revised some of his pet theories had he known how fast news travels on an island."

Gammidge smiled behind his hand.

Crisp reached into his pocket and produced a small, crumpled brown paper bag. He emptied an assortment of penny candies, rubber bands, matches, seashells, and a little bundle of fabric into his hand. "I was up at the other end of the island and I found these—"

"This is unbelievable," said Hanson. He looked from Crisp, a doddering old bird with his handful of sweets and trinkets, to Gammidge, who seemed to be studying the molding in one of the farther corners of the room, and back to Crisp again.

". . . in a tree," Crisp concluded.

"Mr. Crisp . . . Professor," said Hanson condescendingly, "it's none of your business. I'm sorry. I don't know how to put it another way. We can't have would-be detectives interfering with the investigation. It's not an easy business as it is. Do you understand?"

Hanson visited his father every other Wednesday at the Bayside Convalescent Center in Camden, trading off weeks with his younger sister. His father was senile and hard of hearing. He found that leaning close, almost brow to brow, and raising his voice was generally the only way to drive home a point and keep the old man to the subject. Unconsciously, he was applying the same tactic with Crisp, who gazed back unblinking, his eyebrows arched slightly. Hanson half expected him to start snoring. "Understand?"

Crisp nodded slightly. "But you should examine these things," he said weakly. Gammidge thought he looked especially feeble all of a sudden. Hanson had him cowed. Crisp seemed stupefied, scratching his head, searching the immediate vicinity absentmindedly. "Very important things," he said.

Hanson huffed through his nose, rolled his eyes, and picked up his cup of coffee and a muffin. "Do me a favor, Professor, keep them to yourself. I'm going to my room," he said. "See you gentlemen in the morning."

"Oh, maybe you shouldn't drink that coffee," Crisp cautioned amiably. "It'll keep you up all night."

"Nothing keeps me up," said Hanson over his shoulder as he walked down the hall. "Fruitcakes included," he added to himself.

"A sound night's sleep is a gift from God," said Crisp softly as Hanson's footsteps thudded up the carpeted stairs.

Gammidge detected a change in Crisp's tone. When he looked up from the fire, the dotty old man was melting away, his place being taken by the cagey reasoner he'd come to know.

"What are you up to?"

"Pardon?"

"That was all an act," said Gammidge, "wasn't it?"

"I tried to turn in some very important evidence and was rather roundly rebuked for my trouble," Crisp said. "Just trying to do my civic duty."

With a quiet smile Gammidge regarded his companion. "You've got Hanson thinking you're a dim-witted old fossil."

"Seems to happen when I go out of my way to make an impression."

"Oh, you made an impression all right," Gammidge said. "Just the impression you wanted, I bet. So?"

"So?"

"What have you got there?"

"Well," said Crisp. "That depends. I mean, do you ask in a professional or personal capacity?"

"Which will get me answers?"

"Well, since it seems Mr. Hanson is in charge of the official investigation, and as he has refused my assistance . . ."

"Personal, then."

"Ah!" said Crisp, the sparkle leaping to his eye. "Well, in confidence then, I found the murder weapon and what I take to be the bottom of the girl's swimsuit."

"You're joking!"

"I wouldn't joke about such a thing."

"A wire, like you thought?"

Crisp nodded. "Wrapped around chunks of wood at the ends."

"Handles."

"And a wadding of some kind in the middle so as not to—"

"Cut the skin," said Gammidge.

"Cut the skin," said Crisp.

"You've got to turn them in, you know," Gammidge said, after a brief silence during which he tried to convince himself otherwise.

"I tried."

"I know, Crisp, but . . ." Gammidge got up and stepped to the fireplace. The howling of the wind outside sent a chill up his spine, though Matty generally kept the house at about seventy-three degrees. It was even warmer in the parlor, with the fire blazing. "I know how you feel, you know. I do. But if Hanson finds out . . ."

"What can he say? I tried to give them to him. I'd gladly have told him the whole story. He wasn't interested. You heard him," Crisp said calmly. But there was nothing of the helpless old man in him now. Another facade had dropped away. Gammidge confronted another Crisp, one whose clear eyes and steady gaze portrayed a thoroughly conscious, calculating intellect. "He told me to keep them to myself."

"But you can't. You made him think . . ."

The ease with which Crisp slipped into his absentminded old man routine, as if he was putting on a favorite pair of flannel pajamas, left Gammidge both perplexed and off-balance.

"Well, I'll tell you what," said Crisp. "How about if we just keep it between us a little while?"

"No," Gammidge said flatly. "Just . . . don't even . . . no."

"I'll tell you what scares me, Nate."

"What?"

"Mr. Hanson strikes me as the political type."

"That may be—"

"That's what I'm afraid of, you see? This could be big, the implications of this case—you heard him. He's the type who's going to grab the first thing masquerading as evidence and run away with it."

"Come on, Crisp."

"He'll have all kinds of people breathing down his neck. Politicians, the media, the public. They just want an answer. They don't care if it's the truth.

"All I ask you to consider is this: Who do you think is most likely to get the truth out of this case? Who's most likely to find out who really murdered that poor girl?"

Gammidge was beat. He sat down and looked at Crisp. "Preconceptions?"

"Confused priorities," Crisp amended. He fiddled with his watchband. "I suppose Mr. Hanson has the pictures with him?"

"Pictures?"

"The Polaroids."

Gammidge had learned that Crisp said very little without a motive. His brain automatically skipped a groove or two ahead. "Don't even think it, Professor."

"Think what?" said Crisp, taking a hurried gulp of coffee as Matty crossed the floor at the far end of the hall in sensible shoes.

"You heard what he said: 'It's none of your business.' He's not about to go flashing pictures all around the place," said Gammidge. "And how did you know they were Polaroids, anyway?"

Crisp felt it unwise to mention Leeman at the moment. His gaze fell to his fingers. "I made a statement, and you didn't correct me," he said. He raised his eyes again. "One of the stronger human instincts, I find, is the need to correct people."

Gammidge shook his head slightly. "Well, he's not going to show them to you."

"I don't imagine he is," Crisp agreed. "Still, he has them with him, you suppose?"

"I suppose." Anticipatory though he was, he couldn't read the subtle gleam in Crisp's eyes. There was a brief silence. "What of it?"

Crisp started slightly, as if he'd dozed off momentarily. "What? Oh, nothing, Nate. I was just thinking." He nodded slightly as if in agreement with whatever he'd been thinking. "Well, it's been a long day. I think I'll go up to bed." He rose from the comfort of the soft, floral print easy chair and held his palms toward the fire. "If only I had Mr. Hanson's facility for sleep, I'd be off at a nod."

The observation was accompanied by a smile that made Gammidge uncomfortable. He wasn't sure why. Crisp doddered off down the hall like an old man, mumbling to himself. "A sound night's sleep is a gift from God," Gammidge heard him say.

"You're not going to do anything foolish," Gammidge called out in a harsh whisper.

Crisp's comfortable old face appeared over the banister. "I never do, Mr. Gammidge," he said with a smile. The face disappeared, and a long shadow followed the old man upstairs.

Gammidge couldn't help but notice that Crisp's footfalls made no sound.

"He's a ghost," he said aloud.

"Who's a ghost?" said Matty as she bustled in from the kitchen, vigorously wiping nothing in particular from her hands with her terry cloth apron. She began to clear the dishes.

"Crisp," said Gammidge lazily.

Matty continued to rustle within her little cloud of clean. "Oh," she said. "He's a poet, too."

C
H
A
P
T
E
R

9

ALL DREAMS HAVE THE SAME DECORATOR, Crisp thought. A capricious gnomess whose motif is liquidity. One who has no intercourse with the conventions of time and space. Her walls turn to waterfalls, her days to nights, her friendly faces to doorknobs, demons, or donkey's tails. No sooner does she establish a theme than it changes. She is at once temptress, tormentor, and torturess. Idylls metamorphose into nightmares at her merest whim. You can be in the middle of either, without knowing which is which, and you learn at an early age never to approach a corner with both eyes open, for whatever waits for you there knows your every fear profoundly.

His was never a deep sleep. The slightest unfamiliar sound would wake him, an attribute that had saved his life many times in the past but in his declining years had become a curse. Seldom did his sleep filter beyond the shallow pools that dotted the shore of the Blessed Abyss. Pools that teemed with life and refracted light in such a way as to confound reason. Within that realm this malignant sorceress exercised a broad brush, using the full scope of his memories to splash upon her palette. She would often paint him awake with familiar terrors.

There was a woman at the edge of his dream tonight. He knew that it was Amanda Murphy, though he saw no more than her silhouette from time to time.

He was following her, and though she never moved, try as he might he could get no closer. She inhabited the dream and was, therefore, above space and time. He, only a visitor, was mired in them, bound to reality by the tenuous tether of life. He tried to call her name, but the words knotted and tied themselves around his heartbeat. She spoke, too, but he couldn't make out the words. Every time she opened her mouth, blood pulsed from a gash in her throat.

He had something in his hand. A pail of soapy water. That's why he was chasing her—to wash the grotesque makeup from her face, the blood from her throat. As he pursued her the water splashed from the pail, leaving a perfect trail. In the darkness at his back, someone followed.

All the while the world of dreams ebbed and flowed around him.

"Amanda!" The sound of the cry woke him. It was the voice of an old man, clogged with sleep, made brittle by the years. His own voice. Startling. He always dreamed himself much younger.

The household slept on, except for Matty, whose room was next door. She'd never heard him call that name before.

Crisp went to the bathroom and splashed his face with cold water. He looked at himself in the mirror. "Old man," he said. "You've got work to do."

"I don't understand it," said Hanson the next morning at breakfast. He spoke so softly his voice was barely audible above the scraping as Gammidge applied marmalade robustly to his toast. "There were ten pictures in that pack. One is missing."

"I don't see how you can look at those things before breakfast," Gammidge protested.

Hanson's cold eyes draped Gammidge in contempt. "I don't eat breakfast."

"I shouldn't wonder," said Gammidge, biting off a piece of toast and assisting it along the proper channels with a fork full of scrambled egg. "Looking at those kinds of things this time of day'd put anybody off."

Hanson's attention drifted to Crisp, who was sitting in the alcove and seemed to be struggling to remember whether he'd put his pants on. Hanson's unspoken suspicions, though only newly formed, evaporated at the sight. "Someone must have dropped it in all the confusion."

"Someone," Gammidge echoed with a nod. "More than likely someone did."

"Well, it wasn't me!" Hanson said angrily.

"Didn't say it was, did I?" Gammidge didn't look up from his plate.

Matty chugged in under a full head of steam and began collecting dishes. "Has everybody had enough? Inspector? Look at all these eggs left over. Your plate ain't even dirty."

"I'm not hungry, thank you," Hanson said coldly.

"Mr. Gammidge, you're tuckin' in pretty good. You want to finish up these eggs?" Without waiting for a reply, she shoveled the eggs off the platter onto his plate. "Can't give 'em to the cat, you know. Cholest'rol.

"Winston? What are you doin'? You look like you lost your best friend."

Crisp looked up slowly. Matty's breath was almost taken away. "Why Winston, you look a hundred years old!"

Crisp looked out the window. "Restless night, Mat."

"Why not give these to him?" said Gammidge. "He hasn't eaten, has he?"

"Winston?" said Matty. "Oh, goodness yes. He ate hours ago."

Gammidge glanced at his watch. "It's only six-thirty now."

"I know it," said Matty reprovingly. "I half thought you fellas was dead. Ain't easy keepin' all this food warm so long, you know."

Gammidge didn't know whether to laugh or not, so he ate some more eggs.

"He don't look good, do you think, Mr. Gammidge?" said Matty under her breath. She hardly took her eyes off Crisp as she cleared away the dishes.

"Oh, he'll be all right," Gammidge assured her. "He looked like that awhile last night." He peered over his glasses at Hanson, who was scrutinizing the nine remaining Polaroids, oblivious to the ambient conversation. "Brightened right up after a while, though." He looked at Matty. "I wouldn't worry."

"Well," said Hanson at last, rising and brandishing the Polaroids. "These tell us all we need to know."

"And what's that?" said Gammidge.

Hanson saw Crisp turn his good ear toward the words. "That's all right, Professor," he said, planting himself midway between Gammidge and Crisp. "I can't see that there's anything to hide now."

"Not that it wouldn't be all over town 'fore noon even if there was," said Gammidge. Hanson pretended not to hear.

"Our only fear was that, somehow, the Calderwood boy wasn't in the coffin, where he belonged." Hanson explained. "That he'd, well, I don't know what. These fingerprints, well . . . All sorts of crazy things go through your head sometimes when you're faced with facts that don't quite add up." His gaze followed Crisp's out the window.

"You come up with things that sound like they're off the front page of a grocery store tabloid," said Gammidge. "Man Returns from the Dead to Kill Himself type of thing."

"Never underestimate human nature," Hanson observed. "Bizarre things happen from time to time, especially in this business. A man gets a crack on the head, something short-circuits— you can't rule anything out."

Crisp's consciousness appeared to bob to the surface. "Oh, well,"—he started to reach for the bag in his pocket—"then you won't mind taking a look at these things I found."

Hanson smiled benignly at Crisp. "I've got all the trinkets I can use, thanks. Keep them for your collection."

"But Mr. Gammidge seems to think they may be of some importance," Crisp protested feebly.

"Then give them to Mr. Gammidge," said Hanson. "I'm sure he'll find a use for them." He glanced at his watch. "The boat leaves in ten minutes. I don't intend to miss it. Gentlemen." He left to collect his things.

Gammidge's face melted into the most abandoned-old-dog-about-to-be-put-to-sleep expression Crisp had ever seen. An argument Crisp could have thwarted; begging he could have parried or simply hardened his heart against. But against this trod-upon field mouse tactic he had no resource. It touched the poet in him.

"Mr. Hanson," Crisp said flatly.

Hanson stopped at the foot of the stairs. He could make out only Crisp's silhouette against the bay window. "What? Did you call me?"

"Come here, Mr. Hanson, there's something you must see."

Hanson was about to say he hadn't time, but he was so struck by the change in Crisp's voice that he hesitated. "What? What is it? The boat leaves in ten minutes."

"You won't be on it" came the reply. "Come here, please."

"I beg your pardon?" Hanson protested. Nevertheless, he found himself drawn toward the speaker. "If this is your idea of a joke . . ." He reentered the parlor. "What's this all about?"

Wordlessly Crisp took the crumpled paper bag from his pocket and emptied it onto the table. Amid the collection of lint-covered candy, seashells, and rubber bands was the bundle of black fabric, which he spread out on the coffee table. "I found this hidden at the other end of the island." It was a bikini bottom. The Crisp that Hanson had known was gone. In his place was someone else. Hanson listened.

"I also found this"—he unwound the wire—"the weapon that was used to kill Amanda Murphy." He laid it down beside the other items in evidence. "It was wrapped around her neck, and she was strangled with it."

Hanson's objection mechanism sputtered to life. "She was strangled by bare hand!" he protested, holding his own hands up in example. "There were fingerprints—"

"The fingerprints of a dead man," Crisp reminded him emotionlessly.

"Someone got their facts confused," said Hanson. "That's all. We'll find there was just a mistake. Fingerprints don't lie, Mr. Crisp. This is just a case of human error."

"She was strangled with this first," Crisp continued. "Then it was made to look as though she had been strangled by hand."

"The professor said that's why she had those cuts on the sides of her neck . . . the wire, you see." Gammidge pretended to strangle himself with a wire.

"Something wound around her neck after her body was thrown in the quarry," Hanson snapped. "I told you that, Gammidge. Fishing wire or a vine. Besides, who in his right mind would strangle someone with a wire, then his hands?" He looked at his watch. "Where did you get these things?"

"In a hole in a tree."

"Near the beach where the girl was killed," Gammidge interjected.

"Near the beach where the girl was killed," Crisp repeated.

"The beach? What beach?"

"The beach up at McKenniston's, remember?" said Gammidge. "I told you. The professor found that beach sand under her toenails."

"Yes, yes. I remember," said Hanson impatiently. He unwound the kerchief Crisp had tied around the wooden handles. "Handles?"

Crisp nodded.

Hanson thought for a while, then smiled condescendingly.

"Okay. Let's look at your ideas objectively, Mr. Crisp," he said. "The girl is wearing this?" He held up the bikini bottom. Crisp nodded once. "Nothing else?"

"The sweatshirt. There were bloodstains on it. I imagine she was wearing it when she was attacked. Either that or it was lying nearby, and the murderer put it on the body."

"All right," said Hanson. "All right. She's got suntan lotion on. And the makeup?"

"Just the suntan oil."

"Why do you say that?" Hanson was holding the bikini bottom up to the window.

"The makeup was applied later, over the oil."

"Okay," said Hanson, dropping the fabric onto the table. "Okay. When did she put on the makeup?"

"She didn't," said Crisp patiently. "Her murderer did that."

"The murderer put makeup on her?" He cocked his left eyebrow incredulously and cast a sidelong glance at Gammidge.

Crisp nodded.

"After he . . . ?" Hanson finished the sentence in mime.

"After," said Crisp. "She was strangled with that first." He nodded at the wire. "Then the makeup was put on."

"Forty-year-old makeup," Gammidge volunteered. He much preferred life at the edge of the loop. From a safe distance he could toss comments into the wheels of reason and watch what happened.

Hanson became the personification of long-suffering, rubbing his temples. "Then he strangles her again, with his hands, drags her up to the quarry six miles away, and dumps her in. Oh, but first he has to chip a hole in the ice, doesn't he? I mean, it's December, right? Do you suppose the beach was crowded in December, Mr. Crisp? More sunbathers than you can shake a stick at?"

"It was September," Crisp said quietly. "Just after Labor Day."

Hanson went to the entry to get his coat from the rack. "And that's where your whole theory begins to fall apart, you see?" He pulled on his coat, then came back into the parlor and sat down opposite Crisp. "Listen, Mr. Crisp, I appreciate all the thought you've given this case. I do, really. But this whole sunbathing idea— you see how ridiculous it is, don't you? I mean, think about it. It *had* to be December. At *least*. That's when the ponds first froze. We checked. Almost Christmas. There was no bathing suit connected with this crime. Couldn't be. That's just . . . I don't know. Some kid stuck it in the tree, hiding it from a skinny-dipper. Who knows? I'll tell you this: she was strangled and tossed in the quarry." He picked up his suitcase. "Don't look at me like that. *I'm* not the one who's crazy around here.

"Now, anyone who didn't catch a ride on the helicopter this morning will be waiting for us down at the motel, Gammidge. Let's get moving."

"But the fingerprints . . ." Gammidge objected.

"They got mixed up at the lab," said Hanson surreptitiously. "We'll sort it out. All you need to do is apply common sense. Granted, this may seem like a sensational case on the surface, but it'll all boil down to simple common sense." He tapped his temple. "Common sense will answer all the questions in the end. Are you coming, Gammidge?"

"All right," said Crisp, a little feebly. "I guess I just let my imagination get the best of me. Perhaps you're right, Mr. Hanson, about life on an island. You have to be disposed to it, you know?"

"Of course you do," said Hanson with a smile. "Of course you do. Granted, there are some difficulties, but don't you worry, Mr. Crisp. The answers will fall into place, all in good time. We'll get to the bottom of this. It's been a pleasure meeting you." He shook Crisp's hand. He was surprised at the old man's grip, and uneasy beneath his gaze. "Now, Nate, get your coat on or we'll miss that boat. You settled with the lady?"

Gammidge nodded. "I'll take care of it," he said slowly, and left to do so.

The day was knee-deep in blue. Clear. Cool. A pussy willow just outside the window had pushed out a few green shoots, determined to be the first one into summer. Hanson's words echoed in the stillness of the room. Crisp didn't add to them. He didn't have to. They were hollow. Unsatisfying. Hanson sat down again. For the first time since he got to the island, he pushed himself all the way back in his chair. "They're going to be all over me about this," he said, half to himself, half to the angels.

"Bosses?" Crisp ventured.

"Bosses? They're the least of my worries." Hanson leaned forward and poured himself a cup of coffee. Crisp decided there might be a person in there after all. "The press. The politicians." He looked at Crisp. "What on God's green earth prompted you to look in that tree?" His voice was almost pleading. "I mean, why did you go up to the McKenniston's in the first place?"

"The beach sand."

"You found beach sand under her toenails, so you went up to the McKenniston's and looked in a tree?"

"Well," Crisp replied softly, "in a manner of speaking, yes. One thing leads to another. Sequential logic."

"I can't wait to hear the sequential logic that had you poking around in old trees on the evidence of beach sand." Hanson settled back a little farther in the easy chair, prepared for a long story.

Crisp sat down, too. "I had made certain assumptions beforehand, I confess," he said. "The first being that this crime has many layers. The evidence is being manipulated."

"What do you mean?"

"She'd been strangled twice. Why, when the first effort clearly did the job?"

Hanson folded his hands under his nose and rubbed the back of his knuckles thoughtfully against his teeth. He stared at the table full of evidence. Especially the length of rusty wire and its crude handles. "To cover up the first one?"

Crisp smiled. "Right. The first time was very neat. Very clean. There are no fingerprints in the suntan oil beneath the makeup, other than the victim's. This indicates that she applied it herself."

"In December," Hanson reminded him.

"For the moment, let's assume that's a separate problem."

"And in the makeup?"

Crisp shook his head. "No fingerprints. None at all. Then a wire was used to—"

"I understand," said Hanson.

"And there are no fingerprints on the handles. I've studied them."

"Gloves?"

"Rubber, probably," said Crisp. "The wood is very rough—just stumps of branches, as you see—but there are no traces of fabric, as you might expect if the murderer wore cotton or wool gloves. And why did the murderer put this knotted rag in the middle of the wire?" Pause. "To crush the windpipe and the larynx, while leaving as little of the wire mark as possible. Then there's the problem of the buttons."

"Buttons?"

Crisp reached into his shirt pocket and drew out a snapshot, which he dropped to the table.

"That's the missing picture!" said Hanson, stepping to the coffee table. He picked it up and looked at it. "You were in my room!"

"You wouldn't have let me see the picture, would you?" said Crisp.

"Of course not! It's evidence—"

"Look at the buttons," said Crisp, handing Hanson a magnifying glass.

"They're plain brass buttons," said Hanson. "What of it?"

"Look at the buttons on the sleeves."

Hanson did so. The corpse's hands were folded neatly in front of the body, so the buttons were presented for easy inspection. "Chain and anchor," he said softly.

Crisp nodded, took the picture from Hanson's limp fingers, and slipped it back into his pocket. "I wonder why."

"THEM INVESTIGATORS was stayin' up to Matty's last night, wasn't they, Pr'fessor?" Petey Lamont picked up the peppermint wrapper that Crisp had tossed at the spittoon and ran it under his prodigious nose. He'd have preferred butterscotch, especially this hour of the morning. Of course he knew perfectly well who had stayed at Matty's the night before, as well as their weight, hair color, shoe size, and ancestral heritage. Just like everyone else in town. Not that the information in circulation was necessarily accurate, but reliability was of secondary consequence. Volume was critical.

No one knew Alfred Hanson firsthand, but there were a lot of Hansons on the mainland with whom various islanders had communicated through the ages, and their composite became the template used to create a portrait of this particular Hanson. The apple principle applied: if you wanted to know an apple, study the tree. Information gleaned in this manner sufficed to the satisfaction of most and, as Crisp had learned over the years, although not notoriously accurate in particulars, was probably not too wide of the mark in general.

Crisp nodded and stuffed the peppermint into his right cheek with his tongue. "Mr. Gammidge and Mr.—"

"Hanson," said Drew. The last piece of wood he'd put in the stove was too big, and the little cast-iron door wouldn't close all the way. Now and then smoke would puff out in wisps and billows and drift up to join the blue-gray cloud that floated just below the tin ceiling.

"Hanson," said Crisp.

"There's lots of Gammidges over on East Haven," said Drew.

There were nods of agreement.

"I don't 'member any bein' out here, ever," Petey said. "D'you, Stump?"

"Never was," said Stump, reviewing the lengthy parade of islanders that passed before his brain. " 'Cept one who used to go out seinin' with Mo Osgood. But he was from East Haven. Jus' come over durin' season's all."

There was another lapse during which the fire editorialized in pops and crackles. "What'd they have to say about it?" said Pharty.

At this point the two layers of conversation, the audible and the inaudible, merged. The customary formalities having been observed, this question was launched to bridge the two. "They" were the investigators. "It" was the opening of Andy Calderwood's casket.

"Well, I guess they just wanted to make sure he was in there," said Crisp.

The wood had finally burned enough so Drew could shove it the rest of the way into the stove and close the door. " 'Cause of them fingerprints," he speculated.

"I can't figure that out at all," said Petey. "Can you? I mean, Andy Calderwood was already dead before that girl come to no good. They seen 'er over to Rockland a coupla days after them boys was killed. Who was it said they seen 'er over to Rockland, Drew? I know Mostly did."

"Becky Gable."

"That's right," Petey continued. "Becky Gable seen 'er over there after them boys was killed."

"And Evelyn Swears," Pharty amended.

"Yessir," said Petey. "Evelyn did. And Mostly. That's at least three seen 'er over there. Well, then, if all them people seen 'er after them boys was killed, how did Andy's fingerprints get on her neck when he was already gone more'n two, three days?"

The eyes of each man had found a favorite place among the pots, pans, hardware, and old photographs and settled there, but all ears were turned to Crisp. "I believe they're just as confused," he said softly.

"What'd they expect to find?"

"Well, I get the feeling they didn't really know what to think. They had some evidence that didn't seem to add up. As you said, Petey, how could the Calderwood boy's fingerprints appear on the girl's body if he died before she did? I guess, unless you believe in ghosts, you have to think that either people were mistaken when they said they saw the girl on the mainland after the boy died, or the boy didn't really die."

"But it was an open casket wake, f'r pity sakes," Petey objected. "Lots've people was up there. Saw both them boys."

"Charlie did a good job," said Stump.

"That leaves us with the alternative," Crisp suggested. "It's interesting that nobody saw her come back to the island."

Petey wondered if it was. "She musta got back out here someways."

"Maybe just nobody noticed, is all. Lot've people on the boat that time've year . . . 'bout Labor Day," Pharty observed.

"True," said Crisp. "But—"

"I don't know," said Drew. "She was one've those people who

attract attention. I've seen lots of 'em over the years. Isadora Duncans, I call 'em. Not that they mean to, but they do."

"There's a lot that do go out of their way for it," Stump said, and for a few minutes the conversation spiraled off to diatribes against the times.

Crisp, with a remark interspersed here and there, gently returned the speakers to the topic. "But the Isadora Duncan types are different?" he said.

"Oh, yes," said Drew. "Night and day." He tilted his head and lobbed an addendum over the top of his horn-rimmed glasses. "Not that they *mind* the attention, you understand."

Crisp forgot what he was going to say, then he remembered. "She was a very pretty girl." Even cold and dead she was pretty.

"She was," said Drew. Others nodded. "Some pretty."

"Well, I know times have changed since we were boys, but, as I recall, a pretty girl wouldn't go unnoticed on the ferry," commented Crisp.

"You got that right," said Pharty. "Even if it was crowded as the ark."

"Especially if it was crowded as the ark," Crisp corrected. "The bigger the crowd, the more boys. The more boys—"

"More eyes to notice," said Drew.

Everyone nodded.

" 'Specially the way she dressed."

"Distinctive, would you say?" Crisp asked.

"That's just the word I was lookin' for," said Drew. "Distinctive is right. She always wore these real tight outfits."

"Body stockin's, Almy said they was," said Petey. "That's what they call 'em. Dancers wear 'em."

Drew approved. "Well, that's a good name for 'em. I seen lots of women wear 'em . . . most shoulda been shot for it. But she could do it."

"Wasn't flauntin' neither, though," said Pharty.

"No, that's the thing," Drew agreed. "Somehow she could wear them costumes and get away with it. Like she didn't give it a thought, you know? I guess that's where personality makes a difference."

"That's all she wore?" said Crisp, draping inquisitive wrinkles over his eyebrows. "Just these dancing costumes?"

"Oh, no," said Drew and Petey.

"Skirts," said Petey.

"Big, colorful skirts, like gypsies wear," added Drew.

Pharty launched a cheek full of tobacco at the spittoon. "Real feminine," he said.

"Flowers and things," said Drew. "Then she always had these big ol' scarfs—"

"Bandannas," Petey corrected.

". . . in her hair," finished Drew.

"Bright red hair," said Pharty.

"Bright red hair," repeated Drew.

"That's how come they noticed her on the mainland," Pharty concluded.

Crisp thought of the bright red wig pinned to the bright red hair of the corpse in the morgue. Nonsense oiled the gears of suspicion. "Doesn't sound like a girl who'd escape notice on the boat," he speculated. One by one, the others nodded in agreement. "But as far as we know, nobody saw her, going or coming."

The statement was directed at Petey, but Pharty answered. "Must've. Like you said, you don't miss somebody like that."

"That's what I mean," said Crisp. "If somebody saw her on the boat, they didn't come forward when the FBI was investigating the girl's disappearance last year. Curious, isn't it?" said Crisp. "So many people on the boat that time of year, but the only three people who saw her were in Rockland."

Evelyn Swears lived at the end of Clamshell Alley, a narrow lane at the water's edge that followed the contour of the harbor. The water side was occupied by lobster shacks in various stages of repair and disrepair. Most of the lobstermen had been out on the water for hours by this time; their trucks were wedged at odd angles in openings here and there. One or two of the shacks showed signs of life, though. Lethargic wraiths of smoke moored themselves to tin chimneys and, congregating at an altitude of twenty feet or so, refused to go any farther.

The residential side of the lane was lined with a series of neat white cottages, built on granite ledge, three stories in front and two in back, so their second stories admitted an enviable view of the harbor over the roofs of the lobster shacks.

Jeannie MacQueston's crocuses, little kings of spring, were already up and aggressively trying to out-purple one another among the remaining islands of snow and ice in a sea of matted wheat-colored grass. The air, although not warm, whispered promises of summer in Crisp's good ear, and as he walked his stride became somewhat less purposeful. Once again he hadn't slept well. He was tired. He would have liked to lie down among the crocuses and let spring grow up around him. This year it would grow up around the Calderwood boys and Amanda Murphy. His turn would come in time—perhaps next year, or the year after. A welcome prospect. He wondered if he'd get any closer to the fire in the meantime.

A tidy white picket fence, about waist high, held Evelyn Swear's little patch of yard in place, and everything therein was as perfect as human hands could manage. She had crocuses, too, but they didn't grow just anywhere, as was the case with Jeannie MacQueston's. They were arrayed with military precision: the vanguard of spring venturing toward the strange new world of summer. There was no snow or ice in the yard. Evelyn had determined that that sort of business was over with for the year. Accordingly, she had Snotty Spofford and one of the other neighborhood boys remove the residue and prepare the various little planters, which would soon be invisible beneath their burden of flowers.

Crisp lifted the latch, walked through the gate, and took the four or five baby steps along the brick path to the glass-paned door. The knocker was a brightly colored pine woodpecker. He gave two sharp tugs to the little string that made its beak bang against a wooden plate, then he folded his hands and waited.

Presently a female form emerged into the bright shaft of sunlight from the shadows within and opened the door. "Hello?" said Evelyn Swears. She'd seen this man before, but whether on TV or at a bean supper she couldn't recall. Crisp detected the doubt in her voice.

"I'm Winston Crisp, Evelyn."

"Winston . . . ?"

"I stay up at Matty's place."

"Matty? . . . Oh. Oh . . . the professor." The fire of recognition quickly swept into her eyes. "Yes, yes! Come on in, won't you?" But she stopped halfway across the threshold and gripped his forearm with her firm hand. "Did you close the gate?" Crisp double-checked. He had. "If I don't keep that gate shut, the dogs get in," she said contemptuously, closing the door behind them.

"You're lucky I was down here doing laundry," she said as she led him across the basement to the stairs. The smell of clean, warm linens hung neatly in the air. "I wouldn't have heard you knock upstairs."

As he followed her up the steps, Crisp noticed that Evelyn, like Matty, wore sensible shoes. Perhaps all women grow into them in time, if they live long enough, he thought. Amanda Murphy would never wear sensible shoes. She would always be young, lovely, and impractical. And dead.

"I'm sorry about the mess," Evelyn said as they stepped into the kitchen. Crisp looked around. Moving from his own place into Matty's, he had learned that *mess* is a relative term; how distantly related he began to appreciate as he looked from Evelyn's spotless floor to her sparkling windows, to her gleaming dishes, arranged in descending sizes in the dish rack. "If I'd known you were coming, I'd've baked some sticky buns." He knew she meant it. There was a smell of baking in the air.

"Oh . . . well, I shouldn't have just dropped in on you like this, Evelyn."

"Oh, I love company," she said. Now her puttering had a purpose.

Crisp didn't remember being invited to sit, but there he sat, and before he knew which end was up, she had set the table for tea and produced a warm blueberry muffin from thin air. It sat steaming on his plate. A small pat of butter slid off its crown and oozed down its sides. "I haven't even put the dishes away. Cream and sugar?"

"Uh . . ." said Crisp. "Uh . . ."

Cream and sugar were placed on the table. "Look at me," Evelyn said, busily sorting herself out with her hands. Crisp looked at her. "I must look a mess." Crisp didn't think so. Evelyn was a thinner version of Matty, except that she wore slacks, which Matty would never have countenanced. Evelyn was a modern woman. She had a puckered little face with cheery cheeks and perpetually smiling little crescent eyes that peered at the world through gold-rimmed bifocals. The effect was completed to perfection by a pair of those magically capable hands that seemed the hallmark of her generation.

"Isn't that awful, them finding that girl up at the quarry like that," she said. Crisp had planned to ease into the topic. He had rehearsed a whole series of little statements that, from segue to segue, would cause Evelyn to broach the subject. He'd have to save them for another time.

He felt like an invited guest. She didn't ask why he'd come. He wasn't made to feel a nuisance or an imposition. Ample room was made for him in the routine of Evelyn's day, and she accommodated herself to the intrusion as if it had been expected. Some places in the world had forgotten the term for such behavior. Happily, Penobscot Island was not among them. It was simple neighborliness, the act of putting oneself aside. "Eat that muffin 'fore it gets cold. I don't expect it's very good. I just threw a batch together this morning. Had to use store-bought blueberries." She sounded ashamed. "Another month or two and we'll have fresh, though. 'Course, rhubarb will be up in a few weeks. You'll have to come back for some fresh rhubarb pie. Do you like double cream?"

"Double cream?" Crisp said with his mouth full. He noticed Evelyn wasn't eating. "Aren't you going to have a muffin?"

"Oh, no," said Evelyn, as if the thought had never crossed her mind. "I don't care for blueberry. I just like the smell."

Crisp swallowed hard. "You just bake them for the smell?"

"Well, one reason is as good as the other, I guess," Evelyn responded matter-of-factly. "If you bake 'em to eat, why not bake 'em to smell?" The teakettle had begun to whistle. She got up and poured the boiling water into a teapot. "My Harry loved blueberry muffins," she continued. "I'd make 'em all summer long in those days. I guess the smell of blueberry muffins and summer got to be about the same thing to me, you know? So, I was feeling a little tired of winter this morning and figured if I got the smell of blueberry muffins in the house, it'd hurry up summer a little." She poured a steaming cup of tea and placed it in front of him. He looked at her with all his eyes.

It was a good muffin, and summer did seem a little less distant.

"You saw her on the mainland . . . that girl?" Crisp asked.

"Poor girl," said Evelyn.

"Poor girl," said Crisp.

"Yes. Becky Gable and me were going up to the coffee shop for some breakfast."

"Oh, you were together?" Evelyn nodded. The number of actual sightings was reduced from three to two. "And you took the first boat?"

"Yes," said Evelyn. "And just as we got there, she come out of the bookshop. You know the bookstore next to the coffee shop?" Crisp knew the bookstore. It was one of many that would probably never carry a volume of his poetry. "Well, she come outta there and struck off up street at a good clip."

Evelyn went on for a while about how good the food was at the coffee shop since the new owners took over. She couldn't remember where they were from. New York or New Jersey. Something with "New" in it. "Could be New Guinea, for all I know. I think I'm getting forgetful. Happens at our age, you know," she lamented. " 'Course you do," she added, as if it was obvious.

It suddenly occurred to Crisp that, though there was a preponderance of people eighty and over on the island, he couldn't think of a single case of senility or Alzheimer's among them. Everyone he knew was razor sharp and completely aware. Of course, there was the possibility that they were all senile, himself included, and seemed cognizant only by comparison, but he didn't think so.

Something struck Crisp as curious. During a lapse in Evelyn's prattle, he stuck in his oar. "She came out of the bookshop, you say?"

Evelyn nodded.

"And . . . you were on the first boat?"

"Oh, yes," said Evelyn. "Wouldn't have time to get much done if we went over on the second boat."

"You just stayed the day then?"

" 'Course we did," Evelyn replied, a little taken aback. "I ain't about to get stranded over on the mainland all night. No sir."

Crisp smiled an understanding smile. "No. No, of course you wouldn't want . . . You know, I'm surprised the bookshop was open that hour of the morning."

It struck her as curious, too, come to think of it. "You're right, you know. The boat gets in just after eight."

"How long did it take you to walk to the coffee shop, do you think?"

"Oh, probably ten minutes."

"Ten minutes?" This struck Crisp as too long a time to walk the fifth of a mile from the ferry to Main Street.

"Well, it's Becky, you see. She fell on the ice last winter when she was down getting the mail, and she broke her hip. Dog ran in front of her. They should pass a law, as far as I'm concerned. Put 'em all on leashes. I'm sorry. I like dogs as well as anyone, but you can't have 'em just going around crippling people like that, can you? Just bills, too," she said.

"Bills?" said Crisp. The thread of logic was unraveling and he had the feeling that if he didn't get a hold of it pretty tightly, it would be lost forever.

"From the mail," said Evelyn. It wasn't an answer, just a response dropped into a tiny opening in her commentary that would otherwise have been occupied by a "my goodness" or an "oh, my word."

"And they put in one of them stainless steel hip joints or whatever it is. They tried to put in plastic, but she wouldn't have that. It's not biodegradable, you know. Becky's awful keen on the environment. So I'd say ten minutes."

Crisp massaged his brow. It would not be difficult to get information from Evelyn Swears. Sorting it out could be another matter.

"Did you see her?"

"Yes," said Evelyn, sounding not the least bit indignant. She knew what happened to the minds of people Crisp's age. "I just said that, dear. Me and Becky Gable saw her come out of the bookshop."

"No, no," said Crisp with a smile. "I mean, did you see her face, or was she walking away from you? You said she went up the street . . . away from you."

"Well now, let me think," said Evelyn, and she thought. "No," she said finally. "No, I can't say I saw her face. 'Course, I can't speak for Becky, but I doubt she saw her until I pointed her out, because she walks with her eyes to the ground."

"Becky Gable does?" Crisp hypothesized.

Evelyn nodded. "Because of her hip. Makes her awful cautious, it does. Well, it would, wouldn't it?"

Crisp sipped his tea and listened as Evelyn, sufficiently fueled to run until her supply of firsthand knowledge was exhausted, babbled on.

Not that her oratory was in any way restrained within the borders of firsthand knowledge. Within a two-and-a-half-muffin time span, Crisp had been presented with an entirely new angle on island history and hearsay—what he would come to call the "beauty parlor perspective."

"How'd you happen to ask that?" Evelyn said finally, having circumnavigated the full range of topics.

Crisp hastened to catch up. What had he asked? "Oh, uh . . . the girl, you mean?"

"About seeing her face."

"Well . . . uh, you see," Crisp mumbled. His thoughts had been wandering far and wide, scouting out the strange new terrain of the woman's point of view. It was no easy task to marshal his thoughts against this sudden frontal assault. Many thoughts had difficulty finding their way and tripped over one another in their confusion. "I heard you had seen her. But only you three—Mostly Sanborn saw her, too."

"Oh, yes. I know that. The FBI asked us all about it last—when was that? September? October?"

"Yes. Well, I hear she was . . . the men down at the hardware store"—he detected a slight upward wrinkling of Evelyn's nose—"say that she dressed—"

"I can just imagine what they said about the way she dressed," said Evelyn scornfully. "Can't find anything better to do than sit there all summer long and ogle summer girls." The twinkle left her crescent eyes for a moment. "At *their* age," she synopsized.

"Yes," said Crisp. He knew she knew he was one of the men at the hardware store. His comrades had been defamed. How should he answer this slur against their honor? His gaze fell to the floor. "Well . . ." he said limply.

"I imagine she'd be hard not to notice, though." Crisp detected a softening in her tone. Not forgiveness. Surely not absolution. He decided it was long-suffering forbearance. "I expect there's lots of nice things you could say about her. She seemed a nice enough girl, from what I know, which isn't much. But you wouldn't call her modest." Her left brow furrowed ever so slightly in thought. Crisp allowed all the silence she would need to give birth to whatever was on her mind. "She wasn't a floozy, though—the kind they go crazy over down to the hardware store." She lowered her glasses almost imperceptibly, looked at him over them, and dared his denial. He knew she would be amazed to learn the hardware store's opinion of floozies. At least, she'd be amazed if he had the audacity to suggest what he knew to be the truth. He'd been a student of human nature long enough to know that Evelyn knew what all women know: all men are mortally guilty of something, so they sheepishly accept blame for lesser crimes in atonement. In the face of false accusations, a man's silence becomes nolo contendere for the whole sex. "She wasn't a loose girl, just . . . just—"

"Naturally flamboyant?" Crisp suggested.

"If that means what I think it means—colorful—that's it exactly," said Evelyn, brightening.

Once again she was bustling. In a twinkling the table was cleared and the dishes were washed and arranged neatly in the dish rack.

"That's how we noticed her in the first place over in Rockland. She always wore these bright skirts."

"Like a gypsy?" Crisp suggested.

"Just like a gypsy," Evelyn concurred. " 'Cept clean."

"But you didn't see her on the boat going over?"

Evelyn was very deliberate when asked a question. She thought carefully. Rare, Crisp thought. Most people's responses were reflexive: they reply on impulse, leaving themselves to defend ludicrous positions. Generations of lawyers have successfully capitalized on the trait in their efforts to dismantle justice. They have classes in it at law school.

"No," she said. "I didn't. Neither did Becky. She said so when

we saw her . . . the girl, I mean. She said, 'I don't remember seeing
her on the boat, do you?' What I was trying to think of was if I
saw her on the way coming back, and I didn't. Somebody asked
me that before, one've them FBI men back when she turned up
gone. I was just rethinking in my mind, to make sure. I can't say
she wasn't on board. Like I said at the time, I don't go in the smoking cabin, and she could've been in there. Or out on deck. I don't
go out there, either. So I can't say she wasn't on the boat. There's a
lot of people going back and forth that time've year. But I didn't see
her get on or off, and that's when I would've seen her. She would've
stood out like a butterfly. So," she said in closing, "she must've gone
over the day before and come back later."

"She must have," said Crisp. As he got up from the table, his
coat, gloves, and hat manifested themselves in Evelyn's hands. She
helped him put them on as if he was her elderly, imbecile son she'd
been doing for every day of his life.

"Well, I'm so glad you came by," she said as she walked him to
the back door. It led out to the top of the ledge and a muddy little
path that cut across a field to the road. "Take care you don't slip
on that ice at the bottom there," she said, pointing to a place where
ice used to be. "Next month I'll have some fresh rhubarb pies.
You come back then, Professor, and I won't send you off hungry."

Crisp minded his step at the bottom of the ledge. What would
Matty say if she found out he'd had someone else's muffins?

"**W**ELL, DID YOU FIND any more bodies up there?" Mostly Sanborn's distinctive voice tugged Crisp too quickly around, and a letter or two slipped from the little stack of mail in his hands. There were no letters from publishers among the flyers and bills. No rejections today. Of course, that meant no acceptances, as well. But no rejections meant his poetry was still out there somewhere, being read by someone. Reviled, most likely, but read nonetheless. There was hope. Having been rejected so many times, he imagined he'd achieved a certain notoriety among editors and readers of unsolicited material as the most widely read unpublished poet of all time.

"Dropped your mail," said Mostly, rocking back on his heels and tangling his thumbs more determinedly in his overalls. Crisp bent his aged frame to retrieve the letters. Some of it was Matty's, or he'd have let it lie. "You startled me, I guess. I was miles away."

"I'd rather be here," said Mostly with a smile. "Not so many surprises when you know where you are."

Crisp smiled, too. "No, I suppose not."

"Find what you was lookin' for up there? You never did say what it was, exactly. Somethin' to do with that girl, I know."

"Well, I found some things, yes, but the police didn't seem interested when I showed them." That they'd shown interest later on, he could keep to himself without prevarication. "Just some little odds and ends. What brings you down to this end of the island?"

"Oh, just had to get some six-inch bolts for the ramp," said Mostly. They began to walk toward the hardware store. "They got three-eighths inch up at Brown's, but I want five-eighths. Don't want to leave things to chance, you know. Been enough tragedies up there without that ramp givin' way under one've the senator's fat friends at low tide. They're likely enough to fall in by 'emselves." He employed sign language to indicate that a lot of drinking went on at the senator's.

"I see," said Crisp. "Then the bigger the bolt—"

"The better," Mostly concluded with a wink.

"The better," Crisp agreed.

There was no one in the hardware store except Drew, who stood by the cash register at the far end of the counter doing paperwork. He looked up when they came in, waved, and ignored them. Mostly took a handful of candy and raisins from the skillet, and they sat down—Crisp in Petey's seat, Mostly in Crisp's, as protocol demanded.

"I was going to come up and see you this afternoon," said Crisp.

"Don't have to now," said Mostly, popping a Tootsie Roll Junior in his mouth. "Saved you a pedal." He doubted there were many pedals left in the professor.

Crisp nodded. "They say you saw Amanda—"

"Mandy," Mostly corrected.

"Mandy. They said you saw her over in Rockland a day or two after the Calderwood boys' accident."

"Yup. I did."

"Where was that?"

"Rockland?" said Mostly, a little puzzled.

"No, I mean where in Rockland did you see her?"

"Oh, gorry . . . she was just comin' out've some store."

"Which one?"

"Shoot, I don't know. They're all the same's far as I'm concerned. Coffee shop's 'bout the only one I go in."

"Did you see her on the ferry over?"

"Didn't come on the ferry."

"How did you get there?"

"Took the senator's launch. She was bein' pulled out for the winter, down to Hank's. They flush 'er out and paint 'er for the next season, you know. McKenniston likes keepin' a boat on the mainland. That way he can get out to the island, if he needs to, after the last ferry's gone." Mostly opened another piece of candy and began to chew on it. "Not that he's ever used it. Doubt if he'd know how to run the thing, myself. But gives him comfort, I guess."

"So, what time did you come over?"

"Oh, just after sunup, there'bouts. Six, maybe."

"And you went to the coffee shop?"

"Oh, that was pretty much later. We had a bunch've errands to run first."

"Someone was with you?"

"Two someones. Sarah Quinn and Marky Williams."

"Did they just come along for the ride?"

"Marky did," said Mostly. "Sarah had to come over to get things to close up the house with. New padlocks, furniture coverin's—that kind've thing. Anyway." It was a rhetorical "anyway."

"They didn't see Amanda . . . Mandy?"

Mostly shook his head. "Jus' me. We was all split up by that time. Sarah went to run her errands up to the hardware store. They open early. Marky went off to do somethin'. He didn't tell me what. Prob'ly lookin' at them girlie magazines up to the bus stop."

"What time was it when you finally went to the coffee shop?"

"Oh, ten. Ten and a half."

"Hey, Mos'. Senator know you're loafin' around downtown on a workday?" Drew had finished doing paperwork, or whatever it was he did behind the counter. He fluffed the cushion in his chair and sat down.

"You're a good one to talk. He's a good one to talk," Mostly said to Crisp with a wink. "Man never done an honest day's work in his life. Sits here in fronta this stove all day, eatin' candy, gossipin', and robbin' people blind."

"Ain't gossip," Drew said matter-of-factly. "It's news."

"Oh, that's right," said Mostly. "It's only gossip when women do it."

"What'd you come in here for? McKenniston still has a bill down here, you know. I was just lookin' at it. You're the one who's supposed to take care of those bills before the season's over, aren't you?"

"What bill?"

"That bill for fifty-seven dollars and eighty-three cents is what bill. Left over from last summer."

"I didn't buy nothin' for fifty-seven dollars and eighty-three cents," Mostly objected, sitting forward in his chair.

Drew swiped calmly at some dust on the stove. "Didn't say you did. I don't put down who done the chargin', only who the chargin' was done to."

"What was it for?"

"What's the matter, you don't believe me?"

"I think you'd rob your own grandmother if you got a chance, that's what I think," Mostly said playfully. He knew full well that if Drew said the senator owed $57.83, then he owed it—not a penny more or less. Nevertheless, for the next few minutes they disinterred each other's ancestors and heaped abuse upon them.

It was finally resolved that Mostly would settle the account his next time in. For now, however, he had to add two six- by five-eighths-inch bolts to it, which Drew allowed, though he was loudly skeptical that he would ever see the money.

"What was we talkin' about?" said Mostly at last. "Oh, the coffee shop. That's where I seen 'er. She was comin' out've some store upstreet from there. Just when I was goin' in, she come out. I called after her—said 'hi,' you know, the way you do when you see someone you know over there. Anyway, she didn't hear, I guess. I don't doubt it, all that traffic. Some awful crowded."

"That was the only time you saw her?"

"Yup."

"And she was walking away from you?"

"Yup."

"Then you didn't see her face?"

"Didn't have to with that girl, did you, Mos'?" said Drew. "Like we was sayin' earlier, Winston. She was one of a kind."

"And that red hair," said Mostly. "There wasn't no mistakin' that red hair. Nope," he said flatly. "It was her, all right."

"Was the store far away—the one you saw her come out of?"

"Oh, not far, no," Mostly replied. "Three or four doors down, I guess. Close enough so I could see her, but far enough so she couldn't hear me when I hollered."

"Hard to believe she wouldn't hear an old foghorn like you," observed Drew, punctuating the comment with a single-syllable laugh.

Mostly's voice was distinctive. High pitched and clear. "That is hard to believe," Crisp agreed.

"I bet she heard, all right," said Drew. "She knew just who it was, and that's why she didn't turn around. I'm surprised she didn't head the opposite direction at a dead run."

"Oh, shut up, you ol' chicken thief," said Mostly, rising. "Well, I gotta get back up to the salt mines," he said. "Drop them bolts in a bag, Drew, will ya? I don't want to lose them washers."

"Bag'll cost you extra."

"Charge it to the ol' man. He's worked for the gover'ment long enough, he won't think nothin've payin' a few hundred dollars for a paper bag."

"Oh, there's a big difference when it's his own money," said Drew. "You know that as well as I do. Some ol' tight, he is."

The door squeaked its good-bye as Mostly opened it.

"One more thing," said Crisp. "How did you get back that day?"

"Took the ferry."

"All three of you?"

"Yup."

"But you'd left your car up at McKenniston's?"

"Truck," Mostly corrected.

"Truck," Crisp amended.

"Yup."

"How did you get it?"

"Just rowed across the Thorofare, got in 'er, an' took off home."

"Across the . . ." A light dawned. "Oh! You took the East Haven ferry."

Mostly's words said, "That's right." His tone said, Of course, you poor old idiot. "Wouldn't make much sense to take the Penobscot ferry when my truck's all the way up to the north end of the island, would it? Marky lives up there, anyways."

"And you gave the Quinn girl a ride home?"

"Usually, yup. Not that night, though. She stayed awhile to put them things she bought around the place—drapin' furniture and whatnot. Straightened up the storeroom out in the barn. Lot more to closin' up a house that size than jus' lockin' the door an' shuttin' off the lights, you know. And the McKennistons're awful particular."

"Then how did she get home?"

"I don't know. Called her ol' man, I imagine. He come an' got 'er sometimes when I had to work late and couldn't take 'er home." He looked at his watch. "I gotta get goin'. See you later, gentlemen."

"Would you mind if I came up and had another look around?" said Crisp. "Tomorrow sometime?"

"Tomorrow's the funeral," Mostly reminded him. "You goin'?"

Crisp hadn't thought about it. "Yes," he said. Strange. It seemed to him as if she'd been buried for ages. "Yes. I'm going."

"Don't know who else'll be there. You can come up to the house after that, if you want."

"I don't think I'll care to then," said Crisp, more than half to himself. "Another time."

"I'll be there in the mornin' day after tomorrow, if that's good for ya," said Mostly. "I've got to go over to Rockland that afternoon to get the launch. Seas'll only be two to four feet, it said in the *Telegraph*. Should be nice and calm if I head back about five or so."

He was halfway through the door when Crisp called after him. "You didn't see Mandy on the ferry when you came home?"

"Nope," said Mostly. The door closed behind him. Crisp watched him through the window. He waved and strolled away.

Drew sat back comfortably in his khaki pants and plaid flannel shirt, folded his hands behind his head, and studied Crisp for a moment. "What was that all about?" he said.

Drew had been the first one to befriend Crisp when he came to the island more than sixty years ago. During World War II they'd both gone into intelligence work and, though Drew labored in a clerical capacity, their paths had crossed on occasion. At the time, Drew realized that his old companion was building a reputation of legendary proportions, working closely with William Donovan and his network of spies at the Office of Strategic Services. But that was only the beginning. Crisp's real forte was cold war. In that dull gray battleground, a dull gray man such as Crisp was completely invisible, and that's when a person of his peculiar talents is most lethal. Drew was the only islander in whom Crisp had ever confided about his work, but not much. And even that in a self-effacing way. "You back in business?" Drew asked.

Crisp sighed long and deep. "Imagine a mouse in a maze, Drew. He knows where to find the cheese, he's seen it, he can smell it, he knows it's just around the next corner, or the next, but just as he gets to it, it's replaced with a picture of cheese. What happens then?"

"Depends," said Drew stoically. "Are you the mouse, the cheese, or the one doin' the experiment?"

Crisp stood up and tugged on his stocking cap, his coat, and his gloves. "That remains to be seen," he said as he opened the door with its loud complaint of farewell. "But I'll tell you something, just between us." He held his gloved finger beside his nose. "*Nobody* saw Amanda Murphy on the mainland that day."

The sky was half sunshine and half rain clouds. Crisp stepped out into the part that was raining.

Drew opened the stove door and stirred the coals with the poker. "I wonder who wants to know the things he's goin' to find out," he said to the ghosts of the old men in the empty chairs.

CHAPTER 12

A LITTLE GRAVEYARD called the Stranger's Cemetery is tucked among the evergreens, near the old lighthouse at the north end of the island. It's reserved for people from away who had been called to glory while on the island. Some were strangers indeed, people whose bodies washed up on the beach from time to time. Others were nonnatives who elected to enrich the soil of Penobscot Island with their mortal remains.

Amanda Murphy's only living relative, a half brother twice her age, had elected on her behalf to have her buried there. He came to the funeral. He struck Crisp as one of those men, somewhat beyond middle age, who spend their lives being busy. One day he, too, would turn and cast a weary eye back over the parade of his years, would strain to hear the music he'd invested with his life, but hear only silence. Vanity, vanity, said Solomon. Vanity, vanity, thought Crisp. The middle-aged man glanced often at his watch and wondered if the service would be over in time for him to catch the next boat.

Neddy McKenniston was there, too. Apparently he and the

brother didn't know each other. Neddy had flown in on the mail
plane and, as Crisp found out later, left on the last boat from East
Haven. He wouldn't return to the island until he'd finished his last
year of postgrad studies at Harvard in another month or so. By
that time summer would be in full swing and the caretaker's com-
mittee would have removed the silk flowers from the grave and
stored them back in the cupboard at the Legion Hall. Neddy was
taller than Crisp had imagined, six foot one or two. Brown hair,
like all the family. Lanky. Athletic. With restless eyes and a smile
that came and went quickly and meant nothing.

Leeman Russell was there, as well. Apparently he'd taken time
off from his job at the grocery store for the purpose.

Waymond Webber attended, standing as close to the casket as
possible, but he still couldn't see anything. Mostly Sanborn stood
beside Crisp, a little distance from the grave.

The brother didn't know any of Amanda's friends, so they
hadn't been invited. He wondered at this odd assortment of mourn-
ers. All men. Imbeciles, as far as he could tell. It was cold. He would
be buried in Florida.

Last of all was the priest who came over from the mainland and
seemed to wish he could say something personal but, since he
couldn't, said what was expected. No one else was there.

The fog was thick and chilling. The lighthouse horn punctuated the ceremony at regular intervals, like a soul in purgatory,
calling, calling into the impenetrable mists, with no reply.

Crisp waxed poetic at funerals.

The priest called for a moment of silent prayer, then the gathering broke up and everyone except Crisp and Mostly filtered away
into the fog. Apparitions.

"Sad there wasn't more people here," said Mostly. "She must've
had friends'd like to've been here. Say good-bye, you know."

Crisp nodded. It had been a long night, during which his dreams had resurrected her again. She was running among the ruins of some rambling wooden structure. Up and down flights of creaking stairs, in and out of dark rooms. He'd chased her, never doubting that it was his dull, heavy footfalls from which she was running, but he was unable to stop his pursuit, lest she get away. It would be impossible to find her again among all those rooms. He was out of breath. Even in his dreams he was an old man now, shackled by the frailties of age. He tried to call her, to tell her to stop running, that he meant her no harm, but no words came out. Just gasps and wheezes. His lungs ached. His feet were sore, and his knees buckled at each step. Stabbing pains shot up his spine and down his left arm. The sound of his heart plugged his ears, and tears poured from his eyes and into the bucket of warm, soapy water he carried.

He'd awakened with a start. His nose was running, and tears puddled deep in his eyes. Someone was in the room; he could make out her silhouette against the window. He rubbed frantically at his eyes with the heels of his hands. "Amanda!" He fumbled for his glasses on the bedside table, put them on, grabbed at the light, and snapped it on. Too quickly. It fell to the floor and went out. But in that split second he saw her plainly in the corner of the room, where the eaves meet the dormer. She was standing, with her hands in front of her, almost reaching out to him, but not quite. She was wearing a frilly blue dress with a satin sash. Her hair was swept into an elegant temple of curls, and a cameo adorned the black velvet choker at her neck. "Amanda," he whispered in the darkness. He strained with all his heart to see her. To hear a reply. But the brief light that burned her image on his brain had temporarily blinded him, and all he saw was its ghost in the dark. He heard her breathing, though. Soft. Slow. Soft. Slow. Each breath added weight to his eyes and sent him to sleep again.

Madmen are those who have discovered that dreams exist in layers. One may wake from one dream into another and keep waking, each time entering a new dream, each more real than the last, but no less a dream.

"I'm sure she had many friends," Crisp said softly. "Many friends."

There was no reason for him to look up at that particular moment. No sudden sound, no motion. But he did, and when he did, he wondered if he was still dreaming. The fog was so thick that the evergreens in the surrounding forest were melded together in a brooding darkness. But in one place that darkness was broken by a slim patch of light, and the shape of the light was that of a young woman. Crisp was breathless, and his heart rose quickly to his throat. "Most! Look over there." But as he pointed, the figure withdrew into the mists and, by the time Mostly drew the area into focus, was gone.

"What?" he said. "Deer?"

Crisp took off his glasses and rubbed his eyes. The residue of dreams. "Probably," he said. "That's probably what it was."

For half a minute Mostly stared at the place in the forest that Crisp had indicated. He didn't see any deer. "Well, I gotta get back to work," he said finally. They began walking down the grassy, rutted road. "How you gettin' back to town?" Mostly asked. "You didn't bring that bicycle, did ya?"

"No," said Crisp with a smile. "Matty's nephew—"

"Billy?"

"Billy. Yes. He's running errands for someone up this way."

"Prissy Hearthstone, I bet."

Crisp nodded. "Odd name."

"Well, you never met a less odder woman in your life, I don't guess," said Mostly. "One've them people, what you see is what you get, though. Nice lady." All during the funeral, Mostly, in wool sports coat and tie, had been swatting at his shirt front in search of a resting place behind the bib overalls he otherwise wore at all times. His hands were like salmon attempting to return to their spawning grounds, little knowing that the river had been dammed in the intervening year. "Matty and Prissy's good friends. He's prob'ly doin' somethin' for her, I imagine."

"Anyway," said Crisp, "he told me to just start walking and he'd pick me up before I got too far."

"Well, that's good," said Mostly. "That's good." He stopped at the edge of the cemetery. "There's a path beats off through here up the shore to McKenniston's," he said. "I'll be goin' back that way. You be all right?"

Mostly rarely took his eyes off the ground, but he looked up in response to his companion's silence. He saw Crisp looking back in the direction of the grave, peering hungrily through the fog.

"See that deer again?" he said, narrowing his eyes and squinting. He still didn't see anything. "They don't usually come out this time of day. Early mornin's when they come out. Late evenin'. Can't see anything in this fog anyway."

Exhaustion could do strange things to the mind. Crisp had seen strong men surrender their most deeply cherished ideals and beliefs for simple want of sleep. He felt as though his head was filled with helium and would float from his shoulders, or burst, if he moved too quickly. And now he was seeing Amanda Murphys wherever he looked. Half a second ago she'd been standing by the grave. Her own grave. A wandering breeze tugged a thick veil of mist across the scene and everything was gone.

Mostly knew that Crisp had had a heart attack not long ago. "You sure you're all right?"

Chills ran down Crisp's back. He manufactured a feeble smile. "Oh, sure. Sure. I'm fine," he said. He patted Mostly on the shoulder. "You go on back to work."

"You sure look awful tired," Mostly protested. "I can go up to the house and get the truck if you want . . . take you back to town."

Crisp had already started down the road. Amazing how thick the fog was. Mostly had almost lost sight of him. "Just take half an hour, if you want to wait," he hollered, his high, nasal voice slicing cleanly through the air.

"I'll be okay," called Crisp. "I'll be up to see you tomorrow, if that's still okay."

"Sure," said Mostly to the fog. "Sure," he said to himself. He stood staring in the direction of the road until he couldn't hear Crisp's footfalls on the gravel anymore. Then he turned for one last look at the cemetery.

"What do you s'pose that is?" he said aloud. He saw something on the far side of the cemetery. For half a second he thought it might have been the deer the professor thought he saw. But it wasn't. It was a woman, standing near the open grave. "Hey, there!" he hollered involuntarily. The woman looked at him. A fleeting window opened in the fog, allowing him to see clearly. He recognized the costume immediately. The billowing skirt of many colors, the dark bodystocking, the dazzling tangle of long red hair. All the excitement of a thousand childhood games of "ghost in the grave-yard" surged over him a hundredfold. He raised a two-syllable soliloquy to heaven, turned, and fled up the path toward McKenniston's as fast as his legs could carry his old bones and their abundance of flesh. Cold fingers of fright pursued him—ran up his back, along his shoulders, and up his neck.

"You don't look too good, Professor." This observation coming from someone of Billy Pringle's perceptions was alarming indeed. When he was no more than six or seven, Billy had fallen off a cliff and landed on his head. The experience had had a profound effect on his personality, bringing into play certain defects that would have rendered him an embarrassment in polite society. Not the least alarming of these was that he punctuated every sentence with a loud raspberry. Once old enough to leave home, he'd removed himself to a small shack at the edge of town and settled into a lifestyle that obviated the need of running water, electricity, combs, and toothbrushes. No one would ever imagine, upon sight alone, that he was related to Matty, even by so much as species. However, his gentle nature and quiet concern for and aid to others betrayed the connection and had, over time, made him the ward of a thousand hearts.

"That seems to be the consensus, Billy," said Crisp.

"I don't know that word, Mr. Crisp," Billy replied.

"Consensus is what most people seem to think," Crisp explained carefully. "Several people I've spoken to recently have said the same thing you said."

"That you don't look well?"

"That's right."

"Consensus?"

"Consensus."

As a rule Billy drove very slowly. When his mind was busy with a new problem or discovery, he drove slower still. At the moment he'd slowed his ancient truck to a crawl. Crisp could almost hear him mentally knitting the word into his vocabulary. He didn't mind that it would be a long ride back to town. He liked Billy.

"Well," said Billy when he'd finished thinking and sped up enough to shift into second, "if that many people say the same thing, you must really look like hell."

By the time Crisp realized the statement was meant not as a joke but as an observation, he'd already started to laugh. He almost choked himself trying to turn it into a cough. "I've just had a lot on my mind lately, I guess. Haven't slept well."

"You don't sleep well when you have a lot of things on your mind?"

"No," said Crisp. "I think about them."

"Why don't you not think about them 'til mornin'?"

One had to marshal one's thoughts carefully before speaking to Billy Pringle. "Well, they sort of think about themselves," he said. An analogy suddenly sprang to mind. "It's like an engine. Once you start it, it keeps running all by itself."

Billy considered this. "Not if you don't put gas in."

Crisp opened his mouth but, realizing he didn't have anything to say, closed it again.

"Don't seem things never change up this way," said Billy after a while.

"Do you come up here often?"

The truck slowed down. Just a little, though. It was an easy question. "Not too often," said Billy. "Nope. Once in a while I run up with an order from Carver's when they got something special goin' on. Matty sends me up to Prissy's sometimes. Chores and things."

"You deliver groceries?"

Billy downshifted into second. "Yup. Sometimes they'll order a whole side've beef or a truckload've lobsters for picnics. They have these cookouts down on the beach, you know. I even brung a whole dead pig up here once."

"A whole pig! Is that a fact? They must be big parties."

"Sometimes," said Billy. "Sometimes there's just family, though. Not more'n eight or ten."

"But why order all that food for just eight or ten people? What do they do with the leftovers?"

"Oh, they just stick 'em in the freezers. Eat off 'em all summer that way." Billy laughed. "Nope. Old money up there. They don't let nothin' go to waste. Barbie Carver says they could survive on the leftovers of an Indian's buffalo." He laughed, raspberried, and laughed again.

"It would have to be a big freezer to hold a side of beef."

"Or a pig, too. Gorry, I'd hate that, wouldn't you?" said Billy. "Goin' in there and seein' a half-ate pig hangin' there with his face all on and everything." He shuddered. "That's how they eat 'em, you know. Cook the thing up whole, head and everything. I seen pictures," he added confidentially. "They stick apples in his mouth, then they just fall to on it. Cut big ol' pieces right out've him while he's layin' there lookin' at 'em."

"Going in? You mean they're walk-in freezers?"

"Sure they are," said Billy. "Just like they got down to the stores. Most of 'em bring their own cooks. And them cooks bring their own food, seems like. Comes over by the boatload, and they salt it away in them freezers. Barbie says that's 'cause food's cheaper on the mainland, 'specially down to Mass'chusetts, where the gov'ment pays for it. She says she don't hardly get any business from up that end've the island. 'Course, they get most've their regular stuff—eggs and milk and veg'tables and stuff like that—over to East Haven, I should imagine. It's just across the Thorofare. But when they got a big party on, I guess they raid most've the places around for one thing or another, 'cept what they got in them freezers."

"Do the McKenniston's have a freezer like that?"

Billy shrugged. "I don't know. I never delivered nothin' up there. They trade mostly at The Island Grocery when they're in town, and Leeman Russell delivers for 'em, you know."

"Oh," said Crisp. "Is that a fact?" After a mile's silence, Crisp asked, "Would you mind dropping me off at The Island Grocery, Billy?"

Billy said he wouldn't mind at all. The regular throb and clang of the engine sewed a ragged hem on the ensuing silence. "Were you home during all the excitement up your way the other night?" Crisp asked finally.

Billy knit his brow and thought carefully. "You mean when everyone was goin' up to the cemetery?"

"Yes."

Once again the truck slowed to a near stop. Crisp realized that, if he wanted to get back to town anytime soon, he'd have to stop asking questions of Billy. "I was," Billy replied slowly. "Seems like the whole town come rushin' by."

"Must have been quite alarming."

"Alarming?" said Billy with a tilt of the head that indicated another holiday in his vocabulary.

"Surprising."

"Oh, yes it was," Billy said. "I knew somethin' was goin' on. I was out turnin' up my garden."

"In the rain?"

"It wasn't rainin' yet, though the sky was lower'n a fat lady's bladder," said Billy. "But that wouldn't've stopped me. Best time to turn's in a new spring rain, my uncle Walt says. Wakes the soil up and gets it activated, he says, and he's got the best garden in town, don't he?"

"So you watched everyone go by?"

"Yup. I just stood and watched. Just like a parade, it was, 'cept movin' faster. All them lights and shoutin' and tires squealin'. 'Course, there wasn't any music. After a little while there was just a few stragglers comin' up the road. Then, 'bout dark, come the last two—you and that girl."

Crisp shuddered involuntarily. "What girl?"

"That one come right up after you, Pr'fessor. I thought you two was together." Then, in response to an expression on Crisp's face, he added, "You know, that redheaded girl. I seen her in the lightnin'. She was right behind you when you was walkin' your bike."

They turned off the road into the little gravel parking lot of The Island Grocery. "Here you go," said Billy. "Say hello to Aunt Matty for me. Tell her I said thanks for that meat loaf she sent up the other day. I'm goin' to eat it, too. One day soon."

Crisp made no motion toward the door. Instead he seemed posed for a portrait of bewilderment: his jaw slack, his eyes focused on something only he could see. "Professor?" said Billy. "Professor, you okay?" He laid his hand on Crisp's shoulder and shook him slightly.

Once again fatigue was obscuring the boundaries between the real and the unreal, forming a tiny vortex of confusion that spun through Crisp's mind, grabbing old memories by their shirttails and tearing them out of seclusion, mixing them up with present perplexities, weaving old ghosts together with new. How is it that someone else was seeing his ghosts?

"Professor? Want me to take you up to Matty's?"

Matty. There was a memory that spanned his whole life. The thought of her swept up all the ghosts, dusted them off, and put them neatly away. "Oh, no. Thank you, Billy. I'll be fine." He got out of the truck, closed the door, and tied it shut. "Thanks for the ride."

"Sure thing," said Billy. "You want me to wait?"

Crisp hesitated. "Yes, please. That'd be nice."

Why had he said that? He knew Billy had offered out of concern for an old man. He'd become accustomed to offers of help in recent years. And he always refused them. Perhaps this ride had signified the turn of another page in his life. The final page. His leg had fallen asleep and he limped as he walked into the store.

"Mornin', Professor." The girl at the cash register, whose smile he always enjoyed, was a Nelson, but he could never remember which one.

"Good morning, Miss Nelson," he said.

"Philbrook now." Mrs. Philbrook, nee Nelson, beamed, displaying a dazzling new wedding ring of proportions only lobstermen could afford.

"Oh! You married young . . . ah . . . young . . . Philbrook, did you?"

"Yup," said Mrs. Philbrook, who didn't seem old enough to be out of school at this hour, let alone married, to a Philbrook or anyone else. She leaned on the counter. "Did Matty send you up for somethin'?"

"Oh, no. No," said Crisp. It was one thing to sound like an old man when it was convenient, but he sounded like an old man now, and he hadn't meant to. He cleared his throat. "No. I'd like to talk to Leeman for a minute. Is he in?" He still sounded like an old man.

"Sure. He's around. Just go up and down the aisles. You'll run into him."

Crisp found Leeman working at the soda cooler. "Good morning, Leeman."

"Hi, Pr'fessor. How'd you get back to town?"

"Oh, Matty's nephew—"

"Billy?"

"Billy Pringle. Yes. He—"

"He gave you a ride, did he?"

"He gave me a ride. Yes."

"You're lucky you made it back 'fore dark, then," Leeman said with a laugh. He had opened a box of soda cans and was stamping them with a device that left the price printed in ink on the top of each can. "I'd've given you a ride if I thought you'd needed one."

"You do that awfully fast, Leeman," said Crisp in admiration. "Don't you ever put two prices on the same can?"

"Not hardly ever," Leeman replied. He stopped and leaned against a nearby tower of boxes that seemed to have been placed there for the purpose. " 'Course, I did when I first started out in the business." He tapped the handle of his stamper. "Been at it almost twenty years now, though." He paused. "Even if I do make a mistake once in a while—might be some pretty summer girl comin' down the aisle, you know, so I go a little faster to impress 'em—they know it up at the cash register. So they don't charge 'em twice, or anything. Ain't the end of the world."

Once again he turned to his work.

Thickity-thickity-thickity. Crisp was mesmerized by the rhythm of the stamper as it bounced across the cans. He might have stood there all day if Leeman hadn't finished the top layer and begun stacking them in the cooler.

"Some sad that was, wasn't it?" said Leeman.

"Sad?"

"That funeral."

"Oh," said Crisp. He was reminded of why he'd come. He wondered if it mattered. "Yes. Not many turned out, did they?"

"I thought half the town would be there," said Leeman. "I guess they figure the excitement's over."

Crisp didn't share the town's evaluation. "Billy tells me you deliver groceries to the north end of the island," he said after sufficient silence allowed an abrupt change of topic.

"In the summertime," said Leeman. He had pulled the cans of soda already in the cooler to the front and was stacking the new cans behind them. "Start up again pretty soon, I guess," he said. "Most of the families don't come up 'til Memorial Day—sometimes

the Fourth, even—but they send their help up—staff, you know—
to get things ready. I guess I'll start gettin' calls in the next week or
two. They're usually clean out've most everything."

"You deliver to McKenniston's?"

"Yup. But they do most've their shoppin' over to East Haven.
I go up now and again, though."

"Would you happen to know if they have a freezer?"

"Sure they do. Great big one in the barn."

"A walk-in?"

"Yup. McKenniston's old man had it put in. He come up in the
fall to go huntin', him and some've his friends. If they got a deer,
they'd store it in there. Not that they minded if they didn't get one.
I think they come up here mainly to get away from the women—
all that high-society carryin' on. You know? They'd come up here,
tie one on for a week or ten days, let it all hang out, as the kids say.
You heard 'em say that?"

Crisp wouldn't have been surprised at anything kids said these
days. He'd lost touch with youth when they got pretty heavily into
the business of burning things. Undergarments. Draft cards. A generation of pyromaniacs. It suddenly occurred to him that Amanda
Murphy was a generation removed from all that. He nodded.

" 'Course, their freezer ain't as big as the Ringling's," Leeman
continued. "They got a drive-in freezer."

"Drive-in?"

"Only one I ever heard of," said Leeman. "Don't work half the
time, though. That is, the generator don't work."

"It's run by generator?"

"Yup. I guess that was a good idea back when we had the island power plant. 'Lectricity was down half the time in them days.
You know that. But since we got that cable over from Central Maine
Power, we don't have that problem no more. So most've the summer places went off the generators."

"The McKennistons'?"

"Oh, they was one've the first. They still got it hooked up, just in case, but I don't guess it's hardly ever used."

Having removed all the cans from one box, Leeman tossed it aside and opened another with a razor blade he kept for the purpose in the pocket of his apron. He turned some of the little wheels in the top of the stamping device and began pricing new rows of cans.

"Well, I'll leave you to your work," said Crisp. "Amazing how fast you do that." The stamper flew even faster until Crisp was out of sight.

"You know, I think I'll walk after all, Billy," said Crisp through the passenger side window.

Billy looked skeptical. "You sure?"

Crisp stood a little taller. "Yes, thank you." He waved as the truck drove off. "I'm much better," he said to himself.

He struck off down the hill toward town. If his step wasn't exactly jaunty, it was distinctly less elderly. For the moment his heart was as light as a schoolboy's. At last he had an answer to one of the questions that had been haunting him. Soon he would have more.

"TELEPHONE FOR YOU!" Matty called as she bustled toward the parlor. Crisp was sitting in his favorite chair, holding a worn, old copy of Longfellow's works close to his nose in the dim light, drenching himself in the cadence of the words, lost in the worlds of their meaning. "Telephone for you, Winston!" Matty repeated as she entered the room. Had she not just taken off her apron, she'd have been worrying it with her animated hands. As it was, she just posed them anticipatorily in the air like a Rubens cupid.

It was not Matty's voice that roused Crisp from his thoughts—she was one of those women who talked unendingly regardless of who was or who was not within earshot—rather it was her immediate presence at his elbow. "What?" he said, a little drowsily. The unconscious part of his brain retrieved the echo of Matty's words from the brink of the abyss. "Telephone?"

"For you," said Matty, as if to say, of all people.

No one ever called Crisp. As he ambled down the hall, he tried to remember the last time he'd talked on the phone. Not since he got to the island, surely. "Hello?"

"Hello, Mr. Crisp."

The voice was immediately recognizable. "Mr. Hanson?"

"Yes, sir." The timbre was the same, but the tone was decidedly different. "I hope I'm not interrupting anything too important."

"I'm reading Longfellow," said Crisp.

"Oh, good," said Hanson. Evidently he was among the many who did not share Crisp's views on poetry. He'd probably end up an editor. "Then you've got a minute to talk. I ran into an old friend of yours this morning."

There was an ironic redundancy in the words. All of his friends were old. "Really?"

"The state attorney general."

Who the heck was the attorney general these days?

"Michael Jessup."

"Jessup?" said Crisp, brightening. "You mean Dickie Jessup?"

"Well, his son, Michael."

The last time Crisp had heard the name Michael Jessup, it was attached to an excitable little towheaded boy of some six or seven summers who had an uncanny gift for clearing one's pockets of nickels. He should be treasurer. "Michael Jessup is the attorney general?" said Crisp. He smiled at the image of young Michael barely visible behind a large mahogany desk in an imposing government office—the flag of state on one side, Old Glory on the other, and the attorney general himself toppling towers of nickels with row upon row of toy soldiers. "Imagine that."

"He told me all about you."

"Did he?" said Crisp. "How is his father?"

"Dead."

The word hung for a moment in the air. Dickie had been in his early forties the last time they met. He'd always supposed they'd get together one day and exchange stories. Closer to the fire, chair by chair. "I didn't know that. I'm sorry to hear." He was.

"Michael told me all about you," Hanson repeated.

"So you said," said Crisp. "Did he tell you about the nickels?"

"What?"

"Nothing."

"He told me about the work you did for the government. Still do, from time to time, I understand."

"Not for a while now," said Crisp. "Little puzzles." To him that's all they were. "Favors for old friends." There was that term again.

"Well, I owe you an apology . . . about the way I . . ."

Hanson sounded uncomfortable. Crisp put him at ease. "Oh, don't mention it, Mr. Hanson. Don't mention it. Apology accepted." People should always be put at their ease. It made them so much more pliable. "What can I do for you?"

"Well, as a matter of fact, I was wondering if you might . . . I know you've been sort of poking around on your own, but I was wondering if you'd mind helping out in a more . . . in an official capacity."

"How do you mean?"

"Well, I told you I'd been talking to Jessup—"

"Michael."

"Yes. Well, it was about this case. I told him about the wire and the swimsuit . . . told him what you said."

"And about the beach sand?"

"Yes, that, too. Everything." He laughed. "I must confess, it didn't seem half as crazy when I was the one doing the telling." He paused. "Anyway, to put it bluntly, he told me to ask you to handle the investigation."

"How do you mean?"

"He wants you to take over. I'll work for you. My whole department's at your disposal."

It wasn't an unusual request. Crisp had heard similar ones many times over the years, some in far stranger cases, or at least far more important cases than this. But he wasn't in his old line of business anymore. He was retired. He was a poet. And he was in a race to solve Amanda Murphy's murder before he lost his mind. But he had to act independently. To assume an official role would be to assume rules of conduct and mounds of regulation. Administrators don't solve crimes.

"No, no," said Crisp. "I couldn't do that. I'm honored, but—"

"I know it's a lot to ask, Mr. Crisp, but to tell you the truth, I'm just plain flummoxed."

Crisp detected the tone of a few sleepless nights in Hanson's voice. "You got the fingerprints back?"

There was a brief silence at the other end of the line, through which Crisp could hear the manufactured laughter of a television comedy in the background. "Andy Calderwood's, definitely."

Crisp nodded, and both men draped themselves in a moment of deep reflection. Finally Crisp spoke. "I can't take over the investigation, Mr. Hanson."

"But—"

"Much as I appreciate your confidence in me, I'm afraid I'm just too old." He did sound a little feeble. "But I'll make you a proposition. Let me have a free hand, let me just keep poking around on my own, and I'll let you know anything I turn up."

"You're sure?"

Crisp was sure.

"Deal," said Hanson after some thought. "What are you going to do?"

"Oh, I think . . . I think you'd rather not know . . . in an official capacity," said Crisp. "Give me a couple of days, and please don't tell anyone that we're . . . that I'm . . ."

"I understand."

"Thank you," said Crisp. "I will tell you one thing I've found out."

"What's that?"

"Nobody saw Amanda Murphy on the mainland after the Calderwood boys' accident."

"But the FBI report—"

"Only repeats what the witnesses said. I've spoken to them, and none of them saw Amanda Murphy—only someone they thought was her."

"An imposter?"

"I believe so."

"A woman, though."

"Probably . . . definitely not Andy Calderwood."

"But that changes the chronology. He could have killed the Murphy girl!"

"Possibly."

"And the imposter would have to be either an accomplice . . . or a coincidence."

Crisp doubted it was a coincidence. Amanda Murphy was an original. "It would seem so," he said. "It would seem so."

"I don't see how that sorts out the confusion much."

"I disagree," said Crisp. "It's been my experience that the truth is not a puzzle you put together, it's a puzzle you take apart. Each fact, each piece you remove, no matter how obscure in itself, reveals a bit of the picture beneath. If we pick away at those pieces long enough, Mr. Hanson, the truth will show itself. Or at least we'll see enough of the truth to guide us to certain conclusions."

"I suppose so," Hanson said reluctantly. Crisp's unorthodoxy echoed like heresy in the halls of his formal indoctrination.

"The important thing is not to discard a fact because it doesn't seem to make sense, or because it doesn't fit a theory," Crisp continued. "That's what's wrong with science today, don't you think? Rather than letting the facts lead them to truth, scientists have adopted the habit of imagining a truth and forcing the facts to fit it. You see, any theory that isn't fluid enough to be altered by fact atrophies, becomes this monolith that people of little imagination suppose to be truth. Evolution, for instance. The Big Bang . . ."

Crisp was beginning to heat up on topics that had drawn him into debates with old friends at the Smithsonian and the National Academy of Sciences that lasted until the small hours of the morning. He could hear the silence at the other end of the phone raise its eyebrows and roll its eyes. "Anyway," he synopsized, "the truth never changes, only the way in which we perceive it."

Hanson had been listening. He realized that as he looked at the crime through the eyes of this old man, the world that came into focus would be one in which he was a stranger. "There's something else you'll want to know . . ."

Crisp let the silence prod the remainder of the statement from Hanson. "We found some other fingerprints."

"On the buttons?" Crisp conjectured.

The pregnant pause that followed was punctuated with a sigh of resignation. "How did you know?"

"Charlie took a picture of Andy Calderwood at the wake. He keeps an album. I looked at it with my magnifying glass. All the buttons matched."

Hanson concluded a brief mental battle. "I should tell you, when we opened the casket . . . after we took the pictures, we saw one of the buttons was just lying there. I thought that was strange, so I took it . . . and another one."

"Chain and anchor," said Crisp.

Hanson nodded on his end of the phone. "But it was a brand-new coat—so Charlie said. So someone must have changed the buttons for some reason, and in the process—"

"Left fingerprints," Crisp interrupted

Hanson echoed. "Left fingerprints."

"They're not Charlie's prints?"

"No, and they don't belong to any of the Calderwoods. That's about as far as we've gotten with it so far. They're cross-checking against everyone they can think of."

"Of course, there are a lot of people on the island who've never been fingerprinted," said Crisp.

Hanson nodded into the receiver. "We may end up running the whole blasted town through before this is over."

"May I make a suggestion, Inspector?"

"Sure thing."

"Concentrate your efforts on the north end of the island."

"The north end? Why? There's hardly anybody up there but summer . . ." Realization dawned all at once. "Beach sand."

"She was killed on McKenniston's property, I'm convinced of that," said Crisp. "And since there is only one road onto the peninsula, pretty well traveled that time of year, I'm assuming it was by someone whose presence wouldn't have aroused suspicion."

"That's not all you're assuming," said Hanson. They communed for a moment in thoughtful sighs and wheezes. "Anything else?" said Hanson at last.

Crisp thought of the walk-in freezer up at the McKenniston's. "Not for the moment."

"I'll let you know what turns up on those prints, if anything. Good-bye, Mr. Crisp."

"Good-bye, Mr. Hanson."

Crisp was sleeping with his light on now. Not that it made any difference. She would come and stand in the corner, her lips would move, her blood would flow in endless, silent rivulets. Her eyes, though hidden in shadow, would, he knew, be fixed upon him, staring and unblinking. He would pinch himself beneath his covers, but, if sleeping, he wouldn't wake, and if awake, wouldn't sleep.

"Winston."

He heard the word clearly. He saw her lips part before she spoke. He sat bolt upright in bed and stared at the familiar silhouette in the corner. "Amanda?" he said. His voice was hoarse and heavy. He cleared his throat. "Amanda?"

The sleep in his eyes made halos of the light, and for half a second as he stared into the dark pockets in the corners of his room, trying to separate shadows from substance, he saw her as he'd never seen her. Undead. Unstaring. Her bright eyes brimmed with moisture and overflowed with vitality. The ghastly makeup was gone. The rust-edged wound was gone, and her beauty overwhelmed him.

In the quiet of the night, Crisp loosed the ragged tether of his heart and, for the first time in a lifetime, fell in love. Tears welled in his eyes and washed the vision away.

"Amanda," he said softly.

He was awakened by the smell of coffee. He'd moved to the little straight-backed chair in the ell sometime during the night and fallen asleep there. He was sore in places he'd forgotten he had.

Slowly he opened his eyes. A colorless, lifeless light washed through the window and across the room, turning his jumble of bedclothes the color of a burial shroud. It was raining in sheets of perfect, perpendicular lines. He massaged his forehead and temples with both hands.

"Winston!"

Here was a voice of flesh and blood. Matty's voice, melting through the gloom like the rattle of a key in his cell door. "Five minutes!" said Crisp.

"What?"

"Five minutes!" Crisp bellowed as loud as he could through the sleep in his throat.

At the bottom of the stairs, Matty mumbled something about his food getting cold and him lying in bed all day. He smiled.

By the time he had breakfast and Matty had read him the parts of the paper she thought he should hear, the sun had won its battle for the morning and was celebrating its victory in the water drops on the pussy willow outside the kitchen window. A slight breeze had picked up and was tossing the chickadees back and forth between the trees and the birch feeder that swung from the clothesline.

"Well, it'll be a nice enough day yet," said Matty, who had been talking all along, but this was the first thing that had made it through the sleep that clogged Crisp's brain.

"We may get summer this year after all," said Crisp. Two blue-jays had descended on the feeder, chasing the chickadees away. And a squirrel was busily tearing the suet bag to shreds.

"Least you don't have to go to no funerals today," Matty rejoined. "Not much of a crowd there, I hear." She topped off his coffee.

Crisp had ceased to be amazed that Matty knew everything there was to know. "Not many."

"You want to talk about it?"

Instantly his defenses were up and about, stirring one another with sharp jabs to the ribs and climbing the battlements. He'd always had the nagging suspicion she could read him like a book. He was determined not to let her get past the first chapter or two, if he could help it. "About what?"

"Oh, anything that's on your mind," Matty replied disinterestedly. She cleared the table. "You just seem a little preoccupied, is all. I didn't know but what you might want to get something off your chest. Helps to talk things out sometimes." She scraped leftovers off his plate into the old blue plastic bowl she put outside every morning for neighborhood dogs. "You don't have to tell me anything if you don't want to."

She draped a newspaper over her head and stepped out through the curtain of water that cascaded from the roof in the aftermath of the rain. She put down the bowl on the porch.

"I've just been dreaming," said Crisp. He knew she couldn't hear with the runoff pelting on the newspaper that covered her head. He was trying it out.

"Did you say something?" said Matty. She closed the door behind her, shook the newspaper over the sink, and spread it out on the sweater rack to dry before throwing it away.

"I haven't been sleeping well, I guess," said Crisp. He considered this admission less likely to elicit unwanted probing. He was quite sure he didn't want probing. Quite sure.

"Could be that mattress," Matty replied. They both knew it wasn't the mattress.

"Mmm," said Crisp.

"Been dreamin'?"

There was no defense against someone who was tall enough to peek over your walls. He didn't respond.

" 'Bout that girl," said Matty. This time it wasn't a question.

"Tell me something, Matty," Crisp said sleepily. "How do you know these things?"

Matty shrugged. She wasn't going to tell him he talked in his sleep. Or that she listened. "Just . . ." She shrugged again.

"Well, it's awfully uncomfortable."

"I guess I thought you'd sleep better once she was in the ground," said Matty. "Hoped so, anyway."

"Too many questions," said Crisp. He put a little more Sweet 'n Low in his coffee and stirred it with his fork handle.

"Like what?"

Crisp got up and walked to the window. He thrust his hands deep into the pockets of his khaki pants. "Who's the maestro?" he said, almost beneath his breath.

"What?" said Matty. She was already in the pantry.

"I feel like everything's been planned, Matty."

" 'Course it is. God planned it."

"Well, I wasn't thinking on such an elevated plane, I'm afraid." He walked to the pantry and leaned against the doorpost. "Whoever murdered that girl has . . . has . . . it's like I'm a pool of water."

Matty was bent over the laundry. She twisted the furrows in her forehead into a question mark.

"Be patient, now, I'm just trying to make a point," said Crisp.

"Well, make it in English," said Matty.

"I am. You have to listen to the whole thing."

The furrow relaxed.

"Imagine a little pool of water in the dirt. Now, what happens if you trace a little line in the dirt right up to the pool?"

"The water flows down the groove."

"Exactly," said Crisp. "I'm that pool of water, you see? And I'm going right down the groove that somebody put there. The groove they want me to go down."

"We're still talkin' about this girl?"

Crisp nodded. "Yes, Matty."

Matty nodded. "And you don't think she was murdered by the Calderwood boy?"

Crisp shrugged. "I don't see how."

"You think it was somebody else?"

He shrugged again.

"Now you think that somebody is leadin' you along by the nose?"

Crisp nodded.

"And you think he knows what you're goin' to do even before you do?"

Crisp nodded.

"Well," said Matty—it was her philosophical "well"—"he must be some clever."

THE MCKENNISTON ESTATE consisted of the main house, a guest house, and a barn. It crested a swell of earth that, to the north, rolled across grassy fields and disappeared into the forest and on the south tumbled abruptly down crags and crevices past the boathouse to the unsettled sea. Casual turn-of-the-century elegance had given way to the casual neglect of the mid-1900s. The tennis courts were overgrown, their fence posts leaning toward the ground like a gaggle of old men looking for pennies in the tall grass. The novelty of the swimming pool had worn off a quarter century ago, so the elements had recommissioned it as a receptacle for their refuse.

The houses themselves were in good repair and had recently been painted red with white trim. They had always been painted red with white trim. The shingles of the barn, which was knotted among a stand of ancient evergreens, had been weathered a deep gray-brown and were rotting at a leisurely pace. The rust red trim was peeling in places, missing entirely in others. The structure seemed to have grown where it stood.

Contrapuntal to the quiet nostalgia of the scene as Crisp entered was a distant mechanical thumping punctuated by the sound of a tortured feline. His stomach churned with a horror that was not mollified by his feeling of impotency. How could he, an old man on a bicycle, with imperfect hearing, locate the source of the sound and extricate the animal from the machinery before it was torn limb from limb?

His search led him to the cliff overlooking the Thorofare. The wind was blowing briskly, and the sea crashed on the rocks below. He strained to separate the plaintive wail from nature's cacophony. It emanated from the boathouse. How long could the hapless creature endure such obvious extremes of pain? More to the point, thought Crisp as he hastened down the ramp, what sight would he soon have to add to the waxworks of horrors that constituted his memory?

Once at the bottom of the ramp, he bounded across the deck, threw open the door, and stood akimbo in the doorway, transfixed by a blast of rock-and-roll music from the oil-soaked abyss.

His pulse seemed to be keeping time against his eardrums with fists of thunder. He could feel the veins in his neck marking the downbeat. He was too old and White to know anything about backbeat. "Hello?" he said into the darkness.

There was no response. None was expected. He knew that his voice couldn't be heard over the noise. As he stepped in out of the sunlight, objects in the room oozed into view. The offensive noise was coming from a large portable radio that hung by its strap from a crossbeam of a boat cradle. Squinting, he could make out the extension cord, which he followed to a bare outlet in the plank wall. The umbilical cord that sustained the "cat" in unspeakable misery, doubtless against its will. He pulled the plug.

Peace.

The patient had died but was happier for it.

It was not an unbroken peace, however.

"Hey!" said someone under the cradle.

Crisp watched carefully as, bit by bit and hind end foremost, a body emerged from below the boat, to the accompaniment of a commentary calling into question the parentage of whoever had conducted the mercy killing on the radio. Crisp still held the plug in his hand.

When fully birthed by the inky blackness, there stood before Crisp—rather below Crisp in the well of the boat slip—a youth of about seventeen summers with the physique of a poorly fed scarecrow and a mane of dirty hair that seemed to weigh his head to one side, leaving only one eye operable. This eye he trained on Crisp and the plug. "Huh?" he said.

"You must be Marky Williams," said Crisp, draping the electrical cord over a nearby beam a safe distance from the outlet.

"Yup," said Marky Williams. It occurred to him that this could be one of the doddering old friends or relations of the people who signed his paycheck, so he reined his indignation. "Need somethin'?"

"Well," Crisp said slowly. What, now that the cat had been saved? "I was wondering if you had a key to the barn."

The boy jerked his head to one side; the hair flew temporarily out of his eyes and fell promptly back into place. "Nope," he said.

"Oh . . . well, do you know where I . . . is there someone . . . perhaps Mostly has one?"

"He ain't here."

"I see. Well . . . and there's no one else with a key?"

"Nope," said the monosyllabic youth. "Nobody's got one."

"Oh."

"It ain't locked."

"Oh?" said Crisp, who, in the space of forty-seven seconds had become a devout adherent to the concept of a generation gap. "Well, then . . . that's good."

"It ain't even got a lock, as far's I know," said the boy, the words flowing forth in a comparative torrent. "Even if it did, you could still get in fifty different ways."

"I see," said Crisp. "Well, I'll just go . . . and . . ." He expected the boy to ask him who he was, what he was up to, and why he wanted to get into the barn. The inquisition was not forthcoming. The boy just nodded.

"Would you mind pluggin' that back in?" he said. "I go crazy if it's too quiet."

Cringing inwardly, Crisp stuck the plug in the outlet. The silence, sung to by the rhythm of waves and lilt of seagulls, was swept away by a bulldozer of noise. The boy smiled and crawled back under the boat. Crisp left the building, shut the door as tightly as possible, and made all the haste his legs would allow to separate himself from the scene.

Marky Williams had exaggerated when he said there were fifty ways into the barn, but there might as well have been. Time had burgled the huge cast-iron hinges on the barn doors, lowering the left door two to three inches into the soil, where it had taken up permanent residence. The right-hand door was held closed by a two-by-four, one end of which was wedged under a wooden bracket that seemed to have been made for the purpose, the other stepped deep in the ground. It took a good deal of effort to remove it. This done, the huge door sprang open about six inches, then stopped abruptly.

Crisp, who had leaped out of harm's way, tugged the door open a little more and stuck his head inside.

The air was thick with pleasant smells. Hay. Kerosene. Paint. Ancient, dry wood. Hemp. Sawdust and sea salt. The wind, having nowhere in particular to go, sneaked in at odd angles through broken windowpanes and numerous cracks and crevices in the walls and tossed the smells together in an aromatic salad. Bird droppings and feathers covered every surface, silent memorials to the generations of sparrows and pigeons that had made their home in the rafters.

The roof had held up well. It was dry inside the barn.

Crisp took inventory as he made his way gingerly over and

around the decaying remains of an old ice sled, a weather-beaten dory, and a '28 Ford roadster. Two wooden canoes with wickerwork seats were tucked among the rafters overhead, together with fishing poles, several sets of rawhide snowshoes and cross-country skis, and other items long enough and low enough to be suspended between the crossbeams. A workbench occupied the entire north wall and was littered with every imaginable implement conceived for the purpose of putting together or tearing apart. Hundreds of capless jars held thousands of rusting screws, nails, washers, bolts, cotter pins, and the congealed remains of various pungent fluids, some of which had fused with the paintbrushes, stirrers, and rags that had been placed in them and forgotten.

The two-horse stall at the opposite end of the structure had become a catchall for everything that couldn't find a proper home among the chaos. A row of decrepit windows over the workbench barred entrance to all but the weakest wash of sunlight, giving the scene a Wyethian aura, that of a world frozen in time and forever beyond waking.

A three-quarter wall of vertical pine boards ran the length of the building immediately to Crisp's right. Its surface, too, was crowded with the relics of a hundred years. License plates and calendars. Double-ended saws. Ropes, chains, and wires. Cracked mirrors and empty window frames. Door frames. Bedsprings. Air pumps. Inner tubes. Wheelless bicycles and broken toys. All the things someone meant to fix one day and never got around to.

The wall was punctuated by three doors ten to fifteen feet apart, and Crisp was determined to examine each room in sequence.

The first had once been home to the groom or stable boy. An iron spring-frame cot lay against the right-hand wall, covered with equine flotsam. A plain wooden washstand, wearing its nonmatching chipped porcelain bowl and pitcher at a jaunty angle, stood on tiptoe trying to peek out the window. A small rectangle of carpet was the room's only concession to comfort. Otherwise, austerity, if not monasticism, seemed to be the decorator's motive genii.

The world had been a different place when the dust in this room was last disturbed. It felt like a museum display, the only difference being there was no velvet rope to keep the present at bay.

Crisp closed the door on his way out. Whatever ghosts resided there were not his to trouble.

Access to the second room was barred by the Ford roadster. Crisp climbed in the driver's side, slid across the crushed velvet seat, rolled down the passenger window, and examined the door to the room. Ancient movie posters and risqué picture postcards from France were thumbtacked to it in profusion. Wedging his head and shoulder between the car and the door, he was able to extend himself enough to reach the thumb latch. It clicked easily up and down, but the door didn't open. He removed a shoelace and, tying the latch open, lay back across the seat with his feet sticking out the window. He placed them against the door and pushed until it squeaked open enough to offer a provocative glimpse into the room.

A glimpse was sufficient to suggest that ingress had been impeded by design, and that he had doubtless not been the first to gain entry via the roadster. This was the boys' secret room. The clubhouse. The haunted mansion. The vestibule of ill repute. The smoking room. The hiding place. Their own Barbary Coast with all its delicious promise of iniquity.

Crisp poked his head through the door as far as possible. It was dark. Such places always are. Over the years the sun had managed to poke a few holes through the tattered green shade that covered the window, but there was not enough light to see what all the whispering was about, only enough to suggest shapes in the darkness and the sins of the past. Cigarette butts and cigar ends, their stale perfume long since absorbed by scolding breezes, rested on can lids and mason jars.

The walls hosted a varied exhibit of pornography through the ages. The subject of even the most recent of them was a grandmother by this time. Crisp didn't need to investigate this room any

further. Its secrets were those that boyhood, in all its splendid per-
fidy and inconsistency, held in common. He had been a boy once,
and, like many men, had spent most of his life fleeing the memories of its clinging pleasures.

He closed the door, rolled up the car window, slid across the
seat, got out, closed the door—locking it first—and brushed off
his hands.

The third and last door stood wide open. Directly opposite it
was an oversized outside door, opening onto the pool patio. Here
the debris was less antiquated, indicating recent use. There was
the customary abundance of unrelated junk, but garden tools and
custodial implements formed the bulk of the inventory, which included a well-used golf cart. The doors of a crude wooden wall cabinet stood open, revealing work gloves, boxes of Miracle-Gro, and
an assortment of mosquito repellents and insecticides. Below this,
behind a stack of screens and old storm windows, was an old
steamer trunk, covered with autographs and pasted with playbills,
train ticket stubs, and theater tickets.

Crisp's heart raced as he noiselessly set aside the screens and
windows. It wouldn't do to attract attention. Not now. It wouldn't
do to have the juvenile junk music aficionado training his cyclopean
eye on what was about to happen. And wherever Mostly was, Crisp
hoped profoundly that he would stay there.

The trunk was locked. The only thing in the building that had
been. Perhaps the only thing on the estate, or the peninsula, maybe
the whole island. It was a good sign.

His fingers had a memory of their own. In twenty seconds he'd
popped the lock. Without a sound. Without a sign. The lid issued
a long rasp of relief as he raised it. The contents matched his suspicions so perfectly that he could almost have described them
blindfolded.

It was Trudy Rutherford's theatrical kit, full of things that had
been new when he was young. A large tortoise-shell hand mirror, lying face up atop a heap of feminine props, reflected Crisp's keen

eyes. There were numerous shoes and stockings, and here and there, floating free or half wrapped in tissue paper, were an assortment of wigs, pads, and similar devices that actresses use to supplement deficiency or minimize abundance. In the middle, like a crown on a velvet cushion, was a shoebox-sized wooden case. It was covered with gaudy silk brocade and rested among folds of costuming. He lifted the lid. A small battalion of glass makeup jars stood at attention, awaiting inspection.

Pay dirt.

The lid came off the first jar easily. Too easily. Its contents were cracked and dry, a miniature desert the color of mustard gone bad. The second was the same. The third yielded, but not without stern resistance. Its contents were supple. Almost fluid. Still usable.

In all, there were eleven jars. Three had been left partially open and were useless. The rest were sealed tight and had been for a long time. Crisp put the three jars in his pocket, returned the rest to the case, and closed the trunk.

"P'fessor!" The voice was unmistakably Mostly's. "I thought somebody was in here when I seen that door open. Watcha up to?"

Under most circumstances Mostly's presence would not elicit stark terror. This was not one of them. Beads of sweat had formed on Crisp's brow in an instant. The veins pulsed visibly on his wrists, and his heart was attempting to flee the scene via his mouth.

"I . . . I . . ."

The village of Eze sits atop a barren hill in southern France, near the Italian border. In recent times it has become an artists' colony, a tourist trap. In the days immediately after World War II, however, nearly deserted and rat infested, it formed the backdrop for darker deeds. Stephen Caton had been stabbed in the back one night while attempting to retrieve a roll of microfilm from the baptismal in an abandoned church that squatted on the hilltop.

Crisp had found Caton there, still warm. Blood hadn't had time to congeal around the blade of the curved dagger that stuck in his back. His eyes, staring orbs of horror, bulged toward the crucifix-shaped vacancy on the blackened wall at the back of the chancel as if glimpsing hell and begging forgiveness. Crisp couldn't help but wonder if he'd received it. The body had to be moved so he could see if the microfilm was still in the small cleft above the baptismal spigot.

It was there—in the dead of night, with a Luger in one hand, Caton's body in his arms, and knowing that the murderer wasn't far away, possibly in one of the shadows cast by holy ruins—that Crisp had last sweat. It was the last time he'd been caught.

Perhaps he'd lost his touch. At any rate, Mostly wouldn't pay the price that was paid that night. Another waxwork.

"You startled me," he confessed.

Mostly, his thumbs hooked around the halters of his overalls, arched an eyebrow and nodded knowingly. "You been gettin' into things, ain't you?"

Although it had been a long time since Crisp last sweat, it had been even longer since he blushed. He did so now. "Well . . . I spoke to the young man in the boathouse. He said the barn was open, and . . ."

Mostly smiled. "I don't care," he said. "Look around all you want. You can take half this stuff home with you, as far as I'm concerned. Then take a match to the rest. Junk, most of it." Crisp brushed off his hands. "Find what you was lookin' for?"

"Half," Crisp replied. He finished stacking the screens in front of the steamer trunk.

"Mrs. McKenniston's theater stuff?"

Crisp nodded.

"You found the key, then." Crisp hadn't used a key. His face showed it. Mostly bent over and rattled the ornate little key that hung on a hook on the side of the trunk. "Easier that way," he said with a larger smile than usual. "Somethin' to do with Mandy?"

Crisp continued nodding.

Mostly resumed nodding and fell silent for a moment. They

both looked distractedly around the ghosts of McKenniston's past. Each object was haunted by its own aura, the memory of the sights and sounds that had accompanied its days of usefulness.

"You seen her up there, didn't you?" Mostly said finally. He rarely said anything of consequence. Like the majority of natives, he would keep his thoughts to himself and take them to his grave. His communication with the world would thus be amiable but superfluous. These words had not come easily.

"Who?"

"Mandy."

"Where?" said Crisp. Once again his heart was straining in anticipation.

"You know," said Mostly. "Up to the cemetery."

Crisp grasped Mostly by the arm. "You saw her there?"

"You did, too," said Mostly. He writhed slightly, but Crisp didn't relax his grip. He seemed unaware how hard he was squeezing. "I remember the look on your face."

Crisp's head was swimming. He knew that the thin mental membrane separating fact from fantasy in his own mind had atrophied almost to nonexistence, but could his dreams even spill into the reality of those around him?

Mostly's stoicism was no proof against the hungry, desperate eyes that beseeched him for answers.

" 'Member how foggy it was?" he said. He managed to extricate himself from Crisp's grasp. "You was just headin' off down the road and I was goin' to take the shore path back up here. Well, I just happened to look back up there toward the cemetery, toward the grave, and there was a break in the fog for half a second, and . . . well . . ."

"You saw her."

Mostly nodded. "I sure did."

Crisp was suddenly exhausted. The implications of what Mostly was saying were too profound. Too perplexing. First Billy Pringle, now Mostly Sanborn. Of course, there was the possibility that he was dreaming again, or still. That would explain everything. There was an odd comfort in the notion. He stared out the window. "What did she look like?"

"Like always," said Mostly without hesitation. "Just like always. You know how she dressed . . . and all that red hair . . ."

The thought hit Crisp like a thunderbolt, instantly dispelling all the fog and confusion. "Pinch me, Most'," he said. Once again he put the window screens aside. This time, though, he threw them.

Crisp ransacked the contents of the trunk, collecting all the wigs he came across. When he was done he had seven in all. Long and straight. Short and curly. Brown, black, and blond. "No auburn," he whispered, holding them up for inspection with the eager appreciation of a savage admiring his haul of scalps.

"Red?" Mostly speculated hesitantly.

Crisp nodded. "Mrs. McKenniston played a redhead on at least one occasion in her early days. "She must have had a red wig."

"But there ain't one there?"

"Exactly," said Crisp with a smile. The sun was coming out slowly. It would be spring soon. "But she must have had one . . ." He let the sentence hang. He wanted Mostly to form the same conclusion, as if to validate his own thoughts.

"Then . . . she lost it," said Mostly, almost to himself. He, too, was suddenly emboldened by an idea. "Or somebody took it," he said.

"Why would anyone take it?" Crisp coaxed.

"Well . . . could've been the kids. They was always into this stuff. Wasn't s'posed to, but . . ."

"It probably would have turned up, if that had been the case," Crisp thought out loud. "Why else would anyone want the wig?"

Mostly thought. "To use it."

"Why?"

Mostly cringed slightly. He wasn't accustomed to interrogation. "I don't know."

"Yes, you do," said Crisp. "Think, Most'. Why would someone wear a wig?"

"Well, lots of women wear wigs, don't they?"

"Not wigs of an entirely different color than their own hair!"

"Well, then"—he brightened briefly—"for a costume party!"

"Or?"

"Or a play, like this redheaded character you just said."

"Or?"

Mostly pillaged his brain. Wigs were at no ready point of reference. A jumble of random notions, themselves only newly formed and inseminated by Crisp's gentle persistence, all at once fell together and gave birth to a single, cogent thought. "To look like somebody else?"

"Who?" Crisp prodded.

"A redhead," said Mostly.

"Which redhead?"

Mostly found himself in a box canyon. There was no way out. Given the context of their conversation, there was only one redhead in the world. "Mandy," he whispered. He studied the word in disbelief as it hung in the air. The longer he studied it, the more sense it made. "Mandy!"

"Bingo," said Crisp with a sly smile.

"It wasn't Mandy we saw up at the cemetery," said Mostly. He slowly turned his eyes to Crisp from the floor where they had been wandering blindly. "It was somebody who looked like her!"

"And how much like her would they have to be—in the fog, wearing her clothes and a red wig—at that distance?"

Mostly sat down on a barrel of pool chemicals. He took out his handkerchief and wiped his balding head. "Not much," he said. He was staring at the contents of the trunk.

"And this," said Crisp, flipping open the lid of the makeup kit, "was the makeup Mandy was covered with."

Mostly looked up at him with helpless eyes. His brain had absorbed all it could. "Huh?"

"Never mind," said Crisp. "Leeman Russell told me there was a freezer in here. I don't see it."

"He must be thinkin' 'bout over to Spencer's," Mostly replied, jerking his thumb to the south. "Theirs is in the barn."

"Then there isn't one here?"

"Oh, sure. Everybody up here's got 'em. Ours is up to the little house."

"Can I see it?"

As they stepped from stone to stone up the sloping path, Crisp learned that the little house, which sat in the shade of three huge old oak trees a few yards down the slope from the big house, was the kitchen and servants' quarters. It also contained two or three spare bedrooms for those occasions when the big house was full.

They crossed the porch. Mostly propped the screen door open with his rump and rummaged through a prodigious number of keys on his key ring. "I didn't know people locked things on the island," said Crisp.

"Oh, well, it's the McKennistons' orders," said Mostly. "I guess comin' from the mainland, they're just naturally suspicious. Mass'-chusetts, you know."

"I see."

"Makes 'em feel good, I guess."

Crisp nodded. Mostly extracted yet another key and stuck it in the lock. It worked.

"There she is!" He turned the doorknob. " 'Course, we always keep a window or two unlocked in case we forget the keys."

As the door swung open, they were greeted by the outrushing of dead air, heavy with the perfume of mothballs and crisp linen. It was colder inside than out, and their breath formed in clouds that hung for an instant in the air, then vanished.

"This way," said Mostly. The pine-board floors creaked beneath their feet and echoed through endless whitewashed rooms as they threaded their way among mounds of sheet-shrouded furniture.

"Why would anybody do such a thing is what I want to know," said Mostly. They were in the kitchen. "The freezer's down through that door there," he said, motioning toward a small archway at the far end of the room. He led on. "I mean, if someone's fool enough to show up at a funeral dressed like the person that's gettin' buried . . . Here it is. This is the pantry and that's the freezer." He pulled open the thick insulated door, disclosing a small sheet metal–lined room about five feet wide and six feet long. "The light's right on the left, there."

Deep shelves lined the wall on both sides, leaving an aisle about two feet wide down the center. Directly over the aisle was a rail, firmly embedded in the wall at both ends and supported in the middle by a brace suspended from the ceiling. Four meat hooks hung from the rail. Against the wall at the far end, also suspended from the ceiling, was a small cooling unit.

"If someone's fool enough to do that," Mostly continued, "why didn't they pop out sooner, so everyone could see?"

"That's a good question," said Crisp. He stepped to the back of the cooler and began inspecting the meat hooks. "Could you pass me a chair, Most'?"

Mostly handed him a step stool, which was kept under a pantry counter. "This do?"

"Perfectly."

"They musta wanted us to see, don't you think? I mean, she just stood there, didn't she?" He shivered. "Man, I tell you, I still half think it was her ghost, you know?"

Crisp climbed on the stool and studied the meat hooks for a few moments. Then he climbed down and began to examine the floor. "You can take the stool, Most'," he said. "You wouldn't happen to have a flashlight handy, would you?"

There was no response. Crisp looked up just as the door closed. The click of the heavy metal latch as it slipped into place was followed immediately by another as the exterior bolt was shut. He was locked in. It had all happened in an instant. He hadn't even had time to get off his knees.

"Most'?" he said softly, in disbelief. "Mostly!" he shouted. He didn't get up. He crawled to the door and pounded on it. Once. Twice. "Mostly! Let me out!"

His voice was stuffed back into his ears by the thickness of the soundproof walls. He might as well have been shouting in the grave, pounding on concrete. "Mostly!" he said weakly.

He wasn't surprised when, with a series of kicks, thumps, and wheezes, the generator kicked on. Already he could feel the blast of frigid air. He'd been on the island too long. He'd forgotten to trust no one.

CHAPTER 15

FOR WHAT SEEMED A LONG TIME, he tried to loosen the metal latch plate with one of the meat hooks, but his strength gave out long before the latch was compromised. The warmth from his exertion had created condensation on some of the piping, and already it had turned to frost. It was a very efficient cooling system, he thought. Perhaps a bit too large for the room.

The single lightbulb was recessed in the ceiling and protected behind a sturdy metal cage. He was unable to get his hands close enough to it to keep them warm, only close enough to partially blind himself. His arms got tired, so he held them up one at a time, thrusting the other into a pocket in the interval.

Within thirty minutes he knew he was freezing to death. His extremities had no sensation. He gave up trying to warm his hands. Perhaps his brain was freezing, as well. He wasn't afraid. He'd anticipated this day all his life. He'd tempted it. Taunted it. But it had to come. He hadn't won the war, but he'd won a lot of battles. For what it was worth.

He thought again of Steve Caton's eyes and the crucifix-shaped shadow on the wall. He thought what a luxury to have a few minutes to anticipate death. A few precious moments of cognizance in which to organize his thoughts and make his peace. He prayed. Not for the first time, but the first time in a long time. It was a very practical thing to do, given the circumstances.

It wasn't long before he couldn't keep his eyes open. He was completely exhausted. The needlelike pain was lessening now. He even felt warm. He wasn't sure where exactly, but there was a sensation of warmth somewhere. He lay down in the corner. Sleep was the thing. Sleep.

For the first time in as long as he could remember, his brain was empty. The myriad of thoughts and worries that had occupied every waking minute of every day, all his life, had been frozen to silence. The insistent snatches of poetry that bolted across the realm of his consciousness like comets, daring him to catch them, surround them with words and commit them to paper . . . gone. The everpresent, overarching, omnipotent feeling of failure that wrapped his every thought and feeling in shadow . . . gone. The chamber of horrors, the faces of the dead whose hollow, staring eyes had haunted him for eternity . . . gone. None of it mattered anymore. None of it would follow where he was going.

His cheek rested on the floor. His eyes closed. Already death was blissful.

"You're going to die?"

The voice wasn't human. It didn't come to his ears, it was in his head. He opened his eyes. Amanda Murphy was sitting in the corner by the door with her legs crossed. She was wearing the same thing she'd worn at the graveside, and she had the makeup on again. It was peeling and cracked in places, missing in others—the same as when he'd seen her in the morgue. He couldn't tell whether or not she was bleeding. Probably. He tried to speak, but the necessary apparatus had ceased to function. Bits of him seemed to be preceding him into the afterlife. He smiled weakly and nodded.

"You don't know yet."

He shook his head ever so slightly. No. He didn't know. He thought he did. Just half an hour ago he felt he had the puzzle by the tail. Then Mostly Sanborn shut him in the freezer. Mostly Sanborn, of all people. That threw everything out the window. He didn't know anything now, except that none of it mattered. His unconscious had risen to the surface and was doing all his thinking, all by itself concocting idiocies and impossibilities out of thin air. He let it run.

Would he still be old after he died? Didn't he read somewhere that we're all supposed to be thirty-three in heaven? Amanda Murphy wasn't thirty-three, but she hadn't really died completely, had she? She was still holding on, somehow.

Why would she want to?

Maybe she'd fall in love with him if he was younger. He imagined a broader smile on his face. He suspected she'd just hang around until someone sorted it all out. Maybe she had to. You hear so many stories about the afterlife.

His field of vision had been reduced to two small orbs of light whose fuzzy edges were rimmed with halos of darkness, and his eyes were too heavy to keep on her. His gaze drifted from her face, down her dress, over her feet, and back across the floor to a faint, oily smudge not a foot from his face. He knew instinctively what it was. Theatrical makeup. Very old. Lead based.

He'd been right, after all. Amanda Murphy's murderer had painted her face with makeup, then put her in the freezer. She'd lain in the same place he now occupied . . . and Mostly was the murderer. It all worked out, after all. He certainly had access and opportunity. Motive? Well, it wasn't too hard to imagine one or two. You never know what goes on in people's minds.

It didn't matter. But it was nice to know he'd had the right idea.

When he looked up again, Amanda was gone.

He wouldn't stay around and haunt people after he died. He wanted to get as far away as possible.

The floor began to feel warm. He would have liked a pillow.

Of course, there was the problem of Andy Calderwood's fingerprints, speaking of haunting. And why the makeup in the first place? And who had played the part of Amanda Murphy in Rockland? Surely not Mostly. And why? Why all the elaborate subterfuge? Of course, murderers often try to incriminate others, but why someone who was dead at the time of the murder? What sane person would do such a thing?

What sane person?

That was the whole point, wasn't it? What if the whole thing had been meticulously planned to make no sense? It would have to be the work of someone completely cold, calculating, and unbelievably ruthless. Someone who had simultaneously planned the murder and the defense—not guilty by reason of insanity. The type abounded in his former profession.

The murderer had nothing in common with Mostly Sanborn.

The more he thought about it, the more questions remained unanswered.

He'd have to stop thinking about it.

Surprisingly, it wasn't difficult.

Sleep was the thing.

He huddled a little closer in the corner, not because it warmed him, but because it was comfortable. His eyelids threatened to collapse under their own weight, but he'd fight for a minute more. No rush.

His heart had slowed almost to a stop. His hands and fingers were bright blue and one and a half times their normal size. The color didn't match his plaid shirt. Charlie Young would know what to do. He could hide them, put them in white dress gloves, if they weren't too swollen.

They looked like the hands of an old Black lady. He couldn't feel them. Couldn't move them. Maybe they belonged to someone else after all.

There was a memory tied to the tail of that notion. Something Leeman Russell had said about his bicycle seat. It didn't look right. Didn't fit.

Didn't fit.

That was it. Suddenly he knew how the fingerprints of a dead man ended up on Amanda Murphy's neck. Simple really, for someone mad enough to conceive it.

The biggest hurdle had been overcome, thanks to Leeman. Thanks to the cold and his big blue hands.

Something else occurred to him, too. In his time he'd come up against people who were capable of almost anything, people whose mere presence could make the blood run cold.

They'd have taken off their hats to this one.

It was going to be good to exit a world through which such a person could pass undetected, but he shuddered to think that he was leaving this particular murderer behind.

Of course, only the how had been solved. The why remained. That would be someone else's problem.

It was time. He hadn't breathed in a minute or so. Nor did he want to, particularly. He closed his eyes to die.

As if attending that cue, the cooling fan shut off. There was a rattling at the door. No! Crisp thought. No! He couldn't open his eyes. He didn't want to. He was ready to go. He was eager to go. If someone found him now . . . he felt the inrushing of air. Frantic hands were already on him, under his arms, pulling, dragging. One person, probably. Breathing very hard and heavy. Crisp tried to speak. Tried desperately. Leave me alone! I beg you! Nothing came out. Please . . . The freezer door closed behind him. Amanda!

"IT WAS A GOOD THING Marky Williams was there, is all I can say." It was Matty's voice, without the jam and flour smell. He recognized the hospital smell immediately. His hands and feet felt as if they were immersed in lava. The pain was excruciating. "If he hadn't been . . . well, I hate to think. I just hate to think."

Crisp hated to think, too. He hated to think he was still alive. He wanted to cry, but apparently his tears were frozen. Other parts of his body were rapidly tingling to life, screaming in protest at being dragged from the grave's edge with deafening coruscations of exquisite pain. He opened his mouth. He meant to cry, to scream, to let out the anguish, but nothing came. Finally the tears welled in his eyes, collected at the corners, and coursed down his face. He tasted their warm salt on his tongue.

"Oh, Lord in heaven!" someone was yelling. Another woman. Not Matty. "Dr. Amburst!" she cried. "Dr. Amburst!" The electronic echo of her voice reverberated through the corridors.

"Look at him!" Matty screamed. "Do something! Do something!"

There was no peace anymore. The world was within him and around him. Pain was perfecting itself throughout his body. It may kill him yet. Please, God.

"One finger and two toes," said Matty. "That's all you lost."

Six days had passed in a sort of physical blitzkrieg, bombardments of pain followed by long, dreamy stretches of listless stupefaction under the spell of whatever drug they were administering him. Matty was sitting at his bedside, knitting. It seemed she'd been there constantly. Whenever his leaking ship hove close enough to make out a little shoreline through the fog, she was there. Knitting. Talking. Lightly brushing his hand now and then. He couldn't see her clearly—just this round, animated figure that was all soft and buttery about the edges.

"Well, I finally got a chance to talk to Marky," she continued. Crisp didn't know whether she knew he was awake. Maybe she just had a little program of bedside conversation, and when she reached the end, it just looped back to the beginning and repeated the same thing all over again. "He said he was all ready to go home . . . I gather he was workin' under a boat or something . . . anyways, he likes to listen to his radio pretty loud, I guess. You know what kind of music they listen to today. I guess "Mairzy Doats" sounded like Armageddon to our folks, don't you? Anyways, he shut his radio off when he was ready to go home and noticed the generator was on. He says they keep their own generator up there because of the way the power was, you know? I don't blame 'em, either. You never know when it's goin' to go down . . . and with a freezer load of meat. Well, that one they got's just for the freezer, as far's I can make out from what he said.

"Anyways, he noticed it was on and it wasn't s'posed to be, so he run up to the house to shut it off. That's when he found you. Of course, you know that. Boy, I bet you was never so glad to see a fellow human being in your life, was you? Even if it was Marky Williams."

What about Mostly? Where was he?

"Now half the town's waitin' to find out how you come to lock yourself in that freezer," Matty continued. "Not to mention how you happened to turn the thing on 'forehand."

His lips felt like dried fruit. It seemed he should say something, but he decided against it. He closed his eyes and pretended he was asleep. Just one finger and two toes. He *was* entering the hereafter in bits and pieces. In less than two minutes he wasn't pretending.

The next time he awoke, the process was so gradual there was no clear definition of when sleep ended and waking began. Someone was poking him, lifting his eyelids and tapping him in places. How long the procedure had been going on, he had no way of knowing. He hoped the person was a doctor.

"How are we feeling today, Professor?" It was a woman's voice. The use of the royal "we" betrayed her as a nurse.

"We wish we were dead," said Crisp. His voice didn't sound strange or strained or even particularly grave. Surprising.

"Ah! You found your tongue after all!" said the nurse. She put some things in a white plastic bag, tucked him in, and fluffed him up with hands far too mechanical to minister comfort to any degree. "We had bets whether you'd pull through," she continued cheerfully. "You just cost me five dollars."

"I apologize," he said. "Believe me, if I'd had my way—"

"Now, now, don't you talk like that, Winston." It was Matty. "You're goin' to be just fine." She patted his hand. He took hers and squeezed it. Reflexively she tried to pull away, but he wouldn't let her.

"Matty," he said softly. He dragged his eyes into focus. He thought she'd look a spectacle, having been at his bedside for who knew how long, knitting and talking. She looked the way she always looked—a self-contained hurricane of domesticity. "I was going to say you should go get some rest, but you look fine."

The nurse filled her quota of poking and fluffing and went away.

"Well, they don't have a word for what you look like," she rejoined, "and if they did you'd never hear it in Sunday school. But at least you're alive. And," she added in consolation, "you don't sound too bad. Now maybe you can tell me how you got in that freezer."

"I was locked in," said Crisp. He tried to open his eyes a little wider in emphasis, but the process admitted too much daylight to his brain, so he closed them again.

"I know that," said Matty patiently. "But how did you manage it is what everyone wants to know."

"I didn't lock myself in, Matty."

"Don't be silly, of course you did. Marky Williams said the door was locked when he got there, and—"

"That's true," said Crisp. "But somebody else locked it. Not me."

Her needles stopped clicking. "What do you mean, somebody else? You're bein' silly now. You mean somebody didn't know you was in there?"

"Oh, they knew, all right."

"Then that proves it, doesn't it? Nobody would lock you in if they knew you was in there." Matty's logic, if it could be called that, was ineluctable. "That's too dangerous." The needles resumed.

"Where's Mostly Sanborn, Matty?"

The needles stopped again. "Why, it's funny you should ask that, of all things," she said. "He's gone, Winston. Gone!" She either snapped her fingers or clicked her needles in emphasis. "Nobody's seen him for days . . . well, since you got locked in that freezer, come to think of it. That very day Mostly turned up gone." She continued knitting. "His mother's frantic, I shouldn't wonder. Poor thing."

Crisp had the feeling her sorrows had only begun.

"How long have I been here?"

"Eight days."

"We're in Rockland?"

Matty made the affirmative noise that was invariably accompanied by three or four nods of the head.

"And you've been here the whole time?"

"Well, you know how long it's been since I had a regular vacation, on the mainland and everything."

"This isn't much of a vacation."

"Oh, I think it is," said Matty. "I'm stayin' over at The Ledges. Now, how's that for fancy! You know," she added confidentially, "they don't have teapots and fixin's in the rooms." She sighed the sigh that was always followed by, what is the world comin' to? "What is the world comin' to? I'm sure I don't know. Sixty-five dollars a night, and no tea in the rooms!"

"You ring for room service, Matty."

"Room service! I'd rather conjure up the dead with a Ouija board. That oily little man in the funny hat comes wheelin' everything in on a tray as if he couldn't carry it just as easy in one hand . . . makes a big production out of it. Just for tea! And then he holds his hand out. You know what that means. Not in this life. No sir. And the tea's cold, on top of everything. I saw it all in a Bob Hope movie.

"All I require is more teakettles in sixty-five-dollar-a-night hotel rooms and less pointy-headed little foreign people with their hands out, thank you."

The knitting needles kept time during the ensuing silence.

"How d'you feel, Winston?"

He hadn't thought about it. That signaled an improvement. "All right, I guess, Matty."

"All things considered?"

He nodded. "All things considered."

"Mmm." Matty made some half-humming, half-about-to-say-something sounds. "That policeman was here."

"Mr. Hanson?"

"He has a dissipated frontal lobe."

"Beg pardon?"

"Phrenology. You know, how the shape of people's heads makes 'em geniuses or mass murderers."

Crisp nodded. "I've heard of it. Back about the turn of the century it was quite popular."

"Well, see? We should learn from the mistakes of the past, shouldn't we?" Matty said thoughtfully. "I wonder what a phrenologist would say about that man's frontal lobe."

"You don't suppose Mr. Hanson is a mass murderer, do you?" said Crisp with a smile. At least he was working his smiling muscles. He couldn't feel whether the signal had made it to his face.

"Well, he's no genius," Matty concluded, as if dubious about there being a middle ground between the options. "He said he'd be back about two."

About two, Hanson showed up.

"Good, you're awake."

Mass murderers, in Crisp's experience, seldom exhibited such punctuality. Matty would have been impressed had she not left his bedside fifteen minutes earlier to attend to "some lady things."

"Hello, Mr. Hanson."

"How's the . . . ?" He massaged the fingers of his left hand with those of his right.

Crisp held up his hand. It was hidden in a mitten of bandages. There was no pain. For all he could tell, all his fingers were present and accounted for. "Oh, well. All right, I guess," he said. "I don't . . . it doesn't hurt or anything. Strange."

"*Strange*—that's the word of the week."

"What happened?"

"Well, first you end up in a freezer, and . . . how did that happen, anyway?"

"Somebody locked me in," Crisp said immediately and with emphasis in order to dispel any contrary notions.

"I know that," said Hanson. "It would've been a little difficult for you to slip a bolt lock from inside the freezer. Why do you think I've had guards stationed out in the hall the last week?"

"Well, that's a relief. I hadn't even thought of it before, but now that you mention it, I heard the bolt in the lock. To hear Matty tell it, half the town thinks I tried to commit suicide."

"If you ever get to that point, let me know. I can suggest a thousand easier ways." Hanson smiled. "Did you see who did it?"

Crisp shook his head. "That's the craziest part of this whole business—"

"You haven't heard the craziest part yet," Hanson interrupted.

"Pardon?"

"Never mind. You finish your story first. Then I'll tell you mine."

"Well, I was just checking out a theory. Mostly had let me into the house. He showed me where the freezer was, opened it, and just stood there by the door while I poked around. He was rattling on about this and that, like he always does. I turned to hand him this little stepladder I'd been using . . ." He paused for a minute, trying to picture the sequence of events clearly in his mind. "You know, he hadn't said anything for a few seconds before that. I was too caught up in what I was doing to notice at the time, but . . . Hmm."

"That was unusual, I take it."

Crisp nodded. "Very," he said. "Anyway, I held out the stepladder for him to take, but he didn't. I looked up, and the door was closing. I was on my knees, so there was no way I could—"

"So you think this Mostly character did it?"

"I did in that first instant, but, no. I don't think so," said Crisp.

"He's disappeared, you know."

"I know. That's what worries me."

"How so?"

"I think Amanda Murphy's murderer was in the house."

"And that's who locked you in the freezer?"

"And Mostly stood between him and that objective."

"So . . . you think he's dead?"

Crisp didn't say anything. Somehow it seemed that if he agreed, even if he nodded, it would make it so. He lowered his eyes and rested his chin on his chest.

"What did you find out? Anything?" said Hanson.

Crisp became slightly more animated. "Amanda was murdered in September. Makeup from Mrs. McKenniston's theatrical trunk, which is kept in the barn, was painted on her neck and face."

"Old makeup."

"Very old." He patted the pockets of his pajamas. "I had the jars—"

"We found them. I've already sent samples off to Augusta."

"Mmm. Well, then she was put in the freezer."

"Until the hard freeze."

Crisp nodded. "Until the hard freeze, when she was dumped into Lawson's quarry."

"Wouldn't someone have noticed the generator running?"

Crisp hadn't thought of that, but it didn't present a big problem. "I doubt there's anyone up there that time of year. Why would there be? Everything's been closed up for the winter. It's not 'til spring that Mostly and Marky Williams go up there, to start getting things ready for the family."

"But you left out the fingerprints," Hanson protested. "How did they get there?"

A chill ran down Crisp's spine. "I'm not going to say until Andy Calderwood's body is exhumed again."

Hanson's first instinct was to bridle, but it was suppressed by his second instinct. "Why?"

"Because something doesn't fit."

Hanson laughed. It was meaningless and involuntary, so he changed it to a sniff. "All right. I'll order it. When?"

"As soon as possible."

"But you're not well enough to travel. The doctor says you're going to be in bed another ten days, at least."

"And there's nowhere I'd rather be," said Crisp. "Fortunately, I don't have to be there. It'll take you about five seconds to find out what I need to know."

Hanson shuddered visibly. "I hate this business."

"Oh, and this time I suggest you get one of your own people to do the digging. Perhaps you could just quietly slip over toward evening—"

"No more helicopters, huh?" Hanson said, cringing. He shook his head, collected his weary frame, and rose to leave. "Tell me something—why the makeup?"

"If I told you what I suspect . . . Let's wait until after we have another look at Andy Calderwood."

"Well, you've sure given me an earful. I guess the least I can do is return the favor."

Crisp waited.

"The fingerprints on those buttons? They're Neddy McKenniston's."

It was something to think about.

C
H
A
P
T
E
R

17

S OMEBODY WANTED CRISP DEAD. That was something else to think about. It had been a while since anyone had tried to kill him. It was hard not to consider the attempt a compliment, of sorts. At least he hadn't ceased to be effective.

Of course, the only suspect that came readily to mind was Amanda Murphy's murderer, or murderers, the type of person or persons who would not be favorably impressed by his resilience. Perhaps they would try to remedy the situation. Although he was glad there was a guard outside the door, he couldn't help but wonder how easy it would be to dupe a small-town cop, more accustomed to directing traffic at school crossings than dealing with diabolical murderers, into leaving his post for a minute or two. That's all it would take.

One or two minutes at the mercy of this particular murderer would be far too long. Something had to be done.

"Mr. Crisp?"

The voice belonged to a wholesome-looking young lady in a red-

and-white-striped hat who had opened the door slightly and was peeking around it. "Oh, good. You're awake."

She pushed the door open the rest of the way and dragged a meal cart into the room after her. She was dressed in a pink uniform, and her thick dark brown hair was pulled into a ponytail, tied with a scarlet and gold ribbon.

"They say you're ready for some solid food," she said. In a single, efficient motion she propped up his pillow, swung his bedside meal tray into position, and transferred to it from the cart a stainless-steel covered dish and a glass of milk. At some point in the proceeding she leaned close enough to him so he could make out her nametag. "Sarah." She removed the cover on the dish, revealing a small, angular, quaking pile of green Jell-O. No less did Crisp quake, inwardly, at the thought of eating it. "Well," she said, apologetically, "almost solid." She took a spoon from the cart, wiped it on her apron front, and, flinging down the gauntlet, placed it beside the bowl.

"There was a different nurse in here this morning," he said, picking up the spoon. He gazed at Sarah. She was really a very attractive girl. Large busted and healthy but not overweight. Probably Norwegian stock.

"Linda Dickins," said Sarah. "She gets off at ten."

"Sarah?"

"Sarah Quinn."

Crisp's ears stood at attention. "Sarah Quinn . . . from the island?"

"That's right."

"I've heard of you."

"Well," said Sarah with a warm smile, "don't you believe half of it, good or bad." Her laugh, though covering only a small segment of the scale musically, was ready and pleasant. Whatever Sarah Quinn his imagination had compiled from the little he'd heard of her came crashing down like a despot's statue.

"I didn't know you worked here," said Crisp conversationally. He'd wanted to talk to this girl, but he was so taken aback by the disparity between the Sarah Quinn he'd heard described and the Sarah Quinn in his room that he'd forgotten what he'd wanted to learn from her.

"I got here the day after you did," said Sarah. "They were advertising in the paper for help. I had to call and remind them they'd had my application for ages."

"You've moved over here, then, to the mainland?"

"Oh, no," Sarah said quickly. "No, I've got to take care of . . . I have a baby, you know."

Had the baby a father? Crisp wondered.

"And Daddy needs me, too. You know how it is. No, I come over on the first boat and return on the last. That gets me back in time to pick up J. T.—my baby—at my sister's and get home to make supper for Daddy before he gets there. I still put in an eight-hour day if I don't take time off for lunch."

"Sounds like long hours," said Crisp, still trying to form a question.

She smiled. "Mmm. Well, you do what you have to, you know?"

"I thought you worked up at McKenniston's."

"Oh, no," she said. Her bustle of activity quickened, just like Matty's did when she was flustered or embarrassed. "I'm not going to do that this year. They'll just have to get along without me, for a change."

"You've . . . worked up there a long time."

"If you don't eat that Jell-O, I may lose my job," she said. The momentary flush had left her face like a summer cloud leaves the sun. She was composed and professional. "It was time for a change, I guess. I've always wanted to work in a hospital."

"I seem to remember someone saying you went to school."

She laughed. "My great college career! The best-laid plans, you know." The laugh dissolved into a smile, soft at the edges.

Crisp smiled back. "Well, you're young yet. Maybe you can pick up where you left off someday."

It seemed as though she had been puttering aimlessly, just like Matty always seemed to putter aimlessly, yet somehow everything got done. She'd even folded the dirty linen over her arm. She looked out the window. "I don't think so, Mr. Crisp." There was nothing left of the unsteady smile. Her expression was one of stoic resolve. "Some things just weren't meant to be."

Crisp understood that. He nodded. He was nodding a lot lately. People do when they reach a certain age. Sarah turned from the window, looked at him, and smiled. Her eyes were pale and deep with thought. "Oh, well," she said. "This is the next best thing, I guess. I'll be back in before I leave to see if there's anything you need."

Crisp looked forward to it. He couldn't remember the last time he'd spent a pleasant few minutes with someone from the Dark Ages between twelve and twenty-five.

Before he knew it he'd eaten a spoonful of Jell-O. "Oh, Miss . . . Sarah . . ." The question he'd been trying to formulate came to him, but it was having difficulty getting out of his full mouth.

"Everything okay?" asked Sarah.

"I'm fine, thank you," Crisp replied. "Do you recall, by any chance, when the McKennistons left the island last summer?"

Only her eyes reacted to mention of the name. A spark, if that, passed too quickly to identify the emotion behind it. If not smothered, contained. "I really don't remember, exactly," she said. Her voice quivered almost imperceptibly with the aftershocks of the brief flush of feeling.

"Generally, then," he coaxed gently.

Some linens had slipped from her hands. She retrieved them from the floor. "Usually . . . Labor Day weekend." She was having to struggle to maintain her composure. Neddy McKenniston? The baby? It stood to reason. The smile that followed was quick and insincere. "I have other patients, you know," she said. "We don't want them jealous now, do we?"

"Just one more thing," said Crisp. "Last year, did anyone stay behind, after Labor Day?"

"I really don't know," Sarah replied quickly. The slightest trace of tension tinted her voice. "Daphne—she's the senator's daughter—came up with the kids one weekend. Everything was shut up, though. They stayed over on East Haven."

"And the young fellow—Ned. Is that his name?" said Crisp. He watched her reaction.

She guarded it closely. "Neddy," she corrected. "I don't remember. He was always . . . He came and went, you know? I don't think he stayed after Labor Day."

She was uncomfortable. Crisp put her at ease with a smile. "Ah, youth," he said dreamily. He looked out the window at a small patch of blue-gray sky embroidered by the branches of an evergreen. "Do you think spring will ever come?"

Sarah looked out the window, too. But she didn't see what he saw. "Spring," she said. There was no inflection to the word. It was as if she was phonetically repeating a word in a foreign language.

They stared in silence for a moment, until someone dropped something in the corridor. "I've got to go," said Sarah, and she did.

The telephone woke him in the late afternoon. The lowering sun had draped the windowsill and the few Spartan furnishings in its immediate vicinity with fool's gold. The phone had been ringing in the dream from which he'd been awakened. He looked at the device. A human making that much noise would be animated, flailing arms and legs, jumping up and down. The phone just screamed. It couldn't care less if anyone heard it or not. It had no share in the news it brought. He won the staring match. It finally stopped ringing.

Microscopic scribbles of dust floated across the shaft of sunlight. He followed them with his eyes and let his mind wander.

Whose voice is that I hear from time to time
Calling in the canyons of my mind?
What childhood cantata, bold and free
Searches for its echo now . . . in me?

He'd have to write that one down.

The phone rang again, but this time it proved irresistible.

"Hello?"

"Crisp? Hanson."

"Hello, Mr. Hanson."

"Two things," said Hanson. "Actually, three things. First, the lab gave me the rundown on that makeup. It all checks out like you said. I've got it right here. Let me see"—he made the sounds of someone trying to find their glasses, then putting them on—"ah, there. Evrington's Theatrical Makeup—that ring a bell?" It did. "Well, that's what it was. Lead base, just like you said. I think it makes what they call the 'foundation.' I guess you'd know that better than I." He would. "Anyway, this is the old formula, before it was outlawed."

"In 1932."

"In 1932, that's right. After that they changed everything. It matches what we found on the girl."

Crisp was nodding again. He caught himself this time, and stopped—not without some effort. "What was the second thing?"

"I'm re-exhuming the Calderwood boy Saturday."

"Good."

"Is it?" said Hanson. "I can think of better ways to spend my evenings, you know."

"And the third thing?"

"Third," said Hanson with a sigh. "Worst of all." He paused. "They found the Sanborn fellow . . . at the bottom of the cliff in front of McKenniston's. He was wedged in the rocks."

"Dead," said Crisp, almost reflexively.

"Seems he was in some kind of golf cart or something. Went

straight over the edge and . . . well. It was in this little cove. Out of the way."

"Did they do an autopsy?"

"Autopsy?" said Hanson incredulously. "Why? He drove off the cliff and died."

"Did he?"

Hanson stopped breathing for a second. "Didn't he?"

"There should be an autopsy."

"Do you really think it's necessary?"

Crisp let the silence answer in the affirmative.

"What reason can I give?"

"You don't need to give a reason."

"Well, then, what reason can you give me?"

"I'm sure I don't have to give you one, if you think about it," said Crisp. "Mostly Sanborn didn't lock me in the freezer."

"He could have done it accidentally," said Hanson, jumping in without looking. "Then he goes out, jumps in the golf cart, rushes off for help, loses his way in the fog or has mechanical difficulty, and"—he made a whooshing sound—"off he goes!"

"And who turned on the freezer after the door was shut?"

"Well, of course—"

"And he couldn't have 'jumped into' the cart. It was down in the barn, if it's the one I'm thinking of. And even if he did decide to go dig out the golf cart and run for help rather than simply opening the door or using the telephone or getting in his truck, what would he have been doing near the cliff? The road is in the opposite direction. And—"

"All right! All right! I get the message," said Hanson. "So, somebody knocks him out while you're in the freezer—"

"Slams the door shut—"

"Turns on the generator, gets the golf cart?"

"Gets the golf cart," Crisp agreed.

"Drags the body out of the house, puts it in the cart, drives to the cliff—"

"Stops, puts Mostly behind the wheel, and . . ."

Hanson added his whooshing sound.

It suddenly struck Crisp that Mostly was dead. His heart sank. There was enough room in the emptiness of himself to admit the fact, as it had the loss of so many over the years, but the addition of a new member to the fraternity of terrors stirred the old ghosts. They lamented loudly and whispered the horrible secrets only he knew.

"Why kill Mostly Sanborn?" said Hanson. "Who'd do something like that?"

Crisp knew. There was always the expedient. Sangé Timor, attaché to the Turkish embassy in Sebastopol, had died similarly, the only difference being he was in a car, and the cliff in that instance overlooked the Caspian. He and Hanson shared a pungent snifter of quietude.

"You still haven't told me what I'm looking for," said Hanson.

"Pardon?" Crisp was a little startled by the voice in his ear. He'd been watching the nurse inject something pink into a little tube attached to his IV and had forgotten he was on the phone.

"The Calderwood boy. What am I looking for?"

The nurse concluded the particulars of her routine with hardly a troubling of the air and left the room. The residue of her presence, a musk-based perfume, settled softly on the linens.

"Hands," said Crisp. He was having a hard time concentrating. "Look closely at his hands. Especially the wrists."

"Is it that important?" said Hanson.

"I think so," Crisp replied. He was wondering what was in the pink solution. Potent, whatever it was. Maybe they'd give him some to take home.

"Why?"

"Why?" Crisp echoed. He felt as though he was talking from the bottom of a large, deep oil drum. He knew he was thinking the words, but he couldn't tell whether he was voicing them.

"Why is it important?" Hanson said. He sounded as though he was in an oil drum, too.

"You'll see . . . when you see," said Crisp, not meaning to be enigmatic. His senses were swimming, and the synapses in his brain seemed to be bridging oceans of green Jell-O."

"Are you all right?" said Hanson a little sharply.

Crisp's hand had stopped tingling. He looked at the neatly wrapped bandage and realized he didn't even know which finger was missing. "Besides," he said, but he couldn't get a handle on whatever thought had engendered the word. His head felt weighted with rocks and tossed into the depths of his pillow. The linen crinkled loudly in his ears. His eyes seemed knit together, and the pink liquid was pulling what was left of his consciousness into the leaden abyss of sleep. "Medication," he whispered.

"Go to sleep," said Hanson. "I'll talk to you later."

"I DON'T THINK THIS IS A GOOD IDEA." Sarah Quinn objected to the fact that Crisp had decided to remove himself from the hospital Saturday, having spent only nine days of a two-week stay. Despite the medication, he'd had a bad night. What little sleep he managed to get was interrupted at regular intervals by nurses who, he determined, subscribed to the concept of sleep deprivation as fundamental to recovery.

This morning he felt much worse. The phantom pain where his finger and toes used to be was nearly unbearable. How does one scratch an itch when the extremity that itches isn't there? Unfortunately, the only treatment was more medication, administered by what seemed like buckets full, and that was worse. Clouding his mind. Fogging his reason. That he couldn't abide. If he was going to die, it would be with a clear head, and that was available to him only outside the hospital—back on the island. At Matty's.

Of course she'd tried to talk him out of it when she stopped by the room before breakfast. Halfheartedly, though. Deep down inside she couldn't see how anyone managed to get better in a hospital. She'd much rather have him home, where she could take proper care of him.

"What about the pain?" she asked.

He smiled weakly. "It clears the head."

His head was sublimely clear as, with nine fingers, he pulled on his clothes. The third finger of his left hand was missing. One of his favorites. He'd stolen a glance when the nurse changed his bandage before breakfast. Very neat. Squared off at the end with loose skin pulled over it and sewn together like a little bag.

"You'll want medication," Sarah said. She helped him button his shirt. "Can you walk?"

He did feel lopsided. He'd been standing only a few minutes and already his remaining toes ached with the strain of compensating for their fallen comrades. His lack of balance was further augmented by the wadded bandage around his foot, which made him feel as though he was perpetually walking uphill. The analogy was not lost on him. He wondered if the disability would affect his bicycle riding. "I'll get along," he said.

Clear as his brain might be, he still couldn't recall what he'd wanted to ask Sarah. Something important.

The last button poked its head out. "Well," Sarah said resignedly, "I guess you're old enough to know what's best." If he wasn't, no one was. "But I can't take care of you like I wanted to." She'd already pulled the sheets and pillowcases off the bed and put them in a wire cart in the hallway. She completed a second circuit of the room as he looked on. It was as if no one had even been there. It could have been a display in the Smithsonian. "And on the left, ladies and gentlemen, a typical hospital room of the mid to late twentieth century. Note the television on the wall. We know this diabolical device was often used in prisons of the time, presumably to torture intractable inmates. Its presence in a place of healing, however, is mystifying. Of course, there are a number of theories . . ."

"I could stop by your house now and then to see how you're doing," Sarah suggested as she fit him to a walker. "I could make it by after supper once or twice, or on weekends. When are you having the stitches out?"

They'd told him, but he didn't remember. "I'm not sure."

"Well, probably ten days or so. I can make it over a few times in the meantime. Make sure you're comfortable. Bring your medicine."

Matty would be hard enough to deal with on that score. She'd make him stick out his tongue to be sure he swallowed it. She was a suspicious woman.

Crisp didn't want anyone reminding him to take medicine. Nevertheless, he'd been trying to think of a way, short of remaining in the hospital, to get a few minutes alone with Sarah. He smiled warmly. "I'd like that, Sarah," he said. "If you wouldn't mind."

"Not at all," she replied. She seemed almost relieved.

"I know you've . . . there are a lot of demands on your time."

Sarah brushed a lock of hair from her forehead. "Oh, no trouble at all. Really," she said. "I'll be over in a few days. Matty Gilchrist's, right?"

"Here, here, now! You march right on out! You can't go up there!" Matty's voice was rising by octaves as she delivered this broken address to person or persons unknown. Two sets of footsteps on the stairs. One man in sneakers or deck shoes, one woman in pumps. Whoever they are, thought Crisp, I can't let them see me like this. Matty'd be embarrassed.

He sat up, straightened the bedclothes, and scooped an armload of debris from the nightstand and stuffed it under his pillow. Further housekeeping was preempted by a loud rap on the door.

"Professor Crisp?" said the sneakers. The pumps were still ascending the stairs. "Daniel Levinson, *Rockland Telegraph*. Can we come in?"

Crisp hadn't even time to deliberate on how a Daniel Levinson could be plural, nor to respond, before the door flew open. In came a short, animated man with a wide face, unruly black hair, and too much waist for his pants.

"Can I help—"

"Where do you want me to set up, Dan?" These words announced the arrival of a tall woman with long braided hair, a narrow torso, and a large bottom—a configuration, thought Crisp, that put her at low risk of a heart attack. She dressed the way women did in the sixties. A time-warp baby. She looked at him. "That's nice," she said. Crisp smiled. "Good light there. Can we lose the specs? I'll set up here out of the way. Excuse me, sir," she continued. "Could you take off your glasses? We're going to get an awful glare if you—"

"Why do you want to take my picture?" said Crisp, deducing from the camera pointed at him that this was her intention. He left his glasses on.

"To put in the paper," the once-young woman replied. "Get a light reading on him, will you, Danny?" She handed the busy young man a little black gizmo with a white knob on it.

"How's your finger?" said the young man, selecting one of a family of pens from among its brethren in his shirt pocket. He produced a tape recorder and flipped open a notebook. Crisp wondered which of the two he mistrusted most.

"Pardon?"

"The finger," repeated the reporter. "It was the finger, right?" He was looking at the photographer.

"And two toes," said the woman, completing the inventory of missing items. "I think he's a little hard of hearing. Speak up."

"Yeah. Finger and toes," Danny said much too loud for print. "How are they?"

"Missing," said Crisp. He'd never cared for the press, and these two, it seemed clear, were determined to reinforce his opinion. "How are yours?"

The female contingent of the journalistic assault popped the flash on her camera. "Good. Great. Let's do it."

"All right," said Danny. He pulled a chair to the bedside and sat down. It was an old wicker chair that Matty had inherited from her great-grandfather, a sea captain. She'd made pillows for it, and they were fastened by little ribbons or something. It hadn't been sat on for years. In fact, Matty had specifically asked Crisp not to sit on it. "It's just for decoration, you see," she'd said. Now there was an over-weight reporter in it, and it was creaking. "Tell us all about it."

He set the tape recorder on the mattress.

"I don't know if you should be sitting on that chair," Crisp cautioned. "It belonged to Matty's great-grandfather—"

"It'll be okay, Professor," said the reporter, a good deal louder than necessary. "I'll worry about the chair, you worry about trying to remember all the facts."

Crisp's eyes clouded. His hand began to shake and his head bobbed a little.

"I think we're losing him," the woman whispered. "You'd better talk fast."

"Here, here, now!" Matty fumed as she bustled into the room. "Who do you think you are, busting into a woman's home like this!" She turned to Crisp. "I called Luther Kingsbury," she said, then, turning to the intruders, added, "he's the police."

"We're from the *Rockland Telegraph*," said the reporter, thus apparently absolved of the civilities common to the rest of society.

"Oh," said Matty. She never missed an issue of the *Telegraph*. Unconsciously she primped her hair and straightened her apron, just in case. "Oh, well. What do you say, Winston?" she asked, a little flustered. "They're from the *Telegraph*."

"I'll be all right, Matty," Crisp said.

"Just look at this room!" Matty cried. Immediately she began putting things right.

"That won't be necessary, ma'am," said the photographer. "We'll just be getting close-ups."

Her words were wasted. "What are these people going to say to their friends, Winston? They're going to think we don't know how to keep house on the island."

"Really," said the reporter as he ushered Matty to the door, "we won't breathe a word."

"Well," said Matty, already on the landing with the door closing behind her. "If it's all right with Winston."

"I'm sure it is," said the reporter as he lifted the little wrought-iron latch into place. Then he returned to his seat. It showed the power of the media, Crisp thought, that Matty hadn't even noticed his sitting on her great-grandfather's chair.

"Now then," continued the reporter, "word is that you were locked in a freezer. Tell us about it. Why? How? By whom? That kind of thing."

"Why?" said Crisp, with a senile little tilt of the head.

"Why what?"

"Why do you want to know all that?"

Danny was speechless. Not so the photographer. She was a woman. Women are sensitive to these things. She understood the problem. She came to the bedside and, lowering herself on one knee, patted Crisp's hand and spoke to him as if his lights had all gone out. "We're from the paper, Mr. Crisp—"

"Professor," Danny reminded her.

Solicitousness was one thing; deviation from the facts was something else. "He's not a professor," said the woman. "That's just a nickname. I asked around."

"Maybe he likes it," said Danny.

Crisp had been looking from one to the other of them during the exchange and, inwardly, was shaking his head. Externally, he nodded only slightly.

"All right, all right," she relented. "Professor, I'm Bobbie Wheelright, and this is Danny Levinson. We're from the *Rockland Telegraph,* and we want to ask you a few questions about what happened to you."

Crisp held up the hand with the missing finger. "You mean this?"

"Yes," said Danny. Now they were getting somewhere, he thought.

"I had an accident," said Crisp matter-of-factly.

"What do you mean?" said Danny. He shut off the tape recorder. "We heard you were locked in a freezer up at the McKenniston place."

"I was."

Levinson turned on the tape recorder and spoke a little louder. "You were locked in a freezer up at the McKenniston place. Is that right?"

"That's correct," said Crisp.

"By who?"

"Whom."

"Whom," said Levinson. "Someone locked you in?"

Crisp looked surprised. "They did?"

Levinson's thin veneer of professional *hauteur* was fading rapidly. "They say someone locked you in the freezer, then turned on the generator."

"Dangerous," said Crisp, scratching his head and looking bewildered. "Somebody could get hurt that way."

"Somebody did," said Ms. Wheelright. She was speaking even more loudly than Levinson. "Wilbert Sanborn's dead."

Wilbert, thought Crisp. Mostly did have a name, after all. He preferred Mostly. "Was he in the freezer?"

"What?"

Crisp's eyes were watery and distant as he turned them to the camerawoman. "How did Mostly get in the freezer?"

"Mostly?" echoed the woman.

It was Levinson's turn to toss in a lifeline. "That was Sanborn's nickname," he said. "Everyone on the island's got one."

That was true, Crisp reflected. They should do a story on nicknames. He could guarantee it would be much more interesting than the one they'd get from him.

"Nobody locked him in the freezer," said Ms. Wheelright. "He drove off a cliff. What's he talking about?"

Levinson shrugged. "You get the picture, I'll get the story." The woman's face disappeared behind the camera with a comment Crisp really couldn't make out but seemed to be directed at her partner. "Listen, Professor, " Levinson resumed, "we've got a noon deadline. Help us out here, will you?" Crisp tilted his head to the other side. "How did you get locked in the freezer?"

"I'm not sure," said Crisp.

"Who do you think did it?"

"What makes you think someone did?"

"Our sources said—"

"What sources?"

"I can't reveal that."

Crisp rested his chin on his chest. "Poor Mostly." He raised his eyes. "I don't remember his being in the freezer."

Levinson stood up abruptly, folded his notebook, looked at his watch, and began pacing the room. "The biggest story to hit the mid-coast in forty years, and our only witness is an imbecile," he whispered to the photographer. "Listen, Mr. Crisp—"

"Professor," the woman reminded him snottily.

"*Mister*," Levinson volleyed. "Our sources said someone locked you in the freezer, then hit this Sanborn fellow over the head with a heavy object, put him in the golf cart, drove him to the edge of the cliff, and . . ." He used sign language to illustrate. "The question is, who would have done it, and why? Was it the same person who locked you in?"

"I wouldn't know," said Crisp. His voice was weak and gravelly. Mostly's autopsy must be finished, and these people knew the results before he did. Good sources. "I was in the freezer."

"You didn't see anything?"

"I saw the door close."

"Then?"

"Then it got cold."

"So," said Levinson, warming to his task. "Somebody turned on the compressor."

"Generator," Crisp corrected.

"Generator. Then you passed out?" said Levinson. He was writing furiously, and Crisp wondered whether he'd presupposed an answer.

"Lost consciousness," Crisp amended.

"Same thing. Then?"

"Then?" said Crisp.

"What happened next?"

"I don't know," Crisp replied. He had to concentrate to keep from smiling. "I was unconscious."

Levinson sat down as abruptly as he'd stood up. "I mean—" The flash went off. "Hey! Wait a minute, will you?"

"Sorry," said Wheelright, though she didn't seem to mean it.

Levinson rubbed his eyes. "I hate that," he said. Willing enough to subject others to it, though, thought Crisp. "Where was I? The freezer?" He looked at his notes. "Oh, yeah. You were asleep. What happened when you woke up?"

"I found out I was alive," Crisp replied thoughtfully.

Levinson propped his palm on his leg, stuck out his elbow at a forty-five-degree angle from his body, dropped the glasses down on his nose, and leveled a severe gaze at him. "Mr. Crisp. You're not being helpful. How do you expect us to get the story if you won't get serious?"

Even Crisp, poet that he was, could not find the words to convey how little he cared whether or not they got their story. He did wonder, though, where they got their facts. Before one can plug a leak, one must determine the size of the hole.

"I'm very serious," he said. "After that, I was in the hospital." A brief silence punctuated the statement as Levinson scratched it down.

"What about the buttons?"

Crisp was startled. Although his expression didn't change, his eyes did. Ms. Wheelright, focusing for a close-up at that instant, was so alarmed by their sudden clarity and coldness that she failed to take the picture. By the time she gained her senses, the look had gone, in its place a benign, almost witless mask. "Buttons?" he said distractedly.

"Some buttons were just sent to Augusta for analysis. Do you know anything about them? Where did they come from? Did you lose some buttons while you were in the freezer?"

Crisp made some sounds in the back of his throat. His eyes became soft and dreamy. "We used to play that when I was a kid. 'Button, button . . . who's got the button?' Mamy Harding always had it. If you caught her behind the oriental screen, she'd let you kiss her for a penny."

"This is getting more like the twilight zone every minute," Levinson commented under his breath. "Listen, Professor, one last question. Concentrate, will you? Who could possibly want you dead?"

No one who knew where he was. "You mean who would want Mostly dead, don't you?"

"*You* were the one locked in the freezer!" Levinson shouted in exasperation. "Sanborn was killed because he saw who did it!"

"Of course," Crisp said slowly, "if you look at it another way, what if I was locked in the freezer to keep from identifying Mostly's killer?" His grandfather had been right; he'd have made a great lawyer. "After all, he's the one who's dead." More's the pity. "I'm very tired. I think if you want to know anything else, ask your source. He seems to know more than I do."

"She," said Levinson. His need to be the one correcting, at that instant, overwhelmed his journalistic common sense.

If Sangé Timor had been this easy, there would be one less set of bones in Crisp's closet. Of course, there would be other little Timors scurrying from hole to hole in northwest Turkey, popping out of shadows now and then, to swear to lies or slit people's throats.

Wheelright dropped the camera onto her chest with a thud. It wouldn't have thudded on Matty's chest. Sarah Quinn's either, for that matter. "Danny! I can't believe you—"

"I want to go to sleep," said Crisp, his voice etched with fatigue.

"I just want to sleep. Forget about it." He closed his eyes and let his head drop to one side.

Levinson collected his reportorial paraphernalia and stood up. "I don't think he heard—"

"Of course he heard," Wheelright scolded. She tossed her things into a leather case and stepped briskly toward the door. Levinson, his tail between his legs, was at heel.

"No, I mean, he didn't understand. Look at him. He's sound asleep."

"Did you see the look in his eyes when you mentioned the buttons?"

Levinson shrugged. "Probably had gas."

"He scares me."

"Who? Him?"

"You didn't see what I saw. Lucky for you he's half deaf."

"Don't tell Mitch, okay?"

As the door closed, Crisp's eyes opened. Determined people, armed with a little knowledge and a lot of ink, scared him. Things were unpredictable enough without these bulls upsetting the china. Still, music can be played on any instrument, provided it's tuned properly. And someone was playing them beautifully. Crisp had little doubt that, should he find that person, he would find much more than an informer.

It had been a fruitful interview. Everything had changed, of course.

A LAND MINE HAD EXPLODED under Private First Class Timothy Hill. Crisp had watched as the gangly young man was propelled about thirty feet in the air and landed in the lower branches of a tree. Shaken, understandably, but completely unharmed. Freak things like that happen in war, especially in a place like the Ardennes, littered with explosive debris from two world wars. But fate wasn't finished with Private Hill. As he jumped down, the trigger of his M14, which was still strapped around his shoulder, caught on a branch and released a round of ammunition at a nearby rock, from which it ricocheted into his chest.

Crisp had never seen so much blood. He watched unblinking as a nineteen-year-old medic performed emergency surgery to dislodge the bullet from the left ventricle and patch up the gaping hole left by the flattened bullet.

Hill was conscious throughout. Crisp didn't know if there had been any anesthetic available. None was asked for. None was offered. The medic poured alcohol over the wound while Private

Hill bit on his rifle strap, praying and cursing and screaming out of the corners of his mouth.

Now, all these years later, Crisp realized that that image had crystallized his concept of bravery. As he looked at the bottle of pain medication on his bedside table, longing for the relief that a pill or two would bring, he remembered that young soldier and forbade himself the comfort. He would be brave.

At the same time, he knew that Matty would be up any minute. She'd discover that he hadn't taken his 11:30. She'd scold him; he'd complain. She'd fuss; he'd refuse. She'd insist; he'd relent. Then, absolved of cowardice, he'd "be a good soldier" and take his medicine. Relief.

Maybe Private Hill would have behaved differently if Matty had been on the battlefield. Of course, she wouldn't have allowed all those bombs lying about in the first place. One should clean up after a war.

Matty was late.

Leeman Russell, on the other hand, was right on time. "Professor?" he said, opening the door just enough to poke his head in and get a good look, just in case Crisp was asleep. He couldn't tell the gang at the poolroom he hadn't seen anything. "It's me," he said, lest there be any doubt. "Okay if I come in for a minute?" He was in by this time. "How're you doin'?" He stepped tentatively toward the bed. If only Tim Hill had been as tentative. "Jeez, don't you look some awful!"

"Truth in advertising, Leeman," said Crisp. "It's good to see you. Have a seat." He gestured toward the corner of the bed. Leeman took a seat. "I feel every bit as bad as I look."

"Jeez," Leeman reiterated. This time he was looking at Crisp's bandaged hand. "I bet that's some rough, losin' a finger like that at your age."

"Not easy at any age, I should imagine." Crisp held up his hand so they could both have a better look at it.

"No," Leeman agreed. "But you had it a lot longer than someone who ain't so old."

He had a point.

"Makes it harder to get used to. Hurt much?"

"Just between you and me, Leeman," Crisp confided, "it hurts like blazes."

"Shoot!" said Leeman. "I forgot them goshdarn flowers."

"Flowers?"

"The girls up to the store got together this little basket. Some flowers in it. Candy, too . . . like they got down to the hardware store. Card. Stuff like that. I left it down in the car."

"Maybe you could bring it up before you leave."

This arrangement left something to be desired. "I hate walkin' up all them stairs again," Leeman concluded. "I'll just give it to Matty. She comes up to see you, don't she?"

Crisp smiled and nodded. "Quite often." She was still late.

"Good. Then she can bring it up one of these times." Leeman tried to steal a peek at Crisp's toes, but they were covered by the blanket. "Where is she anyways?"

"Matty?" said Crisp. "She's not downstairs?"

Leeman shook his head. "Nope. I didn't see her."

"Strange."

"That's what I thought," said Leeman. "Jeez, you look some awful."

"So I gather."

"One finger and two toes, wasn't it?"

Crisp wondered if the *Rockland Telegraph* hired stringers. "One finger and two toes," said Crisp.

"Froze off, was they?"

"I guess you could say that," said Crisp. "Frostbite. They had to amputate."

Leeman nodded. "Some talk downtown."

"I can imagine," said Crisp. It was easy to do.

"You don't have to talk about it if you don't want," Leeman offered. It must have killed him to say it.

"That's all right. I don't mind telling *you*." Talking would take his mind off the pain. A thought occurred to him. "In fact, I'm going to let you in on a little secret. You might be able to help me out."

"About . . . that?" said Leeman, pointing at Crisp's finger. This was almost too good to be true.

"Not really," said Crisp. "It's about Amanda Murphy."

"Even better," Leeman said aloud, though he hadn't meant to.

"The attorney general has asked me to investigate."

Leeman bounced off the bed as if he'd been stung. "I knew it!" he said. "I know all about your work with the gov'ment, you know."

"You do?"

"Sure," Leeman affirmed. "You worked with the NSA."

"And what did I do there?" Crisp inquired gently. It was never safe to assume the obvious . . . about anyone.

"Oh, well, I don't know specifics, if that's what you mean," said Leeman, a little flustered. "Just that you was . . . that you worked there. They do codes and stuff?"

Crisp's reflexes relaxed. "That's right. That kind of thing."

"Stands to reason then," said Leeman cryptically.

"What stands to reason?"

"Well, that they'd call you in on all this business," said Leeman. He was warming to his subject, and Crisp was only too happy to apply a little kindling. What Leeman knew, the town knew, and vice versa. "Police around here ain't equipped to handle this kind of thing." He tapped his temple. "You know what I mean? This girl—"

"Amanda Murphy."

"Amanda Murphy. Right. Dyin' the way she did, and all that

business of diggin' up Andy Calderwood. I knew there was somethin' going on!

"Hey! I bet that's why somebody locked you in that freezer,
'cause you was gettin' too close to somethin'!" He stared at Crisp
and lowered his voice. "They was tryin' to kill you, you know."

"You think so?"

"No doubt," Leeman replied. "I mean, think about it. If you
was just locked in there, that's one thing. You can put the fear of
God into someone that way. But they turned on the generator.
Yessir. They meant to kill you." He snapped his fingers. "Yessir.
You must've been gettin' close to somethin'." There was a time
Crisp had thought so, too. Now he was beginning to wonder if he
was close enough. "Did you?"

"I've found out a few things," Crisp replied.

"I knew it!"

"Now, that's just between you and me, Leeman. Right?"

"Right," Leeman affirmed solemnly. How good that word
would be remained to be seen.

"Can you help me out?"

"You bet," said Leeman. "You name it!"

"I want you to find out if Neddy McKenniston has a blazer . . .
or a sports jacket—"

" 'Course he does. Them kind of people got hundreds."

"That may be," said Crisp. "But this one will have buttons missing. I shouldn't be surprised if it's navy blue."

Leeman thought for a moment. "It's important?" Crisp nodded.
"Evidence?"

"Could be."

"I don't s'pose you'll tell me why."

"Not yet," said Crisp. "Not 'til I'm sure. Can you do it?"

"Sure I can."

"Thanks." Crisp patted his new apprentice on the arm. "Let
me know as soon as you find out anything." Leeman got up to leave.
"And thank the ladies for me."

"Ladies?"

"For the flowers."

"Oh, the girls. Sure I will."

Thirty minutes later, Matty still hadn't come home. Crisp had dressed; that is to say, he'd pulled on his slippers and tugged his favorite cardigan—the one Matty hated so intensely—over his pajamas. He was sitting in the cane rocker by the window, watching three ladies from the Eastern Star putting little flags around the quadrangle in preparation for Memorial Day observations. He couldn't make out who they were.

A cold, steady, mist-heavy wind tore at the red, white, and blue banners, making them seem like butterflies pinned to a board. Another lady removed a year's worth of beer cans, rocks, gum wrappers, and other debris from the mouth of the cannon. Wouldn't do to litter the landscape with rubbish when they touched it off at the conclusion of "God Bless America."

That cannon would be a nice place to be, thought Crisp. To have his head tightly wedged in it when it went off. Boom. All over. Just like that. No more pain. Just crisp little pieces of Crisp raining gently over the island and blowing out to sea.

Where was Matty?

He hobbled to the nightstand and, after a brief battle with his inner man, picked up the little brown bottle, opened it, and poured two pills into his palm. He took them without water, chewing them to a fine paste on his tongue. The taste almost made him vomit. It was his way of atoning for weakness.

Almost at once the familiar tingle surged across his shoulders and up the back of his neck, the welcome harbinger of blessed relief. But it didn't come without a price. It demanded the sacrifice of reason, for a time, the erasure of that fine line between sanity and madness.

He didn't want to stay in the room; the ghosts were crowding in—Timothy Hall, Amanda Murphy, Mostly Sanborn, Sangé

Timor, and a host of others. The longer he remained there, under the influence of the drug, the more corporeal he knew they'd become. He pulled his robe over his shoulders and started down the stairs.

"Professor!" The voice came from the far end of the hall. It was Nate Gammidge. "There you are. I've been looking all over for you." He was talking with his mouth full. Apparently he'd started his search in the kitchen.

With both hands on the banister, Crisp continued his descent. Nate was now at the bottom of the stairs. "Nate?" he said. He was having difficulty focusing; the medicine seemed to set his eyes adrift in their sockets.

"I just found this little piece of apple—" Gammidge's eyes settled on Crisp. "Winston! Do you want some help?" He placed the pie plate on the radiator and ran up the stairs. "Should you be out of bed?"

"Should I be out of the grave?" Crisp whispered hoarsely. Keeping one hand on the banister, he wrapped his other arm tightly around Gammidge. "I'll be all right," he said. "It's the medicine they gave me . . . makes me a little foggy."

"How long ago did you take it?"

"About thirty minutes."

"Well, don't take this the wrong way," said Gammidge. "But you look like hell on a bad day."

Crisp smiled. It came easy with a head full of helium. "That seems to be the consensus." Billy Pringle would understand. Further conversation was suspended until Gammidge had installed his charge in the porch swing.

"There, now. How's that? Better?"

He had no idea how much better. It dawned on Crisp that, with the exception of being shuffled back and forth between cars and ferries, he hadn't been out of doors in nearly three weeks. He took a long, deep, satisfying breath.

The air still had a sharp edge to it, burdened by brine, pine, juniper, and sweet grass. He exhaled and breathed again. More than sight, sound, touch, or taste, smells seemed to stir up a cauldron of dormant memories. Friendly ghosts awoke and looked about, laughing a distant though familiar laughter, singing songs with words he'd thought forgotten.

He was glad to be alive, at least for the moment. He wanted to sing, or laugh. He did neither. If someone had played a jig, though, he doubted his capacity to resist a turn or two about the garden.

"Much better," he said. "Thanks."

"Pleasure," said Gammidge. He sat in the wicker chair opposite Crisp. "Professor?"

"Nate?"

"I'm here on business."

Business, his own or anybody else's, was the farthest thing from Crisp's mind. "I see," he said dreamily. "Well . . ." There wasn't anywhere to go. "Well, I see."

"You're sure you're all right?" Gammidge had dealt with a lot of drunks, and Crisp was doing a perfect impersonation.

"I'm fine," said Crisp. He smiled a stupid smile in affirmation.

"Maybe too fine," said Gammidge under his breath.

"Pardon?"

"Somebody's been leaking information to the press," Gammidge said bluntly, realizing that anything approaching subtlety or finesse was out of the question, given Crisp's present state of mind. "Hanson wants to know if it's you."

Crisp's head bobbed up and down and side to side. He knew that Gammidge had said something important. Something crucial. But he couldn't bring himself to care. "Me?"

"Did you leak to the press?" said Gammidge flatly.

"Take a leak?" said Crisp. "Not right now, thanks." He knew he wasn't making any sense. But it was amusing to hear how things came out.

"Winston," Gammidge continued earnestly, taking Crisp by the shoulders and looking him in the eye. "I've got to know. Did you tell the press about"—he looked around and lowered his voice—"about the fingerprints being on those buttons . . . anything about fingerprints?"

Crisp shook his head as if to dislodge the fog that had taken up residence in his brain. "Didn't tell," he said with great effort. "Said nothing. Why?"

"Because they're asking questions. Somebody's talking, and there aren't that many who know."

It was hard not to smile. Crisp felt happy. He wanted to write a poem about happiness, about dancing with gossamer-clad sirens and tripping down alpine hillsides festooned with edelweiss. Something told him he shouldn't ask Gammidge to dance, but he wanted to. It was at that moment he saw a trail of blood on the floor. He knew whose it was. He knew where it would lead if he followed it.

He didn't want to follow.

"Amanda," he said softly. The smile dissolved from his face like sugar in bitter tea and, with it, happiness. His eyes brimmed with tears, and they flowed freely down his face.

Nate wasn't sure how to proceed. "Professor," he said gently. "Winston." He placed his hand on Crisp's shoulder. How much of this imbecility was the by-product of the medicine and how much was attributable to the recent strain, it was impossible to tell. However, if the old Crisp was in there, he had to be found. Gammidge shook him lightly. "Winston, if the press finds out half of what's been going on—"

"Winston!" It was Matty's voice.

"There you are!" she said as she flung open the French door. "What on earth are you doin' down here? Hello, Mr. . . ."

"Gammidge."

"Gammidge, that's right," Matty replied. "Well, how in heaven's name . . ." She proceeded to straighten Crisp's robe about him. "I've just been next door havin' a little chat with . . . You'll catch your death out here, Winston. Did you take your eleven o'clock? Never mind, I see you did." She turned to Gammidge. "His medicine takes away his senses. The pain, you know. It's too much. His eyes get all glassy, like a stuffed animal. What can we do for you, Captain?"

Gammidge wasn't sure how he'd come by the promotion, but he decided it might be expeditious not to argue the point. "I just wanted to see him," he said, not altogether untruthfully, "and talk about a few things."

"Oh, no point in that," said Matty. She'd produced a quilt from somewhere and was arranging it in Crisp's lap. "Not when he's on his medicine. Takes away his senses, like I said . . . I said that, didn't I?"

"Yes," Gammidge confirmed.

"See, I'm not as silly as they say." She smiled at her hands, which were busy doing something. "No Gammidges on the island, are there?" she asked conversationally.

"Yes, as a matter of fact," said Gammidge. "Quite a few." He'd had enough experience with islanders to know that talking to them would be easier if he could demonstrate a relationship, however distant, with a native.

"Really?" said Matty, looking at him squarely. "You don't say? Now, how is it I—"

"They're over on East Haven."

Matty's lips curled at the corners. He didn't understand. "Oh. East Haven. Well, that's not the same, is it?"

"It isn't?" said Gammidge weakly.

"Of course not," said Matty with a little wag of the head. "Do you get out there much?"

Gammidge was deflated. "No," he said. "Hardly ever."

"Not close family then," Matty guessed.

"Not real close," said Gammidge. He didn't even know any of their first names. "Not really." So much for the presumption of affinity. "My wife and I have vacationed out here a few times," he said, wishing at once that he hadn't mentioned it. "She has family out here."

Matty bustled from the porch for a moment, but that didn't stop her from talking, which she did steadily in a chirpy singsong until she returned with the half-eaten pie and a cup of hot tea. "Did you ever go up there? . . . Tea, wasn't it? This is yours, isn't it? I've warmed it."

"Tea, yes," said Nate, juxtaposing the answers as he took the cup. "Thanks. Yes, that's mine. I hope you don't mind."

"Not a'tall," said Matty, who was rather more flattered than offended.

"What was your question?" said Nate with his mouth full. The pie was even better warm.

"Did you ever go up there to the dance?" said Matty. She placed a cup on a little tile-topped table beside Crisp. She doubted he'd take any tea, but she would keep an eye on him just in case. He'd need help. "Didn't you hear what I was sayin'?"

"I'm afraid not," said Gammidge. "I was—"

"I was talkin' about the time I went up to East Haven, back in the thirties. There was a dance at the yacht club. This young man asked me up there. I can't for the life of me remember his name. Well, you wouldn't know it to look at me now, but . . ."—she blushed a little—"well, there was a boy or two who looked my way in those days."

It was Gammidge's turn to smile. "I don't doubt that at all."

Matty smiled coyly. It fit her. "Well, I don't recall exactly how we met, but . . . oh, yes I do, come to think of it. Lanky Pinkham introduced us. They was havin' a play at the Memorial Hall . . . or a concert . . . somethin' like that . . ." Matty sipped her tea. "Of course, come to think of it, I don't know how Lanky came to know him." She brightened. "Anyway, I wasn't more than fifteen or sixteen, and he asked me if I'd go to the Labor Day dance up at the yacht club. Well, I tell you . . . there were stories about them dances!" Matty flushed slightly but plowed bravely forward nevertheless.

" 'Course, I wouldn't have gone alone . . . just me and him, I mean. But there was generally a wagon load of kids went up there from here. Let me tell you, that was a sight! We all had to wear pink or yellow gowns—chiffon mostly, in them days—and the boys all wore white pants, muslin shirts, and blue blazers—"

"Blue blazers!" said Crisp. The word had poked through his muddled consciousness like a needle.

Matty and Gammidge watched him for a moment. Matty's expression was one of forbearance and understanding; Gammidge looked worried and confused. Nothing else was forthcoming.

"He does that sometimes," said Matty. "Calls out like that when he's under the medicine. Don't mind him. Anyway, where was I? Oh, blue blazers and white sailor hats—that was the tradition up there. Still is, I hear. That's what I mean about there being a difference."

Gammidge, not nearly as adept at following the thread of Matty's conversation as Crisp, was shaking his head, trying to sort things out. "Difference?"

"Between the islands," said Matty cheerily. "That kind of thing would never happen here. We're a fishin' town. East Haven . . . well"—she leaned closer and lowered her voice—"that's for summer folk, don't you know?" She lowered her voice a little more and leaned a little closer. "They've got a golf course up there, you know." She lowered her head gravely and stared at him over the top of her glasses.

"I see," Gammidge said. He was beginning to. "So, that was quite a treat?"

"Oh!" said Matty with a high, tinkling laugh, "I should say so! I never forgot it all these years . . . though I can't for the life of me remember that boy's name . . . but oh, my goodness, I should say it was a treat! Dancin' 'til one o'clock! The food! You wouldn't believe!" She lapsed into a moment's silent reverie. "Never did get up there again."

"Never?"

Matty shook her head. "Once is enough. Spend too much time in that kind of life . . . well, you start thinkin' more of yourself than's proper."

Crisp couldn't tell if his eyes were open, but he was seeing both Matty and Gammidge as well as a roomful of young women in pink and yellow chiffon dancing with straight-backed young men in white slacks and blue blazers. And threading her way through the dancing couples was Amanda Murphy, radiant in her black body stocking, billowing multicolored skirt, and flowing red hair. Her back was always to him now. Always walking away, never responding to his calls.

His consciousness was trying to rally from the quagmire of his thoughts. "Buttons," he said. "Labor Day dance . . ."

"Did you hear that?" said Matty. No young mother could be prouder of her infant's first words. "He picks up bits and pieces of what we say. Who said anything about buttons?" she asked herself aloud. "Will you be stayin' to supper?"

The phone rang and Matty rushed off to answer it.

"Don't leave me now," said Gammidge. He shook Crisp gently by the knee. "The water's too deep for me."

All of a sudden the dancers were up to their ankles in water. The music played on, but Amanda ran toward the door, screaming. He called out to her. "Stay where you are! I'm coming!"

Of course, she was already dead. Someone else would have to save her now.

"That's Mr. Hanson on the phone, Mr. Gammidge," said Matty. "He wants you." Crisp convulsed slightly. His mouth was moving, but he only groaned. "He's havin' one of his dreams," Matty explained.

Gammidge rose slowly and made his way toward the hall. "Does he do that often?"

"A lot lately," Matty replied. "Ever since they found that girl up at the quarry. I've never seen him so upset."

Matty sat down, emptied a small bundle of fiddleheads into her apron, and began removing the stems. She couldn't make out Gammidge's end of the phone conversation, nor did his responses give much away. Not that she was listening intentionally. That would be eavesdropping, so she listened unintentionally.

She heard the phone replaced in its cradle and anticipated Gammidge's footsteps, but they didn't come. He must be just standing there, she thought. Doing nothing. The longer he did nothing, the more she wanted to find out why. "What do you suppose he's up to?" she whispered to Crisp. She rose halfway and craned her neck toward the kitchen door. "Can't see anything."

All at once she heard his footsteps approaching. "Here he comes!" She sat down a little too promptly, spilling a handful of fiddleheads onto the floor. "Oh, now there, I've done it!" Folding her apron carefully around the fiddleheads still in her lap, she got down on her hands and knees and began retrieving the escapees.

Gammidge helped her. "When does the medicine wear off?" he asked. His face was flushed, his tone insistent.

"Well, that depends when he takes it," said Matty. She resumed her seat, cradling the young fern fronds in her lap.

"No, I mean how long does it usually take to wear off? You know, the . . ." He tapped his forehead with his forefinger.

"Oh," said Matty, "he's usually himself in three to four hours. That's how long it seems to last. Hard to get him to take it durin' the day, the way he's s'posed to. I usually have to get after him somethin' fierce. He must've been hurtin' bad."

"He took it about a half hour ago."

"He'll be out like Rip van Winkle for a while now," said Matty.

"I'll be back this afternoon. I've got a few errands to run," said Gammidge. "Would you mind if I stayed here tonight?"

"Not a'tall," said Matty. She was a more-the-merrier type of person. "The more the merrier! I'll have supper at five-thirty . . . I know mainland folk like to eat late. How's pork chops, applesauce, candied yams, rice, fiddleheads, and sweet pickles?" She'd made it up as she went along. Nice to know she hadn't lost her touch despite a long, cold winter and bodies frozen in ice.

"Sounds wonderful!" said Nate. All he'd had to eat all day was a stale doughnut and the slice of pie, for which it was hard not to feel guilty.

"I don't have a thing for dessert," Matty apologized, "just some leftover apple pie and ice cream. 'Course, there's that banana bread, but that's days old. And some molasses cookies, but I'd have to defrost 'em. There is that lemon meringue pie I got over at the ladies circle supper night 'fore last, but you don't know who made it. I just buy them to help out, don't you know? Winston eats 'em, but he's been a bachelor so long, he don't know better. Never you mind," she said, patting her new lodger on the back. "I'll bake a thing or two this afternoon."

"I need to talk to him when he . . . when he—"

"Wakes up," said Matty.

"Wakes up," Gammidge echoed. He was going to say "recovers." "It's very important."

"I GOT THE INFORMATION straight from the horse's mouth," said Leeman. He gave his black corduroys a hitch and made himself comfortable by the fire. "My sister's brother-in-law Hubby collects the dry cleanin' over there. He knows them people personally. You get to, you know, when you work on their laundry like that."

Being back among the living was a double-edged sword for Crisp. It was good to be lucid. It was not good to be lucid and in pain. It wasn't as bad as it had been, though. Perhaps life would return to relative normalcy one day, or as normal as possible with a deficit of fingers and toes.

It took a long time, upon waking, for dreams to separate themselves from reality in his mind. Eventually, however, he distilled the things he'd seen, heard, and thought from those he'd only imagined.

"So, young McKenniston did have a blue blazer?"

"Sure," said Leeman. "Sure did. Blue as . . ." He wanted to come up with the kind of clever analogy so highly esteemed in the poolroom, but nothing came readily to mind. The only thing he could think of was the sky, but it wasn't that kind of blue. It was dark blue. Navy blue. "Blue as the navy," he said, then winced. He hated analogies. "I just called him up and asked him to look in his records."

"That was good of him," said Crisp.

"Would've been if he'd had to," Leeman replied. "But he didn't."

"No?"

"Nope." Leeman leaned back, folded his arms behind his neck, and crossed his legs. "He knew right off the top of his head, just like that." He snapped his fingers. "Like I said, he knows all them people real well. Sees 'em every summer."

"I see."

"He said Neddy wore that same jacket every year, just for the Labor Day dance. Kept it there just for the purpose. Them folks can afford to do that—buy a jacket just for one dance."

"The Labor Day dance," Crisp repeated thoughtfully, remembering Matty's comments to Gammidge. "And did he go to the dance last year?"

"He sure did," said Leeman. "That's why Hubby remembered right away. One of the McKenniston people, staff you know, they picked up the outfit a day or two before the dance, like always—he left it with Hubby all year—but the coat never came back."

"What do you mean?"

"The coat . . . it never came back with the rest of the outfit—the white pants and shirt—to be dry-cleaned and put away."

"Strange."

"I'd say so," Leeman agreed. "Every year the whole outfit got dry-cleaned."

"Perhaps it was torn, or soiled," Crisp hypothesized.

"Well, even if it was, Hubby would've ended up with it. That's what he does, clean 'em and mend 'em."

"Lost, then?" Crisp ventured.

"I doubt it," Leeman said confidently. "Not much place to get lost up there at the club. 'Sides, they're a pretty close group up there. If he laid it down somewheres, somebody would've got it to him, or least've got it to Hubby. He called, but the house was closed up by that time. Everyone left right after Labor Day."

"Excellent!" said Crisp.

"That helps?" asked Leeman. He couldn't see how. "I didn't do much. Just a phone call."

"Don't underestimate your contribution, Leeman," said Crisp. "Now, I wonder if I could get you to do one more little chore."

"Sure!"

"Well . . . it may involve some risk."

Leeman instantly regretted having volunteered so hastily. "What kind?"

"Well, you may have to do a little climbing, " said Crisp, taking the measure of his man.

"How high?"

"Just a foot or two, on a stepladder."

"Oh, shoot," said Leeman. "That's nothin'. I spend half the day on a stepladder, more than a foot or two. Have to reach them top shelves in back. You seen them little pine tree deodorizers up on that shelf near the milk cooler? I got to get up and dust them once or twice a year. That's the highest place in the store, I guess," he said proudly. "Good thing I ain't prone to nosebleeds."

It was impossible to tell whether he meant this as a joke, so Crisp ignored it.

"Good," said Crisp. He doubted that Leeman would undertake the mission if he knew the real danger—being discovered with his fingers in the belly of a certain tree. "Then it will be easy for you."

Crisp acquainted his assistant with the particulars of the task. "I think you'll find what we're looking for way down in the hole. You may have to dig around a bit."

"What is it?"

"You'll see," said Crisp.

"The plot thickens," Leeman said behind his hands, with a wink and a roll of the eyes.

As long as it wasn't further thickened with Leeman's blood, thought Crisp. Leeman was a favorite. "But it's very important that nobody knows," Crisp said. "Don't let anybody see you. Understand?"

"Sure," said Leeman, a little disquieted by the look in Crisp's eyes and the earnestness in his voice. "Sure. No one will see. I know how to get down there without even goin' up by the house. There's that old path down by the shore."

The path Mostly had taken from the cemetery the day they buried Amanda Murphy, thought Crisp. Mostly was dead.

"No one will see," Leeman reassured him.

"It's very important they don't," Crisp reiterated. "That would ruin everything."

"Winston, there's a young lady to see you," said Matty. It was strange to see her so flustered. "Says she come to check up on you."

"Well," said Leeman, "I'll be off to do that . . . errand." He winked. "I'll let you know what I find out."

Crisp stopped him halfway out the door. "Leeman!" Leeman turned. "Thanks. I appreciate . . . everything."

"No problem," Leeman replied with a wave and a smile. Crisp couldn't shake the feeling that this would be the last anyone saw of Leeman Russell alive. He hoped he was wrong.

"He's not sneaking you food off your diet, is he?" The question preceded Sarah Quinn as she passed Leeman in the doorway.

Leeman greeted her a little nervously, the way he greeted all pretty girls. "Hi, Sarah."

"Hello, Leeman." The good-bye remained unspoken as Leeman went off on his errand.

"I think I'm being a pretty good patient," said Crisp. "You can ask Matty." Sarah wouldn't have to go far to do so, since that worthy was at her shoulder. "Matty, have you met Sarah Quinn?"

"Sarah Quinn?" said Matty, putting a chubby arm around the girl's waist. "Why, I haven't seen you since you was this big!" She held her hand about thigh high. "My, haven't you come up a lovely

thing! Go on in and sit down! I'll bring you some tea. Winston says
you took good care of him," she continued as she bustled down the
hall to the kitchen. "He said you might be comin' by to check in on
him!" she hollered. "But I was half expectin' . . . well, I don't know
what I was expectin'! She's a fine-looking young woman, isn't she,
Winston?"

Crisp knew Matty was yelling at him, but he couldn't make out
what she said. "What did she say?" he asked Sarah.

"It's not important," said Sarah. She sat on the footstool beside his chair and put her bag on the floor. "How are you doing?"

The patient nodded a so-so nod.

"No better?"

"A little, actually."

"Have you been taking your medicine?"

He thought of Timothy Hill. "Yes," he said sheepishly.

She positioned herself in front of him. "Let me see your foot."
She lifted it carefully and, rearranging the billowing folds of her
oversized Yale sweatshirt so she could see what she was doing,
started to unwind the bandages. "I'm sorry I didn't come by sooner.
Things have just been too busy."

Her head was bent to her work. Crisp watched her hands; their
motion was experienced. Fluid. Had the bandage been an instrument, the music she made on it would have been flawless and lovely.
As the last of the wrapping fell off, he looked away. He didn't want
to see what wasn't there.

There was a commotion in the entryway. The door slammed,
and heavy footsteps padded down the hall.

"That will be Mr. Gammidge," Crisp said quietly.

"Winston!" said Gammidge as he bowled into the room. The sight
of Sarah brought him up short. "Oh, I didn't know you had . . .
a nurse?"

"Guardian angel," said Crisp. Sarah smiled. She didn't look at
Gammidge, though. She was applying the new bandage. "Sarah
Quinn, this is Nate Gammidge."

"Pleased," said Nate. Sarah smiled and nodded slightly. "Anyway," Gammidge continued, "I need to talk to you." He was clearly agitated. "All hell's broken loose."

Crisp held his finger to his lips and shook his head slightly. "Let's not trouble this young lady with all that," he said softly, though the meaning in his eyes was severe.

"Here's your tea," said Matty as she entered the room with a platter laden with cups, saucers, and assorted baked goods. "Why, Mr. Gammidge. I didn't know you was here. Was you the one who made all that noise a minute ago? I looked out but didn't see anybody." She arranged the pastries on the tray according to color and placed it within easy reach of Crisp and his guardian angel. "Thought the front porch roof must've caved in again." She winked at Sarah.

"Sorry, Matty," Gammidge apologized. He caught Crisp's eye. "How much longer will you be?"

"Sarah?" said Crisp.

"Done!" said Sarah. She patted the new bandage lightly and stood up. "I'll get out of your way. Don't forget to take your medicine. Here's the new supply Doctor Pagitt ordered. You can throw away the others—they were just for the time-being." She wagged a finger at him. "You be good, now."

"What about your tea?" Matty fussed.

"How about if we have it in the other room?" Sarah suggested. "So the men can talk." She picked up the implements and tucked them in her bag, which she left on the piano bench.

The ladies left the room. Their uninterrupted flow of chatter from the kitchen was music to Crisp. Amazing, he thought, how women can talk and listen at the same time, often about completely unrelated subjects. "Take a seat, Nate," Crisp offered, indicating the one nearest him. "Now, what's happened?"

Gammidge pulled his chair so close that he was practically nose to nose with Crisp. "Remember what I said this morning, about someone leaking information to the press?"

"You suspected it might have been me," said Crisp. He did recall.

"Well, you have to look at every possibility," Gammidge replied with an apologetic shrug.

"Of course you do," said Crisp. "I understand. However, let me assure you—"

"I know you didn't," said Gammidge. "Besides, it's all out now."

"What is?"

"Everything!" Gammidge stood up and began pacing à la Hanson. "Mitchell Pomfrey called Hanson from the paper—"

"A reporter?"

"The editor," said Gammidge. "He wanted to corroborate some facts."

"There were reporters here this morning," said Crisp.

Gammidge was taken aback. "Here? For you?"

Crisp nodded.

"How could they possibly know you had anything to do with—"

"Oh, I think it was more about my . . . accident. They were curious, naturally, with all the stories in circulation. They were grasping for straws, really. They did know about the buttons, though. Nothing specific, just that some buttons had been sent to Augusta to be checked for fingerprints."

"Well," said Gammidge, coming to rest briefly on the opposite side of the coffee table, his hands on his hips, "they're all done speculating now."

"How so?"

"They found out about the Calderwood boy's fingerprints on the dead girl's neck."

"That was common knowledge already."

"On the island, yes," said Gammidge. "But Hanson applied a little pressure to Pomfrey to keep it out of the paper. The *Free Press* got wind of it, though. That's why Pomfrey called, to warn Hanson they'd have to print. Couldn't afford to be scooped in their own backyard on something like this.

"But that's not all. They know we found Neddy McKenniston's prints on those buttons."

Just when it seemed things couldn't get any worse.

"What do you think people are going to make of that when it comes out?"

Crisp's mind was racing. Secrecy was his only advantage. Without it, he lost even the slim control he had over developments. Still, he couldn't help thinking that, whomever he was up against, they would have done well at the NSA. "This came out today?" he asked.

"The story's being written today," Gammidge replied. "Monday the issue hits the streets, and the compost hits the fan." He paused thoughtfully. "Can you imagine what people are going to make of this story? Forty-year-old makeup, sea sand, double strangling, a dead man's fingerprints . . . the senator's son! This thing might make the *Enquirer* after all!"

Crisp held up his finger again. "Let's not alarm the ladies," he cautioned.

"Sorry," said Gammidge. He resumed his seat.

"I think the paper may have to change its story, once the exhumation is—"

"There isn't going to be an exhumation," Gammidge interrupted.

"What do you mean?" said Crisp. The residual softness fell from his eyes, revealing something determined and alarming.

"Hanson called it off," Gammidge stuttered. "The attorney general told him to."

"Michael Jessup?"

"Jessup," Gammidge repeated.

"Get me the phone," said Crisp.

"It won't do any good, Professor," said Gammidge. "He's gone on vacation."

"What?"

"He left this afternoon for two weeks on some island in the

Caribbean. He didn't leave a forwarding address, if you know what I mean."

"I don't understand this."

"He's running for governor next year."

Crisp deflated against the back of his chair. "Politician," he said. He seldom swore. It was a reflexive epithet.

"So," said Gammidge after a brief silence. "What do we do now?"

"I'm sorry to have to say this, Nate," said Crisp. His mind had not been quiet in the interval. "But it's not my problem anymore."

"But—"

"One of the conditions of my agreeing to take an unofficial interest in this case was that I be given complete control," Crisp reasoned. "That's no longer the case. So," he shrugged, "there's nothing I can do. I wish I could."

Crisp stood up and retied his robe. "You're right about what's going to happen when that paper hits the streets Monday," he said calmly. "And if the national media gets hold of it . . ." He was halfway to the hall door. He turned and stopped. "But the worst of it," he said, "is that innocent people are going to be hurt. It's been my experience that in a business like this, even when everything's over with, an aura of suspicion follows anyone who was implicated at any stage. They're scarred for life."

"But Professor—"

"Of course, it could all be avoided," Crisp interposed. "The answer is in Andy Calderwood's casket."

"What am I supposed to do?" said Gammidge weakly. Crisp felt sorry for him. He really did. But he had to see the answer for himself.

"Well, I suggest you take a nice hot bath and get dressed for supper," said Crisp. "I'm going to take a nap."

Sarah Quinn came in from the kitchen. "Did I leave my bag in . . . Where's the professor, Mr. Gammidge? What's the matter?"

"Huh?" said Gammidge.

"You don't look well. Is the professor okay?" She picked up his new medicine bottle. "Did he take any of these yet?"

Gammidge took a deep breath and rallied to his senses. "I'm sorry, Miss . . . Quinn?"

"Call me Sarah."

"Sarah," said Gammidge, standing. "What did you say?"

"I asked if the professor was all right," said Sarah. "If he'd taken his medicine."

"I don't think so," said Gammidge with a shake of the head. "I mean, yes, he's all right, but I don't think he took his medicine. He just went up for a nap before supper. Seemed fine." He retrieved a bag from the piano bench. "Is this what you were looking for?"

"Yes, thanks," said Sarah, taking it from him. "I found it, Matty!" she called. "It was on the piano stool! Well," she continued, lowering her voice, "remind him to take his medicine after supper, on a full stomach. Okay?"

"Aye, aye," said Gammidge, snapping to potbellied attention with a mock salute. Sarah laughed. Gammidge was struck, as Crisp had been, by the music of her laughter.

"Then I'll leave the medicine with you," she said, placing it on top of the piano. "Good-bye, Mr. Gammidge."

Gammidge watched after her as she collected her coat, picked up her bag, and started down the hall, her shadow trailing dutifully behind. He wondered how many shadows he was trailing.

Dinner was conducted in relative quiet, meaning there was little conversation between the men. Matty, of course, held forth as usual. Gammidge didn't hear what she was saying, though. He was too preoccupied by Crisp's calm silence. It implied something. Demanded something. Once or twice he glanced at Crisp, half expecting him to be staring back. But he wasn't. He was eating his pea soup, nodding at Matty now and then with a benign smile. What does he want? Gammidge thought. What does he expect from me?

Nothing interrogates a man so deeply as silence. Crisp had planted a seed, what he called a "conscience worm," and he could almost hear it working its way through Gammidge's thought process. You have to know your man, and Crisp knew his, evidenced by the fact that Gammidge, no mean devotee of the dinner table, was playing with his food absentmindedly. Thought had so jammed his mental works that even the mechanical process of eating had slowed to a standstill. Billy Pringle probably ate the same way.

"Mr. Gammidge," said Crisp. Gammidge, surprised from his intricate web of thought, dropped his spoon in the soup.

"What? Yes?"

"I was wondering . . . ," said Crisp slowly, "would you pass the butter?"

Gammidge passed the butter.

"No you don't," said Matty, intercepting the artery-clogging cube. "I don't know how you think you could get away with that, Winston. Right in front of my eyes! Your brain must be foggy. You have margarine." She supplanted the margarine for the butter and passed it along.

"You know," said Crisp to Matty, though he was looking at Gammidge, "I could sneak down to the kitchen tonight and open up the refrigerator and take out the butter, and you'd never know."

What was that supposed to mean? thought Gammidge. What did butter have to do with anything?

"Oh, you think so, do you?" chortled Matty. "Well, just you try it and you'll see what happens."

"Not a thing," said Crisp with a sly smile. "It would be very late at night. The whole town would be fast asleep." He looked at Gammidge. "Penobscot Island has very little nightlife, Mr. Gammidge. As you may have noticed. People generally turn in quite early."

"Oh," said Gammidge. The conscience worm finally drilled its way home. "That hasn't been my particular experience."

"Be that as it may," said Matty. "This old house creaks like Methuselah's knees. I can just see you tryin' to sneak past my room now!"

"You must want that butter awful bad," Gammidge ventured.

"Oh, he does!" Matty affirmed. "Butter and chocolate and eggs and bacon. He'd have 'em all for breakfast if he could. And top it off with ice cream."

"I'd have it all by breakfast," Crisp nodded into his plate.

"What if you got caught?" said Gammidge.

"Well, I was speaking figuratively," said Crisp, looking up. "I wouldn't get it by myself. Matty's right. I'd be too clumsy. I'd need an accomplice."

"An accomplice?" said Gammidge.

"This is the silliest thing I've ever heard," said Matty with a giggle. "Two grown men plottin' to come down and steal the butter! Besides, what would you put it on? There isn't anything for toast except that horrid packaged white bread I use for stuffin'."

"I think just the butter would be enough," said Crisp.

Gammidge spoke hopefully. "In fact, I doubt we'd even have to take it out of the refrigerator. Would we, Professor?"

"Butter?" said Matty incredulously. "By itself?"

"Just a peek would do."

"I think both your trolleys have jumped the track!" said Matty. She laughed heartily. "I'll tell you what. If you want to peek at the butter, you can do it right now"—she waved the butter dish under Crisp's nose—"and save us all a lot of trouble. There! How's that?"

"Just not the same, Matty," said Crisp. "The best time to steal butter is about midnight. Wouldn't you say so, Mr. Gammidge?"

"Oh," said Gammidge. "I really don't think . . . I don't think it's a good idea. You never know how much trouble you can get in trying to do something like that."

"Probably fall down stairs and break your neck," Matty prophesied. "And even if you don't, you'll have me to contend with sooner or later. And cholesterol in the meantime. That's what. Now, stop this talk and make sense for a change, let's."

Crisp tapped the place his watch would be if he had one and mouthed the words "twelve o'clock."

"I don't know . . . ," said Gammidge.

"Oh, honestly!" said Matty. She stood and began gathering up the plates.

Gammidge looked at the old grandmother clock in the hall. "Five hours," he said. "You'd better take your medicine now if you want to be up stealing butter at midnight."

Crisp took the proffered bottle. "I think I'll turn in early, Matty," he said as he rose slowly. He winked and patted her on the shoulder as she whisked by. "Been years since I stole butter."

Matty shook her head and frowned a not-too-convincing frown. "Boys," she said.

Crisp tottered off up the stairs, leaving Gammidge alone amidst the residue of dinner and the whirlwind that was Matty. The up-stairs landing creaked loudly under Crisp's weight.

So that's what Methuselah's knees sounded like.

"Midnight," said Gammidge to himself.

WHEN CRISP AWOKE AT 11:30, he was swaddled in pain. Everything hurt. Especially his head. And his hand. And his foot. And his throat—that hadn't hurt in a long time. He fumbled in the darkness for the brown plastic bottle, popped it open, and greedily swallowed two pills. Maybe three or four.

He lay there in a thick sweat, breathing rapidly and irregularly, waiting for the pain to subside. In a few minutes he felt much better. This time, though, there had been no tingle. Instead, the relief came in a block, all at once. The periphery of his reason was embroidered with fuzz. Paradoxically, the core of his brain seemed completely free of its customary clutter. He could concentrate with absolute clarity; if only he could find something to concentrate on.

He sat up in bed and swung his feet to the floor. They didn't want to stay there. They were filled with helium and wanted to float like balloons. Big orange and yellow balloons with happy faces painted on them. He put his hands on his knees, pushed as hard as he could, and giggled.

"Winston."

Suddenly the carnival that was setting up shop in Winston's mind collapsed. She was back, standing by the little wicker chair in the corner, with her body in the shaft of soft blue light from the street lamp and her head in the shadows. He didn't look. He didn't have to. He knew.

"Amanda," he said. His heart was beating him to death, and his skull seemed to expand and contract with every pulse of blood to his brain. He hung his head and cried aloud. "I can't do anything!" he sobbed. "Stop bleeding!" His voice fell and his tears trailed away. "You're not supposed to be here," he said. "Stop hurting."

There was a movement in the shadows. She was walking toward him! He saw her feet through the haze in his eyes as they crossed the wicker web of light traced on the floor by the chair. She stood in front of him. "Amanda!" he whispered between sobs. He slid from the bed and onto his knees and threw his arms around her legs. She was cold as slate. Her skirt folded around his face and shoulders. It was damp and smelled of sea salt and lilacs. "Amanda!" he cried, not daring to look up at her. "Don't be dead!" He was thinking with such clarity and focus that the ragged edge of his thoughts cut deep gashes in the membrane of logic.

"Why?" she said quietly. Her hand, brushing softly over his head, tore his heart from him in a torrent of uncontrolled anguish and tears.

"Because I love you!" he shouted. He'd never said those words before, not even to his mother or father. He'd always held the words suspect. They came too easily. Without a price. Even now they sounded strange in his ears, but there were no other words that could frame his feelings. A drop of liquid fell heavily on the nape of his neck. Warm. Thick. It oozed down his back. If only it had been the blood of Christ. "I didn't mean to kill you!" he bawled in extremes of sorrow.

Her hand continued caressing his balding head.

"Did I?" he said, his words echoing in the silence. The clockwork of his reason had come apart. Gears and wheels were falling from their hubs and crashing into one another. He began frantically rubbing his eye sockets with the heels of his hands. "What did I say?"

There was no answer.

"I didn't kill you, did I?" he asked, almost frantically.

Still no answer. She was gone. He was alone on the floor, knee deep in tears. "So many," he whimpered. He raised his eyes toward the window, and the light edged his tears with softness. "All loved by someone." The smell of mist was thick through the open window. The foghorn off Lane's Island croaked its lonely note of judgment. "I've killed them all." His conscience worm had come home, and it was a monster.

"Crisp!"

Gammidge's voice came from the hall. He was tapping on the door with his knuckle. "Crisp? You awake?"

Did it make a difference? He couldn't tell anymore. He got up from his knees, stumbled to the door, and opened it.

"Good Lord!" Gammidge exclaimed as Crisp nearly collapsed into his arms. He dragged him to the bed and sat him down. "Are you having a heart attack?"

Crisp shook his head. Unfortunately not.

With one hand Gammidge grabbed a straight-backed desk chair from the corner and pulled it to him and with the other hand held Crisp steady on the bed. "What happened?" he asked. He was face to face with Crisp, searching his eyes intently. "Do you want me to call Matty?"

Crisp tried to respond, but he couldn't. He simply shook his head and mumbled.

"Can you sit there for a moment?" Crisp nodded. "Good."

Gammidge reached for the wash basin, wrung out a facecloth, and dabbed Crisp's face with it.

The cold water, wiping away the tears and the fevered sweat on his brow, was like a slap in the face. Crisp inhaled sharply and began blinking rapidly, each blink scraping away a layer of fog from his brain. The room came into focus and, shortly thereafter, so did Gammidge.

"Gammidge?" he said weakly. "Nate?"

"That's right," Gammidge reassured him. "I thought I'd lost you for a minute. What happened?"

Crisp rubbed his face vigorously with the palms of his hands. "I'm not sure," he said softly. "I guess the operation is . . . taking its toll on me. I'm not recovering as fast as I'd hoped." It occurred to him that he wasn't recovering at all, but he didn't say so.

"Have you taken your medicine?" said Gammidge, picking up the bottle and inspecting it. It was still open. "Seems so. Doesn't help?"

"I can't tell," said Crisp. "I can't imagine the pain would be worse if I hadn't taken it. Still, I wouldn't want to find out."

"Well, take some more as soon as we're done . . . with the butter," Gammidge commanded. "Then you can see if you can get it changed in the morning."

"Good idea," said Crisp. "The doctor's coming by."

The bones in Crisp's legs seemed to collapse as he tried to stand. He sank back on the bed. "Everything seems to be going at once," he said. Maybe this was what it was like to die of old age. He wondered if his finger and toes had been given a proper burial. They'd served him long and well.

"I think we'd better give this up for tonight," said Gammidge, making no attempt to conceal his relief. "You're not up to it."

Crisp protested. "If that news gets out—"

"It's too late to make any difference anyhow," Gammidge replied. "Paper's already set, like I said."

"But if we can prove . . ." Crisp began in protest. Once again he tried to stand. But it was no use. Even with Gammidge's help he couldn't take so much as a step. Gammidge directed him back to the bed. "You take some medicine and get to sleep," he said. "We'll just have to play the cards as they come." He read the directions on the bottle: " 'One or two as needed every four hours for pain.' When did you take it last?"

Crisp was trying desperately to think. The fog was closing in around his consciousness again. He hated the feeling. Did the medicine bring it on or ease it? He couldn't remember. "I don't remember," he said wearily. "I can't think straight."

"Well," said Gammidge as he emptied a pill into his hand. "I don't guess one more will kill you. Here, take this and get some sleep." He tipped the pill into Crisp's hand and passed him the glass of water from his bedside table. "We'll talk it over in the morning and decide what to do."

Crisp meekly took the medicine and lay down on the bed. In a moment he felt much better. Foggier, yes. But much better. The pillow crinkled around his ears like a nicely starched shroud. Perhaps Amanda Murphy was under there somewhere, with all the others. It was an inviting thought. At least they were his ghosts.

A profound darkness imploded on his consciousness and, for the first time in a very long time, he slept the dreamless sleep of the dead.

Sunday morning was clear and cool. Spring was building more and more insurmountable defenses against the possibility of a surprise resurgence by straggling troops of winter, lost on the retreat northward. There was very little wind, and what there was moved slowly, burdened by the heavy scents of the season.

Matty was not moving slowly, though. She was up early and, without even taking time to bathe or make her bed, rushed downstairs to check the butter. However, as she reached the bottom of the stairs, her investigation was interrupted by a knock at the door.

"My land sakes," she said as she hitched the purple cotton cord on her robe a little tighter under her bosom and bustled down the hall. "Who do you s'pose that could be at this hour?" She cast an inquiring glance at the grandmother clock. "Six-thirty," she said. "Later than I thought." She could see a sun-drenched silhouette through the frosted glass. "A girl." She opened the door a crack. "Oh, it's you! I might have known! Come on in!" She opened the door the rest of the way, and Sarah Quinn drifted in on the sunbeam.

She'd taken time to bathe, thought Matty. *She* looked chipper and lovely, her hair was done up, and her bed was probably made as well. Matty didn't often feel shabby. She did now. She gathered her collar a little tighter around her neck. "If you don't mind waitin' a few minutes, I'll have some fresh coffee on." She was hanging up Sarah's coat. "I overslept this morning somethin' awful! I think my alarm must not've gone off. Come with me, dear. You can sit in the kitchen while I mix up some muffins."

"Actually," said Sarah, stopping at the foot of the stairs. "I've already eaten, thanks. I just dropped by to see how he's doing." She gestured upstairs.

"Oh," said Matty, hesitating slightly. There were several things to be considered, propriety not the least of them. After all, she wasn't a *real* nurse. "Well, he's probably sleepin'."

"I hope so," Sarah replied with a smile. "I hope he had a good night."

"Well, don't you think you might just wait 'til he comes down?" Matty suggested, although Sarah was already halfway up the stairs.

"I can't," she said in a strong whisper. "I have to catch the boat. Don't worry, I won't be a minute. I just want to make sure he's okay and see to it he gets his medicine on time. Then he can go back to sleep, if he wants."

"Well," said Matty weakly, but she was talking to herself. Sarah was gone and Winston's bedroom door had already closed behind her. "I don't know what I'm supposed to do anymore," she said as she trundled off to the kitchen. "I know *I* wouldn't go to a gentleman's room. Not if he was Moses and I was Florence Nightingale."

All at once there was a cry from the top of the stairs. Matty, who hadn't yet crossed the threshold, stopped in her tracks and looked up at the landing. Sarah was standing there, clearly in a state of shock. She was holding something in her hand. "Matty!" she yelled. "Call Doctor Pagitt!"

"What's the matter?" said Matty, starting up the stairs.

"Don't waste time, Matty," Sarah ordered. "The professor's in a coma. I've been giving him the wrong medicine!"

"You what!" said Matty, frozen on the stairs. "How did you do that?"

Gammidge's door opened and he emerged from his room, his plaid bathrobe hanging from his shoulders. "What's going on?" he said sleepily. "What's all this noise?"

"Matty!" Sarah said sharply. "Go call Doctor Pagitt now! Don't waste any more time!"

Matty ran down the stairs to the phone and began scanning the list of emergency numbers on the wall. There were only three. "Merciful Lord," she said. "What's the number? Ah, there it is!" She began dialing.

By this time Gammidge was at Sarah's side. She was looking at the bottle of medicine and mumbling over and over, "I can't believe I made such a stupid mistake!"

"What is it?" said Gammidge. He took the bottle from her. "Didn't he take his medicine?"

Sarah laughed at the irony. "Oh, he took it all right," she said. "If only he hadn't!"

"What do you mean?" said Gammidge, gripping Sarah by the shoulders and shaking her. "Talk sense, girl. What happened?"

"I gave him the wrong medicine!" she replied. No sooner were the words out of her mouth than she burst into tears. "I think he's dead!"

Gammidge ran into the bedroom and found Crisp lying peacefully on his bed. His hands were at his side. His mouth was slightly opened. He could be sleeping, but there was no movement to in-dicate breathing. The chair Gammidge had used the night before was still at the bedside. He sat down and placed his fingers on Crisp's pulse points. Nothing. He shook him. No response. He ran back out onto the landing and leaned over the rail. "Matty, do you have the doctor?"

Matty was fussing into the receiver. "What am I supposed to say?" she pleaded, looking up at Sarah and Gammidge as if to heaven. "I've got him."

"Tell him the professor's been given the wrong medicine," said Sarah, who seemed to be getting the better of her wits, "and he's had an overdose."

Matty repeated the words into the receiver and listened to the response. "He wants to know what his vital signs are."

"None," said Sarah flatly.

"None," Gammidge affirmed.

"None," Matty parroted into the phone. "What does that mean?" Again she listened, then hung up the receiver.

"What did he say?" Gammidge demanded.

"He says to give him some CPR until he gets here. He's on his way," said Matty as she ascended the stairs. The letters were as fa-miliar to her as Nubian hieroglyphics. "Do either of you have some?"

"I can do it," said Sarah.

"So can I," said Gammidge. "I'll help." He took Sarah by the arm and dragged her into the bedroom.

"Do you need anything?" Matty offered as she reached the top of the stairs. Not that she could have done anything if they had. She was beside herself. "Oh, my goodness! How could this have happened? Lord be with him!" She couldn't bring herself to go in, so she stayed on the landing listening with all her might as Gam-midge and Sarah Quinn made life-giving noises. She couldn't imag-ine what they were doing.

A sheet of plywood between the box spring and mattress provided sufficient resistance, so Gammidge decided to forego the option of moving Crisp to the floor. He crossed his palms on Crisp's chest, pushing for all he was worth while Sarah tilted Crisp's head back, clamped his tongue against the back of his lower teeth with her thumb, pinched his nose, and blew deep draughts of air into his mouth. Now and then they would stop to feel for his pulse. Sarah pressed her ear against his lips to listen for a breath. "It's not working," she said frantically.

"Keep it up!" Gammidge ordered as he began pressing again. "Don't stop 'til the doctor gets here!"

"TELL ME EXACTLY WHAT HAPPENED," said Hanson. He was sitting across the coffee table from Sarah Quinn, speaking in soft, matter-of-fact tones in order to calm the distraught girl.

"I've already told them!" Sarah responded sharply. "I told Doctor Pagitt and Mr. Gammidge . . ."

The sound of Matty's pathetic moanings as the doctor and Nate Gammidge descended the stairs charged Sarah's eyes with a new torrent of tears. Hanson gently put his finger under her chin and lifted her face. She opened her eyes, perfect mirrors of doubt and confusion, and looked at him.

"He may be all right," he said quietly. "The CPR might have saved his life."

"But he's in a coma! And I'm the one who—"

Hanson put out a reassuring hand near her shoulder but stopped just short of touching her. "Tell me exactly what happened."

Sarah sniffed back an impending deluge. "I . . . I had two bottles of medicine in my purse," she stammered. "One for the professor . . . Mr. Crisp . . . the other for Mrs. Hadley. Doctor Pagitt had asked me to take them 'round. I offered to . . . and . . . I got them mixed up. It wasn't very light in the parlor last night and . . . No!" she said suddenly, as if her words had taken her by surprise. "I just wasn't thinking! That's all! It's my fault!" Once again she buried her face in her hands, and her body trembled with the aftershocks of grief and self-recrimination.

"Just a mistake," said Hanson. He patted her gently on the shoulder. He wasn't good at this sort of thing. Nothing made him feel more ill at ease than a crying woman. He stood up. "This other medicine—for the woman—I'm sure Doctor Pagitt has already—"

"It's still in my purse," said Sarah, trying desperately to regain control of herself. "I was going to take it to her this afternoon."

"Well, it's a good thing you didn't," said Hanson. It was nice to be able to say something comforting.

"No, it wouldn't have hurt her."

"No?"

Sarah put her arms down, raised her head somewhat, and stared at the wall. "Mr. Crisp was taking one to two of his pills. Mrs. Hadley was only taking half a pill every twelve hours." She turned her head and looked at Hanson. "You see? I'd given the professor Mrs. Hadley's medicine and told him to take one to two an hour! It's amazing he's still alive!"

"I see," said Hanson with a shake of the head. "So, even if the woman . . . Mrs. . . . . "

"Hadley."

"Hadley," he repeated. "Even if she had gotten Crisp's medicine, she'd not have taken enough of it to do her any harm?"

"That's right."

"Well," said Hanson in closing, "thank the Lord for small favors." He wasn't sure what that meant, but no one was dead as a result of the mix-up. Not yet, anyway. That was something to be grateful for.

The doctor and Gammidge entered the room. They'd been in the kitchen comforting Matty. Seeing them, Sarah jumped from her seat, ran to the doctor, and threw her arms around him. "Oh, Doctor Pagitt! I'm so sorry! I can't believe I did anything that stupid!"

Pagitt put his arms around her and patted her shoulder. "There, there," he said reassuringly. "It was an accident." He held her at arms' length and looked at her deeply. "Don't ever forget the lesson of it, though."

The admonition freshened her tears. "I won't!" she cried and fell once again into his arms.

Meanwhile, Hanson drew Gammidge aside. "Well?"

Gammidge shrugged. "Coma, as far as he can tell. Drug induced. No way of knowing how deep or how long, or if . . ." His voice trailed off. Hanson stared out the window. "Surprised to find you here so early."

"I came over in the chopper."

"I see," said Gammidge.

"Left it up at the airport."

Gammidge smiled slightly. "Good idea," he said. He studied Hanson for a moment. "Tell me something, Alfred."

Hanson didn't move.

"Why did you call off the exhumation?"

"*I* didn't call it off," he said a little sharply.

"Well, why did Jessup call it off, then?"

Hanson shrugged and exhaled heavily. "Pressure from Washington."

"McKenniston?"

Hanson nodded.

"Crisp wasn't too happy," said Gammidge.

"I imagine not."

"He said he was out of it."

"I don't blame him. I don't know what's going on." Hanson

turned from the window. "Did you find out anything about the leaks?"

Gammidge shook his head. "Just that Crisp wasn't behind it."

"I didn't really think so," said Hanson. "Crisp didn't have any ideas?"

"No," Gammidge replied. "Not that I know of."

Hanson brooded a moment in silence. "Someone's making a fool of me," he said finally. "And when that paper comes out, the whole state's going to know it."

Gammidge nudged Hanson toward the enclosed porch. "Come in here for a minute." He closed the French door after them. "I guess there's no harm in you knowing now," he said softly.

"No harm in my knowing what?"

"He was going to do it anyway," said Gammidge.

Hanson let his expression ask the obvious question.

"Well . . . we were . . . I should say . . ." Hanson's eyebrows reiterated the question. "We were going to exhume the body ourselves," said Gammidge.

Gammidge had expected a scolding of volcanic proportions from his superior. When it was not forthcoming, he was emboldened. "Crisp thinks there's something there that can clean up this whole mess. He wanted to get at it before the paper comes out tomorrow."

Hanson nodded a little. "Did he say what it was?"

"No," said Gammidge. "He just wanted to verify something. I think that photograph gave him some idea."

"Photograph?"

"The Polaroid he borrowed."

"Buttons?" said Hanson, opening his briefcase.

"Maybe," said Gammidge. "But I don't think so. I think it's something else. He said that something didn't fit."

"Didn't fit?"

"Mmm."

Hanson got the Polaroids from a pouch in the cover of his briefcase and looked through them. "He didn't say what? Didn't suggest anything?"

"Not that I recall."

"Here it is," Hanson said, taking from among the others the snapshot Crisp had singled out. He placed it on the table. "See anything?"

"Crisp used a magnifying glass," Gammidge suggested.

Hanson bent closer and studied the photo for a long time. "I don't see anything," he said at last. "Can't even make out the difference in the buttons without the magnifying glass."

"Well, Crisp did," Gammidge said. "He saw something there, but he wanted to make sure."

"Too bad you didn't get to exhume the body," said Hanson as he gathered up his coat. "I'd like to do it myself right about now."

"Well . . . ," Gammidge hazarded, a little animated.

Hanson held up his hand. "Of course, as officers of the court, we can't countermand a direct order from the attorney general."

Gammidge deflated visibly. "Of course not," he said. "By the way, what will happen to Crisp?"

"He'll be here for the time being," said Hanson. "The doctor has him on an IV. Mrs. Gilchrist will take care of him."

"Mrs. Gilchrist?" said Gammidge. "Oh! Matty! Yes. I'm sure she will. Better than he could get at the hospital, probably."

"No doubt," Hanson said distractedly. His thoughts were elsewhere. "I wish he'd gotten what he was looking for. All hell's going to break loose tomorrow."

"Did you find out about Mostly?"

"Mostly what?"

"Sanborn."

"Oh . . . the body," said Hanson, reducing Mostly to his lowest common denominator. "Well, sort of. There's no telling if he was dead before he went over, but I found blood there . . . at the top of the cliff. I imagine that the murderer cudgeled him, propped him up in the golf cart, and drove to the edge. Then when he transferred the body to the driver's side, it slumped over and some blood spilled on the ground."

"You've had it tested?"

Hanson nodded. "It matched," he said. "Common type, though."

A slow minute or two passed. "Are you going back to the mainland?" asked Gammidge.

Hanson sniffed. "I'd like to copy a page from my boss's book and take off for the Caribbean for a week or two." He stared at Gammidge for a long time but was looking through him. "Somebody's got to face the music, I guess."

Hanson picked up his coat and hat and, nodding a farewell in Matty's direction, made for the door. Gammidge followed. "Meanwhile, you hang around here. Keep an eye on him. Let me know if there's any change."

Gammidge held the door open for his boss. "I hope he makes it," he said half to himself.

"That would be helpful," said Hanson. He pulled on his gloves and glared disapprovingly at some gathering clouds. "Stupid accident," he said. "Stupid girl." He trudged off down the walk.

" 'Dead Man's Fingerprints Found on Strangling Victim.' " Matty's hands were trembling as she read the paper aloud.

Gammidge didn't want to hear it. "Is there any more of that blueberry sauce?"

"Compote," Matty corrected, pushing the compote toward him without raising her eyes from the paper. "Listen to this . . ." Gammidge didn't want to listen. " 'The customary silence of this quiet island community has been shattered by a series of bizarre events. The apparent attempted murder of an elderly retiree . . .' I wouldn't call Winston elderly, Mr. Gammidge. Would you?"

To Gammidge the operative word was "murder," but Matty had known Crisp a lot longer. "I'll have some of that coffee now," said Gammidge, hoping the request would awaken Matty's customary hospitality and pry her from the paper.

"It's on the stove." Matty continued. "Elderly retiree, elderly . . . here it is. . . . 'an elderly retiree on the estate of Senator McKenniston (D-Mass.) prompted an investigation by state and local authorities, which led to the discovery of the body of McKenniston's caretaker, Wilbert Sanborn, at the foot of a cliff on the property.

" ' "He seems to have fallen from the cliff and died from head injuries," said assistant coroner Jaret Polkey.' Some Polkeys have a summer place out on Blackberry Island. You know them?" Matty didn't wait for a reply. "Used to be clam diggers." She looked over the top of her glasses knowingly. "Just goes to show." She resumed reading.

" 'When asked if there was any connection between the incidents and the discovery earlier this spring of the body of Amanda Murphy, a summer guest at the McKenniston estate, in one of the island's quarries, constable Luther Kingsbury said, "There's no evidence that the incidents are related."

" 'At the same time, Kingsbury was unable to answer this reporter's questions, based on information received from sources close to the investigation—' "

" 'Sources close to the investigation,' " Gammidge said in disgust. "Damn press can get away with anything saying that."

"Oh, my Lord," said Matty, who had been reading to herself during Gammidge's editorial aside, "listen to this! 'Unable to answer this reporter's questions, based on information received . . .' " she skipped ahead, " ' . . . that the fingerprints of one Andrew Calderwood were found on the neck of Ms. Murphy, despite the fact that Calderwood and his brother, Herbert, were killed in an explosion aboard their lobster boat two days prior to Murphy's disappearance'!"

"Well, there it all is in black and white, just exactly like folks have been sayin', more or less!" said Matty, looking quizzically over the top of the newspaper. "Now, you tell me how that can be. It wasn't really Andy Calderwood's fingerprints on that girl, was it, Mr. Gammidge?"

Gammidge looked at her pleadingly. "I can't say anything one way or the other, Matty. We're in the middle of an official investigation—"

"Oh, for heaven's sake," said Matty indignantly. "Who's goin' to know? Besides, poor Winston's lyin' up there in a coma."

The purport of the addendum was lost on Gammidge. Nevertheless, he felt especially heartless when he reiterated his refusal. "I wish Crisp would pull out of it," he added.

Matty raised the paper and continued reading. " 'Calderwood's body was ordered exhumed by County Coroner Alfred Hanson . . .' That's our Mr. Hanson, isn't it?"

Gammidge nodded.

" 'Hanson . . . earlier this spring. But information on the exhumation is not available at this time, according to Polkey.' " She lowered the paper to her lap. "I heard about that. That was the night everyone was here. Rained somethin' awful. It's a wonder you didn't all catch your death of cold. We heard that's what they was up to," she said in a single breath. "So, that's why."

"What's why?" said Gammidge. He wanted to know.

"Why they dug up Andy Calderwood . . . to see if he was still in there."

It hadn't been that obvious when it was first mentioned to Gammidge, even though he was involved in the official investigation. Then again, he didn't watch soap operas. Matty did.

"He was though, wasn't he?"

"He was," said Gammidge. He didn't feel he was betraying an official trust by making the admission. Everyone in town knew it.

"Then what's all this silliness about his fingerprints bein' on that girl's neck?" Matty continued. "She was strangled, was she?"

"Can't say," said Gammidge hopelessly.

"Oh, for goodness sakes," Matty scoffed. She finished the article. " 'Sources say other revelations are expected to come to light as the investigation continues.' "

"Now!" Gammidge rose suddenly and slammed the table with

the flat of his palm. Matty nearly had heart failure. "Sorry," he said, "but I want to know how the . . . heck these sources know that 'other revelations are expected to come to light'!"

Matty shrugged. "Newspaper people know things like that," she said matter-of-factly. "That's their job."

For Gammidge, however, the press held no such mystical omniscience. They knew no more than they'd been told. The investigation was hemorrhaging internally. Who? Why? One thing was certain: it wasn't Crisp.

The article had made no mention of Matty's housekeeping. Reporters weren't as observant as she thought. She folded the paper neatly along the crease and tucked it in the little space over the breadbox. "Winston will want to read that." Gammidge lifted his tired eyes and looked at her. "When he gets better," she said, as if his recovery was assured.

"When he gets better," Gammidge echoed with a lame smile.

CHAPTER

23

"ANY BETTER?" Matty inquired anxiously. She'd been hovering at Doctor Pagitt's elbow for several minutes as he took Crisp's vital signs.

Pagitt removed his stethoscope. "No worse," he said flatly. He was going to add "he shouldn't be alive," but thought better of it. "No worse."

"Poor girl," said Matty. "She didn't know what she was doin'."

"She'd better learn," said Pagitt. Matty's circumlocutions were familiar to him. He knew she was referring to Sarah Quinn. He replaced the old IV bag with a new one. "I know she's under a lot of pressure at home, with everyone counting on her and all, but that doesn't excuse this kind of negligence."

"I suppose not," Matty said with a sigh. She stroked Crisp's forehead, something she'd never done before, though she'd always wanted to, especially after his dreams. Comas had their advantages. His flesh was cool and damp. She brushed his thin white hair back toward the pillow. "He'll need a haircut soon," she said to herself.

"I'll be back tomorrow morning," said Pagitt as he collected his things and put them in his bag. "Let me know if—"

". . . there's any change," Matty concluded. "Of course I will." She folded her hands and stood looking down at her charge. Her lower lip was trembling. Pagitt noticed.

"You're doing a good job, Matty," he said.

As she looked at him, tears welled in her eyes. She mouthed the words "thank you," but nothing came out. She turned away. Pagitt tiptoed out of the room and closed the door.

After a moment standing, staring, and praying, Matty's nesting instincts overwhelmed her and she began tidying up the room. As she dusted the nightstand, she brushed something that fell to the floor—a small green loose-leaf notebook, no bigger than a man's hand. She picked it up and, supposing it was a book of poetry, began to read.

" 'Beach sand. Sweater. Bikini.' "

"Sounds like that awful modern stuff," Matty critiqued. She couldn't imagine that Crisp had sunk so low in his desperate desire to be published. She read on.

" 'Lead-based makeup. Why the bottom hole? Amanda Murphy has started to appear in my dreams.' Amanda Murphy!" said Matty. "This isn't poetry. It's a journal!" Undeterred, and with a reassuring look at Crisp, she made herself comfortable on the edge of the bed and began reading in earnest.

" 'Remember the bicycle seat. Show Hanson photo. Exhume either Calderwood. Andy no musician.' What on earth?" said Matty. She scratched her head in an unconscious effort to stimulate her brain enough to make some sense of the enigmatic sentences. At least the handwriting was neat. She was proud of Winston for that. She read on aloud. " 'Murderer was too short to reach top hole. Calderwood boys both over six feet. How tall is McKenniston? Where is blazer? Murderer had knowledge of/access to makeup kit. Someone on the estate.' " It went on in a similar vein for several pages.

She closed the book and held it for a moment pressed between her palms. "Oh, my dear," she said. She placed the book on the bedside table and softly patted the back of Crisp's left hand. "He was worse than I thought." She cast a wary glance at the door and the windows, then bent down and kissed his forehead, as gently as if it was a soap bubble. "Poor thing. You just rest," she whispered. She stood up, went to the door, and, casting a last glance at him before she closed the door behind her, repeated, "You just rest."

"Did you see the paper!" Leeman Russell blurted as he burst into the hardware store. There was a full house. Perfect.

"Can't you ever just say hello, Leeman?" said Pharty, punctuating this critique with a near miss at the spittoon.

"You won't worry about hello once you read this," Leeman exulted, waving the paper in the smoke-stained air. "Just cast your peepers over that and tell me 'hello.' " He dropped the paper into Pharty's lap.

Pharty McPhearson was a man in the mold of Stuffy Hutchin and wasn't about to be alarmed by any news to which he didn't hold the exclusive copyright. He shelled a peanut into the paper. "Don't have my glasses," he said.

Leeman grabbed the paper, letting the shells fall where they may, unfolded it, and began to read the front-page story: ' "Ned McKenniston Questioned About Island Deaths.' "

"What deaths?" said Pharty, groping for his glasses. He really had left them home. He swore under his breath.

"Go on ahead," said Stump. He presided from his seat nearest the stove. There was no fire burning now. "You got our attention."

Drew stood up and motioned Leeman to his seat. Leeman sat with his heart beating hard in this place of honor among the inner circle. The sanctum sanctorum. He read loudly, fully aware that his audience had fewer than three good ears among them.

" 'Authorities have subpoenaed Ned McKenniston, twenty-five-year-old son of the Massachusetts senator, to appear before a coroner's inquest in Rockland next week.' "

"What's that?" said Petey, fondling a wrapped butterscotch excitedly. "Who's he talkin' about?"

"Senator McKenniston's boy's been called to court," Drew explained loudly.

"It ain't really court," Leeman corrected, lowering the paper a millimeter or two.

"Just as good as," Drew said beneath his breath. "If I had to explain what a coroner's inquest is, I'd go hoarse."

"Get on with it!" Pharty commanded. "We'll bring Petey up to date after we've got the story. What's he wanted for?"

Leeman inspected the story. "Says: 'When investigators exhumed the body of island native Andy Calderwood earlier this year, they discovered fingerprints on the burial clothing. After long analysis, they proved to belong to Ned McKenniston.' " Leeman lowered the paper with a vengeance. "That's what they took off him that night they opened the grave! Buttons! I knew it!"

"Sure you did," said Petey.

"I did. You can even ask . . ." Then it occurred to him that Crisp was in no condition to ask.

"Buttons with Neddy McKenniston's fingerprints on 'em?" Drew said incredulously. He leaned over Leeman's shoulder and lifted the paper for personal inspection. " 'The coroner's office will not speculate about the fingerprints or why the buttons don't match those on the sleeves, since, according to funeral director Charles Young, the jacket was new. "The buttons matched when I put him in there," said Young. "I'd notice something like that." ' He would, too. How'd you suppose they got there?"

"Good question," said Pharty. His expression reiterated the question. "How'd they get there?"

Drew continued. " 'It is also expected that McKenniston will be questioned about the presence of fingerprints, apparently those of

Andy Calderwood, on the neck of Amanda Murphy, a summer visitor to the McKenniston estate who was found frozen in ice early
this spring. Calderwood had been dead two days the last time Murphy was seen alive.' "

"You don't s'pose there was any funny business, do you?"

"Well, I guess that's pretty obvious, ain't it?" said Stump.

Petey squinted to hear better. "What'd he say? Why're you
mumblin'? Speak up so somebody can hear, will ya."

"No, I don't mean about all this fingerprint business. I mean
about the Calderwood boys. That's the one thing we all figured
was just an accident. What if it wasn't?" Pharty suggested. The
question draped itself on the pendulum of the old clock and measured the silence for a few moments.

"You mean you think McKenniston had somethin' to do with
that?" said Drew.

Pharty removed the cellophane wrapper from a saltwater taffy
one handed. "That's what we're talkin' about, ain't it?"

"What you're sayin' is, what if young McKenniston was involved with it somehow?" said Stump.

"That's right!" Leeman chimed in. "What if that boat didn't
blow up by accident?"

Drew had been picking the empty candy wrappers from the
cast-iron skillet. He opened the woodstove door and tossed them
in. They'd make nice kindling in the fall. "Why would he do that?"

"Who knows?" said Leeman. "Could be lots of reasons."

"Only takes one," said Pharty.

"Still," said Leeman, "that don't answer how Andy's prints got
on that girl's neck."

"Evidence got mixed up," Drew proclaimed. Leeman had risen
preparatory to his departure. The pool hall was his next stop. Drew
resumed his seat.

"They already double-checked," Leeman protested.

"Then they got it wrong twice," Pharty said matter-of-factly.
Skepticism was his strong suit. "Andy Calderwood didn't kill no-

body. He was dead. Dead people don't kill people. Plain and simple. And Andy's dead, ain't he? That was him in that casket, wasn't it?"

Leeman half nodded and half mumbled. "I s'pose it was," he said. If it was left up to people like Pharty McPhearson, there wouldn't be any mystery or romance in the world. What was life without the broad spectrum of possibilities nurtured by speculation?

"That's all foolishness," Pharty pronounced.

"Still," Drew philosophized, "you've got to admit it's some queer, all this business. The Calderwood boys, that could've been an accident. Maybe we'll never know. But the girl wasn't. Neither was Mostly Sanborn."

"Or the Professor," said Leeman.

"That was an accident, wasn't it?" said Petey. "Somebody got the pills mixed up."

"I ain't talkin' about this time," said Leeman. "I mean when he was locked in that freezer."

"Somebody's behind it," said Drew.

Petey disagreed. "One thing might not have anything to do with the other."

"I'd hate to think there could be more than one person on this island could do things like that," said Drew. "Almost makes you want to start lockin' your doors at night."

Pharty turned to Leeman, who was already at the door. "You seen the professor?"

Leeman released his grip on the doorknob. "Sure I did," he said. "I saw him that same day he went into the coma. I was right there with him, talkin' to him the afternoon before that."

"I thought you said it was the same day," said Stump.

Leeman recanted. "Well, the day before. Same thing."

"I mean since," said Pharty. "You been up there to see how he's doin'?"

Leeman was incredulous. "What for?" he said. "He's in a coma." Leeman departed. The door rattled closed behind him.

Once again the clock took up the narrative alone until joined, at length, by Pharty. "Always was somethin' strange about that young fella, though."

"Leeman?" said Drew.

"No! Young McKenniston."

Stump nodded. So did Petey, but, like Crisp, he nodded a lot. It didn't necessarily signify agreement. Drew stretched out his legs and continued reading aloud from the paper that Leeman had left behind in his haste. "Listen to this: 'Forensic specialists must also grapple with the fact that makeup nearly forty years old was found on the twenty-four-year-old girl when she was pulled from the quarry. Said Assistant Coroner Jaret Polkey, "There are a number of things that make this the most baffling case, or series of cases, in my experience." Pressed for details, however, Polkey had no further comment.' "

Nor did the men at the hardware store. Drew folded the paper and set it on the window ledge, where Leeman could find it easily when he came back for it.

The story was unsettling. It illustrated a kind of madness that had always been peculiar to the mainland. The island was a place apart. A place where stoic reason had always prevailed. These things didn't happen here.

Until now.

The men all gazed at the woodstove.

In the days that followed, the gentle thrill of an island summer was overwhelmed by members of the popular media who latched onto the story and trod the thin line between fact, fancy, and fiction into oblivion in their efforts to outscoop one another. After all, one never knew what might be true. At any rate, what began as a remote possibility became a full-grown likelihood: Neddy McKenniston had killed Amanda Murphy, probably because she'd threatened to tell his wife about his infidelities.

"THE WAY IT HAPPENED WAS LIKE THIS," said Irma Louise to the lady whose hair she was turning blue, a summer resident but newly arrived and, therefore, greatly in need of being brought up to date. It hadn't been a sleepy winter. "The McKenniston boy strangled his girlfriend about Labor Day last summer, up at the beach on their property."

"I thought you said they found her in the quarry," protested the customer, who should have been protesting what was being done to her hair.

"Just a minute, Marydale," Irma Louise admonished. "You just won't believe what they say. By the way, you're not going to want it over like that are you?" she indicated a hairdo in the magazine Marydale was looking at. "Don't you think that'd make you look too old?"

"I s'pose you're right," said Marydale, and she continued flipping through the pages. "I just thought I'd like to try something different."

"That's what gets us presidents like the one we got now," said Irma Louise. She cast another in an endless series of glances at herself in the mirror, primped her jet-black bouffant hairdo, and redistributed a pocket of rouge on her cheek with the little finger of her right hand. Her other hand remained in Marydale's hair. Irma Louise was a professional. "Anyways," she continued, "I couldn't believe this when I heard it, but I'm not crazy. You can ask Therma. Isn't that right, Therma?"

"That's right," said Therma, a heavyset lady with an affinity for stretch polyester in contrasting bright colors. "You mean about him draggin' her body up to the funeral parlor?" It was important to make sure they were talking about the same thing. She poured herself some coffee.

"What!" Marydale exclaimed, nearly wrenching her neck due to the contrary effect of having Irma Louise's hand embedded in her hair when she spun to face Therma. "Ow, Irma!"

"Sorry," said Irma, glancing in the mirror. There was that one eyelash that kept coming in white. She couldn't figure out why it wouldn't hold mascara. She couldn't pull it out though; that would be worse. She turned from the mirror and resumed construction. "That's right. I wish you could've heard the gossip around town after that."

"After what?" Marydale pleaded. She'd missed something. "What about dragging a body?"

"The girl's body," Irma Louise said matter-of-factly. Inside, however, she was thrilled to have a new pair of ears to pour the story into, unsullied by the inaccuracies inherent in lesser tellings. Hers was the King James version. "Turns out he killed her up at the beach—"

"Strangled her with a wire," Therma interjected between sips of coffee. She helped herself to one of the powdered doughnut holes that were neatly arrayed on a Chinet plate alongside the coffee maker.

"That's right."

"With a wire!" said Marydale breathlessly. "Are those doughnut holes fresh, Therma?"

"Ought to be," said Therma a little defensively. "Just got 'em over at the IGA this morning."

"Well, I don't suppose one would ruin my diet," Marydale determined. She held out her hand. "Just one of those little chocolate ones, please."

Therma picked one from the pile and handed it to Marydale. "Oh, my goodness, Therma. You had to pick the biggest one in there, didn't you?"

"Well, I'll see if I can find a smaller one," said Therma, bending over the doughnuts with the focused concentration of a gem cutter.

"Never mind," said Marydale, consuming the doughnut hole in one bite. "Already had my fingers all over it," she explained with her mouth full.

"I like the ones with cinnamon," said Irma Louise. "Are there any more of those, Therm?" Therma shook her head. She'd eaten the last one several minutes ago. "Oh, well, prob'ly for the best. Anyway, what they figure is that he killed her and then smeared all this old makeup on her from his grandmother's trunk."

"More than forty years old, it was," said Eleanor Ripley. "She was in the theater." Eleanor had just come back from the powder room but had heard enough of the conversation to know where to jump in. "You're almost out of paper in there, Irm."

"What was forty years old?" Marydale inquired. "The girl?"

"No!" Irma laughed. "The makeup."

"He put forty-year-old makeup on her?"

"She was nearly naked," Eleanor volunteered, betraying some relation, however distant, to Waymond Webber. Her timing was a little off.

"Naked?" said Marydale, playing catch-up.

"When they pulled her out of the quarry," said Therma.

Marydale was determined to understand the sequence of events.

"Okay everybody. Wait a minute. You just said he strangled her up at the estate, on the beach." She pointed at Irma.

"That's right," said Irma. This was just too delicious.

"But you said they found her in the quarry." She pointed at Therma.

"That's right," said Therma. "She was frozen in the ice."

Blue dye was running down Marydale's neck as she stared from one to the other of the hairdressers. Irma Louise laughed. "Now, that's what you get for interrupting. If you just listen, you'll get the picture."

Marydale sat back, folded her hands in her lap, and lifted her head regally. "I'm not going to say another word. I am woman; hear me shut up."

"Good," said Irma Louise with a pleasant laugh. "He covered her with makeup so the fingerprints would show up better." Marydale was about to respond reflexively, but Irma Louise held up a restraining finger. "He had to use the old stuff because it had lead in it."

"I remember that," said Eleanor, to whom the injunction to silence did not extend. "My mother used to use it. Made her break out in blotches. So she'd use more to cover it up."

"They say that's what happened to the Roman Empire," said Therma. "Lead poisoning. Nero and that crowd, you know."

"Anyway," said Irma with another glance in the mirror. She wanted to see the expression on Marydale's face as she told the rest of the story. "He used that because it wouldn't wash off in the quarry, which is where he took the body."

"But not before—" Therma began.

"Let me finish," said Irma. "But first, he took her up to the funeral parlor, where the Calderwood boys was laid out. You heard about that, didn't you?"

"Oh, my goodness, yes!" said Marydale. "It happened the day before we left the island last summer. It was all the talk on the ferry over."

"Well, this was about two days later. He dragged her in there in the middle of the night—"

Therma shuddered. "This is the part I can't imagine."

"Oh, I know it," said Eleanor with a broad wag of her chins. "Horrible!"

"What did he do?"

"Made it look like she'd been strangled by Andy Calderwood."

"It would have to be Andy," said Therma. "Herbie was too delicate. He was there too, though."

"How did he do it?" Marydale begged.

Irma Louise watched the mirror closely. She wished it was a one-way window with a camera hidden behind it like they had on TV. "He somehow got the bodies facing each other at about arm's length, probably lying side by side—"

"Andy's and the girl's," said Eleanor, lest they end up with an abridged version.

"That's right," said Irma Louise. "Then he put Andy's hands on her throat, the way they would've been if he'd been the one strangling her, then he put his own hands on top of Andy's, like this"—she demonstrated in mime—" 'til the fingerprints was in the makeup. That's why he used the old makeup, so the fingerprints wouldn't be washed off when he tossed her in the quarry. That's when he got his own fingerprints on the buttons of Andy's blazer. That's where he slipped up. There's always something, they say. No such thing as the perfect crime."

Marydale had been looking at the women in the mirror. Her expression, Irma Louise thought, was worth the price of admission. "You don't mean it!" Marydale exclaimed. "That's the most hideous thing I've ever heard!"

Irma Louise smiled a peculiar smile. "Isn't it, though?"

"That's not the worst of it," said Eleanor.

"No!" Therma said, taking up the narrative thread with her whole heart. "He put her in the freezer first!"

"What do you mean?"

"When they took her out of the quarry, she was fresh as my Benny on our first date," said Therma. "That means she was put in just before the hard freeze last December, or thereabouts. But somebody figured that, since she'd been wearin' a bikini bottom when she died—"

"A bikini bottom! I thought you said she was naked."

"She was. But there was a tan line or somethin' that showed she'd been wearin' one of those real skimpy little bikini bottoms you couldn't blow your nose on—"

"And she had that sweatshirt on, too, don't forget," said Eleanor.

"She had on a sweatshirt, too?" scoffed Marydale. "What you mean is she was naked under her clothes. I hate to break it to you, girls, but the same can be said of any of us."

"It wasn't *her* sweatshirt," Therma said, as if it mattered. "It was *his.*"

"His whose?"

"Neddy McKenniston's."

"Oh." Marydale nodded. Apparently it did matter. "So, anyway . . ."

Irma Louise recognized her segue. "Anyway," she said, "she had suntan oil on, and beach sand under her toes, so somebody figured she'd been killed back around Labor Day. That was the last time she was seen on the island. So, how did he keep her fresh in the meantime? Put her in the freezer up at the estate. 'Course, everyone just went ahead and buried the Calderwood boys, with none the wiser."

"Same freezer Professor Crisp got locked in," Eleanor reminded everyone.

"Professor Crisp got locked in a freezer!" Marydale cried. She'd have to see if Harold would be willing to stay through the winter next year. This beat Hilton Head cold. "By whom?"

"Must've been young McKenniston," said Therma, echoing the community consensus. "Word is Crisp was pokin' around up there."

"What on earth was he poking around for?" said Marydale. She was aware that Crisp had been an island fixture for years. She knew what he looked like. They said hello on the street, like everybody did. Other than that he was a cipher.

"He's the one who figured everything out," explained Irma Louise.

"Professor Crisp!"

"Yes, of course," said Eleanor. "Don't you know, dear? He used to work for the government. Intelligence work and so on."

"He did?"

"He did. Sharp as a tack, he was."

"Was?"

As if by prearranged signal, all of the women dipped their heads slightly. "Well, he's—"

"He's not dead, too, is he?"

"As good as, from what I hear," said Irma Louise. "Coma."

"From being locked in the freezer?"

"No. He got hold of some bad medicine. Took too much," said Therma. "That's what Evelyn Swears said. She should know."

"She's Matty Gilchrist's best friend," Irma Louise confided to Marydale via the mirror. "He lives up there, the professor does. Boards." She lobbed meaningful glances at Therma and Eleanor, who reciprocated. "That's where it happened."

"So, the McKenniston boy locked him in?"

"That's what they say," Irma Louise confirmed. "Apparently he was hereabouts that time of year. Alone. Lord knows why. They guess he found out that Crisp was onto something, come out to the island, and followed the old fella around a day or so until the time was right, then . . . 'Course, he must've been some careful. Nobody on the island even saw him that whole time."

"But why didn't Neddy kill him?" said Marydale. She'd have, if she'd been McKenniston.

"Tried to. The professor lost some fingers and toes to frostbite, so I guess Neddy was serious enough all right. But somebody up there heard the generator on . . . it wasn't s'posed to be, you see . . . so, one thing and another, they got him out just in time," said Irma Louise.

"Not in time for Mostly Sanborn, though," Eleanor reminded them.

Once again the heads dipped slightly.

"Mostly?"

"McKenniston's caretaker," said Therma. "Died. You probably don't know him. Looked like a pumpkin. He wasn't hardly ever down this end of the island durin' summer. Got pushed off a cliff up there that same day Crisp was locked in the freezer, though they didn't find him for days."

It took a minute or two for Marydale to ingest these shocking revelations. Irma Louise could see her working the thing through until finally—it took a little longer than usual, but she was from the mainland, so concessions had to be made—Marydale asked the inevitable question. "But why?" She searched the eyes of her companions in the big mirror. "Why would he strangle the girl with a dead man's hands? Everybody knew that the girl was still alive after the Calderwood boys died, didn't they? He'd have to be crazy—"

"That's just what they figure!" said Eleanor, in much the same tone she'd shouted "Beano!" at the Masonic Hall the night before.

"That McKenniston's crazy?"

"No. But he wanted people to think a crazy man was behind it all."

Irma Louise and Therma both nodded. "That's right," said Irma Louise. "And I guess he figured any evidence leading back to him would be pretty cool by the time the police got done chasing themselves around, assuming they ever got that far, which I doubt they would've without the professor."

What followed was, by beauty parlor standards, a long silence of two to three seconds. "But whatever gave him such a terrible idea as that?" said Marydale thoughtfully. "I tell you, you'd have a hard

time convincing me that someone who could come up with something like that . . . Well, I don't care if they think they're sane as
the day is long, they couldn't be, could they?" She sighed. "Why,
just imagine such a thing happening out here."

"I never thought I'd see the day," said Irma. "Never."

"Trial's next month, over at the courthouse in Rockland," said
Eleanor. "The papers say he's staying down on Cape Cod 'til then.
He got bailed out faster than a leaky dory."

"Too bad the professor's not in any condition to know justice
is bein' done," Therma lamented. "Thanks to him. They'd have
never got him otherwise."

"You have to be so careful with medicine like that," said Marydale. "Are you going to eat that last chocolate doughnut hole,
Therm? I'll split it with you."

C
H
A
P
T
E
R

25

S TRANGE. He'd had the feeling a thousand times before—the lightheadedness that precedes waking, that millisecond when the senses stumble over themselves in an attempt to impose order on the world rushing in. But waking didn't come. Just the lightheadedness. The distant, indistinct voices. The chaos of a world in which he seemed to have no part. The place of neither here nor there.

How long had he been like this? A moment? Forever? Had he ever been otherwise? Nothing hurt, though. He noticed that. Something used to hurt, but he couldn't remember what. His eyes felt as if they were made of stone. He wanted to open them, but he was terrified that his body wouldn't respond when his brain gave the order. Even worse, what if they were already open? The thought prompted a reflex and his lids flew apart, admitting a searing blast of light. It seemed to burn a huge hole through his brain and leave in its wake a screaming vortex that sucked the lids shut behind it.

Well, the eyes worked.

He wanted to say something, but his throat was sore and dry. Maybe more things would start to hurt as he woke. He'd rather stay asleep. He wiggled his eyebrows. He could feel them moving. He wiggled his ears. He smiled. He swallowed. Then, realizing he had a tube up his nose and down his throat, he started to gag. Instantly there were hands all over him. The tubes came out; they seemed to take a large part of his brain, esophagus, and sinuses with them. But he could cough. And sneeze! A huge, deep, timber-shaking sneeze that blew a matted knot of cobwebs out of his brain.

"He's come back! He's come back!" It was Matty's voice. He'd never noticed how much it had in common with a heavenly chorus of angels. "Thank you, dear Lord," she said. "Winston. Can you hear me?" Crisp nodded. "He can hear me, Dr. Pagitt! You try."

"Winston?" said Pagitt. He was leaning close. Crisp could feel his breath and smell the Edgeworth pipe tobacco the doctor always kept in his pocket.

Crisp felt his lids being pried open, and once again the light rushed in like sustained lightning.

"Good dilation," said Pagitt as he dropped the lid. It seemed to bang and echo through Crisp's brain. "Welcome back among the living."

Crisp wanted to say, I'm just passing through, but, though his lower lip moved perceptibly and a noise came out, even he couldn't make out the words. Spoiled the joke.

"Don't try to talk," said Matty. "He shouldn't try to talk, should he, Doctor Pagitt?"

"Matty's right," the doctor agreed. "You've had those tubes in a long time. Your throat's bound to be a little raw. Just relax."

A long time. How long? Crisp wondered. Slowly it all began to come back to him. He didn't want it to. He knew that his recent memories were painful ones. But his brain reassembled them all in a matter of seconds, against his wishes. How could it betray him like

that? Then he realized something else. His brain had been unconsciously sorting through the evidence during his absence, and now
it laid the whole thing, chronologically and with perfect clarity, before his consciousness. His mind ordered him to sit bolt upright,
but his body would have nothing to do with it. His arms didn't
move. Nor did his legs. He was paralyzed. He made narrow slits
of his eyes and peered out at the world through layers of crust and
haze. He was desperate to tell the world. He knew who did it! He
knew why!

"He wants to get up, Doctor," said Matty. She knew her Winston.

"Mmm," said Pagitt. "Having a hard time, Winston?" He allowed a moment for response, though he knew none was forthcoming. "Muscles have atrophied pretty badly, I shouldn't wonder. They were probably under the impression you were dead, and
they had every intention of following suit." He laughed, but the
humor was lost on Matty. He stopped laughing. "Let's see what
the story is, shall we?"

He took Crisp's hand in his own and touched the fingertips,
closely watching his patient's expression as he did so. "Do you feel
this, Winston?" he asked. Crisp shook his head almost imperceptibly. Pagitt pressed a little harder. "This?" Nothing. Finally he removed a pin from his vest pocket and, concealing the action from
Matty, who would have objected, jabbed it deep into the palm of
Crisp's hand. Still no response. Conscious that he had to keep his
alarm hidden from Matty, he repeated the process with the other
hand, then the arms, lower back, legs, feet, toes. No reaction.
Maybe he was dead after all, but his body hadn't told his brain.

"Matty, Winston's bleeding a little. Oh, don't worry, it's nothing serious, but could you go get me some nice hot water in a
saucepan or something, so I can clean him up?"

Matty toddled off to accomplish her errand. Pagitt waited until she was gone before he spoke. "Winston, can you hear me?" he
said. "Blink three times if you can." Crisp did so. "Good. I didn't

want Matty to hear this. I hate to have to say it, but you're paralyzed completely from the neck down."

It wasn't a surprise, but the news still sent shock waves through Crisp's nervous system. That seemed to be working nicely. Otherwise he was completely helpless. He couldn't lift a finger. The realization made him sick to his stomach and prompted a desperate urge to scream, to tear his soul from his body and run, anywhere, as fast as he could.

Imprisoned in himself, Crisp felt some bizarre affinity with those who had spent time in hell. The hell he had in mind was on 14th Street in Washington, between Pennsylvania Avenue and Soyo Street. In a little store called Izmy's, a very short, engaging, gnome-faced man will fix your toaster, or your can opener, or vacuum cleaner, or any other little appliance that needs mending. He's been there for years. Very clever with his hands.

In the back of the store, in a small supply closet, there's a door with three locks that opens onto the basement stairs. The smells are overpowering, mold and mildew among them, as you start down the steps to the cellar, where the floor is always wet and slippery. What windows there were have been bricked over, and the ceiling is so low that anyone over five foot eleven has to stoop. In the corner behind the ancient oil furnace is a pallet of old boxes and appliance parts. The pallet swings aside to expose a thick steel door that once belonged to a safe set into the floor. The door lifts open on makeshift hinges to reveal a coarse iron grating in the floor, below which is a simple hole in the ground.

The hole is fifteen inches in diameter and varies in depth, the intended height being two inches shorter than the individual who will occupy it. Those who knew of the hole called it hell. Simple, really. No iron maiden. No rack. No rubber hoses. Just a hole in the ground. Dark. Wet. Cold. Not quite big enough for a man, or a woman. And no one had ever left it with their secrets intact.

The important difference between this hell and Crisp's was that visitors to this hell had their own key. If there was a secret that could free Crisp from the oubliette of himself, he'd part with it in an instant.

"Near as I can figure, you've probably had a stroke," said Pagitt. "I'm not sure, but I suspect that's what it is." He pulled up a chair and sat beside the bed, leaning close to Crisp and speaking quietly so Matty wouldn't overhear. "If that's the case, it could be temporary, all or part. You never know. Could all come back to you at once . . . overnight!" He paused. "Then again, it wouldn't be honest to give you false hope? I mean, you might never . . ."

If only he'd died in the freezer. He'd come so close. Just a few minutes longer. It would have been all over.

"I suppose I should get you over to the mainland again . . . do some tests . . ." Crisp shook his head as emphatically as possible. "No," Pagitt amended. "Maybe that's not such a good idea. I understand. Well, I don't guess you're going to like this much better, but you'll need a nurse. Someone to do everything for you. Do you understand? I mean, that's just the way it's got to be. I could ask Sarah Quinn . . ."

Crisp's eyes widened in horror. Again he shook his head.

"No, no," Pagitt replied. "Of course, if you don't want . . . I don't think she'd make the same kind of mistake again, but I understand. How about Matty?" He waited for protest; there was none. "She's not a proper nurse, I know, but she'd take good care of you, if you'd be comfortable with . . . the things she'd have to do."

Crisp knew the kind of things she'd have to do. Poor Matty. They'd both be embarrassed to death. But certainly there was nobody else. The point was, how could he make her understand?

"I'll talk to her," Pagitt offered as he packed up his instruments and placed them carefully in his bag. "Okay?" Crisp hesitated, then nodded. "Good. I'll be by every other day or so to look in on you. Meanwhile, don't panic about it. That's the first thing people do when they . . . when they're like . . . They panic. It's awful, I know, but things will probably start coming back, one by one. We'll see. You in any pain?"

Crisp shook his head. No pain. None at all.

"Good," said Pagitt. "Could be worse, then, couldn't it? Have to look on the bright side." He put on his hat. He was the only man in town who still wore a real hat, one that didn't have an advertisement on the front. "I'll tell Matty to keep a sharp eye out. If there's any change, she can give me a call." He stopped short of the door. "Sorry, Winston," he said.

All the time Crisp had been trying to think of some way to communicate with the doctor. A hundred possibilities went through his mind, but all he could do was blink, smile, and nod. This made it difficult to broach the subject. As Pagitt reached for the doorknob, Crisp tried shouting, but all that came out was a loud gurgle.

"You keep working on that, Winston," Pagitt said with a smile. "But don't overdo it." He straightened his hat and left the room. Crisp lay in stunned silence listening to the footsteps on the stairs. He didn't really believe he was paralyzed, that the limbs he'd taken for granted for so many years had suddenly ceased to function. But it was true. Nothing worked.

Funny. His brain was working. His heart was pumping. His lungs rose and fell with his breathing. His body looked fine, all things considered. Spotted and wrinkled, like any ancient fabric, but still in one piece. Yet somewhere the edges were fraying.

Any good general targets the bridges first. Perhaps death was a good tactician. He'd done well lately. The Calderwood boys, Mostly Sanborn, Amanda Murphy, and nearly a Crisp for the collection. But only two toes and a finger to show for his efforts. So far.

It was so obvious now. Motive, opportunity, method. He shuddered mentally. Even the red wig made sense. So did the makeup, the fingerprints—everything—once you realized you were dealing with someone sane enough to seem normal, perfectly normal, sublimely normal, capable of saintly devotion, human error, and fiendish malice, but someone whose mental and moral bridges were out.

More than anything, it was the hands that did it. He was reminded once again of the bicycle seat. So narrow. Too long and delicate. Out of place on the man in the photo. They were piano player's hands. Herbie was the piano player. Of course, the operation must have taken place at the mortuary the night after the wake. That would have taken some nerve, and just a little knowledge of surgery and the composition of the wrist. Otherwise there would have been a lot of sawing.

True, Sarah Quinn was a robust young lady. She could have sawed all night. But she didn't have to. She'd trained as a nurse. She probably used one of Charlie Young's scalpels. A few relatively easy cuts near the joints, remove Andy's hands for future use, then put Herbie's in their place, the sutures neatly hidden by Andy's cuffs so no one would suspect when they exhumed him—which they would, once they found his fingerprints on the dead girl's neck. Nice and clean. No blood, just a little embalming fluid. Once done, she reclosed the coffins. They'd be sealed and buried the next morning. No chance anyone would ever dig up Herbie as well as Andy. Why would they? Andy had hands where hands should be. Who would ever suspect they weren't his?

Where were they? In the tree? In the quarry? Where was Leeman? What had he found? Was he still alive?

The red wig was easy. It had been taken from Mrs. McKenniston's trunk and used to impersonate Amanda Murphy on the mainland, an Amanda who was always walking away from the witnesses. Almost anyone could have pulled that off—the red hair, the distinctive dress. Besides, the witnesses were all older people with less than perfect eyesight. Not a coincidence.

Brilliant. Affixing the wig to Amanda Murphy's red hair, probably while the body was still in the freezer—what better way to hide the evidence?

But there was other evidence. The little trove in the bottom hole of the old tree. Why not the higher one, where it was more likely to escape detection? Because it was as high as she could reach. That simple. Neddy McKenniston could have reached the top hole. So could Andy Calderwood, had he been alive.

Crisp would bet his life that the red wig was no longer where he put it in the drawer at the funeral parlor. It was required for the impromptu encore at Amanda's funeral. That appearance was a loose thread. What was the point in taking such a risk?

The makeup, also from the theatrical trunk, was both grotesque and practical. It would throw any investigation into chaos, and retain Andy's fingerprints forever, once she'd taken his hands and pressed them around Amanda's neck. They'd have to dig him up, just to make sure he was really dead. And what would they find? Neddy McKenniston's fingerprints on the bright brass buttons. Retribution would be perfected when Neddy was trotted off to prison for the murder of Amanda Murphy, while Sarah stayed at home and raised his child.

It was then that Crisp realized, more by revelation than deduction, the ultimate irony of the whole tragedy. Neddy was a Harvard man. He'd never have given his girls Yale sweatshirts. Yet both Amanda and Sarah wore them like banners. Billboards advertising the fact that their man was a Yaley.

The baby wasn't Neddy's, it was the senator's!

Neddy was both procurer and fall guy for his own father! Nothing more than a pawn in the whole hideous business.

Amanda was absolved of falling for his crass bravura. She and Sarah had succumbed to the wiles and lies of a much more accomplished and sophisticated seducer. The senator.

And now Neddy was the pawn again. Sarah hadn't attacked the senator directly. She chose to get to him through his son, the one through whom she'd come to ruin. Odd he had no alibi.

"Are you awake, Professor?"

The voice startled Crisp. His thoughts had exhausted him and, without being aware of it, he'd fallen asleep. With effort he drew the speaker into focus. It was Sarah Quinn.

"OH, GOOD," SHE SAID SOFTLY, closing the door gently behind her. She was dressed in her uniform and carried a shopping bag over her arm. "I just thought I'd drop by." Crisp's heart began pounding wildly as she came closer. His eyes opened wider and wider with each step. He couldn't help it. He had no other way to respond.

"You know, don't you?" she said. She dropped her arm, and the bag slid down and caught on her fingers. She held it in front of her with both hands. "I can see it in your eyes. I thought you did. That's too bad." She lowered her voice and looked directly at him. "You must think she's a terrible person."

She sat on the edge of the bed, her back perfectly erect. She didn't look at him as she spoke, but rather at the wall. "It had to be that way, you know. Gruesome, like that," she said. "Murder's so common today, isn't it? I mean, if it was just an average murder, he'd have been out of prison in a year and a half. That's the national average for first-degree murder, Professor. Did you know that? I looked it up. A year and a half. That wouldn't do any good. It had to be especially awful, you see? So it would be in all the papers, and he'd be in for a good long time. Forever, maybe. Should be, too. A terrible, gruesome murder like that."

She wrung her hands continually. "I got the whole idea from Mrs. McKenniston's trunk," she said. "I was out in the shed putting things away—the grandchildren had found the key and got stuff out to play with—and then I saw that wig. It looked just like Mandy's hair.

"I remember, I just stared at it for the longest time. All kinds of things went through my mind—J. T. and what happened to Andy and Herbert and other things—and by the time I got done staring, the whole thing was there in my mind, like it just got there all by itself, you know? I didn't sit down and work it out . . . cold blooded like that. It was just there. All I had to do was . . .

"But even that wasn't like me doing it. It was like somebody else, and I was just watching. It's funny. You don't think of yourself as a murderer, even when you're right in the middle of it, you know? It's like you're acting out a play, and you get to have everything just right, but later—you don't think about later." She sighed. "Like now, when I do what I have to do, I'll think in my mind, he'll get up later, and everything will be all right." For a second she stopped wringing her hands and fixed him with a gaze that threw a frantic dance of shadows on the wall of his soul. "Does that make me crazy, do you think?"

She began to unbutton her blouse. "I know you're paralyzed. Doctor Pagitt says there's not much chance of your getting better." She left his bedside, stepped into the shadows by the kneewall, and continued to undress. "But I can't take any chances, you see? I have to think of Papa and J. T. I was hoping it wouldn't come to this."

Crisp didn't look at her. He heard the rustling of the bag. It wasn't the fact that he was going to die that terrified him. It was the method. Sarah Quinn, though relatively new to the field, was an original thinker. He didn't even want to speculate about what might be in the bag, or why she was undressing.

"I wish you could talk," she said softly. "I thought I had everything so perfect, you know? I guess I really did though, didn't I?" She stepped from the shadows and stood over him. She was wearing a red wig, a black body stocking, and a billowy, multicolored skirt. Even head on, from a little distance, she could pass for Amanda Murphy, though much more voluptuous. "I guess you know that Neddy McKenniston's been tried and sentenced. Life imprisonment." She smiled. "Without parole." She laughed halfway up the scale. "Anytime the senator wants to see him, he'll have to go to jail." She completed the scale. "How do I look?" She spun around gracefully, stopped, and returned to the bedside. "Everybody thinks Neddy planned everything to make it look like it was done by somebody who was insane. Neddy! He couldn't plan his own funeral.

"Of course, that's the way it was supposed to be. It worked out just the way I wanted. The only thing that kept messing things up was you." She sat down beside him. "I was watching you in the barn, going into all those little rooms. Then you found the trunk. I was standing behind you with an ax in my hand when I heard Mostly out on the patio."

Crisp's eyes widened. She laughed lightly. "I thought that was my last chance, but then you went into the freezer. I couldn't believe it! Of course, Mostly was there. He saw me just before I . . . I still had the ax. Neddy was out fishing, like always, poor fool. All alone. No alibi. But you didn't die!

"I decided to call the hospital. I'd applied for work before, like I told you, but there weren't any jobs. So I volunteered! They always take volunteers. I asked to be assigned to your room." She was delighted with the cleverness of it all. "And they said okay because, well, we're both from the island, aren't we? Practically family.

"I had everything ready, planned and planned. I was going to tell them I had to leave early to run some errands. Then I was going to sneak in the back way—there was a door just down at the end of the hall, and nothing but the bathrooms and a linen closet between there and your room—and I'd smother you with your pillow, while you were asleep.

"Then you checked out!" she exclaimed. She was almost in tears. "Again! It was like there was some angel or something watching out for you. I couldn't believe it!"

Where was that angel now?

She stared at him for a moment. "I told you then I wanted to take care of you.

"Then I had the idea about the medicine," she said. She was staring at the wall again. "That was one of my jobs, to throw out the old medicine. What could be better? It would look like an accident, and no one would even know it was missing! Isn't that a good idea?

"Mrs. Hadley's medicine, that was just lucky. Coincidence, you know? Of course, I was sure it would kill you. I want you to believe that. I didn't want you to suffer." She stared at him. "They didn't suffer, you know. Amanda . . . it was all over in a minute. And Mostly, I liked him, so I made sure to hit him real hard. I'm not sure he was dead when he went off the cliff, but he never knew it.

"It wasn't easy getting him to the golf cart. One of his feet got caught in the screen door. I had to lay him there while I undid the spring. I was scared to death someone was going to come along!" The thrill of excitement tickled her. She laughed demurely with her hand over her mouth. "But they didn't.

"Now," she said, looking at him with a sincere sadness. "Let's take care of you."

She held up a syringe and pressed the plunger. A thin, silvery stream of liquid spouted from the needle and arched through the air. "The funny thing is, I almost wish I could tell everyone I did it," she said. "People don't think I'm very clever, you know? I hear them talking about what happened and I want to say, I did it!" She rolled up his sleeve. "I can tell you, though. Can't I? You can see how right you are." She rubbed the crook of his arm with alcohol. Ever the nurse in training. "Don't worry," she said. "Nobody will think to look for signs of foul play. It'll be just like you had another stroke.

"Isn't Amanda terrible, doing such a thing? But don't you worry. She's been punished already." She slid the needle into his vein and emptied its contents into his arm. "There," she said, removing the needle and daubing the puncture with the gauze. "I'm afraid you may get a little uncomfortable in about five or six minutes. I wish you could just go to sleep, but unfortunately that's not how this drug works, and it's all I could find in the garbage."

How could anyone be so analytical, so thorough, and so mad all at once? Crisp wondered.

"And there isn't anyone to help you. Matty's . . . gone."

Poor Matty, thought Crisp.

"I waited outside until she left to go to mail her letters."

Poor Crisp, thought Crisp. He imagined Matty returning home with a letter from some magazine, informing him that his poem had been accepted, only to find him dead. Poetic injustice.

"I almost hate to stay and watch," she said, looking at him. "But I have to make sure." She smiled the same warm smile he'd noticed when she fed him Jell-O. "Besides, like I said, I can tell you while we're waiting.

"The fingerprints . . . you figured that out, I know," she continued. "I could tell from what Leeman and Mr. Gammidge were talking about, even though they didn't understand what they were saying. You did.

"At first I was afraid the hands wouldn't come off and I'd just make a mess of it. That's why I did Herbie's first. His wrists weren't so thick, you know? I was surprised how easy it was. Andy's weren't hard, either. But it wouldn't have worked without the scalpel. Thank heavens Charlie had some!"

Crisp doubted heaven had anything to do with this particular stroke of fortune.

"That made all the difference. Once the flesh was out of the way, I just sawed through the bones with Papa's hacksaw." She rubbed her left wrist with her right hand. "That was hard work."

"Amanda, well, she never knew what happened. Like I said, it was over very quickly. She never saw me."

Sarah turned her sincere blue eyes to Crisp. "I didn't have anything against Amanda, you know. Not really. She couldn't help it." She looked away again. "You don't know how the senator can be. But it was because of J. T. He couldn't just leave me like that, with his child. It's not natural, is it, for a man to do such a thing? But he did. Come Labor Day he was gone. Back to Washington. Not a word all winter, even though I called his office. I left messages.

"Then in the spring, I got a call from his housekeeper in Massachusetts, telling me to go up and get the house ready, like always. Just like that. Like nothing ever happened. And here J. T. was just born, and nobody even knew who he was! I mean, I guess they thought Neddy was the father, but,"—she leaned close and spoke into Crisp's ear—"I can tell you this about Neddy. He'll never be anyone's father, if you know what I mean. He just got married because his father made him. Just for appearances.

"Then he showed up with her." She shook her head and the red hair settled on her shoulders. "I knew what that meant. I'd seen it before. He'd get girls for his father, pretend to be their boyfriend, then he'd leave them here and go back to his boyfriends in Provincetown during the week.

"I'm sure he'll be very popular in prison."

She turned and looked at him. There were tears in her eyes and on her cheek. "I told them I'd open and close the house—I needed the money—but I wouldn't work there. I wouldn't be there at the same time as the senator.

"All summer long I thought and thought about how to get back at him. I was thinking mostly how to embarrass him, but I couldn't come up with anything that wouldn't humiliate J. T., too. Then, the day after Andy and Herbie's accident, I was there closing up and putting things away in the trunk, like I said. It was all perfect. It all came to me at once. Mandy and Neddy were the only ones who stayed on after Labor Day. Perfect. Everything just fell into place . . . the hands, the wig, the makeup. Even the freezer and the quarry. All at once, like magic!

"And Neddy's buttons . . . that's why it all worked. His fingerprints were all over them after the dance. All I had to do was snip a few off and sew them on Andy's coat at the same time I . . . Except one I just left lying there, loose, so they'd see something was wrong. It all worked just like I wanted!" She looked at him, laughed, and shivered. "I tell you, I was sure I was going to get caught. Charlie'd come barging in, or something. I've never been so scared in my life. I'm a little scared now, but not as much."

A sudden jolt of pain gripped Crisp's stomach and lower abdomen. He gasped as his body began to convulse reflexively.

Sarah put her hand on his and patted it. "It won't last too long," she said sympathetically.

"I put all the odds and ends in the old tree. Then you found them!" She looked at him deeply. "That's when I knew something had to be done about you. Whatever made you look in that tree? I wish you could talk."

Crisp wished he could scream, but all he could manage was a rasping croak as another seizure gouged at his insides.

"I don't see how Amanda can bring herself to put you through this," Sarah commiserated. He knew she was squeezing his hand, but he couldn't feel it. How was it he could feel his insides so well?

"I had to keep an eye on you. Going up to the cemetery that night, I got soaked. Nearly caught my death of cold. But I found out what you were up to, and I knew you were using Leeman Russell. That's all I needed to know.

"Leeman can't keep a secret," she said with a smile. "Everybody knows that. All I had to do was let him give me a ride home a few nights. He practically begged me to let him tell me everything. But he swore me to secrecy. He found the jacket, Neddy's, in the tree. Just like you knew he would. He asked me what to do with it." The laughter that followed the comment was not musical. It was almost frantic. "I told him to hold on to it until you came 'round." She giggled. "He gave it to me, and told me to do it!"

She paused thoughtfully. "I'm glad he didn't dig any further. You know what was in there, in the bottom, don't you?" She stared at him and nodded with her eyes wide. "I threw it in the ocean.

"I'm glad he didn't find it. He wouldn't have understood. Like I said, Leeman can't keep a secret. I'm still not sure what I'm going to do about him. He knows so much, you see, but he doesn't know he knows it." Her smiled broadened, but it collapsed the instant Crisp succumbed to another convulsion.

"I'm having that feeling like I'm a million miles away from everything, you know?" she said. "Like I'm watching television or a movie and you're just acting."

"I'm not acting!" Crisp screamed, but all that came out was a gurgle.

Sarah looked at the needle. "This was all I could find," she said. "I wish it could be sweet and quick." She stroked his brow. Her hand was soft and cool. "Don't worry. Just another minute or two and it will all be over.

"I couldn't stay and watch you suffer like this," she said. "I don't see how Amanda does it." She ran her fingers through the hair of her wig.

Amanda. The word was like an elixir surging through his being. Maybe there was a heaven and hell. Maybe not. But there was something, some other level of existence. He was sure of it. Any minute now, she'd be showing him around.

It turned out that Sarah knew her medication. She was right. Any minute now. His old body couldn't take much more of this.

Sarah got up, walked to the shadows, and began to change her clothes. "Matty told me you were having dreams about Amanda," she said. "Well, actually she told Mr. Gammidge. You talk in your sleep, I guess. I overheard.

"So, I thought maybe I could make you think you were going crazy, you know? That's why you saw Amanda at the funeral. I wish Mostly hadn't seen, too. He wasn't supposed to. How could you think you were going crazy if someone else saw her too?

"Anyway, I could see you were going to mess things up, so I called the newspaper and told them what you were finding out, about the makeup and Neddy's fingerprints and everything. I couldn't figure out why those things never got out like they were supposed to. That's the one thing that didn't work right. Then I figured you were keeping things quiet. It was ruining all my work. So I had to help things along.

"But I needed to know what you were up to. So I bought this little tape recorder." She took it from her bag and held it up, but he wasn't looking. "I kept it in my bag. Remember when you and Mr. Gammidge were talking and I came back to find my bag? The tape recorder was on the whole time! I heard everything." She laughed in the shadows. "It's on now. I'm going to listen to it later, to make sure all the facts are right, just in case. You never know. It takes a lot of rehearsal: don't say this, don't do that. You can't do anything that might make someone suspicious. Even though it's all over, I have to be very careful.

"You were suspicious though, weren't you? I wonder how much you knew. You had a very suspicious nature, you know?"

It didn't escape Crisp's attention that she was already referring to him in the past tense.

"Oh well," she said in summation. When she emerged from the shadows, she was again Sarah Quinn. She came and stood at his side, took his hand in hers, and looked at him with eyes of deep compassion. "Look what she's done to you, Professor!"

Crisp had broken out in a profuse sweat. His nose had begun to bleed, and the eardrum in his good ear seemed about to explode from the pressure that had built up in his head from holding his breath when a spasm began.

"What a wicked girl."

At that moment the front door slammed.

"Yoo-hoo! Winston!" came Matty's familiar voice. "I'm home! I'll be up to see you in a minute, my dear! Soon as I put these greens in the . . ."

Both Crisp and Sarah Quinn listened with all their might as Matty's voice trailed off into the kitchen. Crisp saw that Matty's unexpected return had a deeply unsettling effect on his murderer. "It's too soon!" she said sharply. "The medicine isn't working fast enough." She began to wring her hands.

Crisp, unwilling to run the risk of alternative expedients, rode the next swell of pain to its desired conclusion. He feigned death, and held his breath.

"Professor!" Sarah whispered excitedly. "Professor!" She grabbed his arm and felt for his pulse. At that moment Matty's footsteps began to thud up the carpeted stairs. Sarah dropped his arm before detecting his faint pulse. "Good," she said to herself. "Good." Crisp could hear her rubbing her hands. "Everything's going to be all right. I just . . . I just stopped by to see how he was doing, and . . . and he was already dead! I was just on my way to phone Doctor Pagitt . . . that's it!" she said. "That's it. This will work!"

Crisp listened as she stationed herself by the door. She put her hand on the knob and, just as Matty grasped the other side, pulled the door open.

"Oh! Matty!" said Sarah. She sounded genuinely surprised and out of breath. Remarkable. "He's gone!"

"Gone?" said Matty. "Gone where? What are you doin' here?"

"I just came by, and he was dead . . . ," Sarah said nervously. Not enough rehearsal. "I mean . . . to see how he was—"

"Dead!" cried Matty. She rushed under Sarah's arm, which had been holding the door open. "Winston!" She ran an anxious hand over his brow. "Oh, my Lord. Look at him! What happened?"

"I checked his pulse," said Sarah from the doorway. Only tremendous mental effort was keeping her from bolting. "He's probably been dead half an hour. I'm so sorry."

Meantime, despite Crisp's best efforts, Matty had discovered a weak pulse in his neck. "Oh, you foolish girl," she scolded. "He's still alive! Go call Dr. Pagitt!" She pulled the covers up around his shoulders.

Sarah rushed to the bedside. "Oh, no. He can't be! I felt . . . there was no pulse!" She picked up Crisp's hand and felt for his pulse. There it was. Almost imperceptible. "How can he be?" she said, almost to herself.

"Go!" Matty commanded. "Call now. Tell him to hurry!" She hadn't taken her eyes off Crisp. "There, there now, Winston. You just hold on. Help's on the way."

Too much was going wrong. Sarah staggered to the doorway and down the stairs like a drunkard in a dream. Before she knew what she was doing, she had dialed Dr. Pagitt's number. She lifted the phone to her ear.

"Hello," said a voice on the other end of the line. It was Jennine, the doctor's wife. "Hello?"

The voice brought Sarah back to her senses. She was leaning on the doorpost, staring into the pantry. Her eyes focused on an assortment of kitchen knives arranged neatly in descending order on the wall.

"Hello. Dr. Pagitt's residence." No response. "Is anyone there? Are you in trouble? Do you need help?"

Sarah hung up the phone. "No," she said as she walked through the kitchen and into the pantry. "I don't need any help."

As soon as Sarah had left his room, Crisp opened his eyes and started blinking frantically in Morse code.

"Winston!" said Matty. "You're back! You're goin' to be okay.

Doc Pagitt's on his way. Do you have somethin' in your eye? Just a minute, I'll get the facecloth from the basin." She put the statement into action. "Here now, let's have a look and see what's there."

She bent as close as she could, narrowed her eyes to a squint, and examined him closely. "I don't see anything in that one," she said. "You have to stop blinkin' for a minute if I'm goin' to find what's botherin' you." She began her scrutiny of the other eye. "That silly girl, I swear. I'll have to get Dr. Pagitt to do somethin' about her. She thought you were . . ." She chuckled. "You know what? You just blinked an 's.' " She stood up. "Blink, blink, blink. Fast like that," she said, blinking three times fast. "That's an 's' in Morse code." She stared at him with a silly smile on her face. This was his last chance. "That's an 'o'! You just did an 'o'! Three times slow!" She blinked three times slow. "You know!" she exclaimed suddenly, "if you knew Morse code, we could communicate! That's an 's.' You just did another 's'. S-o-s. You just signaled SOS! That's amazin'! I'll have to teach you, so you'll know what you're doin'. That's an 'n' . . . no, an 'm.' That's an 'a' . . . Winston, you're blinkin' Morse code. Did you know that?"

Suddenly it occurred to her. "Winston. You do know Morse code, don't you? 'Course you do! Are you spellin' somethin' on purpose? What was it? S-o-s. Did you mean SOS?" Crisp nodded with all his might, and his head moved slightly in the affirmative. "You did? What was the rest . . . 'm,' 'a,' what else? 'T,' 't' . . . you already did that. Oh, two 't's?" Crisp nodded again. This was going to take forever. " 'Y.' M-a-t-t-y. That's Matty, Winston. You spelled my name! This is wonderful!"

If only there were an abbreviated way to spell shut up and listen, Crisp thought. All at once his shoulders contracted violently. His back arched and his heart started pounding uncontrollably. Once the spasm had subsided, he opened his eyes.

Matty was nearly beside herself, mopping his brow and his bloody nose and his tear-filled eyes all at once. "What's happenin'?" she said. "Sarah! Have you got Dr. Pagitt on the phone?" she called over her shoulder. There was no answer. "Where'd that girl go?"

Crisp shook his head frantically in an effort to get Matty to stop wiping his eyes. He blinked s-t-o-p three or four times before she got the message, stopped what she was doing, and stared at him.

D-o-n-t t-a-l-k, he signaled. Of course, she said each of the letters out loud.

"You don't want me to talk?" said Matty. "But what's happened to you? D-i-t-t-o? What does that mean? Ditto what? Ditto don't talk?"

Y-e-s.

"All right," said Matty, sitting on the edge of the bed. "Go on."

S-a-r-a-h t-r-y-i-n-g t-o k-i-l-l m-e.

Matty pronounced each of the words under her breath. Once the sentence was assembled, she sat back, folded her hands, and smiled condescendingly. "Oh, Winston. You haven't lost your sense of humor," she said. "That's a good sign. Still . . ."

Fortunately she was looking at him and stopped speaking when he started signing. S-h-u-t u-p.

"Shut up?" Matty repeated. He'd never told her to shut up. No one had ever told her to shut up. But it finally dawned on her, from his expression, that he was deadly serious. "What makes you think such a thing? Why, she's callin' Doc Pagitt this very minute."

Q-u-i-e-t, Crisp blinked frantically. S-h-e k-i-l-l-e-d M-u-r-p-h-y. M-o-s-t-l-y. C-a-m-e f-o-r m-e.

Matty's eyes were widening. "You can't mean it!" Crisp rolled his eyes. "I'll shut up."

G-e-t o-u-t. T-a-k-e b-a-g.

Matty was on her feet. "What bag? What about you?"

B-a-g.

Matty's eyes lighted on the shopping bag. "That one?"

Crisp nodded. It was then he saw Sarah's shadow on the half-open door, preceded by the silhouette of a knife in her hand. B-e-h-i-n-d y-o-u.

Matty's talents were a little rusty. It took half a second for the translation to settle in, but when it did, she reacted instinctively, spinning around just in time to see Sarah raising the knife over her head.

She screamed and with both hands shoved her attacker against the wall. The force of the impact sent the knife flying from Sarah's hand to a loud landing somewhere on the other side of Crisp's bed.

Sarah, meanwhile, stunned when her head hit the wall, tried desperately to gather her wits while fending off the blows Matty was leveling at her head with the shopping bag. She kicked blindly, landing a painful blow to Matty's delicate left knee. Matty cried out in pain and collapsed as Sarah flung herself across the bed, knocking the wind out of Crisp. She snatched the knife from the floor at the same instant that Matty grabbed her by the heels and pulled her back across the bed.

"Stop it!" Sarah shouted. "I'll kill him!" She raised the knife over Crisp's chest as she slid across him. Matty dropped her legs and Sarah struggled to her feet, holding the knife over Crisp's throat. "Go sit down! Over there!" She pointed to the chair in the corner. The one Amanda often occupied.

Sarah massaged her forehead. She was confused. "I can't do this," she said to herself. She laid the knife on Crisp's chest, picked up the shopping bag, and withdrew the red wig. Crisp knew what this meant. The executioner was being called in.

Still visibly shaken and not thinking clearly, she stumbled as she put the wig on. Matty started to get up. "Sit!" Sarah screamed. "Sit down. Don't move." Her voice trailed off as her head dropped. She took the clothes from the bag and stared at them as if unsure what to do next. Finally, she tossed them on the bed and began to undress.

"Amanda will do it," she said.

"What on earth are you doin', child!" Matty cried.

"Sit!" Sarah snapped, picking up the knife and shaking it in Crisp's direction. Matty sat. Winston was blinking, but Matty was too far away to see what he was saying.

When Sarah's uniform hit the floor, she kicked it away and pulled the body stocking over her head, charging the wig with static electricity. She dropped the skirt on the floor, stepped into it, and pulled it up to her waist.

"Now I know what to do," she said. She took the syringe from the bag and filled it from a small brown bottle. "You have more lives than a cat," she said as she threw Crisp's covers aside. "I've got just enough left for the two of you." Again she pressed the plunger and released some of the fluid. "I don't know what they're going to make of this."

Crisp's insides were already filled with acid and fire. He couldn't take another dose. Summoning all his strength and concentration, he made one last heroic attempt to push her away. Nothing happened. His eyebrows arched mightily, but otherwise he lay still as a stump. No one would ever know how valiantly he'd fought.

Sarah stuck the needle into his vein. At the same instant, the front door crashed open and a confusion of footsteps tumbled up the stairs. "Matty? Professor!"

It was Doc Pagitt. Matty lunged at Sarah, grabbing her around the legs and toppling her over the chair. They both landed in a heap on the floor. The needle dangled from Crisp's arm, still full.

Pagitt burst into the room followed by Leeman Russell and Luther Kingsbury. "Matty?" said Pagitt as he bent to help her up. "What's going on?"

Matty sat breathless on the edge of the bed, pointing at Sarah.

"Who have we here?" said Kingsbury, helping Sarah up. "What happened?" he said with a smile. "You ladies fall down?"

Leeman was studying Sarah closely. "That's Sarah Quinn," he said, reaching out and lifting the hair off her face. "It sure is."

"Sarah Quinn?" said Kingsbury, bending to peek under the auburn cascade. "Why, what are you doing with that wig on, Sarah?" he said, still mildly amused.

Pagitt, meanwhile, saw the needle sticking in Crisp's arm and suddenly became aware of something sinister. "What's this?" he said, removing the needle and holding it up to the light. Matty, still unable to speak, pointed at Sarah. "What is this, Sarah? What were you doing?"

Sarah merely hung her head and said nothing.

Finally Matty burst forth in a torrent. "She tried to kill him!" she screamed on the exhale. "She killed everyone!"

Luther Kingsbury's expression of amused befuddlement fell from his face like a Mardi Gras mask. "What's she talking about, Doc? What're you talking about, Matty?"

"Jeez!" Leeman exclaimed.

Pagitt began testing Crisp's vital signs.

Matty exhaled again. "She killed that girl up at the quarry! And Mostly Sanborn! And she was tryin' to kill Winston!"

"Now, now," said Luther, slow to accept the notion that such a thing could happen under his jurisdiction. "You don't mean Sarah actually killed anybody—"

"Hell I don't!" Matty screamed. Matty never screamed. And she never swore. This was very serious. "Winston told me so. And I heard what she said just a minute ago, just before you got here. She was goin' to shoot both of us with that stuff!"

Pagitt picked up the bottle from the floor and read the label. He looked at Sarah. "Sarah, how could you do such a thing?" He examined Crisp.

Kingsbury had been holding Sarah loosely by the arm ever since he helped her to her feet. Suddenly she screamed at the top of her lungs and pushed him. He fell back against Leeman, who, in turn, fell over the chair. Both landed in a pile as Sarah ran down the stairs and out the door, still screaming.

Kingsbury struggled to his feet and stumbled off in pursuit. Leeman tried to decide whether to stay where the action had been, or go where the action might be. That was the question. He looked from Crisp to Pagitt to Matty and opted to follow Kingsbury.

"It's a good thing she didn't have a chance to give him any of this," said Pagitt as the last of Leeman's footsteps thundered down the hall and across the porch. He could be heard in the distance calling for Kingsbury.

"She did," said Matty. She'd regained her breath and was looking at Crisp, reading his eyes.

"I don't think so," said Pagitt. "The syringe is still full."

"That was the second shot," said Matty on Crisp's behalf.

"What do you mean?" said Pagitt. "You saw her give him a shot?"

"No," said Matty. "He told me. Sign language."

Pagitt looked at Matty to Crisp and back to Matty. "He can't move, Matty."

"He can blink," said Matty. She looked at Pagitt. "Morse code."

Pagitt looked at Crisp. "Is that true?"

Crisp nodded.

"Then, you can communicate?"

Crisp nodded. Nodding wasn't such a bad thing after all.

"Is Matty right? Did Sarah . . . was it really her behind the murders?"

Crisp nodded again, then started blinking.

"What is he saying?" Pagitt asked.

It took a minute for Crisp to get the whole message out and Matty to interpret. "He says she was tryin' to frame Neddy McKenniston."

"It worked," said Pagitt. "If that's the case."

"What's goin' to happen to Winston?" Matty whispered. "That first shot . . ."

"He should be dead," Pagitt replied. He looked at the bottle. "It's antivenin. Lifesaving in small doses, but too much . . ." He shuddered. "That would be an awful way to die."

It was, thought Crisp.

"The only thing I can think is that it must have lost its potency. Still, I'm amazed." He'd been taking Crisp's pulse unconsciously. "His pulse is a little more regular. Must have been pretty bad, Professor," he said. Crisp slowly closed and opened his eyes in response.

"The worst is over," said Pagitt. "You'll have some pretty bad cramps, but nothing like what you've been through."

"Well, you showed up just like the cavalry," said Matty. "How?"

"The phone rang a while ago at the house," Pagitt replied. "Jennine answered it. But nobody was there. She said all she could hear was this ticktock, ticktock in the background." He smiled.

"The grandmother clock!" said Matty. She patted the doctor on the shoulder.

"I was afraid something might be wrong. I couldn't imagine what, but I hopped in the ambulance and came up."

"And Leeman and Luther?"

Pagitt's smile broadened. "I had the whirly lights on. They wouldn't miss it."

Crisp gurgled to get attention and began blinking.

"What's he saying?"

"He says he thinks the story's in the bag."

"In the bag? What bag?"

Matty picked up the shopping bag. "This?" Crisp nodded. She opened it, reached in, and took out the tape recorder. She held it up. "It's still goin'," she said.

"You mean it's been on all this time?" said Pagitt, taking it from Matty and turning it off. "Play and record," he said, looking at the buttons. "It got everything."

Crisp closed his eyes. If he woke up in this world, he'd never see Amanda again. He knew that. If he woke up in the next, she'd be there. Whole. Alive in one way or another. So would he.

> You showed me in the shadow of myself
> A love that can exist by simply seeming.
> I know that as I close my eyes to sleep
> I awake again to sleep from dream to dream.

There would be no dreams tonight.